Charles Hammond. The most powerful man in the world, he was helpless in the hands of a kidnapper who wanted more than money . . .

Helen Thorp. She had made it to the top, but if she didn't get Hammond back it would all come crashing down . . .

Lady Janet Isling. She was as deadly as she was beautiful, and the only thing that kept her going was hatred. She wanted Hammond for reasons all her own . . .

Pete Chamberlain. He was the "hired hand" of a billion-dollar consortium. He *had* to get Hammond back, no matter what the price . . .

THE AUCTION

ALEXANDER COLE

A JOVE BOOK

THE AUCTION

A Jove Book/published by arrangement with
the author

PRINTING HISTORY
Jove edition/July 1983

ISBN: 0-515-06534-X

Jove books are published by The Berkley Publishing Group,
200 Madison Avenue, New York, N.Y. 10016. The words
"A JOVE BOOK" and the "J" with sunburst are trademarks
belonging to Jove Publications, Inc.

PRINTED IN THE UNITED STATES OF AMERICA

For G. H.
for whom I will always be A. C.,
and with love and thanks for A.L.S.
who'd have been A. C. for her too.

BOOK I

1

In Munich they bracketed the limo with guard cars. When it stopped they hit the pavement fast—machine pistols in hand, eyes raking the traffic, sidewalks, doorways, rooftops.

Rome was worse. In Rome they put Mr. Hammond in a plain Fiat, doubled the guard, shuffled routes and hotels daily, and prayed the Pope would declare martial law.

But this was London, and you didn't pile out of cars waving guns in London and Mr. Hammond wouldn't ride a Fiat in London, so when his black Daimler limousine rolled magisterially past Harrods department store, Wheeler, Hammond's chief of security, followed at a distance in a quiet gray Jaguar sedan.

Wheeler was thinking that London was one of the last decent cities left where riding around in a classy limo wasn't an open invitation to getting snatched. They'd had hits in London, for sure—IRA bombers, Arab fanatics, Balkan umbrella psychos—but they were the fringes of distant political arguments and, besides, Charles Hammond wasn't a political target. He was a go-between, a dealmaker for big honchos, a fixer, not a fighter, a fixer who worked hard not to make enemies because enemies got in the way and Mr. Hammond's job was to get things *out* of the way so people could do business.

The Daimler turned off busy Sloane Street and stopped moments later in front of a Dutch-facade row house on Herbert Crescent. Wheeler parked a hundred feet back on the quiet, narrow street and spoke by radio to the sidemen in Hammond's limousine.

Hammond, as usual, was already halfway out of the car. The sidemen jumped after him. They were good, and before Hammond had reached the front steps, they had caught up and hidden the smaller man between them. Hammond was expected at the house. The door opened when they reached the landing and shut behind them a second later.

Wheeler glanced around the residential street, which was deserted but for the cars parked along the curbs, and relaxed. He was tired. Mr. Hammond was working something big and they'd gone nonstop since before Christmas. The last two weeks were a blur of airports and hotels. Now it was almost over. They'd be aboard the Jetstar in a couple of hours, and in New York for New Year's Eve. No one knew they were coming, which meant no meetings, no escorts, just a last minute party at the Comptel suite with some friendly rented ladies, and a late sleep New Year's Day.

There'd be UN appointments the next day, maybe a quick meeting at Comptel with Ms. Thorp, then the long flight to Tana to celebrate the Malagasy elections—whichever side won. Mr. Hammond was friends with both. Wheeler lowered his window. It was warm for winter.

When he saw a London bobby round the corner of Herbert Crescent, Wheeler appraised him professionally. Big man, six-four at least, and looking even taller in his high oval helmet. A man that size who could move fast, and this one walked like he could, was a dude to be reckoned with if he had a brain to go with his machinery.

Wheeler checked his rear-view mirrors. The street and sidewalks were still deserted. He saw the bobby draw abreast the Daimler, bend down to look through its smoked glass window, and spot the chauffeur.

Wheeler reached for his radio.

"Stay inside," he told the men in the house.

"Righto," came the reply.

They were English, regulars with Hammond's London office. Wheeler traveled with Hammond, as did Rice, Hammond's exec, and Rice's secretary, an ex-FBI man who doubled conveniently as Rice's protection. The rest of the support staff was local. Hammond had offices in London, Tokyo, Washington, and Tananarive, to back him up in Europe, the East, the States, and Africa.

Wheeler switched channels and spoke to the chauffeur. "Just give him your license and registration."

The chauffeur was Maltese, a new man, highly recommended, but still nervous and eager to please. "Yes, sir."

"If he gives you any trouble, send him back to me."

"Thank you, sir."

Wheeler watched the bobby walk around the Daimler to the driver's side. The chauffeur lowered his window and handed over his license and registration. One of them fluttered to the street. The bobby backed up and waited; the chauffeur got out of the car, stooped awkwardly, and picked up the paper.

Wheeler nodded his approval; the bobby was right not to expose himself, even in an obviously routine situation, just as he was right to check the Daimler's business outside the Overseas Club. Despite the fact it was a legitimate private club for retired intelligence operatives—mostly British and American—its members' former calling might attract the wrong kind of attention. Idly, Wheeler wondered what business Hammond had there.

The bobby returned the chauffeur's papers and strode back to the sidewalk. Wheeler readied his own papers and murmured "All clear" into the radio.

"Righto," his man in the club said with relief. Hammond was always in a hurry and no one liked telling him he had to wait.

The bobby spotted Wheeler in the gray Jaguar and again stepped into the street.

"Good morning, sir." He touched his helmet.

"I'm waiting for a gentleman in the Overseas Club," said Wheeler, handing over his international driver's license.

The bobby held it between two thick fingers and angled it to read in the pale sunlight. Like most English cops, he looked like a tough, young farm boy and very sure of himself. His hard eyes flickered quickly from the license to Wheeler's face.

"Have you a permit for that firearm, sir?"

Tough son of a bitch, thought Wheeler, annoyed that the bobby had noticed the almost imperceptible bulge in his expertly tailored wool blazer. He's got no gun and asking about mine as if I couldn't kill him in a second. "In this pocket."

"May I see it, please?"

"Sure." He glanced at the Overseas Club door. What the hell would he do if Hammond came charging out and headed for the airport while London's finest was checking his bodyguard's right to carry? He handed the cop his permit and picked up the radio mike to tell the sidemen to wait inside.

"The pistol, sir?"

"What for?"

"Serial number."

"Right."

He put down the radio, pulled the gun out of his jacket, snapped out the clip, and handed the gun out the window, butt first. The bobby reached for it with one hand and returned his license with the other. Wheeler took it and knew the instant both hands were full that he had made a lethal mistake.

The bobby's left hand was filled with a gleaming sliver of metal. He was moving with a grace astonishing in such a big man. He was thrusting like a dancer, lightning fast, and the stiletto extended like a snake's tongue from his enormous hand. It flashed in the sun, then disappeared in Wheeler's throat, just below the knot of his necktie.

The bobby slid the blade out of Wheeler's neck, laid his face against the steering wheel, wiped the thin blade clean on Wheeler's sleeve, and resumed his measured steps toward Crescent Garden at the end of the street.

Charles Hammond came out first, the sidemen scrambling after him. He was a short, stocky fifty-year-old man with ginger hair, bushy brows, and a full bristling mustache. He bounded down the steps like a tightly inflated ball.

The sidemen caught up with him at the bottom of the steps and hid him from view as they had on the way in. One of them was speaking into his radio, trying to raise Wheeler in the Jag, cursing the atmospherics that were blocking his signal; the other, who knew that Hammond's ruddy complexion stemmed from a dangerous heart condition, was worrying about how to slow him down. Racing him wasn't the way.

Hammond beat him to the Daimler's door handle—a basic tenet of Wheeler's security drill was that the chauffeur never left the wheel to open doors—and he yanked the door open and jumped in the back.

Leaning forward to rap the glass partition in his usual impatient let's-go signal, he called, "Gatwick!"

The partition was already open; Hammond stabbed irritably at the button that closed it. "I told you to keep this damned thing shut!"

The chauffeur turned around with an ingratiating smile and the lead sideman was halfway into the car before he saw the weapons in his hands. The chauffeur fired with his right hand and a cloud of white vapor spewed into Hammond's face.

The sideman thought it smelled like peaches. He arrested his forward movement and started to push himself back through the door. The chauffeur dropped the gas gun over the rising partition—freeing a hand to protect his face from the fumes which floated through the passenger compartment like a breath in cold air—and fired the silenced automatic in his left hand, twice.

The first shot went over the sideman's shoulder and cut down his partner; the sound of the bullet hitting him was as loud as the *pock* of the muffled report. The second shot slammed the sideman out of the car and sent him sprawling onto the sidewalk.

The Daimler lunged forward, smacking shut the open passenger door, whipped around the corner at the end of Herbert Crescent, and disappeared toward Sloane Street.

Wheeler held his face to the steering wheel and moved trembling fingers to the ignition key. There was blood in mouth, but the steel must have missed the aorta because he was still breathing. He clamped his fingers around the key.

His mind dulled by shock, he forced himself to wait. It seemed forever. If he was wrong, he'd wasted his only chance to track Hammond. He heard a car start. Seconds later a white Viva pulled out several spaces behind his and raced away.

The watchdog turned the corner and only then did Wheeler start his own engine. Moving as little as possible to contain his bleeding, he steered the Jaguar out of the parking space. He caught up on Sloane Street. The Viva, all boxy and bright with glass, was racing toward Knightsbridge, hustling to make the same traffic light as the Daimler, which was turning right in stately procession through a jostling horde of black taxi cabs.

Wheeler nudged his accelerator. The Jaguar shot forward, faster than he had intended. He careened through the turn as the light changed to red and dropped behind a newspaper truck to hide from the Viva. He felt no pain, only a dull numbness that spread from his throat like a warning he had drunk too much booze. He knew he was handling the car badly, as if the steering wheel and the accelerator were operating in mirror image.

The newspaper truck pulled off beside a newsstand, revealing the Daimler closely trailed by the Viva in heavy traffic. Wheeler tried to get the police on his radio. The controls were on the microphone, but when he got the right channel, he couldn't talk.

Carefully, he inclined his head and let the salty blood pour from his mouth. It splashed on his twill slacks and he thought, as he did every time he put them on, that a hundred fifty bucks for a pair of pants was pretty good for a retired U.S. Army MP. He'd worked for Hammond for years when one day Mr. Hammond announced, as if seeing him for the first time, "You look like hell," and marched him into the best store in whatever city it was and bought him clothes while Rice was having kittens because they were late for a meeting with a bunch of bankers.

Emptying his mouth didn't help. He still couldn't speak. And he knew he couldn't drive well enough to force the Daimler off the road, not with the Viva protecting its flanks. He could do nothing but follow.

Hammond's form was partially visible through the dark back window: he was still sitting upright, but his square head lolled to the side as if he were sleeping. The Daimler changed lanes abruptly and Hammond's body fell out of sight, onto the seat. A voiceless curse bubbled in Wheeler's throat. If they'd wanted to kill Hammond they wouldn't have bothered gassing him; but if they'd wanted him alive they wouldn't have used gas—if they knew about his heart.

The Daimler veered left of the Wellington Arch underpass and swung onto Park Lane, gaining speed in thinning traffic, then passed Marble Arch and took the Edgware Road. They were taking Mr. Hammond north, out of the city. Wheeler followed doggedly, his hands and feet numbing, his vision alternately blurring and clearing, dread spreading like the numbness as he began to realize that he couldn't follow much further because he was dying.

2

The *Grand Choeur Dialogue* stormed from Saint Thomas's twin pipe organs, shaking a hundred candle flames; they tossed dancing lights on an elaborately wrought stone arras that soared behind the altar of the church on Fifth Avenue in New York.

Wrapped to her chin in deep, shimmering sable, a beautiful woman with hair darker than her coat apologized to the deacon at the door for being late. She walked confidently up the center aisle and entered a pew halfway to the altar. It was chilly in the cavernous church; she left her coat on her shoulders, scanned the New Year's Eve Celebration Concert's program, sat back, and let the thundering music guide her thoughts.

Although it was past eight-thirty, she had come directly from Comptel's offices on Sixth Avenue, and the day's work reverberated in her mind. She made some mental notes, culling the echoes until the useful were safely stored and the useless had begun to fade.

The organists finished Gigout and took up Bach and the candle flames danced a more intricate step. She gazed at the stone arras and thanked God that the holidays were almost over. Christmas Day with small nieces and nephews had been a treasure, but it could have ended right there. She caught herself chewing her lip, removed her glove and smoothed her lipstick with the tip of an exquisitely manicured finger. She wondered how Hammond was enjoying his New Year's Eve.

There was a stir among the people behind her and a familiar voice whispered into her ear. "Ms. Thorp? I'm sorry to bother you, but Mr. Cowan needs you."

She looked into the plain face of Mildred Saks, Alfred Cowan's private secretary. Mildred was wearing bright makeup. A long, flowered party dress hung below her beige coat. Alfred had plucked her from a party. Helen felt the excitement rising in her, filling her chest. "I'll be right there," she whispered.

"He sent me in the car," Mildred said pointedly.

"Then I'll meet you in the car, Mildred," she replied, her tone a trace less cordial. Mildred caught her gist and hurried back down the aisle.

Helen Thorp sat a moment longer, letting the excitement clear the music from her mind. She donned her glove, and when she felt completely in charge, rose and swept out of the church. She stopped at the door to slip a folded twenty-dollar bill into the contribution box. She had allowed the usher to see the denomination. Now she smiled at his appreciative nod, full face, as she did for maître d's and bartenders, so he would remember her, and hurried down the shallow stone steps to Fifth Avenue.

Alfred's chauffeur helped her into the Cadillac and drove quickly around the block to the Comptel building. She ignored the guards at the lobby sign-in desk, Mildred fluttering grimly in her wake, and boarded a private express elevator to the top of the fifty-story building.

Alfred Cowan, president of Comptel, was a paunchy, balding man in his fifties. He was hunched over his desk, leaning on his powerful forearms, in his let's-get-down-to-it posture. An unknotted black bow tie dangled from the open collar of his silver-studded dress shirt. His dinner jacket was splayed across an armchair.

"Good party?" asked Helen.

"My wife thought so."

"What's up?" She shrugged slowly out of her coat.

Cowan grinned the way he did when he had her at a disadvantage. "Guess who got himself kidnapped."

"Who?"

Cowan had already stopped grinning. "Your boy."

"Hammond?" The sable slid to the floor and piled around her legs in deep, shimmering folds. "When? Is he all right?"

Cowan shrugged. "I got a call from London. Crocker. He's something like third v-p for—"

"I know who Crocker is."

Alfred had a maddening way of talking slowly at the beginning of a crisis. It was his way of keeping cool, of maintaining perspective, but it was still maddening. "Seems the rest of our London office took off for the south of France, en masse. Goddamned holidays. Anyway, Crocker heard it on the news. He tried to get Rice to confirm it, but that snake-eyed bastard wouldn't talk to him."

Helen crossed the room in two quick strides and dialed the direct code to London on Cowan's telephone. She drummed her pearl gray nails on his desk. Having gone straight to the church from work, she was still wearing her office uniform—a tailored, slit skirt that showed her beautiful legs and a two-hundred-dollar silk blouse. The blouse was gray today, a perfect color bridge between her pale skin and thick jet hair. Fine lines beneath her dark eyes and a full, sensual mouth often made her look wiser, more mature, more knowing, than her thirty-three years.

The phones were slow tonight. Holiday traffic. Alfred caught her eye. She shook her head in disbelief. "Hammond can't have been kidnapped."

"You got any proof that he isn't?"

"Of course not. Alfred, do you realize what this means?"

"That's why we're here." Cowan glanced mournfully at his dinner jacket, pulled the tie from his neck, and dropped it on his desk like a soiled napkin.

Helen was overtaken by a flood of memories. She'd met Charles Hammond in Paris five years ago, on one of the first trips she'd made as Alfred's representative. At the time, the French government was underwriting a microwave net in Mozambique. Comptel wanted to build amplifying stations and Hammond was brokering between Comptel and the Mozambique telephone company under the maternal eye of the French. It was exacting work and he handled it beautifully, managing in the process to direct some of the subcontracts to Comptel's French subsidiaries. Throughout the meeting, throughout the most subtle complexities, he didn't take his eyes off her.

He asked her to dinner. She had already made up her mind. He was too powerful for her to handle. He would demolish every one of the vitally necessary walls that she had erected between business and her private life. She refused his invitation. She'd been right, then.

The lines engaged and the insistent *burr-burr* of the English connection was picked up instantly.

"All Seas, Limited. Good morning."

Helen glanced at her Piaget. Nine o'clock. Two in the morning, New Year's Day, London time, and Hammond's staff sounded like business as usual. She often wondered how he got people to work so hard for him.

"This is Helen Thorp. I want to speak to Rene Rice."

"I'm sorry, Ms. Thorp. Mr. Rice is not in the office."

"When will he be back?"

"I'm sorry, I don't know."

"Please ask him to call me at Comptel in New York."

"Ms. Thorp at Comptel in New York."

"Thank you." She had a sudden thought. "Could I speak to Mr. Hammond?"

"I'm sorry. Mr. Hammond is en route to Tananarive."

Helen thanked her and hung up.

"Stonewalling?" asked Cowan.

"With boulders."

"I gather they were waiting for a ransom call."

"Sure. Have you tried the police?"

"Crocker said that Scotland Yard is investigating. All he knows so far is what he heard on the radio. Two of Hammond's bodyguards were shot dead and a third is missing along with Hammond."

"Dead?" She sank into the chair beside Cowan's desk.

"Any bright ideas?" he asked.

"Not without more information. We should find out how much they ask Rice for. I'd better go to London and talk my way into Rice's office." She was already changing her mind when she saw Cowan frown. "No. I'll do better here. We need help, Alfred. Somebody who knows something about this. Who was that guy who negotiated the South American kidnapping? Remember, I was in Nairobi?"

Cowan smiled his approval. "Chamberlain. I got him as soon as Crocker called."

"Didn't you put him in the Washington office?"

"Right, but Mildred tracked him down in Connecticut. He's here if you want him."

"Wonderful. Let's have a look."

Cowan buzzed Mildred and went to the door.

Helen swiveled her chair to watch.

Her breath caught in her throat. Hammond must have looked like Chamberlain when he was in *his* thirties, athletic, broad in the shoulders, and not particularly tall. A solid chest and a light step.

She shrugged off the thought. Aspects of other men often reminded her of Hammond. It meant nothing. Already the differences were more apparent than the similarities. Hammond pounced into rooms, as if to devour the occupants. But Chamberlain entered warily, eyes quick and alert, like a medium-size predator ready for a deadly defense if it couldn't escape.

"Pete, good to see you," said Cowan, taking his hand. "Sorry to break up your holidays."

"That's all right, sir."

"Home with your family?"

"Yes, sir. My parents."

"Oh. We probably have mutual friends. Greenwich? Darien?"

"Sandy Hook."

Cowan looked blank. "Where's that?"

"Near Danbury. Town built around an old firehose factory."

"Oh. Well, my apologies to your parents too."

"I think they were kind of impressed."

"Great. Hey'd you put that bonus into Eurodollars like I said?"

Chamberlain grimaced. "No, sir. I went in with some friends who were building condominiums in Danbury."

"Wonderful. Make out?"

"We have a problem with the septic systems. I kind of wish I was in Eurodollars."

"That's the breaks," Cowan said jovially, drawing the

amenities to a close. "Come on over here, Pete. I want you to meet somebody. Helen, this is Pete Chamberlain. Pete, my associate, Ms. Thorp."

Helen took his hand but remained seated. "Nice to meet you, Pete. Or Peter?"

"Pete's fine."

He was nervous, which was understandable. Alfred, despite his cheerful interest in an employee's private life, was president of the fifteenth largest corporation in the world. Anyone familiar with Comptel's inner workings, as Chamberlain should be if he was doing his job right, would know that Helen Thorp, executive vice-president for international investment, was Cowan's closest confidante.

She let loose one of her more dazzling smiles, to put him at ease. He had some small scars on his face, scattered randomly as if received at different times, blue gray eyes, and a hand thick with hard muscle.

"Didn't I read your report on security in the East African plantations?" Helen asked.

"I was kind of winging that one. I don't know much about Africa yet." He smiled into her eyes, probing intimately like a man used to women enjoying him. "I had no idea my reports reached such exalted levels, Ms. Thorp."

Helen smiled back thinly. She was familiar with the probing eye and practiced at handling men who used it for extra leverage. Chamberlain had compounded the offense by placing a hair too much emphasis on the *Ms.* for her taste, and there was a mocking note in his exalted levels remark. "We draw on all sorts of sources at exalted levels, Pete. What do you know about Comptel's relationship with Charles Hammond?"

Alfred interrupted. "Pete does more than write security reports. He's sort of a troubleshooter, if you know what I mean. He keeps up."

"In the Washington office," Helen replied coolly, "troubleshooter means ex-army, retired FBI, or has-been CIA." She studied Chamberlain's handsome face. "You look too young to be retired FBI and too smart for the army. That leaves the CIA."

Chamberlain grinned sheepishly. "Guilty on two counts. And I don't know how smart I am. I was a navy SEAL before I joined the spooks."

Helen continued to bore in. "Did you leave the spooks on friendly terms?"

Cowan answered for him. "After Pete got back our South American guy, I made him an offer he couldn't refuse. I know a few people. I smoothed things over for him."

Chamberlain said, "I can still go back for favors, if that's what you're asking, Ms. Thorp."

His *Ms.* had shed its excess weight. He sounded unsure of himself, which would make it easy to slap him down when he stepped out of line. "Okay, Pete," Helen said. "What have your favors told you about Hammond?"

"Not much so far, Ms. Thorp. They nabbed him in broad daylight, two blocks from Harrods. It was very neatly done, including a phony cop and maybe a planted chauffeur. Very, very well planned."

"How the hell did they get inside Hammond's security?" exploded Cowan.

Chamberlain shrugged. "I'll find out eventually, but I doubt it matters. The point is they did it well and professionally, which is a blessing."

"How?"

"They want to keep Hammond alive."

"Obviously," said Helen. "They're going to demand ransom. The question is, Alfred, how much do they want and how much should Comptel contribute."

"He's not an employee."

"Also," Helen added, "what can we do to help Rene deal with them? Rene Rice is Hammond's chief assistant," she explained to Chamberlain.

"He's not an employee," Cowan repeated. "He works for a bunch of different companies."

"Alfred—"

Chamberlain interrupted her. "If I may suggest. Since Mr. Hammond works independently for several corporations, maybe you and Ms. Thorp could poll the others and put together a fund. Share the burden."

"Wonderful idea," said Helen.

Chamberlain looked pleased.

"Maybe," said Cowan.

One of the teletype machines behind his desk clattered to life, startlingly loud in the thickly carpeted office. Cowan swiveled around to read the printout.

"It's probably Crocker in London," Helen said to Chamberlain. She was grateful for his suggestion. It showed more sense than she expected from military types.

Chamberlain was eyeing Cowan's communication consoles with open admiration. "Is that the private link?"

"Yes."

Comptel Inc.'s original conglomerate base was in telecommunications, and it was known in the industry for its especially exotic internal communications network, including two separate telex systems. The first was for regular company business and communication with the rest of the world. The other was reserved for contact between plant heads, district managers, and the highest company officers. Six people, including Helen Thorp, had access to the second system in the New York City corporate headquarters.

The machine ceased typing. Alfred, who had watched it fill the paper, broke the long silence that followed by ripping the paper from the platen. He turned around slowly and placed the sheet on his desk. He looked bewildered.

"Crocker?" asked Helen.

"No."

"Who?" She sensed Chamberlain tightening beside her.

"I don't know." Cowan twisted the paper sideways so she could read it.

"YOUR BID IS EXPECTED AT THE PENDRAGON AUCTION. LANCELOT."

3

Lady Janet Isling awakened in darkness, her hair prickling against the linen pillow case. Silently, she edged her hand under the pillow. She was inches from the gun when powerful hands seized her wrists and jerked her upright.

A flashlight blazed in her eyes, blinding her. She struggled, but when they turned the room lights on she realized that there were two of them and the one holding her was too strong. She went limp to save her strength and put them off guard.

Burglars was her first thought, house breakers surprised to find her sleeping in the seemingly empty villa. Many of the big houses were closed at this time of year, when their residents abandoned the south of France for Paris or Christmas skiing in the Alps.

That they would try to rape her, having found her naked and alone, she had no doubt. Nor did she doubt that she would shoot them both as soon as she could reach the gun. It lay in its usual place—behind the second pillow, the lace-covered one she propped up to lean against while she read herself to sleep.

As her eyes adjusted to the bright light, she saw that the

one who held her arms was a fleshy, round-faced youth in his twenties, French, by the look of his heavy nose and the sloppily cut suit and open shirt favored by local working men. He looked like a typical Marseilles street hood, stupid, but smart enough to wait for orders from the second man, who was watching her with an expression of gloating anticipation. She took in his clothing, and meeting his eyes for the first time, felt fear.

He was a direct opposite of the man who held her. He was very tall, so lean as to be skeletal, his face a mask of hard, straight lines unsoftened by any excess flesh. Glittering dark eyes held hers in a brutal gaze. His clothes—slacks, jacket, roll-neck sweater, shoes—were all black. He wasn't French. There was an Oriental look to his face, but Lady Janet couldn't place a nationality. He carried a black wooden cane with a knob of carved ivory as white as his face.

He spoke. The accent struck her ears as Slavic.

"Where is Lancelot?"

Again she felt fear. They weren't house robbers. Nor were they here by accident. Not if they knew about her and Grandzau. But what a foolish question. If they knew about Grandzau—and knew his code name—surely they knew the answer.

"Grandzau is dead."

The man in black spoke again, as if he hadn't heard.

"Where is Lancelot?"

"I've told you, he's dead." Lady Janet's voice, with its accent of upper-class English ease and privilege, grew insistent. "Will you instruct your man to let my arms go? He's hurting my wrists."

"Where is Lancelot?"

The man's long fingers left the ivory head and traveled down the cane. He was wearing black leather gloves and in the silence of her bedroom, Lady Janet thought she could hear the creak of leather as his fingers moved along the black wood. The grip on her wrists was as tight as before. She'd been trying to edge closer to the pillow, but she was still too far from the gun, and since she was held from behind, she hadn't enough leverage to break the man's grip on even one wrist.

The man in black shifted the cane in his hands, took hold of the ivory head. The movement caused his jacket to open slightly and she caught a glimpse of a Beretta in a shoulder holster. She'd get only one chance for her gun.

"Where is Grandzau?"

"Grandzau died three years ago," she insisted. "He died in a car wreck in the Alps. He's buried in a churchyard just south of the Italian border."

"You are lying to protect him," said the man in black.

"I can't protect a dead man."

"You are lying." He twisted his hands. The head of the cane turned with a sharp click. He drew his hands apart, separating the halves of the cane. Lady Janet's belly clenched. It was not the sword cane she had supposed, not a weapon, but a vicious instrument, a long, black leather riding crop.

He dropped the scabbard end of the cane, stepped closer to her bed, and reached toward her. Without a word, he caressed her with the whip. It tapered to a thin, flexible lash. He traced her breast, then her nipple, then her other breast.

She watched his glittering eyes as she felt the supple leather descend toward her belly, lazily zig-zagging across her taut, suntanned skin until it was stopped by the bed sheet. The man in black paused, the whip resting on her navel, reached out with one gloved hand, and flicked the sheet off her body and onto the floor. Then he resumed tracing the lines of her bare flesh, skirting her pubis, exploring her thighs. She drew her legs together as the whip sought to part them. The stiff yet flexible lash continued its gentle exploration. She'd ridden with the kind; it had a bamboo core. Then he stopped, tapped her belly gently a couple of times, and asked, "Where is Grandzau?"

"He's dead," she said, struggling to keep her voice calm. The man was changing subtly. She sensed a crescendo of emotion beginning to build behind his icy facade.

"You're lying."

He lifted the whip and tapped her breast—a little harder, but soft enough still so that even though the second tap touched her nipple, she felt no pain.

"Where is Grandzau, Lady Janet?"

"He's dead. You can check it yourself."

"You're lying."

"I'm not," she protested, determined not to plead.

The thin black whip rose high over his head. His eyes

passed reflectively along her body. She stiffened for the stroke. Where would it land? Her breast? Her thighs?

"Turn her over!"

Her chance. The man holding her wrists hauled her around. She let herself go easily, building momentum, putting all her concentration into freeing her right hand at the crucial moment.

She twisted her wrist sharply toward her body, dragging all her strength against his thumb and fingers, pulling herself toward the pillow even as she loosened the weakest part of his hold. The Frenchman grunted in surprise when his fingers slipped on her flesh. She pulled harder, gathering her legs under her to spring for the pillow, but his fingers closed like steel wire, bit into her wrist bones, and an instant later she was spread-eagled across the bed, her arms still pinioned, stretched apart, her naked back exposed from her neck to her ankles.

The man in black walked around the bed, drawing the whip through his fingers. Lady Janet twisted around and watched over her shoulder, terrified, sickened by her failure, her fear, and the helpless knowledge that she'd lost her only chance. She drew a breath and clenched her body as he raised the whip.

It descended in a blur, parting the air with a whistle, a sharp cutting sound she knew from the hunt, from urging horses to take gates they were afraid to jump. The leather cracked like a gunshot straight across her buttocks. A sharp trail of pain made her body jerk convulsively and drew a strangled gasp from her clenched teeth and, an instant later, a scream, as the pain traveled into her thighs and up her back, coursing through her muscles like flame.

"Where is Grandzau?"

"He's dead," she gasped, fighting to regain control before terror and panic ravished her mind. She swallowed hard and tried to slow her breathing.

The gloved hand slapped her face.

"Open your eyes."

She hadn't realized they were closed. The black glove was inches from her face. It held a sheet of paper, white, rough-cut at top and bottom. Letters swam before her eyes.

"Read it!" demanded the man in black.

It was printed in capital letters and she recognized a cablegram:

"YOUR BID IS EXPECTED AT"—her eyes widened—"THE PENDRAGON AUCTION. LANCELOT."

"Do you wish to continue lying?"

"But he's dead!"

The man in black twisted her long blond hair around his free hand and jerked her head back until she was staring into his eyes. The pleasure she saw in them was terrifying. Nothing she could say would stop him from doing this to her. He lifted his other hand and Lady Janet flinched as she heard the whip cut the air again, racing to meet her naked flesh.

4

"What the hell is this supposed to mean?" growled Alfred Cowan.

"Pendragon?" asked Helen Thorp, staring at the telex. Chamberlain got up and stood behind her, reading it over her shoulder.

"King Arthur," he answered, touching the name with a large, meticulously cared-for index finger that looked slightly crooked, as if it had been broken at least once.

"Head dragon," Alfred Cowan agreed.

"What?"

"The Malory tales of King Arthur and the knights of the round table," explained Cowan. He grinned at Chamberlain and added, "Before television, my dear."

"Who's Lancelot? And don't tell me he's a nice knight."

Chamberlain said, "I wonder how he got into our private telex?"

"Maybe he works for us." Helen picked up the message and read it again. "Who's Pendragon supposed to be? . . . oh."

"Head dragon." Chamberlain nodded. "Charles Hammond."

"Oh for Christ's sake," said Cowan.

"Is this supposed to be a ransom note?" Helen asked.

"Why would they send *us* a ransom note?" snapped Cowan.

Helen shook her head.

"Excuse me, sir," said Chamberlain, "but I think they sent a lot of them."

"What makes you think that?"

"It says auction," Helen answered. "You invite a number of bidders to an auction. 'Your *bid* is expected at the Pendragon auction.'"

"What kind of a nut plays dumb word games. Lancelot! For Christ's sake. Auction, ransom. They're still kidnappers. Bastards!"

Helen enjoyed strategies and intrigue more than Cowan, who regarded them as an obstacle to getting a job done. "Maybe it's his way of saying who he is."

"How?"

"A code name."

"Well it doesn't make too damned much sense to send code to people who don't have the key. Right, Pete?"

"I think Ms. Thorp has a point. He's using a code for a reason. He figures somebody will recognize it."

Cowan glared at him, then turned back to Helen. "Do you think Rice got one of these too?"

"There's one way to find out." She picked up the phone and dialed London.

Chamberlain took the message and walked around the room reading it.

Alfred Cowan said, "What makes you think Rice'll talk to you now?"

"Watch."

The girl in London answered on the first double ring. "All Seas—"

Helen cut her off. "Lancelot calling Mr. Rice."

Cowan grinned and Chamberlain stopped walking in circles.

"Please hold the wire."

Helen heard a moment of whispered conversation, then Rice's familiar French accent. "This is Rene Rice. To whom am I speaking?"

"It's Helen Thorp at Comptel, Rene. We got one too."

"What? Who—"

Helen could imagine Rice's dark face contracting into a wrinkled ball of little eyes, slash mouth, and long narrow nose. The Madagascan, like many of his island, was of wildly mixed blood—parts French, Indian, Arab, and native Malagasy.

"'Your bid is expected at the Pendragon auction.' Who else got one, Rene?"

"I have no idea," Rice replied stiffly.

"But you do admit that Hammond was kidnapped."

"You seem to have deduced that yourself, Miss Thorp. With the help of the media. Yes. Mr. Hammond was kidnapped."

"What are you doing?"

Rice sounded exhausted. "Scotland Yard is investigating. Beyond that, what can we do but wait for their demands?"

"What other companies is Hammond dealing for at the moment?"

Rice hesitated. "I can't disclose that information. We owe our other clients the same confidentiality we accord Comptel."

"I'd like to suggest," Helen said evenly, "that someone, you or us, find out who else got these messages. Comptel is considering contributing to a ransom fund, if other of Hammond's clients will too."

"I see."

"Do you want to call them, or shall we?"

Rice's accent grew more French, and less clear. He was practically mumbling when he finished saying, "How can we be sure that they too received such a message?"

"By asking."

"But what if they didn't?"

Helen controlled her impulse to shout. "Then they didn't, Rene. It doesn't matter. They'll know by tomorrow anyway. Talk to your staff," she added gently. "See what they say. I'll call you in an hour with Comptel's contribution."

Alfred Cowan was glowering dangerously when she hung up.

"*What* contribution?"

"Rice sounds terrible. I thought he'd handle it better. He's usually pretty cool."

"*What* contribution?"

"We have to offer something, Alfred."

"Why?"

Helen started to answer, noticed Chamberlain sitting in a chair puzzling over the telex message. "Listen, Alfred, why don't we discuss this while Pete . . ."

"Right," snapped Cowan.

Chamberlain was already on his feet. "I'll make some calls. If it's got a secure phone, I'll like the office next door."

"Okay with you, Helen?" asked Cowan.

She nodded.

"Thank you, sir. Thank you, Ms. Thorp."

Chamberlain headed for the door, pausing to pick up Helen's sable coat and drape it reverently over a chair. He wanted very much to hear their discussion, but at the same time he was relieved to be out of that charged atmosphere for a minute. It had been like reporting to the bridge on a flagship and finding the captain and the task-force admiral waiting for your bright ideas. The kind of stuff that took a little getting used to.

He'd met Cowan once before, last year when he'd hired him away from the Agency, all smiles and promises in a D.C. hotel lobby. The Comptel president had been generous, a twenty-five-K bonus for ransoming the kidnapped regional manager if Chamberlain would come to work for Comptel security.

Chamberlain locked Helen Thorp's door behind him and took a deep breath. A guy like Charles Hammond ought to be worth a lot more than a regional manager. A lot more, if he played it right.

He leaned against the door and scanned the lavish office with a tiny electronic receiver. It lighted softly in his palm, confirming what a surreptitious sweep of Hammond's office had already indicated. Comptel's executive suites were bristling with electronic jammers and detectors. If he tried listening in on their meeting in the next room with the miniature eavesdropper he carried in his pocket, he'd provoke a shriek from their antibugging alarms.

He paced around her office, snapping his fingers in frustration. She'd been a surprise, younger, more beautiful, and tougher than company scuttlebutt had pegged her. Much tougher.

She lived very well. Her handsome desk was tucked into an alcove, while the main body of the room contained two separate seating areas, one with a fur-covered couch, an elaborate stereo rig, and an antique bar made of wood veneers and leaded glass. Chamberlain shook his head hopelessly, stymied for a way to listen in. As the international conglomerates operated further and further beyond the control and protection of national governments, they had to get tougher about their own security. Those that owned communication hardware subsidiaries were the hardest to crack. Comptel even had scramblers built into its top-level internal telephones, just like the KGB.

The bar! He selected a crystal highball glass and held the mouth against the wall between Helen Thorp's and Cowan's offices. Then he pressed his ear to the bottom of the glass in time to hear Helen Thorp say, "But last year Hammond agented ten percent of Comptel's business."

Chamberlain moved the glass several inches until he located a wall stud that conducted the sound better than the insulated hollow part. He grinned and whispered "genius" to himself.

Alfred Cowan's voice rumbled through the wall like the belly of a large and hungry animal. "Hammond's got too big a piece of our action."

"It's a little late to worry about that now," Helen Thorp replied. Chamberlain couldn't hear much of her tone, but the swift cadence of her reply had an angry beat.

"As a matter of fact," said Cowan, "I've been worried about Hammond for some time now."

"Alfred, for God's sake, do you want to do *less* business?"

Cowan's retort was so soft that Chamberlain could barely hear. "Maybe I want *you* to do less business with Hammond."

After a short silence, Helen said, "And more business elsewhere? Is that what you're saying?"

"Maybe you've gotten stuck in a rut with Hammond. Maybe you should be expanding elsewhere."

"This is a hell of a time to tell me."

"Have you ever heard bad news at a good time?"

The silence that followed was so long that Chamberlain thought they had turned around and were speaking in the other direction. But when at last he heard Helen Thorp, he knew he hadn't missed a word.

"That bad?" she asked flatly.

"Yep. This just brought it to a head."

"Alfred, how could I miss this? Why didn't you say anything?"

"You didn't listen."

Again there was silence.

Chamberlain waited, digesting the strong impression that Hammond was about to be abandoned. Sure enough Helen Thorp asked, "Are you suggesting we forget about him?"

"I don't know," Cowan said gloomily.

"Because if you are, it will cost us a lot."

"We'll survive."

"Four years lost profit?"

"Three," Cowan snapped too quickly.

"Settle for three," said Helen Thorp. "Will the board allow you that much time?"

"If I feed it to them a year at a time. Hell, our stock's up."

"We can't pay bills with paper profits."

"It won't be a happy couple of years." His voice took on a hard edge. "But I'll be better off than you, sweetheart."

"Yes, Alfred. I know that I am utterly dependent on Hammond if I want to have your job when you retire."

"Which you do."

"Yes, Alfred, as we both know."

Cowan laughed. "You're in worse trouble than you think. If the board cans me, the last person they'd put in this seat would be my favorite protegée."

"I'm aware of that," she replied coldly.

"I wouldn't want that to happen," said Cowan.

"The question is what are we willing to spend to get him back."

"Maybe I'll swallow the loss."

"You won't, Alfred. Because it'll kill your expansion plans."

Cowan snapped an angry retort. "Why did that stupid son of a bitch get himself snatched? What about his security people?"

"He probably didn't listen to them."

"That would be just like Hammond. Why in hell did I let you get me so tied up with him?"

"Because the arrangement worked. We're repeating ourselves, Alfred."

"Why the hell can't we just have employees do what he does?"

She replied patiently. "Because any employee who has the ear of Egypt's defense minister, the chief of staff of Kenya's army's private phone number, and goes whoring with the prince who buys communication hardware for Saudi Arabia would be pretty dumb to remain an employee."

"Screw," said Cowan.

Helen Thorp's voice cut insistently through the wall and swirled around the empty glass. "Nor do we want Comptel employees paying baksheesh."

"True."

"If Hammond pays bribes out of his commission, it's his own business."

"So why the hell did he get himself kidnapped?"

"Moving right along, Alfred. Let's make a decision before it's forced on us. How much do we contribute to his ransom?"

"What do you need?"

"How do I know? It's an auction. They'll ask for the moon. What will Comptel contribute?"

"Fuck!"

"How much, Alfred?"

He answered quietly and Chamberlain wasn't quite sure he'd heard him say one million dollars.

"Not enough," said Helen Thorp, and Chamberlain wondered what Comptel would pay for him if he were snatched. Thirty thousand dollars stuck in his head in a nasty way.

"Five! And that's it."

Chamberlain whistled soundlessly. Raising five million cash, hiding the fact it was paid, and recouping it would engage a platoon of accountants for the better part of a year.

Cowan's voice hardened, the pitch wavering as if he had stood up and was walking around his office. "But it's your job to get him back. No fuckups. That money goes nowhere until you know we've got him back. Clear?"

"You're doing the right thing," said Helen Thorp. "Shall I call Rice?"

"For five million he can pay for his own call."

"Where are you going?"

"My ass isn't as far over the line as yours, and seeing as

how there's no point in both our evenings being wrecked, Happy New Year."

"What about Chamberlain?" she asked.

"He's a hitter. You might need one."

Chamberlain shrugged. He'd never have made it into Cowan's office with ordinary abilities, but the term still rankled.

"How good is he?"

Before Cowan answered, Chamberlain heard the doorknob rattle, followed by a brisk knocking and Mildred calling loudly, "Mr. Chamberlain? Are you still in there, Mr. Chamberlain?"

Helen Thorp listened to Alfred Cowan skim aloud through the thick dossier he'd had ready on his desk. He hadn't hired Chamberlain as casually as he had implied.

"The CIA was not happy to lose him. They even tried a little pressure on me, but Comptel scratches too many backs to worry about that stuff. A lot of good guys had left already . . . you can read all this . . . he left graduate school for the navy, went into demolition diving, a lot of hairy stuff in Vietnam I'm sure he'd just as soon forget, then into the Agency by invitation. They gave him some field training and he did a little field work in South America, but he switched into data analysis. Computers."

"Ambitious," said Helen Thorp.

"How so?" asked Cowan, wrinkling his brow.

"That must have been about the time the Agency went so heavily into electronics."

"And out of the field. Right. So he went with the good stuff."

"Or what he thought was the good stuff. Now they're going back into the field. He guessed wrong."

"Anyway," said Cowan, "that's how he helped us. Got some stuff out of the machines on the guerillas who kidnapped our man, figured out what they wanted, and gave it to them. They had a falling out and a couple of them tried to kill our man, probably assuming that Chamberlain was a desk man. Our employee said Chamberlain had the fastest hands he'd ever seen. And that's from a guy who boxed in college."

"But what's he *like*?" persisted Helen. "Where's his head?"

Cowan snorted. "His head? He was a navy demo diver."

"Alfred," she said exasperatedly. "You know I don't share your love of military types. What does a navy demo diver mean to you?"

"They've taken chances most of us haven't. It steadies a man."

"*Physical* chances, Alfred. You take chances every day that would turn an ordinary person's hair white."

"It's not the same."

"What makes a guy like him work for us?"

"Money."

"Ambitious. Like I said."

Cowan said, "Not like you or me. I think he's got a vague idea he'd like to make a lot of bucks."

"Straight bucks or bent bucks?"

"Very straight. He's a little funny that way. He refused to take money under the table."

"Maybe he was being careful."

"More honest than careful," said Cowan.

"You like him."

"Yes, I do. . . . Phil Block out in Cleveland asked him about the South American kidnapping when Chamberlain was going over his plant security—incidentally, I don't want this one getting into the papers the way that one did. Especially the ransom. Every yo-yo in the world gets the idea to snatch an executive—anyway, Phil asked. Chamberlain told him all about the negotiations. He was really proud of them. But he never *mentioned* the hand-to-hand stuff."

Helen Thorp grinned at her boss. "Sounds like you hired a sort of all-around modest, opportunistic, honest superspy."

"Let's just say he'd be a nice guy to have along at a mugging."

"Whose side?"

"Yours, if you want him. That's what we pay him for."

Mildred asked why Chamberlain had locked Ms. Thorp's door. Chamberlain replied with a smile that he was about to pour himself a New Year's drink. Would she care to join him? She looked like she'd left an empty space at a good party.

Mildred ceased her suspicious inspection of the room and smiled back. "*My* party. My husband's going to kill me."

"What would you like?" He grinned. "The boss is buying."

She placed the papers she was carrying on Helen Thorp's desk. "I couldn't, thank you . . . I just wanted to see if you needed anything."

"I'm fine," said Chamberlain, walking her back to the door and thanking her with another smile. "Like your dress."

He locked the door again and anxiously pressed the highball glass to the wall in time to hear Helen Thorp laugh as Alfred Cowan said, "How do you judge a guy who's trained to hit people? I guess if he's still standing he's pretty good. . . . Seriously though, I hired the guy because I thought he'd be handy to have around to deal with situations beyond ordinary security, and like you said before, it's good to have a pipeline into the CIA. Some of the guys we've had awhile were drying up, so it was time to ship them to Albuquerque and get somebody new in the Washington office. . . . He's yours if you want him. Happy New Year, dear. Call me if you need help." The thin wall trembled as Cowan's door was opened and shut.

Chamberlain found a bottle of Pelligrini water in Helen Thorp's bar refrigerator and poured it into the listening glass, noting with surprise that it didn't bubble like Perrier. Then he sat at her desk and dialed Langley, Virginia, on her private phone, which bore a lingering hint of her perfume.

Cowan had sounded a lot less enamored through the wall than he had when he'd hired Chamberlain face to face. So far the job had turned out to be that of a highly paid, glorified guard, visiting Comptel facilities, inspecting security, and turning in expense vouchers and trip reports.

He enjoyed the travel, the first-class treatment, and the deference paid him by the outlying conglomerate branches, all anxious to please the man from the Washington office. But it was routine and routine didn't go anywhere because there was no way to pull off a big move that counted, especially if the head of the company regarded you as a hitter with a diminishing number of favors in store at the CIA.

Recently he'd begun playing squash with the rest of the

middle-level executives in his office. It gave him the willies, because he'd always believed that pastimes and hobbies were for people who'd given up trying to do things that counted.

When Langley answered, Chamberlain played it straight and gave the operator a short list of names. Then he waited while she tried to run them down on New Year's Eve to ask if they would speak to a former friend about Charles Hammond, whose rescue might count a lot.

5

Something had changed. Something enormous, but indefinable. Her body still leaped and bucked and she still heard her voice shriek hoarsely, but after a while she realized she no longer heard the awful whistle of the lash, nor did she feel it add new pain to the agony that ripped her. She identified the pounding in her ears as her own heartbeat.

"Open your eyes."

She opened them. The letters on the yellow paper swam before her. She cringed as the man in black touched the signature with the tip of his lash and tapped it again and again. Lancelot, Lancelot, Lancelot.

"Where is Grandzau?"

Through the agony that burned her whole body, her mind screamed that someone was using Grandzau's old Malory code.

"Do you wish to lie some more?" asked the man in black.

Who could know it? How could she convince him that Lancelot couldn't be Grandzau? The fat one holding her had shifted his grip. He held both her hands in one of his.

"Where is Grandzau?"

She wrested free and reached toward the pillow. The pain

slowed her, contracted her body even as she tried to stretch. He caught her easily and forced her back on her belly.

"Where is Grandzau?" For the first time he sounded impatient, and she realized again that he had beaten her for his pleasure. Now he expected the truth, but she had already spoken the truth.

"He's dead. I swear it."

He raised the whip.

As she twisted around in another futile effort to escape, she saw that the man holding her had opened his pants.

"Later," the man in black promised. "When she has spoken."

Wheeler awakened hazily, his brain slowly untangling from a weird dream of telephone wires and giant wheeling hawks. Wheeling hawks. Wheeler hawks. His neck was sore. Gradually he began to realize he was in a hospital. He was tubed and trached.

Whenever Mr. Hammond stopped in Chicago, Wheeler dated a nurse from the Cook County Hospital and from her he knew the jargon for the plastic tubing they'd inserted in his nostrils and the tracheal slit in his throat. Memory closed in on him, and with it the giddy thought that having come in with an already slit throat, he had saved the doctors the trouble.

Hammond! He had to report where they'd taken Hammond.

He tried to sit up, groping for a call button in the dim light. He couldn't find it, but he felt tugs on his chest and scalp and, reaching for the sensations, caught his fingers in more tubing.

He was still puzzling out the new discovery when the room filled with nurses, who crowded around the bed and tried to push him down. He struggled and one of the tubes came out of his chest. He looked at it and saw it wasn't a tube, but a wire attached to an electrode. Pain shot through his throat and he realized, as he fell back, that he was in Intensive Care.

He tried to speak and couldn't.

He lay quietly, gathering his strength while the nurses fussed with the loosened electrode. Then, when they had straightened the sheet and were standing back to admire their handiwork, he motioned weakly for pencil and paper.

The nurses patted the sheet back into place, checked an IV

bottle attached to his left arm, and turned to go. Furious, Wheeler tried again to sit up. Again they restrained him. He made more pencil and paper motions, but one of the nurses approached with a broad canvas strap which they started to tie around his torso and the bed.

"You'll hurt yourself if you move," said one of the women as the others passed the canvas under the bed.

Driven by guilt for screwing up Hammond's security and by the same obstinacy that had allowed him to trail the Daimler for miles out of London, Wheeler reached for his nose tubes, determined to rip them out in a drastic attempt to get their attention.

A man in a white smock burst into the room. Wheeler saw a dark blue sleeve sticking out from the white. He let go of his nose tubes and waited quietly while the nurses reacted to the intrusion. He was lean as a knife and had a little gray pencil-thin mustache. He regarded the wall of glaring nurses with chilly disdain. Reaching under the smock he pulled out a pen and pad, announcing as he did, "I am Inspector Farquhar and that man is trying to communicate something."

New Year's dawn broke behind the East River and laced cold, gray light into Helen Thorp's office atop the Comptel Building. Fifty stories below, the streets were still dark.

It found Peter Chamberlain in quiet telephone conversation in one corner and Helen Thorp at her desk. She cradled her phone with a satisfied nod and scanned the single sheet of paper on which were listed in a small, neat hand the night's telephone conversations. Four cigarette butts sat in her ashtray, one for each two hours.

She waved Chamberlain over. He finished his call with an audible, "The boss beckons."

Tired as she was, Helen watched him with a certain interest as he sauntered across the room. Chamberlain really was built like Hammond, broader and shorter than him, and lacking, of course, Charles's electric vitality. But he seemed to have a sense of humor, though she couldn't imagine him, or any other man, doing what Hammond had done that first time in Paris. When she'd returned to her hotel suite from dinner with the Mozambique telephone officials, she'd found her bed buried under rose petals. She'd slept in them, resolutely alone.

"Who'd you get to?" asked Chamberlain.

"Everyone but Hans Streicher, which isn't surprising."

"No. The arms dealers tend to be independent. He'll come around when he's sure he needs us."

"Mishuma will match us. Lockheed couldn't find anybody who was allowed to say yes, but they want to. Same with Texas Instruments. They don't want their hands dirty, so I think they'll let us represent them."

"Nicely done," Chamberlain said admiringly. "Very nice."

"British Hovercraft is another proposition. They're very comfortable working with military types, so they'll probably stand alone."

"Will they join you when it counts?"

"Of course," said Helen. "It's to all of our advantages. A couple of smaller companies will also come in for smaller amounts. Some of them are in a lot worse trouble than us, because Hammond handles the majority of their sales. They'll do what we tell them to. Also, the Paris office says Dassault has approached us quietly."

"They really kidnapped the right man," said Chamberlain.

"They sure did. Everyone wants him back safe and sound and capable of finishing his jobs for them." She bent her head back and stretched her neck. Massaging it with her fingers, trying to rub out the kinks, she asked, "And how did you do?"

"Two things. I finally located a guy who knew about the Malory code."

"Did he know who uses it?"

"Sort of. A German named Karl Grandzau was selling secrets to both us and the Russians back in the late sixties and middle seventies. He had a small network in NATO and another one in East Germany. The kind of operator who every time you're ready to kill him for screwing you comes back with some good dope from the other side. And speaking of dope, he was trading a lot of the narcotic kind on the side, heroin out of Marseilles, until the Chinese in Amsterdam took over the business. Each of Grandzau's contacts had a code name from the Arthurian legend. Really corny. Grandzau's code name was Lancelot."

"So we'll buy Hammond back from Grandzau."

"Except Grandzau died three years ago."

Lady Janet lay still, her body no longer able to flee the lash. The whip had never strayed from her buttocks, but the pain was everywhere. Sometime after the whip stopped cutting its song in the air, she heard the man in black talking on the telephone.

"She doesn't know. Perhaps he tricked her too."

There was a pause. Then he said, "Yes, I'm sure. I'll have to try the one in Bern." He hung up the phone. Then she heard him say, "Take care of her."

"I'll be awhile," said the flashy one.

The man in black said nothing.

Lady Janet sensed movement and watched through slitted eyes. She was still on her belly, the sheet soaked with her perspiration. The man in black passed into her range of vision, the whip still in his hand, and slipped it into the cane scabbard with a regretful sigh. The instrument clicked shut. He twisted the knob to lock it and walked out of the room.

She heard his heels clicking on the polished marble stairs. She waited, gathering her will. From behind her she heard the rustle of cloth, the thud of heavy shoes, the clink of a belt buckle—the fleshy one removing his clothes.

She didn't know if she could move at all. The pain still coursed through her body. Her arms felt like lead. She tried to orient herself, to see where she lay on the bed, to figure out where the pillow was, to fix exactly the way her arms and legs lay.

He grabbed her ankles and shoved her legs apart. From the window came the sound of a starter motor, then the distinctive rumbly-clatter of a Citroën-Maserati. She forced herself to lie quietly while the man behind her arranged her body for his assault.

He was breathing loudly now, a deep and slow inhalation. His hand brushed her wealed buttocks and the resultant pain compressed her will. If she could only move, the moment was coming. She concentrated on the forward lunge. It had to be perfect. He was too big to fight in close quarters. This was her last chance. He was going to kill her after he raped her.

The bed sagged as he knelt between her spread legs.

She leaped forward, sliding her hand under the first pillow, desperately burrowing for the gun behind the second. He bellowed surprise. She got her hand under the second pillow, but he grabbed her legs and pulled her toward him. Her fingers hit the hard shape of the gun, but he dragged her away from it. She kicked out like a swimmer, straining forward, her hand back under the pillow.

She got her hand around the gun. In a practiced motion, she flicked off the safety as her forefinger slid through the trigger guard. Twisting onto her side, nearly blinded by pain, she brought the gun around, sighting his meaty shoulder, and squeezed the trigger.

He was naked, white as a drowned body. He gaped stupidly at the gun, then tossed a balled sheet at her with cunning speed. The shot exploded loudly in the big room.

Lady Janet fell back on the bed, weeping bitterly.

The man in black would pay for what he had done to her, but the sheet had spoiled her shot and now her best clue where to find him lay dead on her bedroom floor, a bullet through his heart.

"Dead? If Grandzau's dead, who is Lancelot?"

"No one knows." Chamberlain stood up, stretched until his joints snapped, and walked to the glass wall. He stared at his insubstantial reflection superimposed on the gray city. "But we have a worse problem. Much worse."

"What?"

He turned back to Helen. "I think that some of my friends were a little too eager to talk."

"Meaning that the CIA is interested in Hammond."

"Only because the Russians are."

6

"The Russians? Charles Hammond doesn't deal with the Russians. They asked him to handle the grain trades, but he said no way." Helen grinned, remembering. "He says Russian bureaucrats make Arab cement traders look like cake-sale ladies."

"You like Hammond, don't you?" Chamberlain asked.

Helen was too tired to pretend. "I like him a lot. Life moves right along when he's around. He's got a flair. What did the CIA tell you about the Russians?"

"Minute the word was out that Hammond was snatched, the KGB jumped in with all four feet. Tipped Scotland Yard to some IRA cells in London the bobbies didn't know about. Busted a Palestinian safe house with their own men. Thank God Hammond wasn't there. They're not exactly subtle. Now that they've heard about the telegrams, they've started cozying up to Mishuma and Hans Streicher and God knows who else. They want Hammond and they want him bad."

"For what he knows," Helen breathed.

"Looks that way. Hammond knows a lot about a lot of armies, having sold them their best hardware."

"What would they do with him?"

"Wring it out of him."

"Oh God."

"So it looks like we won't be the only bidder at that auction. We might work a deal with Mishuma and Streicher and surely Hovercraft, but the Russians'll bid against us."

"What will the CIA do?"

"They're going to watch everything we do. And if it looks like the Russians are going to get Hammond, they'll kill him."

"Well . . . will the Russians disrupt the auction?"

"No. Hammond won't be there in person. So they can't."

"Well, we'll make a deal with the CIA. Bid together."

"Wonderful," said Chamberlain. "The thing is, the Russians are hunting Hammond already. They won't wait for the auction."

Helen Thorp nodded, chewing her lip. "Right. And the CIA?"

"Watching. Ready to pounce if the Russians get close."

"Right." She stopped chewing her lip and hit him with the full force of her startling eyes. They glowed violet in the dawn light. Her voice harmonized with them, intent, demanding.

"Pete. What do *you* want?"

"Beg pardon?"

"What do you want?" she repeated. "What do you want to get out of this?"

"I'm not sure I understand you."

"A good piece of my career is on the line with Hammond's life. I don't know if I should have you work for me or if I should handle it myself. The Russians complicate my decision. So I want to know more about Pete Chamberlain. What does Pete Chamberlain want?"

Chamberlain hesitated.

Helen Thorp shook her head. "Don't try to make up a right answer. Just tell me."

He spread his hands wide, studied his thick fingers, then met her eyes again. "I want to get ahead."

"How?"

"I want to make money . . . I want to do something that counts."

"So does everybody."

He looked surprised.

"So does everybody," she repeated.

He was silent.

She pushed him harder, seeking the loyalty she would reap if he exposed himself with a deeper confession. "The ones who succeed know a better reason."

Chamberlain turned away from her and looked out the window.

She moved next to him. Down in the street, five hundred feet below where it was still dark, some New Year's diehards were waving forlornly for nonexistent taxis. She found Chamberlain's face mirrored in the glass. The sky was lightening rapidly and when their eyes met it was in the last dim reflection of the night.

Chamberlain spoke softly. "You know what I want?"

"What?"

"I want to feel comfortable walking into Cowan's office."

"So do I."

"You're kidding," he said, turning to her with a grateful smile.

"A little . . . would you settle for my office?"

"What do you mean?"

"Get Hammond back alive and I'll guarantee you'll be comfortable walking into my office. Any time. Any reason. Get him back, Pete. Blank check. *Get him back.*"

The pencil was gone. So was the paper. Inspector Farquhar was still there, but he wasn't alone. A guy in a rumpled gray suit stood beside the Scotland Yard dick. He looked American, he looked in good shape, and he looked like he hadn't slept in two days.

Farquhar noticed his eyes were open and said, "This is Mr. Chamberlain from Comptel, Incorporated, one of Mr. Hammond's clients."

Wheeler fumbled for the missing pencil, and Farquhar stepped nearer the bed. "Feeling better?" he asked, extending a pen and pad. "You started bleeding again and the doctors had to work on you. Do you remember what you told me?"

Wheeler nodded slightly. It was easier than writing.

"Good. It's six hours since we talked. We don't know where Hammond is, but they've sent a sort of ransom note. Anything you can tell me will help."

Wheeler was astonished by the weight of the pen. He felt much worse than before. Nor could he understand Farquhar's urgency. He was tired and nothing seemed that important. Lazily, he turned the penpoint to the paper. It seemed to stick to the pad.

"Try," whispered Farquhar.

The new man brushed past him, gripped the rails on the side of the bed, and leaned over until little more than a foot separated his face from Wheeler's. His head seemed enormous.

"Come on, fella. You're the only break we have. You're the only thing that went wrong for the bastards. You weren't supposed to stay breathing, but you did. Don't blow it now."

Wheeler closed his eyes. The voice hammered at him.

"Chamberlain, go easy on him."

"Come on, Wheeler. Hammond's hanging by his balls. He's waiting for you, man. Spill it."

"Chamberlain!"

Wheeler opened his eyes in time to see the American shrugging Farquhar's restraining hand off his muscular arm. *I know what you're doing,* he thought. *You got to get me moving.* He bunched his muscles, put all his strength behind the pen, and watched its lines trail across the page.

"Good," said Chamberlain.

Wheeler pushed harder. There were dark and empty patches in his memory. He'd followed Hammond's Daimler north out of London, past Hampstead and Highgate. The road flickered light and dark as if he were driving in and out of tunnels, but he saw no tunnel walls, only the closely spaced English houses and storefronts. The Daimler veered off the busily traveled road, took a fork.

He stopped writing. He saw that the Scotland Yard guy had spread a road map out on his bed.

"East or west?" snapped the American.

Wheeler thought. He'd turned to the right. West. No, east. East. Shortly after the fork, the Daimler got onto a two-lane road that cut northeast into the countryside. Wheeler dropped further and further back as traffic thinned. When he couldn't keep even one car between him and the Daimler, he pulled onto the shoulder and waited, aching for another car to come along.

A truck came. He trailed behind it, but it was going too slowly to keep pace with the Daimler. He floored the Jag, shot around the truck, and raced after a distant black dot that grew larger and larger as he caught up but it turned out not to be the Daimler. It was a farm truck, heaped with feed corn, that had joined the road from some road or drive he hadn't seen.

Wheeler panicked, jammed on the brakes, and slowed the Jag around in a controlled slide that caused his mouth to fill with blood. He raced back down the road, saw the intersection, turned into it, and skidded to a stop. It was a dirt road, the road the farm truck had just come from. There was corn scattered at the turn. The Daimler had gone elsewhere.

He started to turn the Jag. The steering wheel grew stiff, as if the servo assist had broken down. He heaved against it, forced the big car to back and fill, back and fill, each turn tighter and more killing than the last. He kept trying to turn the car, growing weaker, his spirit diminishing. At last he surrendered. Wheeler stopped writing.

After a while Inspector Farquhar said, "But we found you a hundred yards from the car."

Wheeler looked into the American's anxious eyes.

"You weren't in the car, fella. What happened after you stopped driving?"

Wheeler drew a question mark.

"Come on. Do you remember getting out of the car?"

No.

"Did somebody pull you out?"

Wheeler wrote "birds."

"Birds?"

"He's around the bend," whispered Farquhar.

"Screw!"

Wheeler bore down on the pen. He remembered the wheeler birds. The wheeling birds. He *had* gotten out of the car. He had forced the door open, lurched out onto his feet, and begun walking toward the main road. He kept hearing the birds crying, saw them. Hoody crows and black crows. Then suddenly they were gone, wheeling off in one direction, roosting in a distant line of trees. He watched them, turning as he did, lost his balance, and fell. He lay staring up at the sky, empty of birds but for one wheeling hawk which dove suddenly out of his line of vision. A roaring sound grew in his ears and he thought he was dying. He had almost reached the road. A stream of black telephone wires passed overhead like a musical staff. The roaring grew louder.

A silver airplane filled his memory . . . straining engines clawing her into the air on fully pitched props . . . the frantic racket of taking off from too short a runway. The plane slashed diagonally across the line of wires, climbed past his vision, and was gone. The sight lay vivid in his brain.

"Did you get its numbers?" snapped Chamberlain.

Wheeler smiled. He could rest now. Mr. Hammond didn't hire idiots. Of course he got the numbers.

"Right," said Inspector Farquhar, cradling his telephone with finality and smiling across his desk at Chamberlain, who'd been ushered in while he was in the middle of his call. "The airports are all on it, and the radar chaps are tracing all of yesterday's intruder reports. Interpol is checking on the Continent. We'll turn up something, with luck. How did you do with Rice?"

Chamberlain slumped, exhausted, in Farquhar's visitor's chair. The Scotland Yard detective had a curiously bland office, a framed picture of his family the only personal object on his desk. "Rice is not very helpful."

"That was my experience too. I had to practically threaten to arrest him before he'd speak to me. Turned out to be a worthless little bugger anyhow."

"I figured Hammond for having a ballsier second in command," Chamberlain agreed. "What if he gets sick in the middle of something big?"

"Or kidnapped." Farquhar smiled.

"I started yelling," said Chamberlain. "Definitely the wrong move. Rice looked like he was going to cry. Unbelievable scene. Phones ringing, staff going crazy . . . Rice's secretary told me that Hammond's got twenty deals hanging fire and Rice is just sitting there with his head in his hands."

Farquhar said, "Some friends who've heard I'm with this case passed on some information about some of those deals."

Chamberlain nodded politely. A highly placed cop usually had a couple of half-decent sources in the intelligence community, especially if he'd ever managed a favor, like looking south when somebody ran north. "Anything interesting?"

"Interesting *sounding*, but it's really little more than raw data. Charles Hammond does more than arrange bank loans, as I'm sure your employers have told you. What they might not have told you, however, is that Hammond has his fingers in some very strange pies in some even stranger places."

"Like where?" asked Chamberlain.

"Mozambique. Hours after Hammond was taken, two Zimbabwe guerilla factions sheltering in Mozambique launched a combined assault on a third faction that they suspected of having kidnapped him to prevent their receiving arms."

"Are you saying Hammond's a gunrunner?"

"Let's say he's a go-between in a lot of arms deals. . . . At the same time, in Brasilia a colonel and a major got into a gun battle on the steps of the presidential palace. Hammond had met with the colonel three times in the past month. The major shot him dead and was not arrested."

"Sounds like he stopped a coup."

"Yes, it does. My sources didn't know any more about it. Perhaps you can ask yours if it was a coup and if Hammond was involved."

Chamberlain realized that it was time to offer something back. "I heard that some of Hammond's friends in Madagascar headed for the hills when they heard he got kidnapped. They've got some kind of problem going on down there with elections."

Farquhar nodded. "Hammond has plantations on the island."

"They were the one thing Rice would talk about," said Chamberlain. "He said that Hammond gets down there about six weeks a year on vacation."

"What's your next move?" asked Farquhar.

Chamberlain hesitated. The Scotland Yard man was being very helpful and could continue to be, but he was no dummy and he'd know right away if Chamberlain was holding back. He decided that Farquhar was definitely worth cultivating.

"Comptel is leading a consortium to buy Hammond. Rene Rice claims he can only contribute a million and a half dollars."

"What?"

"Exactly. I'd like to find out why."

Farquhar gazed at the picture on his desk as if he were viewing mug shots. "Let me give you the name of a fellow in the City. Banking chap. Might know a thing or two about Mr. Hammond's finances."

Lady Janet shot herself full of morphine, concealed a second charged needle and her gun in the small of her back, and flew from Nice to Bern. She had to risk discovery by airport security and Swiss customs because she couldn't travel without the pain-killer and it had been too many years since she'd used her old contacts for drugs and weapons.

The small of the back was the safest spot she knew for sizable items, and her striking beauty and obvious wealth were good cover when the authorities were looking for terrorists who failed abysmally at concealing their middle-class origins. She dozed on the plane in a drug haze, her face veiled by her blond hair. After it landed, she drank coffee to clear the fog from her brain while she waited for her rented car.

She drove into Bern, across the city, and into a section of countrylike houses on several-acre plots concealed by high stone walls. Fleming's gate was unlocked. She rang anyway, but no one answered.

Pushing the gate open, she got back into her car and lay her gun on the floor beside her seat. Then she drove onto the macadam driveway between low walls of plowed snow.

The place looked deserted. The immaculate snow-covered lawns bore no prints, but the walks were shoveled. Behind the house, glinting in the afternoon sun, were Fleming's greenhouses, the heated gardens he had often spoken of retiring to when Grandzau's schemes had paid off.

Lady Janet rolled down the window and listened. There was an eerie snow-damped silence. The walls blocked the noises of the city beyond, and the house, two stories of white brick, was silent. Then she saw that the breeze had blown a fine film of powdered snow over the shoveled paths and that there were footprints in the path to the greenhouses.

She was wearing an unlined Burberry, too thin for the Swiss winter. She shoved her gun into the pocket, kept her hand on it, and got out of the car. She left the door open and walked toward the greenhouses.

The sun was blinding where the snow met the white house, the glare like a blow to the face. She was exhausted and a small part of her mind, a rational piece not driven by hurt and humiliation, was clamoring to stop, to get back into the car, to go to a hotel and sleep until she could handle herself.

I'll have to go to Bern, the man who had beaten her had said. And Bern was where Fleming, one of the two who might have used Grandzau's code, lived. She kept walking, the gun rigid in her pocket, the barrel pushing against the cloth of the light raincoat. This was her only lead. She reached the greenhouse, hearing nothing.

Standing in the partial shadow of the greenhouse, her hand on the door latch, she thought she saw someone inside. She took the gun out of her pocket, opened the door, and stepped in. Ignoring the sight which greeted her first, she pressed her back to the door and shot glances to either side. Then, when she was sure she was alone, she approached Fleming.

His hair had grayed at the temples in the three years since she'd seen him, at Grandzau's funeral on an Italian hillside. His fingers were caked with dried earth. He had started a new rose bed in a raised wooden planter. The homey scattering of trowel, pruning knife, basket, and bone meal spoke as much for Fleming's innocence as the cruel marks on his naked body.

He was hanging by his bound ankles from an overhead irrigation pipe, his wrists tied with a black silk handkerchief. The man in black hadn't struck him more than a dozen times, but Fleming was dead. His lips were blue. She guessed that the old man, with no information to appease his tormentor, had died of heart failure.

Fleming had always treated her with courtesy. Lady Janet cut him down with the pruning knife. He fell heavily. Still holding her gun, she covered his body with sheets of black plastic.

That left Daitch in Brussels, the only other one who could have used the code. Daitch, the junior partner, Grandzau's bodyguard, the man who'd set up hideouts and boltholes so Grandzau could betray all sides and disappear until they gave up the search. Of the three, Grandzau, Fleming, and Daitch, Daitch had been most treacherous, worse really than Grandzau, though he deferred to Grandzau's superior intelligence and brilliant imagination.

Lady Janet hurried to her car. If the man in black knew of him, there was no time to sleep. Daitch was fully capable of killing him before she could. The pain was nudging through the morphine. She let it. It would keep her awake until she was on the plane to Brussels.

Peter Chamberlain lay chin deep in hot water. Through the rising steam he surveyed the striped marble bathroom walls of his Savoy hotel room. They were cream colored with natural black streaks at regular intervals, and in his exhausted state he dallied with the thought that someone had skinned a stone tiger.

A wall telephone between the toilet and the bidet rang loudly, echoing on the hard surfaces of the big, luxurious room. Chamberlain ignored it because he knew he was worthless until he got some sleep. He'd hung a DO NOT DISTURB sign on the front door, but he'd forgotten to tell the desk to leave him alone. It had been thirty-six hours since he'd reported to work at his Washington office. Since that morning he'd flown to New York, driven to Connecticut, driven back from Connecticut, spent New Year's Eve and night on Helen Thorp's telephone, crossed the Atlantic Ocean, and run around London like a two-day package tour.

Now it was one A.M. London time, seven in the evening in New York, and he was damned if he was getting out of the water to talk to anybody. The Scotland Yard man was tracing the airplane Hammond might or might not have been taken away in.

The phone stopped ringing. Chamberlain went back to contemplating tiger stripes and the way his toes occasionally bobbed to the surface. He was so tired that the Scotch he'd taken into the bath sat on the edge of the giant tub untouched.

He dozed for a moment, then summoned the energy to apply some soap. In the midst of slipping back under to rinse his chest, he thought he heard something outside the bathroom door. He stopped moving, waited for the sloshing water to quiet, and listened.

He felt the wet hairs on the back of his neck begin to curl away from his skin; his heart quickened and even though he knew his tired state was amplifying his reactions, he still felt afraid. Someone was moving around the suite and he was lying naked in the tub in an unlocked bathroom. He wondered if he could get to the lock on the door, bolt it, and telephone for help without being heard.

Footsteps, muffled by the carpet, approached the door. Chamberlain wrapped his hand around a heavy glass ashtray.

"Are you in there, Pete?"

He sagged back into the water. "In the tub."

Helen Thorp pushed the door open, gave the soapy bath water a single piercing look, lowered the toilet lid, and sat down. She was wearing a dark, blousy cashmere dress and her hair was free, glimmering thick and black to her shoulders.

"Welcome to London."

"What have you got?" she asked.

"The numbers on a plane they might have put Hammond on. And a lead on one of Grandzau's partners who's retired in Switzerland."

"What else?"

"Rene Rice is an idiot and Hammond's broke."

"What?"

"Neither of which makes sense."

"Nor do you. What are you talking about?"

"Rice treated me like the enemy. He's got himself barricaded in the All Seas offices. He's not making any decisions and he's not supporting his staff. He's pretty lightweight for a chief of staff. Which means Hammond was an idiot for hiring him in the first place."

"What do you mean Hammond's broke?"

"I talked to a banker. He's mortgaged up to his eyeballs on everything he owns. Everything. Which I think is one of Rice's problems. He knows he doesn't have any money for a ransom."

"Hold it. Define broke."

"No money. Maybe a million and a half in assets. For a guy like Hammond, that's no money. He owes on everything he owns. Even his Madagascar plantations. Wait till the kidnappers find out he's broke. Maybe they did. Maybe that's why they're making it an auction."

"Wait. You say Hammond's broke because he's mortgaged?"

"Up to his eyeballs."

"No. It doesn't work like that. For all you know Hammond went liquid to put his capital into barley futures. He stays on top of things and moves fast."

"What if barley futures fell through?"

"It's not like personal finance," Helen Thorp explained

patiently. "You're comparing Hammond to a Scarsdale doctor who's afraid to tell his wife that the kids have to go to public school because he got burned in the market."

"I don't get it."

"Take my word for it. The fact that Hammond's company doesn't have cash for a ransom doesn't mean much."

"But the guy must be worth millions."

"Tied up, at the moment."

"In what?"

"That's his business, Pete. You can't plan a financial strategy in the event of getting kidnapped. Now come on, get dressed. We have a meeting downstairs in ten minutes."

"I've been up since yesterday. I'm going to bed."

"Sorry, I need you. I've ordered coffee. Want some wake-up pills?"

"Christ, no. How'd you get in my room?"

She dangled a key from its brass tag and dropped it into her pocketbook. Chamberlain closed his eyes and sank deeper into the tub, loath to leave the seductive warmth, much less dress and go downstairs. He wondered how she had talked his key out of the impeturbable desk clerk in tails, and decided Comptel probably owned the place. The scent of her perfume drifted over the water. He opened his eyes. It occurred to him that there was something he wanted more than sleep.

She returned his gaze, her eyes wide and guileless.

"What kind of meeting?" asked Chamberlain.

Helen Thorp fished a gold case from her bag, put a cigarette between her lips, made flame rise from one corner of the case, and inhaled deeply. "A shareholders' meeting."

"Comptel's?" He felt himself growing erect, but the deep, cloudy water hid him from her.

"Hammond's. I've got everyone together who's going to buy him back. People from Mishuma, Lockheed, Texas Instruments, British Hovercraft, Dassault, and even Hans Streicher."

"How'd you manage him?"

"The same way I got the others. Comptel moved first, so it's our show and they're all hoping we'll get Hammond back for them." She smiled, crinkling her eyes, and Chamberlain realized that she had slept since he'd seen her last. "Basic rule of business, Pete. Everybody hopes the other fellow knows what she's doing."

"There's another basic rule of business, Helen. Or maybe it's more a basic rule of life: if a lady walks in on a guy in a bathtub and she looks as good as you do he's going to ask her to join him."

She crossed her legs and flicked cigarette ash into the bidet. "You're too tired to be clever."

"Are you referring to words or deeds?"

"I'll get you your clothes."

Ten minutes later, in the elevator, she said, "I'll fly commercial back to New York. You can keep the plane."

"What range does it have?"

"It got me here from New York nonstop."

"Thank you. Listen, do I tell these guys I'm going to kick the door down and hijack Hammond?"

"No. I just want to cover all bases. If you can't find him, these people will put up the auction money."

"Do they know about the CIA interest?"

"They could. I don't know."

"Marvelous."

She led him down a hall to a hotel meeting room. "Ready?"

Chamberlain took a deep breath and worked at straightening his shoulders. "The last time I was this tired I was at the bottom of the South China Sea and a lot younger."

"This'll go quickly. Then bed."

"Are you here in the Savoy?"

"No. There's an apartment I usually stay in in London."

She opened the door, leaving Chamberlain to wonder with whom. A half dozen men were waiting nervously. They stood and shook hands as Helen introduced Chamberlain. Then she said, "Mr. Chamberlain has worked for Comptel for some time. Last year he negotiated the release of one of our South American managers from leftist kidnappers."

"Do you think these are leftist kidnappers?" asked a tall, gray-haired man who represented Lockheed.

"I don't think so, but it doesn't matter. The point is they've got Hammond and they're calling the shots."

Chamberlain was too tired to bother remembering names that weren't important. A man who looked very much like the first and who represented Texas Instruments said, lowering his voice conspiratorially, "My sources in the intelligence community suggest this Lancelot's been operating for some time in Europe. A kind of freelance spy."

The Japanese man from Mishuma nodded his agreement.

"I wish that were true," said Chamberlain. "Then we wouldn't have to worry about some crazy amateurs losing their nerve and killing Hammond. Unfortunately, our sources suggest that the freelance spy you're talking about died three years ago."

This time it was the arms merchant, Hans Streicher, who nodded. Chamberlain gave him a small smile. He instinctively liked the bluff, hearty German. From what he had heard, Streicher was as decent a sort as you'd find in his trade. Of course that wasn't saying much, but he might make a good ally if things got rough. He would look him up in the morning.

They asked some more questions. The gist of Chamberlain's answers remained the same. They would wait for the kidnappers to announce their arrangements. They would play by their rules. They would do nothing to risk Hammond's life.

"What if someone outbids us?" asked the Japanese man.

"Like who?"

"Someone who doesn't want us to have Hammond."

"Who would that be?"

"Mishuma has competitors who would gain by our loss."

"I think that's pretty farfetched," said the man from Lockheed.

"It does seem a bit extreme," said Helen. "Besides, our pooled resources are enormous. Who could outbid us?"

The Frenchman from Dassault, who had not yet said a word, spoke. "The Russians."

"What?" asked Hans Streicher.

"They made a clumsy overture to my aide this afternoon. They offered to bid with us. Back us. In return, they could help retrieve him. It was absurd. But it suggests that they have a reason for wanting Hammond and that reason isn't hard to guess."

"He knows a lot," said Streicher. "Maybe too much."

Helen rose from the table. "Mr. Chamberlain is aware of this and has had considerable experience in the area of intelligence and espionage. He is watching the Russians. Comptel has other employees similarly engaged."

Rene Rice, who had also not spoken until now and who looked emotionally shattered, said quietly, "Mr. Hammond knows many things, negotiating as he does with so many important people, but he doesn't know the sort of things the Russians would want him for. Only the most secret weapons are unknown to the adversary governments; they number but a few. And Mr. Hammond would never be included in such a sale. The Russians have no reason to want Mr. Hammond."

Chamberlain and Streicher exchanged skeptical glances.

"We can't be sure of that, Rene," said Helen.

"I know it," insisted Rice. "They don't want him."

"What about the Brazilians?" Chamberlain asked suddenly.

Rice looked blank. "I don't understand."

"Neither do I," said Chamberlain, "but a Brazilian colonel you people were talking to got shot right after Mr. Hammond was kidnapped."

Rice shrugged miserably. "I know nothing of this."

Chamberlain noticed that Kaga Nagumo, the man from Mishuma, was giving Rice a very hard stare. Helen Thorp glanced questioningly at him too. Chamberlain looked around the room.

"Is anyone who might be on our side missing? You all know something about Hammond. Is there anyone else we should invite into this group?"

"Arabs," said Streicher. "Why are there no Arabs?"

"Good question."

"He often helps me in the Gulf States," said Streicher.

"Mr. Rice?" asked Chamberlain. "Can't you invite Mr. Hammond's Arab clients to join the consortium?"

The Malagasy stared blankly and Chamberlain wondered again how Hammond could have hired such a lightweight.

"Mr. Rice?"

"I'll try," Rice said doubtfully.

Chamberlain didn't believe him. "This is no time to cover up, Mr. Rice."

"I'm not."

"You're holding back. I guess you're used to giving your clients discretion, but it's too late for that now. You know more about Hammond's business than any of us. You gotta stop blocking Ms. Thorp and get us some more contributors."

Chamberlain noticed that the others were nodding agreement.

"Anything," Rice said in a choked voice. "I'll do anything to get Mr. Hammond back. We must get him back."

"Thank you," said Chamberlain. He headed for the door, pleased by the small approving smile he saw on Helen Thorp's lips. "Anyone who needs me, Comptel will know where I am. Good night."

Inspector Farquhar woke him an hour later by standing quietly beside his bed for the ten seconds it took his wearied senses to raise the alarm that he wasn't sleeping safely. He came out of it quickly, sagging back in disgust when he saw the English police officer's face.

"Go away."

"We found the plane."

"Hammond?"

"No."

"Please go away."

"We found Grandzau's partner in Bern. Or the Swiss police did, I should say."

"He's the kidnapper?"

"He's dead."

"Marvelous."

"Brussels." Farquhar waited.

"What about Brussels?"

"Interpol think they've found Daitch."

7

Chamberlain felt a second wind—or was it a third or fourth?—begin to shamble through his body as Inspector Farquhar bore him south over deserted roads in a high-powered police Rover. Gradually, he sat up straighter and focused on the road ahead.

"What about the plane?"

"We traced it north to Stornoway."

"Where's that?"

"It's on the Isle of Lewis in the Outer Hebrides. Scotland. About six hundred miles from here."

"Who was aboard?"

"Well, it didn't stay there."

"Where'd it go?"

"Damned if we know. It seems to have flown directly there, refueled, and taken off immediately. The pilot filed a flight plan for Keflavik, Iceland, about seven hundred miles away, but the Icelandics haven't recorded their arrival."

"Meaning the plane was either lost or flew in another direction."

"Most likely the latter, considering the circumstances. It was a twin-engine Cessna with long-range tanks and extra wing tanks, so they have close to a twenty-five-hundred-mile range."

"What does a twenty-five-hundred-mile circle from Stornoway include?"

"Greenland, the Azores, Europe, North Africa, Scandinavia, and Russia."

"Marvelous. When'd they leave Stornoway?"

"Yesterday afternoon."

"So they're gone?"

"Interpol has sent out an alert for the plane. It will be found. The question is when."

Chamberlain rubbed his eyes. "I really thought we'd have something with the plane. The bodyguard surviving and following them wasn't supposed to happen. I hate to see a lucky break wasted."

"Quite."

"How's the bodyguard?"

"Still alive."

"Yeah. He looked like a tough son of a bitch. Who got killed in Bern?"

"Fleming. The Englishman who was Grandzau's partner."

"Oh yes."

"He'd been tortured, according to the Swiss police."

Chamberlain turned to Farquhar. "Really?"

Farquhar glanced away from the road. When their eyes met, the policeman said, "My people tell me that the CIA is afraid the Russians want Hammond."

"How'd they get to Fleming so fast?"

"The CIA got there first, as a matter of fact. They put Fleming's house under surveillance. Photographed his visitors, tapped his telephone, the usual. But whoever killed Fleming slipped past them."

"Let's hope they remember when they find Daitch."

The English police officer turned the Rover into the airport exit lane. "As I understand my informant, Interpol located Daitch on its own and hasn't told the CIA yet."

"It won't take them long to find out. Interpol isn't very good with secrets."

"I asked a fellow I know about those Malagasy who ran off into the bush, speaking of secrets," said Farquhar. "Hammond's secrets."

"Malagasy?"

"Madagascar. You mentioned that Hammond's friends on the island of Malagasy had—"

"Right. Same place where he has the plantations. His home."

"They've come back. They're campaigning again for the national election. It's an important one. Looks like a change of government for the island."

"How about the Zimbabwe guerillas?"

"They're accusing the South Africans of murdering Hammond."

Chamberlain laughed. "Hammond really had a way about him, didn't he?"

"A Hong Kong gold trader killed himself this morning because Hammond disappearing ruined a deal he was set to sign with an Emirate sheikh. And the major in Brazil who shot the colonel has vanished. They've arrested the colonel's wife. There's a rumor that she was having an affair with Hammond."

Chamberlain laughed again. "I'm sorry. I'm getting giddy, but Hammond sounds like too important a guy to have an affair with only a colonel's wife."

"Her family owns a good part of the upper Amazon basin."

"Oh . . . they think they might find oil up there. Interesting."

Chamberlain looked at his watch. Two-thirty in the morning. Gatwick's deserted roads, quiet runways, and empty buildings were ablaze with light. Chamberlain had the eerie feeling he was approaching a giant space station whose inhabitants had been ravaged by an extraterrestrial pestilence. He shook the image from his mind.

"Can you recommend someone I should see in Brussels?"

"Say hello to Inspector François Aarschot."

"Where do I find him?"

"He'll meet you at the airport." Farquhar pulled up in front of the private craft terminal.

Chamberlain extended his hand. "I think I owe you a few."

Farquhar smiled wearily and Chamberlain realized he wasn't the only one running on no sleep. "You see, they used our uniform to fool Hammond's bodyguard. We can't let that sort go unpunished. Can we?"

They cranked up the Comptel jet's engines as soon as they saw Chamberlain emerge from the terminal. He trotted up the ramp, the door clanked shut behind him, and they started taxiing toward the runway.

Chamberlain glanced around appreciatively. The two gray-haired gentlemen piloting the thing looked like they'd been through more than one war. The steward had the graying crewcut of a retired U.S. Army lifer. He pointed at a bed with turned down crisp sheets and said, "You've got an hour if you'd like a nap, sir." He curtained off the area.

Chamberlain was out of his clothes and between the sheets before the plane finished flinging itself into the sky.

The steward woke him with black coffee and some English tea biscuits. "You got time to have it in bed, sir. We're not into final approach yet."

The coffee was excellent. The steward took the empty cup, showed Chamberlain the bathroom, and passed him his clothes when he came out. Chamberlain shrugged into his gray jacket, noticing that the steward had dispatched the worst wrinkles while he'd slept. Some brigadier had lost a fantastic aide when this guy had retired.

As the jet glided to a smooth stop in a quiet corner of the Brussels airport, the Comptel steward brought him a mahogany box. He carried it in both hands, laid it carefully on a table beside the bed, unlocked the lid, and drew it open. Inside, nestled in green velvet, were half a dozen handguns of varying sizes and calibers.

"In case you want to carry, sir. We can work temporary permits on any of 'em."

Chamberlain shook his head.

The steward opened his own jacket a fraction so Chamberlain could see his .22 pistol. "You want company, sir?"

"No thanks. I'll be with the local police."

"Yes, sir." He closed the gun box and returned it to its cabinet. Chamberlain was glad to see that the steward had the brains to pack a light gun aboard a plane. Nonetheless, he had no intention of wandering around Belgium with an armed man he didn't know. There were enough unknown quantities as it were.

François Aarschot was a short, pudgy man with slick black hair and a face that would have been taken more seriously if it had a mustache. He looked, without it, petulant. He greeted Chamberlain with an irritable glare. His tight lips squeezed out a thick French accent.

"Bon soir, Monsieur Chamberlain."

"Thanks for meeting me, sir."

"I could hardly refuse this opportunity to repay Inspector Farquhar's many favors all at once."

Thinking he might have heard it wrong, Chamberlain smiled uncertainly.

Aarschot cleared it up for him. "Monsieur. Permit me to mince few words. I dislike government spies intensely, and I like industrial spies even less."

"You despise spies? Good. I'm not a spy."

"I know who you work for and I know what you do for them. I promised Inspector Farquhar I would help you find this Daitch, and I will. This way, monsieur."

The Belgian police officer led Chamberlain to a small Mercedes-Benz and drove without another word into Brussels, beyond the rich hotel district, into an older, poorer section not yet gentrified. Careening through a maze of narrow streets, they came suddenly upon a crowd of police vans.

White floodlights played on the front of a low, stone building. A small crowd of civilians in overcoats watched from behind the police lines. The police moved cautiously, ducking and crouching as they scampered behind their vans. Chamberlain spotted several sharpshooters on roofs in the gloom overhead. His breath puffed white when they left the warmth of the car. He jammed his hands into his coat pockets. He'd left his gloves on the Concorde and the cold was brutal.

Inspector Aarschot nodded irritably at the stone building. "Daitch has barricaded himself."

"Does he have Charles Hammond in there?" asked Chamberlain, glancing nervously at the police firepower.

"No. He's constructed camouflaged pitfalls—what you call booby traps. He killed two of my men earlier this evening with a mine attached to the outer door."

The remnants of the shattered door hung from twisted hinges. Chamberlain could see the burned spot on the stone lintel where Daitch had attached the shaped charge. It was a neat job: the stone wasn't even cracked.

"How do you know he doesn't have Hammond?"

"We've spoken to him on the telephone. He hasn't uttered

a word about Hammond. That is why. He is alone, monsieur. I am sure of it." He crossed his hands behind his back, rocked on his heels, and glared defiantly at Chamberlain.

Chamberlain leaned on the Mercedes's roof and surveyed the scene with bleak regard. What if Hammond just happened to be in there? What if Daitch and the rest of his crowd were preparing for a last stand? What if this Belgian waffle were full of it?

An armored half-track clanked around a corner, forcing the bystanders to the narrow sidewalks. Chamberlain caught a glimpse of a startlingly beautiful blond woman on the edge of the crowd. He stared at her, distracted, until the armored half-track blocked his view.

Typical police. When in doubt call in the heavy stuff. Poor Hammond. Poor Helen.

"Inspector?"

"Oui, monsieur?"

"How'd this all start? Were you trying to arrest him?"

"Of course not. We were obeying an Interpol directive to surveille. Suddenly Daitch killed a man."

"Who?"

"Unfortunately, he was with the Soviet embassy. An anti-personnel grenade exploded in the hall and moments later the man came tumbling out the front door, dying. He fell there." Aarschot pointed and Chamberlain saw the white-painted outline of where the body had landed. It looked just about Aarschot size, maybe a little chubbier. "When my men went in to investigate, *poof,* the door exploded."

"What was the guy from the Russian embassy doing there?"

"We don't know. The Soviets took the body and said only that the man usually walked this way to work."

"But what was he doing inside?"

"It's possible the Russian had a woman in a neighboring apartment. She is away for the holiday, the neighbors tell us. These things will be resolved."

"Do you have a floor plan?"

"What for?"

"I'd like to see the situation."

Aarschot stared at him suspiciously. "Very well. Come with me." The Belgian darted from police van to police van, ducking in the spaces between. Chamberlain followed him without crouching. A man who could set a charge like that on the door didn't need guns.

At the command post in the back of a communications truck, Aarschot introduced him to his fellow officers. Each in turn shook hands and accorded Chamberlain a quick nod.

They spread a building plan on a console and showed Chamberlain how Daitch occupied the entire ground floor. "He may have access to the cellar," said Aarschot. "You can see over there how its front windows are bricked up."

"Yeah, I noticed."

"The back is unreachable. The building backs on a solid wall. The way out is the only way in."

"If it weren't, I guess Daitch would be long gone."

"It is a last stand, monsieur. From the look of the traps, he's been preparing his defenses for a long time."

"Why?"

The Belgian corkscrewed a fat finger in the direction of his brain.

"What set him off today? Did he see your men?"

"No! He did not, monsieur. You have my word. No, I think he saw the newspaper stories about his former associate, this Englishman killed in Bern. He went berserk. There is psychology in this work, monsieur, and in psychology you will find the answer to this riddle."

"I want to talk to him."

"Don't be absurd."

"I have to talk to him."

"What would you say that my men haven't already?"

"First I want to make damn sure that he doesn't have Hammond in there with him. And if he doesn't, I want him to tell me who does."

"And how would he do that?"

"Hammond's kidnapper used an old code that Daitch once used. I want to know who else used it."

"You can talk to him after my men have arrested him."

"Inspector, you better get something straight." Several officers looked curiously at him. Chamberlain lowered his voice so only Aarschot could hear. "Nobody is going to arrest Daitch. He's an expert demolitions man. And if he's even half as crazy as you think he is, he'll blow up the whole block before he'll let himself be taken."

Aarschot rocked on his heels. "I have acquitted my debts

to Inspector Farquhar. Good night, sir. A car will take you back to your plane. Or you can wait in a hotel, at your own expense, until we have Daitch behind bars."

"Thank you," said Chamberlain. He stepped out of the communications truck, slipped between two police cars, and walked briskly across the narrow street to the floodlighted house.

The Belgians were shouting at him and one cop even started after him, crouching low, when with a fearful glance at the windows, he turned back. Chamberlain mounted the front steps and an electronically amplified Aarschot shouted, "Halt, monsieur. Halt!"

Chamberlain went up the steps.

"Halt or he'll kill you, monsieur."

Chamberlain went into the foyer. Here, safe from being grabbed by a zealous cop, he probed the dark recesses with his penlight, climbed gingerly over a trip wire the Russian had been lucky enough to miss, and started into the dark hall.

The antipersonnel grenade had pocked the walls with shrapnel. It, or the door device that killed the cops, had blown out the overhead lamps, so here he was totally dependent on his penlights, of which he carried three.

Sleeplessness tended to sharpen his senses. He heard better. Nonetheless, he swept the hall repeatedly with the light, crouching and holding it over his head in the unlikely event someone pegged a shot at it. He was convinced, however, there would be no shooting.

The hall was very long, longer than the beam of his light. He took a miniature microwave Doppler horn from his pocket, set it securely on the floor, and turned it on. Movement within its projected waves would register, via a thin wire, as a mild electric shock in his palm. There was nothing moving. He pocketed the device and started slowly down the hall.

He shied from a loose floorboard, started to step to one side, thought better of it, and inspected the walls. The right wall, opposite the loose board, looked clear at first glance. On closer inspection, Chamberlain saw a thin, seemingly rusty nail protruding at shoulder level. He moved close to the wall and stepped under it. Had he brushed against it while avoiding the more obvious trigger of the loose floorboard, he would have set off something fatal. It was overhead, in the ceiling. A Claymore mine. He swallowed hard. Daitch wasn't fooling around.

He traced the almost invisible trip wire leading from the rusty nail up a groove in the wall to the Claymore. He inspected it minutely, decided it was a simple, one-way trigger, and reached for it with the clipper blade of his customized Israeli army knife.

He got the wire between the jaws of the clipper and bore down gently. He felt his mouth twitching a nervous, private grin; there always came an instant when you defused a charge when you had to ask, Is this right? It was then you waited for the silent explosion. Veteran demolitions men said you never heard the one that killed you.

If Daitch had hair-triggered the thing, he'd find the truth of the saying. Chamberlain released a deep breath. The trap was defused. He crouched on the floor again, pointed the scanner down the dark hall, and waited for the tell-tale buzz in his palm. Nothing. He was still alone.

Behind him, outside, he heard loudspeakers. The police were bellowing something or other. Whether organizing a charge or threatening Daitch he didn't know, because he didn't understand French. He started down the hall again, casting his light from side to side over the floor and up to the ceiling.

Suddenly he stopped short. An odd little hole pocked one wall at waist level. He played the light over it. It looked manufactured, not accidental. He reached to finger it. The outer, dimmer glow of the penlight circle brushed an identical hole at ankle level. He jerked his hand back as if seared by steam.

His breath came short. He'd almost killed himself. He found a third hole at shoulder level. Then he turned the light to the opposite wall. He was not surprised to find a tall, narrow mirror. It was an old one, the edges beveled, the plaster frame once gilded. It had been there a long time. Daitch, Chamberlain decided, was on the edge of brilliant. If he'd seen the mirror first, as he would have if the lights weren't out, he never would have noticed the holes opposite that emitted the invisible laser beams; then as he passed the holes and blocked the beams so they wouldn't reflect back from the mirror, he'd have broken an electrical circuit, tripping an electromagnetic switch on yet another of Daitch's explosive delights.

Problem. They were spaced in such a way that he couldn't crawl past.

He backed up, removed his overcoat, and transferred the contents of his suit jacket to the big overcoat pockets. Then he took off the suit jacket, donned the overcoat, balled the suit jacket into a missile the size of a soccer ball, and hurled it down the hall. He flung himself back and to the floor.

The explosion was so quiet that he could hear the old mirror shattering. He got to his feet, puzzled, and moved forward cautiously. The mirror was in slivers on the floor. A broad jagged line of broken plaster ran the full height of the wall where the holes had been. Whatever had exploded had come out of that wall. He bent down and retrieved his jacket.

The shredded cloth fell apart in his hands. The bomb had thrown a hundred steel lancets across the hall. He saw them now among the mirror slivers. A hundred tiny spears, as if the wall had erupted in a miniature nineteenth-century African war.

"Daitch!" The cry welled up in him, filled his throat, a primitive shout of victory. "Daitch! Open up, you bastard, I'm better than you are!"

His voice echoed to silence and he stood waiting alone, the euphoria draining away, the adrenaline seeping out of him, feeling a little silly and vaguely frightened. Then, to his amazement, a wooden door at the end of the hall creaked open into a lighted room.

He approached cautiously, the hair prickling up his neck, until he could see inside. The man who had opened the door was returning unhurriedly to his chair in the center of an overly decorated Victorian parlor. When he turned around and sat down, crossing his legs, Chamberlain could see he was a middle-aged man who looked like a professor at home for a quiet evening with a book. He wore bedroom slippers and a wool robe over trousers. He reached up and turned on his reading lamp and in the light spill his eyes were bright as marbles.

Hammond stopped in the doorway. "Daitch?"

The man smiled sadly. "Yes. Who are you?"

Daitch looked crazy. Gently, Chamberlain introduced himself. "My name is Pete Chamberlain . . . nice to meet you, sir."

"You're quite good, Mr. Chamberlain. Come in."

Chamberlain took two steps.

"Mind the trap door!"

Chamberlain froze, but it was too late. He was caught flat-footed, smack in the middle of the throw rug that covered it. One of Daitch's hands rested easily on the arm of his chair. The trap release was more than likely under his finger.

Daitch chuckled. "No, sir, you are *not* better than I. It's a twenty-foot drop to the sewer below."

Chamberlain looked around, the balls of his feet tingling for the fall. He realized now that every potted palm, every bit of bric-a-brac, every writing box, every chair, table, and settee was probably booby-trapped.

Daitch lifted his hand and motioned him off the rug. "Come in. We've both made our points. Where did you learn your trade?"

"U.S. Navy SEALS," said Chamberlain, working hard at breathing normally.

"Ah, a diver? See, you could have swum to safety in the sewer. . . . Now, what are you doing here?"

"I'm looking for Hammond."

Daitch looked genuinely puzzled. "*Charles* Hammond?"

"Yes. Charles Hammond. The dealmaker."

"Well I know who he is. In fact I've met him in the past. Charming man. I read in the paper"—he nodded at a pile of newspapers on a tilt table—"that he was kidnapped in London . . . is *that* what this is all about?"

"I'm looking for Hammond."

"What in the name of God would make you think that I had anything to do with kidnapping Charles Hammond?"

"We got an invitation to bid for him in the, quote, 'Pendragon auction.'"—Chamberlain didn't like how surprised Daitch looked—"It was signed Lancelot."

Daitch appeared startled. His bright eyes narrowed. "Is that why you killed Fleming?"

"I didn't kill anybody," said Chamberlain, shaking his head. "But someone looking for Hammond probably did," he added lamely. It looked as if that idiot Aarschot had been right. Daitch was just an innocent basketcase. A very lethal basketcase, he reminded himself. But he still might know something. "If you didn't use the Malory code, and Fleming didn't, who do you suppose did?"

"Grandzau. Grandzau was Lancelot."

"But Grandzau's dead."

"Yes, isn't he?"

"Who else would use it?"

"Why would he use it would be a better question," replied Daitch. He smiled vacantly.

"To identify himself," said Chamberlain.

"Grandzau."

"No. There must be somebody else."

"There was no one else," said Daitch. "Just Grandzau, Fleming, and me."

"It doesn't add up."

A telephone rang, a startling noise in the quiet room. It sat on a tea table with an exquisite marquetry top. Daitch regarded it sourly. "It's those damned police. Would you be so kind?"

Chamberlain reached for the receiver. "Sure." Then he stopped himself, stared at the telephone, looked for extra wires and scratches on the casing. But he wouldn't do it that way. It would be a very sensitive pressure switch, tripped by removing the weight of the receiver. He crouched down and inspected the table.

Daitch giggled. "Not to worry. The telephone is quite safe."

Chamberlain shrugged. It looked safe, and Daitch could already have killed him with the trap door. He picked up the receiver and heard Aarschot's prissy little voice. "Now, Monsieur Daitch—"

"This is Chamberlain. I'm in here with Daitch and we're talking."

"We're coming in," Aarschot snapped after a shocked silence.

"No you're not. Not till I'm done. I left one of his booby traps near the front. I'll disarm it when I'm through."

"Remove it immediately!"

"Just sit tight." He hung up. Daitch was smiling vacantly again. "Okay, Mr. Daitch. Give me a guess. Who else would use the code?"

Daitch focused on him slowly.

"The Malory code?" Chamberlain prompted.

"Each of us retired into ways reminiscent of how we had worked. Fleming didn't like the work. He despised the complex. He became a simple gardener. I, who built the hideouts and protected the group from its enemies—of which we made many—became a recluse. A well-defended recluse, with my back to the wall and my flanks protected. And Grandzau? Grandzau loved secrets. He loved to find secrets. He loved to destroy them, by selling them. And he loved to construct them. Maybe when Grandzau retired he created the ultimate secret."

"Son of a bitch," Chamberlain muttered. "Okay . . . what if he did fake his own death? Where would he hide Hammond?"

Daitch's eyes grew hooded. He smiled. "In a secret place."

"Come on, Daitch. I don't mind kicking it out of you if I have to."

"You've already breached my fortress. What else can you do?" His eyes clouded over. Chamberlain stared at him, powerless to stop him from slithering over the brink of sanity. When he began to drool, Chamberlain turned and walked back down the hall, through the glass and lancets, under the defused Claymore, past the pocked walls; he cut the trip wire in the foyer, leaned out the shattered door, and called to Aarschot.

The inspector came running, followed by a phalanx of Belgian police in flak vests. Chamberlain led them down the hall into Daitch's room. They clumped behind him, boots pounding. The commotion roused Daitch from his stupor. For a moment his eyes grew bright with fear. Then he saw Chamberlain and he smiled.

"I don't know where Grandzau would hide Hammond because I always chose the hiding places and I haven't chosen this one. If he were smart, he would choose a mobile niche. Not a foolish trap like I chose here." He waved his hand scornfully at the room.

Aarschot signaled his men and they converged on Daitch's chair.

"Stay back," Daitch shouted, his eyes burning into Chamberlain's.

Chamberlain was distracted by his own thoughts. "Why

would Grandzau fake his own death and kidnap Hammond?" he asked Daitch as the police grabbed the seated man.

"Not for the money." Daitch smiled, struggling to stay in his chair. He was holding on to the arms desperately. "Not for the money. For the secret."

Chamberlain shook his head. Two cops shouldered him aside and went to help. They began to tear Daitch's fingers loose, one by one. "But he didn't keep it se—*don't move him!*"

The room erupted in a sheet of white flame. The last thing Chamberlain thought about as the flame turned black was the reading lamp. Daitch had turned on the reading lamp when he sat down; he had armed a detonator. And the explosion wasn't silent at all. The explosion from Daitch's final booby trap was deafening.

8

Hammond lay in the bottom of a rowboat, listening to the ancient sounds of water lapping wood and air thumping through the oarsmen's chests. It was night, without stars, and bitter cold. Two men were pulling—one amidships, one aft—their backs to Hammond in the bow. Kidnapped. Now, of all times. Unbelievable. They were in for a big surprise when they got to the ransom. He had to escape.

He lay still. If they knew he'd awakened, they would bind his hands and feet as they had on the plane. They'd given him another shot a while ago, but they were cautious and he had a high tolerance to drugs.

Icy spray cleared the gunnel as the boat made its slow, bumpy way through the chop. The blanket they'd thrown over him was soaked through. Cold water, salty on his lips, had shocked him back to consciousness. He had to escape to finish plans no one knew.

Cautiously, he lifted his head and peered out at the black water. Lights shone dimly astern. There was blackness to either side and he was afraid to lift his head high enough to see over the bow. He knew neither where he was nor how much time had transpired since he'd been kidnapped in London, but he had to escape, find a phone, and report that he was free.

He was firmly tied into a foam life jacket. He wouldn't drown if the boat foundered. They were taking no chances, just as they'd taken none on the plane. Before they had given him the injection, they'd taken his blood pressure and checked his heartbeat. There wasn't a mark on his body. They'd even massaged his hands and feet when they untied him, but he had to escape.

The oarsmen knew their trade. Only now and then did the lead man look over his shoulder to see where they were going. They steered by one of the lights falling astern. Hammond waited for the man to glance over his shoulder again, then raised his own head for a second look. Ahead, at some distance difficult to judge in the dark, was a tight cluster of lights. A ship, a far shore, an island, he couldn't tell.

The water was utterly black. In the small crescent of his vision it appeared only as a dark shine. No white broke its blackness—even where the oars bit in and tongued through it. It looked deep and cold and endless. It looked terrifying, but he had to escape, to close the deal to end all deals.

He was a good swimmer. The snug foam jacket would keep him afloat without impeding his arms and legs. He wormed quietly to the right side of the boat. If the closest oarsman grabbed for him as he climbed out, he would be using his left hand and the odds were he was right-handed. A small edge.

He would swim away from the boat, deeper into the darkness, then make for the lights astern. He tensed, pressing his arm, his hip, his legs, and his feet against the boat's ribs, seeking purchase from which he would convulse over the side. He waited, his heart beating faster and faster. His cold fingers touched sand between the boards. The boat dipped toward his side, as if offering help. He waited too long and it rolled back.

Hammond cursed himself. The dip would have made climbing out easier. Why had he waited? He wondered how long he would last in the cold water. What if it was the North Atlantic? It was winter. The cold might kill him.

An angry, bitter hatred for the coward he was welled up in Hammond's chest. It wasn't the cold that frightened him. He was younger and stronger than people thought—an advantage, as was any fact others didn't know. His enormous energy forced him to exercise every second he wasn't busy on a plane or in a hotel. As for his heart, it was a lot tougher than the nervous doctors knew. But he was terrified of the black water, terrified to leave the boat, terrified to enter the fathomless darkness. Was he that much a coward, that much paralyzed by fear, to throw away the work of ten years, just to save himself this single moment?

The boat rolled again, and again he found himself face to face with the black water. It was getting rougher as they rowed further from land. Could he make a deal with the men straining at the oars? They were probably fishermen picking up some quick money. Would they let him go for a million apiece? For two? Or would they have the cunning to know they'd never survive to spend the money? Then if he tried to deal, they would tie him up again. They'd never deal. He had to escape.

Every second he stalled made the swim back longer. But the water looked like oil. He couldn't imagine breaking its surface. If he slid under it, it would close over his head like a black plastic sheet. He would butt and thrash and punch that sheet until he was exhausted. Then he would sink slowly, spiraling down to ever blacker depths, settling finally in the cold mud at the bottom. But he had to escape.

Again the boat dipped low on his side.

He was a gambling man and he recognized a last chance.

He levered himself onto the gunnel. The wood bit into his chest and groin. The men at the oars shouted. Something flicked against his foot. Hammond kicked it away and fell free, into the water. The cold drove his breath from his lungs. He thought his heart had stopped.

He kicked again, struck the boat, and pushed off, swimming overhand as hard as he could, ignoring the pain in his chest, driving his body through the black water, fighting for distance and warmth, exhilarated that he had conquered his fear.

The life jacket held his shoulders high out of the water. He felt like a child paddling a rubber inner tube, but already he was swimming more freely as his body adjusted to the cold and the shouts of the oarsmen drove him on.

Suddenly something jerked him backward. He thrashed helplessly as it dragged him through the black water back to the boat. He couldn't escape.

Stiffened by the cold, her shoulders sagging with weariness, Lady Janet walked the empty streets back to the center of Brussels. She bought a first class train ticket to Paris and slept sitting up in the station, waiting for the early morning train to depart. If there was one good thing, it was that she was too tired to hurt.

She had not been surprised when Daitch's building exploded moments after the police went in, though she had been astonished that the man who had gone in first had come out alive to signal them. But in the end, it had ended Daitch's way.

It was only on the train, after a few more hours of sleep, stretched out in an empty compartment, that she began to admit the truth about why she was going to Paris.

Daitch's explosion had been almost anticlimactic. By the time it rocked the street, she'd already realized that the man in black wasn't the only one looking for Grandzau's old associates. The Brussels police were, and Interpol too. One of their officers had identified himself in an attempt to take her to dinner. And the Russian who'd tripped Daitch's mine. She recognized his body before the Belgians took it away. KGB in Amsterdam, years ago, a freelance running a little dope on the side. Before the Chinese. And then the man who'd defied the Brussels police and entered Daitch's house. The one who had survived longer than he should have. He'd walked in with the sort of arrogant contempt for the local authorities that used to be a hallmark of the CIA.

She recalled the cablegram the man in black had shown her. YOUR BID IS EXPECTED AT THE PENDRAGON AUCTION. LANCELOT. Where is Grandzau, he had asked. Not where is Fleming. Or where is Daitch. They knew where to find Fleming and Daitch. And they knew where to find her. But they asked for Grandzau.

She admitted that she believed Grandzau might be alive.

Only one piece fit badly. The newspapers said that Charles Hammond had been kidnapped in London. That the dealmaker was Pendragon she had no doubt. If you were going to use the code, then Hammond had to be Pendragon.

But Grandzau wasn't a kidnapper.

It wasn't his way. He traded in words, not bodies. And he

died three years ago. Died in retirement, leaving her the villa, money, and free to do what she chose.

Lady Janet stared at the French countryside flickering past the window of the high-speed express. The wheels made hardly a sound on the endless, seamless ribbon of welded track. She gripped a handrail, reeling from the enormity of what he had done to her. Only Grandzau would have used the Malory code. It had no purpose other than identification. He had been Lancelot. Fleming had been Pellinore; Daitch was Lionel. She was Guinevere. When she had protested that Grandzau should then be her Arthur, the German had laughed. "Such a Guinevere deserves more of an Arthur than a gnome like me."

It had been the only time in her life that her beauty had betrayed her. The little man, thirty years her senior, never could believe how much she loved him. The speeding countryside began spinning before her eyes.

If Grandzau wasn't dead but alive these three years, spinning a scheme to kidnap Hammond, it meant he had deliberately abandoned her—first to an empty life without him, and now to the savage interrogation by the man in black. Grandzau had to know it would happen, that something like it would happen when they came looking for the man called Lancelot.

If she ever saw the man in black, she would kill him. But she wouldn't hunt him. Not if Grandzau was alive. Not as long as Grandzau was alive. But just as the man in black was no longer important—she would hunt the hand, not the instrument—so too hunting Grandzau would be an entirely different proposition. The man in black was someone's soldier—whose she didn't know and didn't care—and there wasn't a soldier in Europe she would hesitate to fight. She was an English aristocrat. Her father had raised her to shoot and ride, to handle a foil; from others she had learned manual killing and how to use a knife. But Grandzau wasn't a soldier. He was the master. And to get the master, she knew she needed help. Which was why she had known since before Daitch's house exploded that she was going to Paris.

Lady Janet registered at a quiet hotel on the rue de Bourgogne where she wasn't known. She shopped for a change of clothes and a warm coat, gave what she'd been wearing to the valet, bathed, slept until dark, and walked out into the city, her left hand grazing the hard edge of the gun in her pocket.

Fluent in French, she read the headlines in the news kiosks as she walked. Hammond had been missing for two days now and the papers were speculating that he'd been taken by rightists, leftists, business rivals, or maniacs, but there had been no word at all from the kidnappers. She wasn't surprised. The sort Grandzau would invite to his auction would hardly bandy it about. It would be a private event, with no reporters, no official observers, no window shoppers.

Consequently, the French government's newest promise to aid its former East African colonies should Indian Ocean tensions worsen had recaptured the headlines. The right-wing newspapers approved arming Mozambique and the island of Malagasy: those on the left were caught between an anti-imperialist stance and a desire for the jobs that would be created by sending more planes and missiles to the western Indian Ocean. Hints of Russian subversion in the area spiced the debate.

She headed for a bar in the fifteenth arrondissement in a tired neighborhood of narrow cobble streets, brick walls showing through crumbling cement facades, rusted wrought-iron street lamps, and peeling wooden shutters. A big Citroën plant squatted on the quai André Citroën a few blocks away. Here and there aging postwar apartment buildings stood between the lower, older slums. Those who worked built cars and were implacably leftist. They mingled easily with the gangsters and mercenaries who frequented the Café 79, named for its number on the rue de la Convention.

She hadn't been in the 79 in years, but it was the sort of place that didn't change until the *gendarmerie* arrested the patrons and bolted the door. Crossing the Seine at the Pont de Mirabeau, Lady Janet saw that hadn't happened yet. A single red neon sign announced the number, shining through the wire mesh that covered the single window. Someone had tossed a grenade at that window during the Algerian war. It had missed the opening, but the owner went to wire mesh regardless.

She raised her head as she entered the smoky front room, her pulses quickening with the old excitement of being where she shouldn't be. She had been nineteen when she'd had her first absinthe at the 79, followed in quick succession by her first heroin, her first man who paid—a mercenary back from Rhodesia who'd gotten full value for his money—then others who rejoiced in such quality at the customary low price, and finally Henri Trefle.

Absinthe had had a romantic connotation for a wealthy and sheltered girl who had known little more than a childhood of bucolic splendor on the Isling Gloucestershire estate and a year of grotty, boring student rebellion. The bitter, potent liqueur had been her first eager step into the alluring depths below, beyond and free of her father, her brothers, horses and their dressage, Range-Rovers, tweedy plus fours, country hauteur, English dignity, and stifling certitude.

Heroin—the best from Marseilles—was a world unto itself. The drug was an occasional companion for a decade, but though it often seized her remorselessly, her wealth shielded her from the addicts' plagues of bad dope and dirty needles. Whoring had earned her a thousand francs—charging the minimum—before Trefle had put a stop to it, a thousand francs she mailed to her father with instructions to invest it in something "suitable."

She sat down at a table with a red-and-white-checked cloth and ordered white wine. One of the things she liked about France was that even a dive like this had a good wine if you had the price. She sat for several hours, smoking, sipping the wine, brushing off the attempts to pick her up. The room was rich with memories of the way she had lived and the way she had changed.

She'd switched quickly from absinthe to wine—whites and burgundies, not the claret of her father's table; she'd been too energetic and impatient in those days to wait for absinthe's apparition of the Green Fairy, not when heroin delivered its visions with the speed of light. The morphine she was injecting for her pain now was the first dope she'd had in a year.

She was unmoved by the stares and leers her beauty drew from the men in the bar. She had whored for the excitement and to spite her father. It, and he, had long since died. But Trefle she needed again. He would help her. Not for love, God knew, but for hate.

She had a shock when Trefle walked in. At first she didn't recognize him. He'd deteriorated in the last four years, put on forty pounds and acquired a blotched face that was vivid proof he'd surrendered to his old enemy. Lady Janet watched him order it at the bar. The barmaid poured Algerian red. So he was broke as well. Now she noticed the threadbare bush jacket, no coat despite the cold, the filthy beret, the run-down jump boots, the faded trappings of a failed professional soldier.

Trefle drained the glass and rapped it on the bar to demand more. Turning around to observe the bistro with a sour scowl, he deliberately jostled a big man beside him—a very big man, larger than himself—and sneered at his protest. Before the man could take it further, his companion grabbed his arm and forcefully led him to the door, his drink unfinished on the bar.

Lady Janet sat back, relieved by the incident. Despite appearances, Trefle hadn't lost his reputation as an expert guerilla with the appetites of a psychotic killer. He stiffened when he saw her and stared in mild surprise. Lady Janet smiled and shifted painfully to the next chair. Trefle never sat with his back to a room or a door.

Taking his second glass and the bottle, Trefle left the bar and crossed the room to her table. Fat, and half-drunk, he still walked like a cat. He had cat eyes, too—knowing, uncaring, quick, and cruel.

"Bon soir, Henri."

"Bon soir." There was something new in his eyes, something that she had hoped to see, a shadow of bitterness that hadn't been there four years ago, a shadow connected to the twisted downturns at the corners of his fleshy mouth. She smiled again. He would do.

"Sit down."

He sat heavily and sloshed Algerian red into her white burgundy, staining her glass pink to the rim.

"Merci," she said with an ironic nod. She knew what he liked, knew how to play his admiration for her breeding and spirit. Raising the glass, she met his eyes. "I *thought* I would find you celebrating."

He slurred his words. "I just wish I had been the one."

"Ah, but you wouldn't give him back. No matter how much they paid."

Trefle blinked slowly. He was drunker than she had thought. He muttered, "I hope they kill him."

"They won't."

The cat eyes leaped to her face. He didn't want to hear that. "If it goes wrong, they will kill him."

"It won't go wrong."

"Kidnappings usually go wrong," Trefle insisted in a dogged slur.

"Not this one," Lady Janet bored in. "I know."

Trefle blinked again and shook his head. She waited for him to ask how she knew, but Trefle shifted to another facet of what he wanted to believe.

"I should have killed him myself, while I still could."

"I've brought you a second chance," said Lady Janet.

Trefle hadn't heard. "Hammond betrayed me," he said.

She knew. It was why she had come here. Trefle had told her immediately after it happened, four years ago, when she had lied to Grandzau and pretended to visit her home in England and had returned instead secretly to the 79, looking for action and excitement and had found Trefle, unexpectedly back from East Africa. Trefle had been wounded and he'd bled in the night and she'd left his blood on her body until she returned to the south of France, as some crazy proof that she could still be perverse even though she loved Grandzau.

"Hammond betrayed me."

Lady Janet forced herself to wait and listen patiently. *Betrayal* was a serious word in the mercenary fraternity—as important a part of their view of life as oiled weapons, spare ammunition, courage, and fear.

Trefle shook his massive head and hunched his great shoulders over the table. One hand toyed with his glass. The other gripped the edge of the table—gathering the checked cloth, threatening the wine—as if he were preparing to hurl the table across the dark room.

"What happened, Henri?" she asked softly. "What did Charles Hammond do to you?"

He recited the story like a litany. It was a short, clear, angry account, obviously oft repeated, and just as obviously the source of a deep, bitter obsession.

Charles Hammond had hired Henri Trefle to raid Mogadishu, the capital of the East African-Indian Ocean state of Somalia. Trefle's mercenaries were to seize the government radio station and the president's palace—the first vital steps in a Hammond-engineered political coup. It was staged from a secret base in Kenya.

"I put my men in three unarmed transports—French, English, and German officers; *negre* soldiers. We took off from Patta Island, north of Lamu, the moment Hammond radioed that the way was clear. It was understood that Hammond would bribe the Somalia airport defense units. There were Russian ships in the Indian Ocean so we flew at wave top, under their radar so they couldn't report us. When we reached the Mogadishu airport, the Somalians Hammond was supposed to bribe opened up on us with all they had."

Trefle spat in the corner. He was staring at the tablecloth as he continued. Lady Janet sat still and attentive, bent forward to hear better his whispering voice. Each word was the same as the night he had bled on her breast.

"Hammond changed his mind. The way wasn't clear. The antiaircraft shot down the planes following. My plane was in the lead and the pig Somalians weren't fast enough to hit us. We headed back to Kenya. Behind us you could see the other two planes burning on the ground. The Somalians scrambled a jet from the runway. Again we flew darkened at wave top, but the jet found us anyhow. I think the Russian ships might have tracked us."

He emptied his glass, refilled it, ignored hers, and spat again. "He was a trainer pilot. All he had was a couple of light machine guns for target practice. Well, he practiced that night. He couldn't shoot us down. We were too sturdy and the gun was too light. But he tried. He made run after run, lacing the fuselage again and again and on every pass more of my men died. My pilot dodged and twisted but the bullets kept tearing through our plane until the bastard ran out of ammunition.

"When we got back to Patta Island, there were twelve of us alive. I forbade them to touch a single dead man. I carried every body off myself. Even the pilot was gone, dead a moment after he touched her down.

"Had I seen Hammond that moment, I would have butchered him." He touched his chest, over his heart, and Lady Janet saw he still carried his long glass knife. It was tempered glass in a fiber glass sheath and no airport X ray would ever spot it.

Lady Janet waited silently.

His cat eyes landed on her face again. "I've told you this

before—the night I returned to Paris and you were here and came to my bed. Why do you pretend you've never heard?''

Lady Janet hesitated, struggling to meet his gaze. She'd let his drunkenness lull her into forgetting how quick he really was. ''I just thought . . . you wanted to say it.''

''What are you doing here? What do you want?''

She recovered quickly. ''Can we go to your room?''

Trefle inspected her piercingly. Then a slow, lazy, sensual smile rambled over his face. ''You still want it.''

''I want to talk.''

''Sure you do. Just like last visit. . . . Pay the check!''

He stood up quickly and brushed past her as she fumbled for her money. Lady Janet twisted slightly to one side and kept her free hand out of her pocket, in case he was checking to see if she had a gun.

She followed him to the door and walked beside him up the rue de la Convention, then into a side street, through an alley, and into a courtyard. Now she went ahead of him, climbing circular stone stairways several floors up in a crumbling brick *pension*. An open door revealed the Turkish toilet that served the floor. Trefle unlocked his door and ushered her in with a mock bow.

She entered quickly, crossed the room, which was dimly lighted by an overhead bulb, and whirled, drawing her gun, halting his rush. Trefle stopped, a drunken smile on his face, his eyes bright and hard.

''Stop,'' she said. ''Back up.''

Trefle came a slow step closer.

''You taught me that the single advantage of a gun is its longer reach. And you said never surrender that advantage. I'll kill you if you come a step closer.''

Trefle stared, then shrugged. ''What do you want?''

''Back up.''

He backed to the wall.

''Good. Now hear me out. Grandzau kidnapped Charles Hammond.''

Trefle spat. ''Grandzau's dead.''

''He faked it.''

''So what?''

''Grandzau won't kill Hammond. He's auctioning Hammond to the highest bidder.''

''Yet another reason I wish I was rich.'' He brightened.

"Maybe somebody will buy him for what he knows. Maybe they'll drag it out of him and then kill him."

"There'll be others bidding to keep him alive. . . . Tell me something, Henri. Why didn't you go after him?"

Trefle snorted harsh laughter. "Money. How does a man like me even track a man like him? He's in Europe one day, Africa the next. Private planes, guards, helicopters. It wasn't possible." He spat again. *"Merde.* If they get him back, they'll treble his security."

"Would you like to find him right now?"

"Shut up, woman. You talk too much."

"I'll finance the hunt."

Trefle stared. "You'll pay for me to kill Hammond? Why?"

"After you kill Hammond I will kill Grandzau."

Trefle laughed. "Because he fooled you? You're crazy."

"I'll kill him and I need you to help me. I'll give you Hammond."

"I don't believe you."

"Move over there. Into the corner. Move!"

Trefle went reluctantly.

"Look at me!"

She shrugged out of her coat, smoothly shifting the gun from one hand to the other. Then she stepped between Trefle and the big mirror. She kept her eyes on his, her gun trained on his chest; she reached back, felt for the switch, and turned on the light by the mirror. Then she bunched the hem of her skirt in her hand and slowly raised it to her waist.

Trefle wet his lips.

"Look in the mirror!"

He tore his eyes from her beautiful legs and looked at the cloudy glass. The weals that criss-crossed her bottom and thighs had turned blue-black.

"Grandzau knew this would happen. He *made* this happen."

Trefle wet his lips again. His eyes flickered between the mirror and her legs, and then back to the mirror. He smiled.

"They say that a woman learns to enjoy the whip."

She shot him and Trefle went down with a scream.

She stood over him, holding her gun in one hand, her skirt in the other, and watched him writhe on the floor. She listened to footsteps on the stair. They paused, then descended unhurriedly. It wasn't the sort of building where a single shot drew attention.

Cursing and moaning, Trefle struggled to a sitting position, spread aside his bush jacket, raised his dirty pullover, and inspected the bloody furrow her shot had plowed through the roll of fat around his waist.

"You crazy woman, you could have killed me."

"You're not the only man who can help me, Henri. Just the most convenient." She released her skirt and smoothed it over her legs. "Get up. I've booked the midnight sleeper to Marseilles."

9

Chamberlain was awakened by a steady ringing in his ears. His immediate sense was one of relief—at last he had slept. Then he realized he was in a hospital. He moved his hands and legs, assessed himself undamaged, and tapped his head to try to stop the ringing. That set off a headache that would last, like the ringing, most of the day. He lay back, shut his eyes, and slowly pieced together the events that had brought him here.

When he looked around again, having dozed a few minutes, he discovered Aarschot in the next bed. The Belgian detective had lost his hair and eyebrows, which lent a comic cast to his otherwise angry expression. Chamberlain nodded hello, igniting a secondary headache.

Aarschot loosed a torrent of irritable French. Chamberlain's blank expression provoked the Belgian to switch to his thickly accented, prissy English. The gist of his tirade was that four Belgian policemen had saved his and Chamberlain's lives and the Brussels mortuary had the bodies to prove it. Daitch, whose warning to stay back Chamberlain had understood too late, was also dead.

Chamberlain felt slightly detached from the event. He was

trying to remember something Daitch had said about Hammond and Grandzau. Something secret. Nurses and policemen filled the room suddenly. The cops congregated solicitously around Aarschot, who preened visibly and shook hands as if he were selling machine parts at a discount.

Chamberlain got the nurses. He had always liked nuns. They fussed over him, twittering in kind and thoughtful French.

"Telephone?" he said.

It sounded like a word that should be the same in either language. Apparently it was because a nun came toward him weaving a long cord around the policemen shaking hands with Aarschot. At the end of the cord was a telephone, which Chamberlain used to call one of his friends in Langley, Virginia.

Again he had the feeling that his Central Intelligence Agency friends were a touch too anxious to help. They already knew about the explosion, Hammond's absence from the rubble, and Chamberlain's survival. He asked about the missing airplane.

"Farquhar in London is on that. He's playing it close to the vest, but I don't think he's got anything yet."

"If he hasn't, I'm not sure where to go next."

"Try Marseilles."

"What the hell for?"

"That's all I can say."

"Oh, come on."

"'Bye, Pete. Glad you made it."

Chamberlain looked at the phone for a moment, then he dialed the operator and asked to be connected to Scotland Yard in London. The ringing in his ears was doing funny things to his memory. He knew he had Inspector Farquhar's number, but he couldn't remember the number or whether he had written it down, and if so, where.

"I think I've used up your favors in Brussels for a while," he told Farquhar.

"Not to worry. How are you?"

"In one piece. Have you found the plane?" He glanced around the hospital room, seeking the closet where they'd put his clothes, hoping they hadn't removed or dropped anything from his pockets. He needed his passport and his tools and he had to get out of here.

"We're making progress," said Farquhar.

Chamberlain remembered the Comptel plane. He'd get that old sergeant to bustle him out of the hospital, onto the plane, and then . . . "What sort of progress?"

"We're pretty sure it didn't go to Norway, Sweden, Denmark, Central Europe, or Algeria."

"Leaving Greenland, the Azores, and Russia?"

"Quite."

"Plus anywhere they could have gone after refueling at one of those places."

"I rather doubt they'd have refueled in Russia."

"We gotta get that plane," said Chamberlain. "It's the only thing in their plan that went wrong."

"I understand you spoke with Daitch," Farquhar said matter-of-factly.

"Sorry," said Chamberlain. "I didn't mean to hold back." He related the entire conversation.

"Interesting," said Farquhar. "It certainly does seem as if Grandzau is alive. Perhaps your friends at the CIA can persuade the Italians to exhume him. What's your next step?"

"Get out of here, get on my plane, and go someplace, though frankly I don't know where."

"Why don't you try Marseilles?"

"Marseilles?" mused Chamberlain, as if hearing the name for the first time. "I guess it would be a good town to put together a little snatch team . . . especially if you used to know people down there in the heroin trade."

"Not to mention the information business. Remember, Grandzau often operated in Marseilles. However, I must point out that you're not the only one thinking along these lines."

"Oh?"

"My friends at MI-Five tell me that their friends at the CIA tell them that the KGB boys are already in Marseilles, knocking down doors all over the waterfront."

"What's with the Russians?" Chamberlain asked irritably.

"Ask *your* friends at the CIA. I hear they're dogging the Russians' tracks." Farquhar chuckled dryly. "I think they're still hoping your little ransom consortium will bail them out."

"Nice to know they'll be so close by if I need them."

"Yes, I imagine you *will* find yourself in the crossfire. Best luck, old boy. Do check in when you get a chance."

"Glad to," said Chamberlain, noticing that a new bunch of

cops were now shaking hands with Aarschot and clucking over his bald head. "Provided they ever let me out of Belgium."

"I rather gather that your Ms. Thorp has already arranged that. Cheerio."

The Belgian who delivered Chamberlain to the airport repeated several times that his government took no nonsense from rich multinational corporations. Chamberlain said he understood, got on his jet, and flew away.

The steward was ready with a sophisticated first-aid station and seemed disappointed that the hospital had found nothing on Chamberlain that needed repair. He brought him breakfast, and watched, fascinated, as Chamberlain took inventory of the contents of his pockets, sipped coffee, and chewed a croissant.

"What's your name?" asked Chamberlain.

"Kreegan, sir."

"I'm afraid I better have a look at that gun case of yours."

"Yes, sir!"

"No, leave that. I haven't finished. Just put it here on the seat beside me and we'll have a look."

Kreegan opened the lid with a flourish. "Captain says we're going to Marseilles."

"The captain's right," said Chamberlain, perusing the contents of the velvet-lined case.

"That's a tough town with small spaces, sir. Little twisty, windy alleys and little dark rooms, bitsy little cars. You want something made for close work."

"How about this?" asked Chamberlain, picking up a beautifully balanced, snubnosed revolver.

"Shit," snorted Kreegan. "You take a guy out with that, sir, and you end up blowing away a fishstand across the street with the same slug. Sir."

"Good point. Something tells me you have a particular weapon in mind, Kreegan," Chamberlain said irritably. The ringing still hadn't stopped, and both headaches were worse. He was glad for the coffee and little else.

"This, sir."

"It looks the same as this one."

"Well it's not, sir. This one's actually a shotgun."

Chamberlain inspected it from several angles before asking incredulously, "A six-shot *shotgun* revolver?"

"A double-action hand shotgun. Six shots as fast as you can pull the trigger."

Chamberlain regarded it dubiously. "What's the tradeoff?"

"Beg pardon, sir?"

"Whenever you fiddle a machine to get more of one thing, you get less of something else. In other words, what *won't* this thing do?"

"Oh. Well, it won't pack much wallop after twenty feet. Of course like we said, you don't have big spaces in Marseilles so range don't matter. The shot spreads real fast, won't hold a tight pattern cause the barrel's so short, but again, you're in tight quarters. And it won't be very quiet."

"How loud?"

"Like artillery. Also, don't try to reload right away."

"Heat?"

"Yes, sir. You'll burn your hand off."

Chamberlain nodded, weighing the gun in his hand. "So it's loud as a cannon, dangerous to be beside, and too hot to reload."

"But the other guys don't know that. Besides, after six shots, who's still going to be standing? . . . More coffee, sir?"

"Thank you." He sat quietly, sipping the delicious coffee, studying the beautiful little weapon, while Kreegan cleared the breakfast dishes and locked up the gun case, and the needle-slim jet murmured across the face of Europe.

The Central Intelligence Agency had never treated him this well. He enjoyed the comfort immensely, but it frightened him a little. There was nothing morally wrong with attentive servants and private jets, but you could lose your life sometime if you started to believe in these trappings and ended up thinking that the button was the machine.

Marseilles was warm. He'd had snow in Washington, snow in New York, damp cold in London, and an icy North Sea wind in Brussels, but Marseilles was blessedly warm. It smelled of spice and gasoline exhaust, tobacco smoke, the salt sea, and tropic heat.

Comptel had a house overlooking the Mediterranean. There

was a bowl of fresh fruit on a table in his bedroom window, and beside it, a telex machine noisily printing out a message from Helen Thorp.

"GLAD YOU'RE ALIVE. RECEIVED 2ND LANCELOT INVITATION. TEXT FOLLOWS. QUOTE. PENDRAGON WELL. AUCTION JANUARY 6. SITE TO BE ANNOUNCED. LANCELOT. END QUOTE. WE HAVE FIVE DAYS. REPEAT. FIVE DAYS."

Ms. Ultra Cool sounded a touch panicky. Chamberlain leaned over the keyboard and typed a reply.

"I'M HERE. I'LL LOOK AROUND. I'LL DO WHAT I CAN."

He waited for an answer, but she was apparently not near her machine. Kreegan bustled into the room, his arms heaped with boxes. Chamberlain had come here by cab and was surprised to see him.

"I said I'd call the airport if I needed your help."

"But you gotta have clothes, Mr. Chamberlain. It's hot as hell here. I'll get right out of your way." Briskly, he tore the boxes open and handed Chamberlain a couple of suits, both tropical weight, one light beige, the other a dark blue. "They're the same size. Put one on, and I got a Frenchie tailor outside'll set you up right away." He slipped the shot revolver's holster over his head.

Chamberlain saw the sense in it. The house was cool, but he'd been uncomfortable in his winter worsted outside. He changed into the beige suit and Kreegan brought the tailor running with a piercing whistle. The jacket was perfect but for a tightness at the holster. The trousers needed to be let out and shortened.

"Do the light one first," snapped Kreegan, "chop chop. You can take a shower, sir, and make some phone calls if you want, and it'll be ready. I brought you some shirts. Fifteen-and-a-half collar."

Twenty minutes later, showered and slipping into a fresh cotton shirt, Chamberlain noticed that his headache had gone away, though his ears were still ringing. The tailor helped him into the jacket and stood back, pursing his lips, to inspect his work.

"Nice going," said Kreegan. "Now you can do the dark one. In case you're having dinner out, downtown, sir. Here's some neckties. You might want to slip one in your pocket in case you don't come back to the house."

Chamberlain nodded distractedly, dealing with the same

problem he always had with summer clothes—where to put his tools so they wouldn't bulge through the light cloth. The shoulder holster made things worse. Its bulk was tailored for, but it still restricted the amount of equipment he could put in his left breast inside jacket pocket. Eventually he got things equitably distributed. He no longer bulged like a shoplifter, but the tailor still clucked at what he had done to the lines of the suit.

"*Portefeuille?*" he suggested plaintively.

"They're full, all right," Chamberlain agreed.

The tailor shook his head. He pantomimed carrying something.

"What the hell is he talking about?" said Kreegan. "Wait a minute." He turned and yelled out the door, "Hey, Pierre?"

"Oui, monsieur," cried a weedy young man who scurried into the bedroom.

Kreegan explained to Chamberlain. "I got you this student here, Pierre, to translate for you—what's the tailor saying, Pierre?"

"*Portefeuille,*" repeated the tailor, continuing his plea in rapid French while Kreegan glowered impatiently.

"Yes," said Pierre. "He suggests that the gentleman carry a handbag for his, um, implements. Tools. Uh. Instruments."

Chamberlain smiled at the tailor. "Thanks, but no."

"He means like a pocketbook," said Kreegan. "Guys carry 'em over here."

"Yeah, well this guy isn't. Thanks for the translator, I'll call him if I need him. I want you back on the plane, in case I have to go quick. Now, everybody out."

Chamberlain waited until he heard the front door close and cars pull away. Then he exhaled noisily, took off his new suit, walked out into the hot sun, and stepped into the blue marble swimming pool. It was late afternoon, but the sun still shimmered on the water. He swam a few laps, pulled over to the side, and leaned against the side of the pool and looked out at the Mediterranean.

It was time to think and what he thought was that if Grandzau had faked his own death and kidnapped Charles Hammond, then he had better find out everything there was to know about Grandzau. It was all very well to fly to Marseilles because Grandzau had operated here, but for all he knew, the

German had a deeper love for and knowledge of Wisconsin and had Hammond hidden in a cow barn ten miles from Milwaukee.

He climbed out of the pool and walked, dripping comfortably, into the house. Here it was cool; he wrapped his shoulders in a generous bath towel. He telephoned direct, got passed through several low-level types until he found a low-level type he knew. The girl sounded like she was expecting to hear from him.

As he cajoled and flattered her into quizzing the Agency computers about Grandzau, he had the feeling that she was running him through his paces for the hell of it, as if she'd already been instructed to give him anything he asked for. Nonetheless, he continued the charade as if he hadn't noticed. If that was the game they wanted to play, it didn't bother him as long as he got his information. Nor did it surprise him. He was quite obviously their stalking horse or point man on this operation. His main problem would be getting out of the way when they changed their minds.

He asked for printouts on Grandzau's entire history, including associates, friends, and enemies. He gave her his computer terminal number, the model—so she'd transmit in the proper mode—and an hour deadline. Then he telephoned Helen Thorp. The Comptel executive operator couldn't find her at home or the office, but finally tracked her down at a private Manhattan lunch club called, too coyly he thought, Le Club, which he remembered as being a bit stuffy and filled with rich business types, like Helen Thorp, entertaining out-of-towners.

"Sorry to drag you away from all the fun, but as long as I'm going through hell in this villa, I'm going to make life miserable for the rest of you."

She laughed and he found himself thinking of the line of her neck as she threw her head back. "They're taking good care of you?"

"Kreegan should have been somebody's mother."

"He's a treasure. What's your next move?"

"I need access to the Comptel computers."

"Sorry. I can't authorize direct access."

"Yeah, okay, I understand you can't open 'em just like that, but give me somebody who has access. I want to search for any info on Grandzau."

"What can Comptel do?"

"How many branch offices do we have in Europe?"

"Thirty-eight."

"And that's just Europe. We could have dealt with him sometime, sold him something, bought something from him, who knows. I asked the Agency for the dope on him. As soon as I get names of companies he's owned and worked for, I want to run them through Comptel's computers. You know what I mean?"

"Right. I'll do it. There's only a few of us with complete access. And if you can't get me for some reason, go straight to Mr. Cowan."

"Thanks. Enjoy your lunch."

"Wait. Did you get my telex?"

"About the new Lancelot message? Yeah."

"Pete, we're running out of time."

"We are."

"Well what the devil—I mean what are you going to do now, aside from tapping computers? What's your next step?"

"I hear Marseilles is swarming with KGB types. Maybe I ought to have a chat with one of them."

They were easy to spot, munching fried fish and dressed like a Russian tourist's idea of how a Marseilles gunman looked. What gave them away more than their black shirts and white suits—an outfit some of the locals still wore—was their size. They looked like a pair of Ukranian plowboys. Back home in Connecticut, they would have been recruited for pro ball in their junior year of high school.

Spotting them was one thing, dealing with them another. He'd already seen one back alley bar they'd reduced to splinters, the stunned patrons stacked like cordwood in the corner. Now they lounged with their backs to the fishstand, surveying the sidewalk with open contempt. Across the busy street their backup squad waited in a black Peugeot. In the unlikely event that someone they'd assaulted called the gendarmes, the Peugeot would decant a middle-level Russian embassy official with diplomatic immunity for the hitters and a fistful of francs for the cops.

Chamberlain lounged in the door of a tobacco shop, working hard at looking French. The beige suit and the open-collar light blue shirt helped, but the *pièce de résistance,* the device that transformed his persona as well as his nationality, was the syrupy, perfumed hair tonic with which he'd slicked his hair down tight to his head. It felt like telephone wire, but if anything could make him look southern European—maybe even like a French cop—it was this glossy head. He'd tried to complete the effect with black wraparound sunglasses, but had given it up at nightfall because he couldn't see.

The KGB heavies finished their dinner and started swaggering down the crowded sidewalk. Chamberlain waited until the black Peugeot started after them before he followed. They walked aimlessly for a while and Chamberlain began to get nervous. Street work wasn't one of his strongest points. The navy had taught him to hide in the water, emerge to wreak havoc, and hide again. The Central Intelligence Agency had honed his aptitude for small things that worked and made him conversant with computers. At Comptel he'd been trying to learn to deal with powerful people and large organizations. But he had little practical experience in street work.

Had they made him? Were they strolling along looking for a quiet hole in the wall to beat his head in while the black Peugeot stood watch? Why weren't they moving with the purposefulness with which they'd reportedly been tearing up Marseilles?

He hung further back. There had to be some way to separate the two gorillas from the car, and then one from the other, long enough to ask one simple question. Two questions, actually. What were *they* asking the people they were leaning on? And what had they learned?

The Peugeot's horn trilled insistently through the street noise of cars and motorbikes, music from the bars, and the click and shuffle of hundreds of nighttime walkers. One of the Russians leaned casually on the roof of the car, watching the street, while a man inside spoke through the open window. The second Russian kept walking slowly, glancing back now and then. Chamberlain went into a boutique and watched through the window. The Peugeot had a two-way radio antenna.

The Russian pushed off from the car and caught up with his companion. Advancing at a brisk walk, they turned abruptly into an alley. The car stayed where it was.

To follow the KGB men, Chamberlain had to pass the car. He hesitated, hoping it would move forward, but it stayed at the curb, its four occupants ignoring the blaring horns and angry shouts of the drivers behind, who had to swing out into oncoming traffic to pass it. Every second he waited, the KGB men were moving further away, closer to the target to which they'd been ordered.

A woman's laughter drifted across the street. He saw two couples, arm in arm, strolling into a club. He was suddenly afraid to pass the car. Not afraid that he'd lose his opportunity if they spotted him, but afraid he'd get hurt. It had to come sometime, and here it was. He'd never questioned the theory that you had to be crazy to be a demolition diver. But now he realized that if it was true, he was no longer crazy.

The Russians solved the dilemma for him. They started their car and drove away. Chamberlain looked for a backup squad, saw none, and went into the alley. It was fairly dark several steps in and it didn't look promising. One wall was the side of a porno theater. A fire escape ran up it into the black sky. The near side was lined with dark doorways. He stepped around a pile of garbage cans and crouched down behind them. Listening for the sound of the men in the car following him, he swept the alley with the microwave scanner, felt nothing, and started rapidly in.

He came to the end of the alley abruptly and much sooner than he had expected. There he found a single wooden door, ajar. He turned around, faced the street, and swept the area. The scanner showed no one following. He pushed the door open, scanned the darkness. Nothing. He hesitated. The scanner was capable of reporting only a moving presence. An infrared scanner might respond to a waiting attacker's body heat, but he didn't have one. He had a flashlight, but he was afraid to draw fire.

Suddenly he heard a loud crash, and a startled cry, quickly muffled. Closing one eye to protect his night vision, he flicked his flashlight for a second in the direction of the sound. In the brief moment of light he saw an open doorway and steps beyond. He ran to it, dodging a pile of flower pots he'd seen between himself and the door.

He went up the stairs fast. The noise had come through an open window a floor above. The struggle was going at full fury in the dark. He heard the thunk of fists slamming into bodies, the crash of bodies hitting walls. A whistling, swishing sound was followed by a scream.

Electric light blazed on, painting a battered, shabby room stark white, half blinding Chamberlain. One of the Russians lay still on the floor, blood oozing from his throat. The second was locked in combat with a man as big as himself who was fighting to free his wrist from the Russian's grip. The Russian was holding on for his life. The man had a long shiny knife, wet with the fallen KGB man's blood.

None of them had turned on the light. Chamberlain whirled to face the rush from behind. What he saw looked impossible. There was a man sitting in the corner, but he hadn't turned on the light because his hands and feet were bound to the arms and legs of the chair. Chamberlain gaped. He had seen the stunningly beautiful woman who was now swinging a gun at his head, on the street in Brussels outside Daitch's house.

He was still trying to untangle the impossible from the obvious when her gun met his temple with a ringing crunch and a vicious blue stab of pain drove him to his knees. The last thing he saw as the pain drew a curtain over the light was the man with the knife breaking free and swinging his shiny weapon with lightning speed. It cut the air with a whistle and it gleamed like a long, thin shard of broken glass.

10

"Herr Streicher."

"Mr. Nagumo."

A wealthy, retired brigadier, down from the country for a week of shopping in London with his wife, stared openly as the slim Japanese man crossed his path in the lobby of the Savoy Hotel and shook hands with the portly German. Both men bowed, Kaga Nagumo inclining his head, and Hans Streicher bending from his ample waist with a quiet click of his heels. They walked toward the Grill, Streicher a full foot taller and twice as wide as Nagumo.

English, the ancient brigadier noted with a grim irony, was their common language.

"I'm delighted that you were free for dinner," said the Japanese man.

The brigadier had lost some hearing in the '14–'18 war, a condition exacerbated by injuries received in the futile defense of Singapore in '42, so he had to strain to catch the German's blunt, "We better talk." Then they were gone.

After they were seated, Nagumo asked, "What have you heard from Marseilles?"

"The police say nothing."

Nagumo ordered malt whiskey, the German ordered vodka.

"There's nothing quite like a single malt," said Nagumo.

Streicher fixed him with a good-humored stare. "We don't have time for maneuvering."

"I suppose not," said Nagumo, clearly uncomfortable with the German's blunt approach.

"Comptel screwed up. We gotta do something about it."

"I was not entirely surprised," replied Nagumo.

"Neither was I, so I've been doing what you've probably been doing."

"Yes?" said Nagumo with a smile.

"I've been checking around."

"Yes."

Streicher had learned his English and much of his manner as a boy in Berlin's American zone, operating in the postwar black market. "I gather your *yeses* mean *me too*. Right?"

Nagumo, who had spent his postwar years selling cheap goods in the European market, had learned his English after mastering French and Italian. "Yes. I too have been investigating on my own."

"I need a drink," gasped Trefle.

Lady Janet looked away from the wheel of her rented Renault for a moment. The coast road was an unfolding black band ahead of the speeding car. In the dim glow of the dashboard lights she saw that the Frenchman's hands were trembling.

"There's brandy in my bag."

Trefle pawed into it, extracted a silver flask with an exultant cry, twisted off the top, and tipped it into his mouth. His neck worked as the brandy poured down his throat. At last he lowered the flask. She took it from him, swallowed quickly, and handed it back.

"Finish it."

"I intend to."

"Why did you kill them?" She knew it was stupid to ask even as she spoke.

"So they wouldn't kill me."

"They were Russian, weren't they?"

"Sounded that way," said Trefle.

Lady Janet concentrated on a series of bends in the road. They'd been questioning the old Legionnaire who ran the rooming house on the courtyard in Marseilles when the Russians had interrupted them. The Legionnaire provided lodging for mercenaries down on their luck in between jobs.

She felt Trefle's eyes on her and she returned his gaze. The brandy had calmed him; the muscles in his cheeks were no longer twitching.

"They were stronger than me," he said. "Not as quick, but stronger."

The confession startled her. Not that he admitted their superior strength, but that he would bother explaining why he had killed them. He wasn't through: "I don't have the strength anymore. I drink too much. And I've aged. But I have the will. And I know how. Better than any of them."

Lady Janet nodded. It was difficult to imagine Trefle in a weakened condition. "Perhaps you should get a gun."

"Perhaps."

They rode silently for a while, each thinking. They had done well in Marseilles until the Russians barged in. Charles Hammond's kidnapping was a subject of great interest among the mercenaries. Many remembered his betrayal in Somalia. Others were fascinated by the audacity of the plot. None had heard of the Pendragon auction, and no one had any idea that Grandzau was alive. They speculated freely about Hammond's captors, and many claimed to know who'd been in on it.

Everyone wanted to have a former comrade in on a big deal. Hard pressed to sift reality from fantasy, Lady Janet and Trefle had weighed the teller's reputation and the nature of his speculation. Those who claimed a friend was in the hire of politicians or business rivals they'd ignored. Those who knew for sure that Hammond had been taken by terrorists they'd passed by, searching for someone who knew some plausible detail of Grandzau's plan.

Then they'd happened upon a mercenaries' brothel that the Russians had invaded. They hadn't killed anyone, but some of the men had been badly knocked about. Trefle started in on them while she questioned the women. They learned it wasn't the first place the Russians had attacked. They were tearing up Marseilles asking the same questions they were. Where was Grandzau? Who had gone to work for him? A frightened prostitute, a nineteen-year-old Greek girl sniffling for heroin, told Lady Janet that a group of soldiers staying in the rooming house in the courtyard by the porno theater had hired on with Grandzau. She'd neglected to add that she had told the same thing to the Russians.

Trefle and Lady Janet had gotten there first and Trefle had just begun to threaten the Algerian veteran who ran the place when the Russians arrived. The man had started to talk and what he told them had them driving to Lyons. They would have taken a plane or the train, but the dead men they'd left behind would have been discovered by the police whose klaxons they'd heard as they'd fled, and the Marseilles airport and railroad stations would be swarming.

The Marseilles police attacked the case of the murdered Russian KGB agents on two fronts. Forensic teams, laboratory technicians, narcotics detectives, and Deuxième Bureau operatives scrutinized the room where they were found for fingerprints, weapons, blood types, scuff marks, nail parings, and hair samples.

At the same time, a pair of Corsican-born homicide detectives dragged Peter Chamberlain into an interrogation room at the back of their precinct house, woke him up with a bucket of ice water, and suggested he would save himself a lot of anguish if he confessed to the double murder. Chamberlain shook his head to clear it. Vaguely he wondered what cumulative damage there would be from the explosion in Brussels followed by a strong woman bending a gun barrel over his head. He saw the man who poured water on him wind up and throw an open-handed blow. He was too groggy to avoid it, and it crashed against his cheek.

It snapped his head back, but the sting cleared his brain.

"Okay, guys," he said, raising his hands to protect himself. His hands were chained together in front of him. They had him seated in a straightback chair under a bright light. They were yelling in French, but when he looked blank, they switched back to the English they'd started with. He felt in his pocket, but his passport wallet was missing. So they knew his name, his nationality, and who he worked for. This was no time to be a lonesome hero.

All his pockets were empty. He spotted their contents on the window sill. Gesturing carefully at the pile of paper and gadgets, he said, "May I have my wallet?"

The cop who had hit him raised his hand, but his partner

eased him aside. Both wore shiny gray suits and dark blue shirts. Both were short men, compactly built, and both looked perfectly content to slap him around until he confessed.

"What?" asked the cop.

"Can I call my company? They can vouch for me."

"Vouch you're a murderer? We already know that."

"If I'm a murderer, who laid me out on the floor?"

"Your second victim struck you just as you slit his throat."

"Wait," said Chamberlain as the second cop came closer to hit him again. The cop kept coming.

"Wait! The guy in the chair. He saw what happened. Ask him."

One cop hit him, the other grabbed his hair and leaned close to his face. "He said you tied him up and beat him and killed the Russians when they interrupted you."

"What?"

They hit him again. Chamberlain tasted blood in his mouth. They closed in and slapped him back and forth between them. A deep and unusual anger rumbled to life inside him. The fact that these clowns spoke English meant they weren't just a pair of weirdos having their private idea of fun. They had their orders to get a confession.

Chamberlain exploded out of the chair, swinging his handcuffed hands like a club, felling one detective with a single blow, then kicking the other in the groin even as he lost his balance and fell heavily to the concrete. The first detective lunged groggily for him. Chamberlain rolled aside and levered himself back onto his feet.

The one he'd kicked lay coiled and writhing, but the first detective was coming for him again, climbing to his feet, pawing a blackjack from his pocket. Chamberlain tried to guess which way he would swing. He'd lost the initiative. All he could hope to do now was minimize the damage.

11

Kaga Nagumo was fascinated by the German.

Only a catastrophe like the kidnapping of Charles Hammond could ever have led to him sitting at the same restaurant table with the arms dealer. Nagumo was Japan's foremost businessman in Europe, a position attained by thirty-five years of hard work selling Mishuma's products coupled with a careful habit of innocuous respectability cultivated when Occidentals in postwar Europe were still very leery of young, fit-looking, Japanese bearing cheap electrical devices and mass-produced cameras.

Streicher, by contrast, was not much less than a simple cutthroat. The arms dealer's manner reminded Nagumo of the jujitsu gangsters who managed Tokyo's vice. He lounged insolently with his after-dinner brandy, surveying the other diners with easy contempt, as if knowing he dealt daily with matters that terrified ordinary men.

His German accent thickened as he got drunk, drawing the notice of the English and Americans at nearby tables. He shoved his big hand between the glasses and the flowers drooping from a silver vase and grabbed Nagumo's hand. Nagumo shuddered from the impulsive contact, then winced as the German squeezed.

"Partners! Ja?"

"Yes," Nagumo replied quietly, glancing around in fear they were overheard. A young couple was still at the table they'd taken moments after he and Streicher had been seated. He'd noticed them because they didn't look as if they could afford the Grill. They were holding hands. He chided himself for being nervous.

Streicher grinned lopsidedly. "Nobody knows what we're partners in," he whispered. "Relax."

Nagumo smiled uneasily. "Yes, of course."

A strange light appeared in the German's eyes and he was suddenly much less drunk than he had seemed. "Order some coffee, Mr. Nagumo. We've got a long night ahead of us. I want an answer on that radar by morning." He grinned again and bellowed in a thick German accent. "Coffee. *Schnell!*"

He grinned at Nagumo. "If the English want to hate me, I'll give them reason."

Nagumo cringed inwardly from the staring people and thought of the things he did for Japan.

Lady Janet shivered in the cold mist that rose from the Rhone and settled in the streets of Lyons. It was three in the morning and she was waiting in the car while Trefle jimmied a lock on a warehouse across the street. He waved. She slipped out of the car, closed the door soundlessly, and ran to him.

Trefle slid the door aside and squeezed into the dark interior. Lady Janet followed and fanned out to the right, drawing her gun, covering Trefle while he closed the door. She was reminded of the final days of Grandzau's drug business, when the Chinese merchants were tightening their grip on the market and sending strongarms to close down independent operations. Grandzau had resisted as long as he could, turning a profit every day, until they fled for their lives. More than once she'd flattened her body to a wall and raked the hostile darkness with her gun.

She heard a sharp click-click and narrowed her eyes. A second after the warning, Trefle flicked on a flashlight. It was a low-ceilinged room stacked with cardboard-boxed wine bottles stored for shipment to overseas markets. Lady Janet recognized the label, an indiscriminate mix of nonvintage *vins rouges* no one would drink locally. She exhaled her trapped breath. They were alone. Having seen from the outside that the windows were shuttered, they turned on the lights.

They searched the room, found nothing but the boxes, and moved on, Trefle investigating the low cellar while she ascended a steep staircase to the first floor. She had just entered a narrow corridor between stacked wine cases when Trefle shouted.

She ran down the stairs two at a time, across the ground floor, and dropped into the cellar, landing crouched and silent. Trefle pointed at a solidly built cabinet. The doors were open and there were gun racks inside, empty but for a single weapon.

"They're gone."

"Bloody hell."

The arsenal cabinet had held six guns. Trefle pulled out the last and inspected it with professional delight. Lady Janet recognized the M76 submachine gun that Smith & Wesson hadn't built in years. It was fast, accurate, and light. With the stock folded it was twenty inches long. Disassembled it would fit in a medium-size handbag.

She found a couple of boxes of 9mm. Parabellum cartridges in the bottom of the closet. "Break it down," she told Trefle. "I'll take it."

"The *patrone* is a good man."

Lady Janet laid a pair of thousand franc notes on the empty rack and closed the cabinet doors.

The door to the Marseilles precinct interrogation room slammed open and a white-haired plainclothes inspector flanked by uniformed cops burst in. The inspector took in the scene with a quick glance.

Chamberlain took a step back. The detective he had kicked struggled painfully to his feet. The other detective put his blackjack back in his pocket and nervously saluted the senior officer. The uniformed men rushed Chamberlain and held him from either side.

The white-haired inspector spoke in rapid French. When he was through, the detectives shook their heads. "Non."

Chamberlain guessed that they'd been asked if he had confessed.

"Can I call my company?" he asked loudly.

The white-haired man looked at him. Chamberlain met his

hostile gaze, his heart sinking. This was no savior. Then he saw Kreegan's crewcut head through the open door. The steward pushed his way into the room. The white-haired man turned to him and it was obvious they had talked before.

"You're not permitted in here."

Kreegan ignored him. "That's Mr. Chamberlain. Can I take him with me?"

"You don't understand. He is going to be charged with murder."

"You're kidding," Kreegan scoffed cheerfully. "Pete wouldn't hurt a fly. Now I've got the American consul coming down here from a nice party just to tell you people that Mr. Chamberlain is a respectable American citizen."

The white-haired man was unmoved. He said coldly, "My answer to the American consul will be the same as my answer to you. This man is to be charged with murder. And no force but a French court will free him from our custody."

"Come on."

"Get out." He snapped his fingers and two more uniformed cops sprang into the room and grabbed Kreegan.

"Goddamnit," said Kreegan. "You're making a lousy mistake."

"I'll arrest you next."

Kreegan faced Chamberlain for the first time. "I'm sorry, sir. They're being real pigheaded about it."

Chamberlain had a sudden thought. "Call the guy at Dassault."

"Right!" cried Kreegan, and the white-haired man raised his brows. Stroking his nose thoughtfully, he watched the police escort Kreegan from the interrogation room. Chamberlain watched apprehensively as the Corsican reached for his blackjack.

The white-haired man stayed him with a gesture. "Dassault?" he asked Chamberlain.

"Yeah. You may have heard of them. They built the Mirage? France's mainstay in the arms trade? Our companies are in partnership."

Again the white-haired cop stroked his nose. "We shall see," he said. He gestured and the Corsican detectives left the room. The others followed and closed the door, leaving a grill open. Chamberlain sat down and waited alone, watched through the grill by a uniformed cop.

It was a long wait. After a while, he stretched out on the hard floor and tried to nap. The clanging door awakened him and he saw gray dawn light spilling through the windows of the outer room.

The interrogation room filled rapidly. The white-haired inspector was back, as were some uniformed officers and Kreegan, looking pleased. A very young and angry-looking Frenchman was wearing a dinner jacket. A scent of feminine perfume suggested that a lady was waiting to conclude a heretofore pleasant evening.

He gave Chamberlain a single look of utter contempt, loosed a loud torrent of French at the white-haired inspector, then waited with crossed arms while Chamberlain's hands were unchained, his possessions, including the shot revolver, were returned, and Kreegan was allowed to lead him away.

"Wait," said Chamberlain.

"Let's go while the going's good," said Kreegan, propelling him through the door.

"Back off," snapped Chamberlain. He brushed past the inspector and said to the man in the dinner jacket. "You're with Dassault?"

"I am," came the tight-lipped answer.

"Thanks for getting me out. Now I want to know what these clowns got out of the old guy tied to the chair."

The Frenchman's eyes rolled skyward. "I want to go home, monsieur."

"Me too. There was a guy tied to a chair in the room where the Russians were killed, where the cops found me. The cops probably have him here. I want to know what he told them."

"Monsieur."

"Mister, if your boss can send you down here to spring me, he can boot your ass across the Pyrenees if I ask him to."

The elegantly dressed man shrugged and raised his open hands high in a what-do-you-want-from-me pose, but he spoke to the inspector.

"Non!"

"Oui!" the young man bellowed. "*Immédiatement!*"

It was the inspector's turn to shrug. He snapped out orders until officers brought him a carbon copy of a typed sheet of paper. It was in French. Chamberlain glanced at the inspector's stony expression and decided he had pushed him as far as he could.

"Thank you." He turned to the man from Dassault. "Come on."

Kreegan led them out of the stationhouse and into a waiting limousine. The Frenchman protested.

"We'll drop you as soon as you translate this thing. Get in."

Kreegan drove, after asking directions on how to get to where the Frenchman wanted to go. Chamberlain sank gratefully into the plush velour seat and said, "What does it say?"

The Frenchman scanned the paper. "This is an official confession form. The witness claims that a man and a woman came to the pension he runs, tied him to a chair, and threatened bodily harm if he didn't respond to their questions. He told them he would comply. They asked if five men who had been staying at his pension had left suddenly. He said they had. They asked where they had gone and he said Lyons."

"Where in Lyons?"

"He didn't tell the police."

"Would he tell me?"

"Not without a serious bribe. You see these veterans and *colons* and mercenaries all know each other and of course stick together. They wouldn't have told him exactly where they were going, but he might have guessed. At any rate, he didn't tell the police."

"What else does it say?"

"He told the police that the five were all marksmen."

"When did they leave?"

"Yesterday morning."

"Are you sure?"

"Yes."

"That doesn't make sense. I'm assuming they were hired by Grandzau—the man who kidnapped Charles Hammond—but that was three days ago." He looked at the early morning sunlight splashing the tops of the houses. "Four days ago," he corrected, half to himself, half aloud. "Oh for Christ's sake. Is this whole thing a wild goose chase?"

"I don't think so," said the man from Dassault. "The veteran mentioned Grandzau's name several times."

"What?"

"The Marseilles police know what you and the Russians

were looking for. They've been watching the KGB and the CIA for days now. So they asked and the veteran claimed that Grandzau had come there a week ago."

"What?"

"Grandzau visited the man's building last week."

"How did the guy know?"

The Frenchman shrugged. Then he brightened. "Ah. My destination. Thank you for the ride."

Chamberlain opened the door and let the Frenchman slip past him. "Kiss the lady for me."

"It will take more than that to appease her."

A sleepy doorman let the Frenchman into the high-rise apartment building. The moment he closed the door, Chamberlain said to Kreegan, "Back to the waterfront. I've got to talk to that guy as soon as the cops are done with him."

Hans Streicher left the Savoy after dinner with Kaga Nagumo, chartered a light plane, and flew to Essen, where he went drinking until late morning. He did a lot of business in Essen. The German city was located handily near Holland, a short barge ride on the Rhine from the great port of Rotterdam, whose sealed and bonded warehouses provided secure storage for weapons in transit.

He drank less than he bought as he pursued a thread of information through the clubs and bars frequented by weapons men, shippers, warehousers, truckers, hijackers, and agents. A shipment of surplus antipersonnel mines had been stolen from a Rhine barge heading from Mannheim to Essen. The occurrence was less unusual than the fact that no one seemed to know who had done it.

The execution of the hijacking had neither the hysterical confusion associated with terrorists or the cold-blooded murderousness expected of professional criminals. Instead, the entire operation, from stopping the barge to off-loading the mines, had been carried out with the cool precision of the best professional soldiers.

Streicher shared several schnapps with a bargeman who'd witnessed the robbery. The old Bavarian was a veteran of thirty years of smuggling. "If I had to guess," he admitted, "I'd say they were mercenaries gathering an arsenal for a coup." He had ducked down out of sight, but they had killed no one, honoring the old military maxim: never use more force than needed, and never complicate an operation. Murder would have brought in the police. Robbery was kept among associates.

Some other bargemen joined them. Streicher stood another round and listened with half an ear while they talked shop. He had employees doing what he was doing at this moment throughout Europe. Somewhere, someone would find a clue to where Grandzau had taken Hammond. It was too risky to wait for the auction. He had met Grandzau a couple of times. Once he'd paid dearly for inside information that had come to nothing.

Grandzau was a smalltime chisler, and that worried him. With the Russians fanging around like mad animals, Grandzau would never be able to make his auction secure. If he didn't find Hammond first, Hammond would be killed at the auction or wherever Grandzau was hiding him. The whole caper had obviously grown to greater and more complex proportions than Grandzau could have imagined when he started. All of which meant that if Streicher didn't find Hammond before the auction, he was out his biggest deal in ten years, a deal that depended upon Charles Hammond being alive.

He excused himself and found a telephone. His office in downtown Essen was serving as a message center. One of his men had found something interesting in Brest. He'd be calling in again to talk to Herr Streicher in an hour. Streicher hung up and went back to buy the bargemen—who'd broken into lusty song—another round and a big breakfast. It was one of the things you did when you expected to make a lot of money.

Kaga Nagumo and the Japanese trade consul in Rome were old friends. Thirty years ago they had crossed paths regularly as they traveled up and down the Italian peninsula, Nagumo peddling cameras and Ohira pushing plastic Madonnas. A generation of poor Italians had worshiped the wares of the now portly man who occupied the most important seat in the Japanese embassy. A plaque on his office wall, presented by the Ministry of International Trade and Industry, attested to his hard efforts and his sincerity.

Ordinarily a cheerful man, Ohira looked as worried as the small, trim Nagumo. A secretary in modern dress completed an abbreviated tea ceremony and left with a respectful bow. Ohira glanced at her shapely legs.

"The prime minister telephoned last night. I had no idea this Charles Hammond had become so important."

Nagumo smiled thinly. "Oil makes anyone important."

"Anyone who has it."

"Or knows where to find it."

"As in this case."

"Yes," said Nagumo.

Ohira said, "The prime minister told me to ask you for the details." Within hours of Hammond's kidnapping, all embassies had been ordered to help Nagumo get him back. Rome had come up with something.

"Yes?"

"Why was Hammond hired?"

"For the same reason that I am overseeing the project. Secrecy. No one must know until the deal is consummated."

"But why you?"

"Who would suspect the head of Mishuma's European operations of forging an oil consortium with the government of Brazil?"

"Good."

"And who would know that Charles Hammond was my agent? He made all the initial contacts. He even inserted the geological survey team. He got them into the country as archaeologists. If the discoveries come in even half the size of the estimates, we will have our own oil supply for the rest of the century."

Ohira smiled wryly. "I wondered why the prime minister called personally."

"Did you get the boy from the Romans?"

"Yes. We brought enormous pressure."

"Where is he?"

"Handcuffed in my secretary's office. He turned suddenly violent."

"I'm not surprised. He'll be in jail the rest of his life."

"As he should be."

"The prime minister authorized us to offer leniency if he'll help."

"Let's see him," said Nagumo.

The boy, and he was a boy, no more than twenty, eyed them sullenly as they entered the office. He was handcuffed to a metal window frame, the window open a crack, the chain passed out and around a steel upright. A cool breeze slipped past him.

Nagumo thought he looked entirely normal, not a bit different from thousands of university students throughout Japan. His hair was neat and clean, his clothes decent, and it was hard to believe that he'd been arrested with a gang of Italian Red Brigaders after a bloody shootout with the police. His name was Hidi Ochi and the Italian authorities had discovered he was an electronics genius who built remote-fired bombs and mines for the Red Brigade, had taught the Italian terrorists how to construct the devices, and had also built monitoring devices with which they tracked the police.

Nagumo had the strangest feeling he was looking at himself thirty years ago, selling the Europeans what they wanted. Ochi wasn't doing it for the money, but neither had he. Cameras, radios, even plastic Madonnas, were sold less for the currency than for the idea of Japan. Nagumo found himself liking the boy even before they spoke. As threatening and lethal as he was, he too was selling for an idea of Japan.

He introduced himself and told the boy he was being returned to Japan to stand trial for crimes committed there and abroad. He then told him he was empowered to offer him great leniency. Conceivably he could go free on probation after his trial.

The boy said nothing, just watched with liquid dark eyes. If he cared, if he hated Nagumo, if he wanted anything, he kept it secret.

Nagumo said, "I understand you told the Italian police that you built an electronic device for a German man."

The boy said nothing.

"I understand you did it for money."

The boy spoke. "We needed cash for explosives."

Trade Consul Ohira snorted incredulously.

"It seemed simpler," the boy explained patiently, "than robbing a bank."

"If you tell me what you built, who the man was, and where he was going, I'll see that you have a swift trial, in Japan, and never spend a day in jail."

The boy shook his head.

"Why not?" asked Nagumo.

"I cannot betray a revolutionary."

"A revolutionary?" Nagumo said in amazement.

"Excuse me," said Ohira. "That's what he told the Rome police. I took the liberty of obtaining a picture of Grandzau and some information that might be interesting to our young friend. May I?"

"Certainly," said Nagumo.

Ohira left and returned with an expensive leather slipcase. He showed Hidi Ochi a grainy, long lens photograph. A spidery-looking little man was climbing out of a car. He was thin and sticklike. His face was barely visible, but the way he held his body seemed like an easily remembered characteristic.

Ochi glanced at the picture.

"This man's real name is Grandzau," said Ohira.

Ochi said nothing.

"He may have called himself Lancelot."

Recognition flickered across Ochi's face and Nagumo felt excitement building. He'd seen the newspaper clipping on the back of the picture. Ohira turned the picture over and showed Ochi the article from an Italian paper. The boy squinted at the writing.

Ohira spoke. "Just before he retired a few years ago, this Grandzau-Lancelot sold the address of a Baader-Meinhof gang hideout to the West German police. They were all shot dead. If he told you he was a revolutionary it was only to get you to cooperate."

Ochi smashed his elbow through the window.

He can't escape, he's chained to the steel, thought Nagumo.

The boy twisted about and slashed his neck on the broken glass. Nagumo leaped at him. By the time he gripped his shoulders bright blood was splattering on the white windowsill. Ohira's cries brought staff running. Several men pulled Ochi from the window, unlocked the cuffs, and forced him to a couch. A nurse came running. Ochi's thick coat collar had saved his life. In ten minutes his cuts were bandaged and a sedative administered.

When the drug took hold, Nagumo knelt by the couch to which the boy had been tied. "You knew he wasn't a revolutionary, didn't you?"

The boy nodded dully.

"It made it easier to do business?"

"Yes. The explosives seemed worth it."

"Grandzau is just a criminal. He'd attack you as readily as he would attack me. The differences between the establishment and the antiestablishment are meaningless to a criminal. We are both in the same community."

"No!"

"Yes. We are both tied to it. You against the way it is. Me for the way it is. But he is outside the community."

"Criminals are your problem," hissed Ochi.

"Our problem. It is like the Yamaguchigumi. Criminals are everyone's enemy."

At the mention of the gangster organization that controlled prostitution, gambling, amphetamines in Tokyo and the port city of Kobe, Ochi looked up.

Nagumo pressed on. "If the antiestablishment were to win, the gangsters would be a worse enemy to you than they are to us. They'd roll you over while you were still trying to get on your feet."

A muscle began twitching in Ochi's cheek despite the drug.

"I'm offering you a chance to go right back out in the street," said Nagumo. He sat back and waited impassively.

"The man called himself Lancelot," Ochi said quietly. "He said it as if it were funny."

"A private joke?"

"Yes. I don't know where he was going, but I think it was near the sea."

"Why?"

"The electronics had to be protected against salt air. Like military specifications."

"What were the electronics?"

"ECM gear."

Nagumo and Ohira exchanged a doubtful look.

"Electronic countermeasures? What kind?"

"To jam radar."

Again Nagumo and Ohira looked at each other.

"What kind of radar?"

"Civilian and military ground stations."

"Why?"

"He didn't say."

12

The old Algerian veteran looked like he'd been indoors a long time. He had the leathery skin and glare-narrowed eyes of a desert campaigner, but his complexion was dead white. It was as if he had fled the sun the day he was mustered out and hidden indoors ever since. He uttered a weary protest when he saw Chamberlain, Kreegan, and Pierre the translator waiting in his spare, neat little apartment.

Pierre had his instructions. He spoke kindly in French, telling the man that Chamberlain wanted to know only what he had already told the Marseilles police. He hastened to add that the *Americain* bore no ill feelings about his false testimony concerning the death of the Russians that couldn't be forgotten in exchange for a quick and honest response. He warned that the *Americain* already knew much of what he had told the police so that a false answer would likely be recognized. Such a response would be regarded as hostile and would prolong the presence of the three strangers in the lodgings of a man who doubtlessly wanted to do nothing more than go to bed.

"Où est Grandzau?"

The Algerian veteran stared at Pierre for a long moment.

His answer ran long and angry, and when he was through, Pierre translated it for Chamberlain.

"He says how would a simple concierge know the whereabouts of the man who kidnapped the great Charles Hammond."

"He said more than that," said Chamberlain.

Pierre hesitated. "Uh, yes. He said that you are as stupid as the stupid police. He asks us to leave."

"Find out when Grandzau was here. How many times. And who he hired."

Pierre spoke in French.

The veteran shrugged and replied irritably. Chamberlain watched his angry eyes, looking for the involuntary narrowing at a lie, wondering what sort of a soldier he had been thirty years ago. He might have served in Nam in the early fifties, when they still called it French Indochina and the Vietnamese hadn't yet formed the world's deadliest heavy infantry.

Pierre translated.

"Grandzau came here twice. A week ago, and a month or so before that. The first time he hired five men. He took them with him. Last week he came back and hired five more, but they didn't leave until yesterday, when they heard that the Russians were searching for them. He doesn't know much about the first five. They weren't here long. The second group he got to know. They were all great marksmen. Twice a week they would drive to the country and practice. He went along once to watch."

"What weapons did they practice with?"

Pierre asked.

"He says they had a rifle and several handguns."

"What kind?"

Pierre asked. He looked worried. "He said that it is time for you to either leave or start paying for information."

Chamberlain nodded at Kreegan, who produced a fat roll and peeled off a hundred francs. The veteran stuffed the bills into his shirt pocket and answered the question.

"Nine-millimeter pistols and an Uzi automatic rifle," said Pierre.

The veteran spoke again.

"He wants more money."

"Give it to him," snapped Chamberlain. He'd lucked out

with this guy and he wanted all the man had. Kreegan passed him a couple of hundred francs.

Pierre translated. "They went to Lyons to get more weapons."

"Where?"

The veteran didn't know. He licked his lips, watching Kreegan's roll, and Chamberlain could see that he wished he knew the location of the arsenal in Lyons.

"What kind of weapons?"

The Frenchman's reply was animated. He was reaching for the money when he finished. Kreegan gave him a hundred francs while Pierre tried to translate. Uncertainty made his accent stronger.

"Smith and Wesson," he said, distorting the Smith with a long "ee" sound. "Submachine gun?"

"Right."

"M seventy-six. He said nine-millimeter."

Chamberlain raised his eyebrows. A beautiful weapon. But why were they only now going into action—four days after Hammond was kidnapped? The first crew did the kidnapping. Was the second for protection during the auction?

"Was Grandzau alone when he came here the first time?"

"He was with a Maltese," Pierre translated. "Both times."

"Where were the others going after they got guns in Lyons?" he asked, with little hope of getting an answer. To his surprise the veteran answered, "Brest."

"Brest," said Pierre.

"I got that," said Chamberlain. Brest, on the northwest tip of France, where the English Channel met the Atlantic Ocean. "Why would they tell this guy that?"

Pierre asked. The Algerian veteran grinned and reached for Kreegan's money. Chamberlain nodded and Kreegan peeled off several more large bills. Pierre translated the answer.

"They made many long-distance telephone calls to Brest this past week. They kept asking him for change for the telephone. Then he heard them make hotel reservations."

"What hotel?" Chamberlain snapped.

Pierre asked.

"He doesn't know."

"Screw!"

Why would Grandzau keep the two groups apart? Easier to

work with a small group the first time? Easier to get away with a small group? Or maybe it was like bringing in fresh reserves. The second group was saved the tension of the kidnapping and the immediate aftermath. And why Brest? The man from Dassault was about to be interrupted again. He needed the long-distance telephone records from here to Brest to trace the hotel. But he needed it done discreetly so he'd get there ahead of the French police, Interpol, the CIA, and the goddamned Russians. On second thought, the hell with Dassault. Comptel probably had good connections with the phone people over here. He'd drop this in Helen Thorp's lap.

There was something else. The veteran was watching him, awaiting another question, eager to dip into Kreegan's roll again. "Ask him who the man and woman were who slugged me and killed the Russians."

The eager expression faded abruptly. The veteran said he didn't know. Chamberlain didn't believe him, but the sudden terror in his eyes promised that neither bribes nor threats would get the truth.

Chamberlain stared him down, then shook his head in disgust. Maybe he didn't know. Maybe it was just a healthy fear of the kind of man and woman who could slaughter a pair of KGB heavies and flatten an ex-U.S. Navy SEAL in less time than it took to think about it. Despite himself, Chamberlain grinned at the vet. Franc notes of enormous denominations blanketed the man's lap and stuck from his pockets like florid lettuce.

"You better get to the bank, old-timer, before somebody mugs you."

Pierre dutifully started to translate, but Chamberlain was already out the door, motioning him and Kreegan to follow. He had no doubt that he'd milked Marseilles dry, but by now there should be answers at the Comptel house to the questions he had asked the night before.

The teleprinters had heaped data paper onto the bright tile floor of the bedroom overlooking the pool and the sea. The Central Intelligence Agency, Comptel's information center, and Helen Thorp had all transmitted. He read the Agency and Comptel reports, then telephoned Inspector Farquhar.

The Englishman sounded very pleased. "We have the airplane in Iceland."

"Hammond?"

"No passengers. The Icelandic authorities are holding the pilot, but he swears he was hired to deliver it from Stornoway to Reykjavik. There are indications that he's telling the truth."

"That means Hammond got off in the Hebrides."

"Probably. We're searching Lewis and Harris right now."

"Should I come up there?"

"I don't think we'll find him here. Even though there are many remote places in the islands, the folk all know each other. It wouldn't be such a safe place to hide. Hammond could be on an outlying croft, but he'd been much more likely spirited away on a fishing boat."

"Could he have flown out?"

"Not from Stornoway, though he might have been picked up by helicopter from an outer island." Farquhar paused, then added reflectively, "I think we can assume he's in our general territory."

"England and Northern Europe."

"Admittedly a large area. However, there's something else that might interest you. And your partners."

What Farquhar told him made Chamberlain telephone Central Intelligence Agency stations in Bonn and Rome. In both cases the name of his friend in Langley got him to a helpful personage who seemed to be waiting for his call. When they were finished, he turned to the message from Helen Thorp.

A teletype machine's full-caps typeface always exaggerated a message's importance, but Helen Thorp's communiqué had the impact of a three-line, seven-column headline on the front page of *The New York Times*. Beginning, WHAT THE HELL DO YOU THINK, it blamed Chamberlain for destroying the agreement among the companies to buy back Hammond, and ended, AND COMPTEL HAS NEVER NOR EVER WILL AUTHORIZE ITS EMPLOYEES TO COMMIT MURDER.

Chamberlain turned on the transmitter and typed, I DIDN'T DO IT. A minute later he picked up the ringing telephone.

"I certainly hope that's true," said Helen Thorp.

"The Marseilles cops believe in me."

"The Marseilles cops believe in the Mirage. Where is Hammond?"

"A short boat ride from Brest."

"What? Brest, France? Are you sure?"

"Reasonably."

"How do you know?"

"I don't *know*, but everything seems to point to Brest. The Agency tells me the Russians are heading there. The mercenary soldiers I just missed here in Marseilles were heading for Brest—with a stopover in Lyons for guns. At the same time, Comptel tells me that a corporation that Grandzau used to use to buy equipment purchased a whole pile of microwave power units from our French subsidiary."

"What the devil do microwave power units have to do with kidnapping Charles Hammond?" demanded Helen Thorp.

"Listen, lady, I've been up all night and people have been hitting me with disturbing frequency, so would you let me just finish the good stuff?"

To Chamberlain's amazement, she was contrite. "I'm sorry, Pete. I get very tense sitting around here not being able to control what's going on over there. Please go ahead."

"I don't know what Grandzau needed microwave power units for, but he needed them in Brest. That's where the order was shipped."

"Oh."

"In addition, a friend in London—"

"Inspector Farquhar?"

"Yes—tells me that Hans Streicher and Kaga Nagumo had dinner at the Savoy last night. Together. Then Streicher flew to Essen and Nagumo went to Rome. So I called friends of my friendliest friend at Langley, who informed me that Hans Streicher left Essen late this morning, about the same time Nagumo left Rome."

"Heading for Brest?"

"Streicher's in a chartered plane. He didn't file a flight plan for Brest, but he's heading in that general direction. Nagumo's flying to Paris. He doesn't have a reservation, in his name anyway, on the connecting flight to Brest, but there's a train that's almost as fast."

"Well what the hell are you doing in Marseilles?"

"Waiting for the plane's landing gear to get fixed."

"What?"

"Relax. Everything can't work right every time. They're fixing it and I'll still get there faster than commercial."

"But that's insanity," she shouted. "We're paying them to do a job!"

"Everything can't work right every time," Chamberlain repeated soothingly, grinning at Kreegan, who had just handed him the message from the airport with a doleful look. Helen Thorp made an exasperated noise on the telephone and Kreegan pounded his fist into his cupped hand like a center fielder who'd dropped an easy fly in full view of the television cameras.

"Goodbye," said Chamberlain. "I'm going out to the airport. If they don't get it fixed, I'll buy a new one. Come on, Kreegan. Let's get out of here." He started to hang up, then remembered the hotel. "By the way, Ms. Thorp. Do me a favor. Get somebody big in the French phone system to trace the calls from this number to Brest in the last month." He gave her the phone number at the pension. "There should be some calls to a hotel. But try to keep it quiet. I think it gives us a leg up over the rest of them."

"Pete," she said softly.

"What?" Was she going to tell him to be careful?

"You really fucked up."

He had to escape.

They'd let him swim from the boat, let him taste victory, then hauled him back like used bait—by a rope he hadn't known about because they'd tied it to his life jacket when he was still out on the drugs. He had to escape.

From whom? From what? He didn't know. Under better circumstances, the irony of Charles Hammond not knowing might have been funny. His life, his work, his skill, and his talent, was information. Who wanted? Who needed? Who counted? He knew the right people, people who counted. He knew their wants. And most important, he knew their needs.

But he knew nothing about his kidnappers. Bedouin revolutionaries or right-wing Poles from Chicago, he didn't know. He didn't know what they wanted, he didn't know what they needed, he didn't know how they intended to get it. The crowd that had him now was a different bunch than those who had grabbed him and those who had him on the plane. The boatmen, he realized now, were locals picking up some extra work—Scots, they'd sounded like. Now his guards were French. Correction, *spoke* French, in a variety of accents.

Maybe the French foreign legion had him. Of course! The feeble joke pointed at a fact. These were mercenaries. He stopped in midstep. He hadn't been thinking too clearly or he would have noticed this before. He took a slow, deep breath and felt a thin smile crease his face. Mercenaries. Professionals for hire.

He had been ignoring, pushing aside, and tamping down a lot of fear. Now it slipped away like a windblown mist. At least they weren't crazy, whoever they were. At least they weren't fanatics who'd kill him for a cause or mail his ears to prove they were ruthless.

Hired guns. Hired by whom? A hundred possibilities raced through his mind. He had a few enemies. Some of his clients had rivals who wouldn't mind seeing him on ice for a while. Some of his clients were engaged in negotiations so byzantine that even *they* might put him on ice.

His speculations seemed farfetched. Enemies would have killed him already. There were simpler ways to stall negotiations. One could always say that one's government was dragging its feet. Or if one represented a government, one could blame the bureaucracy. Which they usually did anyhow, Hammond thought sourly.

He was coming back to life, his mind working, chewing the problem, casting off the lethargy the drugs and shock and fear and confinement had caused. Who and why? Who and why? They'd brought him tea in a tin cup. He banged it loudly on the iron door. Who and why?

A man yanked the door open. His Maltese chauffeur. The one who'd sprayed him in the face. Hammond belted the chauffeur in the mouth and started running down the stone corridor. The younger man caught him easily. His lip was bleeding and he was angry, but he didn't try to hurt him back.

Good. They knew how valuable he was. The guards had orders to keep him intact. "I want to see your boss."

The Maltese started to drag him back to the room.

Hammond doubled over, convulsively gripping his chest. The Maltese went rigid, then raced down the hall while Hammond writhed on the stone floor. He lay still until the Maltese returned with a small, gaunt white-haired man in his sixties.

A couple of armed guards hurried after them, one carrying a field first-aid kit. The Maltese looked terrified. The white-haired man knelt beside Hammond, his face working.

"Can you hear me?"

German accent.

"Herr Hammond? Can you hear me?"

Scared silly.

"Hypodermic," snapped the German, gesturing at the man with the bag. He filled the needle expertly from a vial of Adrenalin.

Knows about my heart, thought Hammond. Organized, and experienced in first aid. The German unbuttoned his sleeve.

"Hold it," said Hammond. "I'm fine." He sat up, grinning.

"You would play games with me?" asked the German stuffily. He sounded embarrassed that he'd fallen for the heart ploy.

"Would you care to tell me who you are and what you're doing with me?"

"That was not a funny trick," said the German.

Hammond asked, "Who are you?"

"Put him back in his room," the German told the guards. They yanked him to his feet, a little less gently than the Maltese had handled him, and dragged him down the corridor while the German went the other way.

"I'll make you a deal," yelled Hammond.

The German turned around. "You're in no position to make anyone a deal."

"Like hell I'm not."

"What do you mean?" He stopped, and turned fully around now, curious.

Hammond knew he had him.

"Anybody with something to offer is in a position to deal."

"You have no more money, Mr. Hammond. Hardly enough for ransom."

So it was ransom. But how the hell did the Kraut know he didn't have any money? "I'm not talking about ransom."

"If you can't offer ransom, you can offer nothing."

"Insurance."

"What kind of insurance?" asked the German.

"If you tell me who you are and what you're going to do with me, I'll insure your scheme against failure."

The German approached him, intrigued. "What do you mean?" He gestured the guards to let him go.

"Told you I had something to offer." Hammond grinned. "If anything goes wrong with your plans and we both survive, I'll pay you one million dollars within six months. Ransom insurance."

"Your ransom will be much more than one million dollars."

"One million dollars will be a lot more than nothing. All this is costing you is some information. Like most insurance, you'll be better off if you don't have to collect it."

"How do I know you'd pay me?"

Hammond's expression hardened. "If you know enough about me to kidnap me, you damn well know the value of my word."

The German introduced himself, smiling, enjoying Hammond. Then he took him to his own quarters, where, in private, he described his plan and, incidentally, how he knew that the dealmaker couldn't afford his own ransom. When he was done, Charles Hammond was sick and trembling.

BOOK II

13

Kaga Nagumo's rented silver Mercedes-Benz topped a rise with a hard-sprung bound. The land dropped away and the gray English Channel spread before his tired eyes, curtained indistinctly under low-hanging clouds and notched in the near distance by a French harbor village.

Nagumo sat between a pair of black-belt Japanese body-guards in neat blue business suits. The one driving saw the coast and gave an exultant grunt. He pressed harder on the accelerator. The car, running hot from the long race from Paris, shot down the gentle sloping road that ended at the harbor a mile ahead. To his left, the west, Nagumo noticed a smudge on the blue, dawn sky, the smoke of Brest.

Gripping the dashboard, Nagumo leaned forward, straining to make out details in the village. The buildings were stone, their roofs slate. They were clustered around an English Channel tide slip—a miniature artificial harbor formed by a pair of rock jetties that thrust out into the Channel, enclosing the natural basin, and protected by a massive steel gate. There was room inside for two or three small coastal freighters.

He felt a wrenching disappointment. The basin was empty. He slumped back in the seat, huddled between the two bigger men. Streicher hadn't waited. The German had double-crossed him. He'd left without him and was probably closing in on Grandzau at this very moment. Nagumo winced at the thought of the reckless German launching a frontal assault which would frighten Grandzau into a panicky defense, during which Hammond would almost certainly be killed.

"Sir!"

The car was slowing at the outskirts of the French village. Again the bodyguard on his right spoke.

"Look, sir!"

They had rounded a low, stone warehouse which had hidden part of the harbor from the road. Tied to the quay beside a squat crane was a sleek, narrow English-built wooden motor torpedo boat. Gray as the clouds, it looked of World War Two vintage, similar to the American PTs he'd fought in the Pacific.

"Stop the car!" He leaped out and hurried out onto the stone quay, casting aside the exhaustion of the long drive, startling the young men, who ran after him, exchanging wary glances with the handful of French dockers and fishermen who were watching with amused detachment the furious action beside the motor torpedo boat.

Hans Streicher was bellowing orders at a gang of tall, husky young Germans who were struggling with tangled chain slings that hung from the squat, rusty, steam-powered crane that puffed and creaked ominously on its revolving station between the motor torpedo boat in the water and a gleaming, amphibious tank aboard a flatbed truck on the land. An old Frenchman in blue overalls lounged at the crane controls, one eye squinted against the smoke from a smoldering cigarette between his lips, his face a mask of doubtful expectation. He nodded occasional agreement with remarks called out by the watching dockers.

"Dumkopf!"

Streicher waded toward his men, pushing and shoving. One went sprawling. He sprang to his feet, catlike, a big man, bigger than Streicher. Streicher turned on him again and he stood respectfully aside. The German arms dealer let loose a torrent of angry invective. His men edged away, grouping beside the tank. There beside the weapon, Nagumo thought, they looked much more at home. One of the French dockers called a remark in fractured German. An angry glance from Streicher's gang silenced him abruptly.

Nagumo stepped forward and saw that the German was struggling to hide a grin. Despite the chaos and his bellowed invective, Streicher appeared to be very happy.

Nagumo winced as the German bounded up the space between them and threw a meaty arm over his shoulders. He felt the bodyguards tense incredulously. Streicher's sweater reeked with perspiration.

"Bonjour, my friend. Bonjour. What a morning!" He took in the rising sun, the bluing sky, the gray channel, and the green hills behind them with a generous sweep of one arm. "What took you so long?"

Nagumo started to answer, but Streicher cut him off. "No matter. We're stuck here till the tide comes in." Nagumo noticed for the first time that rocks were exposed near the mouth of the harbor just before the steel gate. Until the tide filled it, the harbor was closed.

Streicher's gaze returned to the amphibious tank. He frowned at the rusty crane, then slapped Nagumo's shoulder again and grinned proudly. "You see my idea?"

"I think so," Nagumo replied slowly, wishing his bodyguards weren't observing the German's excessive familiarity and the way he allowed it. It was the sort of embarrassment that others would hear of and remember. "I believe the vessel is an English motor torpedo boat."

Streicher nodded vigorously. "She's been converted to a motor yacht. They stripped her guns and replaced her Rolls-Royces with smaller diesels to save fuel." He crossed his arms and grinned at the vehicle on the flatbed truck. "But that is going to give her some teeth again."

"An amphibious tank," Nagumo observed politely.

"A Mowag PIRANHA six-by-six," came the proud reply. "She's got a turbo supercharged diesel engine, Allison automatic gearbox. Twin-screw. One hundred kilometers per hour on land and ten in water."

"And what are those tubes on the turret?" asked Nagumo, edging out from under Streicher's comradely arm.

"Six Oerlikon eighty-millimeter AT rocket launchers."

Nagumo gazed at the six-wheeled angular vehicle with new respect. "Where did you get such a weapon?"

Streicher's good humor faded. He glowered darkly. "I have *four hundred* of them corroding on a dock in Rotterdam, where they will stay until Charles Hammond is free to complete negotiations with the Emirate sheikh who promised to buy them."

"And is Hammond still where we found him?" Nagumo asked softly, so his bodyguards wouldn't hear.

"Yes," muttered Streicher.

Nagumo glanced at the watching French. Across the little harbor he could see women watching from their windows. "Are we safe here?"

Streicher nodded grimly. "The villagers are earning more money today than they have in memory. But they won't help. They won't get involved, except the old man who runs the crane. He wouldn't let anyone else touch it."

Nagumo spoke to his bodyguards. Expressionlessly, they removed their blue suit jackets and their ties, rolled back their white shirt sleeves, and walked lithely to the tangled chain slings. Streicher turned to his own men. "Get everything else on board."

They began loading food, water, and ammunition, while Nagumo's men began patiently stringing the slings under the Mowag PIRANHA. A heavy truck with a hydraulic backlift rumbled through the village and backed onto the quay. Streicher paid the driver with a stack of crisp franc notes. The driver peeled back his canvas cargo cover, revealing two rows of thirty-gallon oil drums, and began lowering them to the ground on the hydraulic lift. Heaving and cursing the great weight, Streicher's men struggled to roll them up the gangplank aboard the boat.

"Extra fuel," explained Streicher. "Where are the black boxes?"

Nagumo led him to the Mercedes. Reinforced-cardboard shipping crates marked FRAGILE in Japanese and Italian filled the back seat. Nagumo lifted them carefully out of the car and stacked them on the ground, cataloging their contents while Streicher watched.

"These are jammers to block Grandzau's radar. We can assume it will be ordinary shipping radar."

"You're sure of that?"

"The boy only built jammers for Grandzau," replied Nagumo. He smiled, relieved to be back in his own world. "I questioned the boy closely, with the aid of several radar technicians. They're confident that this radar is protected with sufficient ECM devices to override Grandzau's jammers. The boy built extremely powerful equipment, but it was relatively unsophisticated. This unit will cut through the jammers and find Grandzau's ship."

Streicher bent down wordlessly, stacked all but one of the cartons, scooped them up in his powerful arms, and headed for the boat. Nagumo grabbed the last box—a portable generator to power the equipment in case the boat's electrical system was inadequate—and struggled up the steep boarding ramp after Streicher.

They had conferred by telephone when he'd discovered the boy in Rome, and had concluded that Grandzau was using radar jammers to make a ship electronically invisible. It was a guess, but a good one. A ship would be a suitable place to hide Hammond, evade pursuit, and even provide a place to hold the Pendragon auction, they had agreed. Then one of Streicher's contacts had provided definite proof that Grandzau was on a ship.

The German had already learned about the hijacked antipersonnel mines. Now, he was told, the mines had been trucked to Rotterdam and put aboard an eight-thousand-ton freighter. The rest had been easy. Armed with the freighter's name, Streicher's sources found the ship was chartered by a small French corporation, a company that existed mostly on paper, a company Grandzau had used in the past to purchase equipment and rent safe houses.

By the time he had reached Paris, Nagumo's sources had learned more about the ship. She was too old, too neglected to undertake a long voyage. Unless Grandzau was suicidal, she would lay close offshore. Japan's ambassadors' security force—the intelligence and protection unit which had provided Nagumo's bodyguards—had contributed a clue as to what shore. The American CIA, it learned, suspected that Grandzau was near Brest.

The motor torpedo boat smelled of fresh paint, old varnish, salt, and machine oil. Streicher put the cartons in the truncated forward cabin. His men had leveled much of the deckhouse to make room for the PIRANHA's cradle. The lavish galley had escaped the destruction. Streicher poured two cups of *café filtre* from the stove, handed Nagumo one, and sat down heavily on a dusty bunk. The boat reverberated with the pounding of paratroop boots as the men trundled the fuel and supplies aboard.

Nagumo sat primly on the edge of another bunk. He should have felt tired, but the hunt was invigorating. He was sure they were closing in.

"Why antipersonnel mines?" asked Streicher, suddenly leaning forward, his big hands embracing the coffee cup like bear paws.

Nagumo thought about it for a moment. "Perhaps he's booby-trapped the ship. A final defense."

"Maybe," said Streicher, suddenly standing up and gazing out a narrow port. "Tide's coming in. We'll be out in two hours."

Shouts on the quay and a confident snort from the steam crane drew them to the deck. The Japanese bodyguards had swathed the PIRANHA in chains and the crane operator had just tried an experimental tug. Streicher's soldiers and the French loungers watched expectantly. Nagumo moved away from the cradle, but Streicher scrambled onto it and resumed bellowing orders, directions to the crane operator augmented by vast and enthusiastic arm signals. The lifting cables tightened and slowly the amphibious armored vehicle's six wheels rose from the flatbed truck one by one until the PIRANHA hung in the air, its wheels drooping like wet pigtails.

To Nagumo's eye, the vehicle, which looked to weigh nine or ten tons, was tilting ominously. One of his bodyguards seemed to be of the same mind; the young man's brows were knitted with concern. The other bodyguard was smiling broadly, however, proud of their handiwork with the creaking chains. Nagumo looked at the crane operator. The Frenchman appeared monumentally unconcerned. Pointedly ignoring Streicher's shouted signals, he lifted the PIRANHA several feet higher and swung it slowly off the truck, over the quay, over the foot of water between the dock and the motor torpedo boat, over Streicher on the cradle. For the first time, he removed his cigarette from his mouth. Then he thrust his head through the open window in his cab and hissed, loudly enough for the entire quay to hear, "'*Raus!*"

He threw a lever and the PIRANHA plummeted to the deck of the motor torpedo boat like a toppling castle. Streicher scrambled off the cradle, grinning mightily, and clapped his hands together when his weapon landed dead center, its wheels nestling into their waiting chocks. The boat settled deep in the water.

"Like a baby in its mama's lap," he called to the Frenchman.

The Frenchman lighted a new cigarette and smoked while the Japanese bodyguards loosed the chains and snaked them out from under the PIRANHA. By the time they had finished and the Frenchman had secured his crane and shut down the boiler and strolled away, the tide had risen to cover the rocks near the harbor mouth.

Streicher took a long look at the rocket-bearing weapon astride the sleek and low-lying boat, then ordered it covered with canvas. "We might alarm the French navy."

Nagumo nodded eager agreement, glad to see that the German had more sense than he had thought. When the vehicle was shrouded, he followed Streicher onto the bridge, just behind the PIRANHA. As he had expected, the vehicle blocked the view from the helm so that a lookout would have to tell the helmsman where to steer.

Streicher lowered his bulk into a worn, leather steering chair, scanned the engine instruments, checked that the twin gear levers were in neutral, and hit the left starter switch. The boat trembled and the exhaust rumbled loudly astern. He jabbed the right switch and the second engine came to life. He set them both at eight-hundred rpms to warm and said to Nagumo, "We'll be lucky to make twelve knots, she's so underpowered."

Scanning the oil-pressure gauges once again, he put his feet up on the dash, leaned back, and held his face to the morning sun. It was warm in the lee of the PIRANHA and Nagumo sat gratefully beside him, out of the chill wind, waiting for the tide.

After a while, Streicher asked, "Do you find that the winters seem to get longer as you get older?"

"And the summers shorter," said Nagumo. "Much shorter."

Chamberlain flew commercial from Marseilles to Brest after repeated delays in the repairing of the Comptel jet. Kreegan flew with him, shared his disappointment that the mercenaries had already left their Brest hotel, and took care of renting a car while Chamberlain checked in with Comptel and the Agency's Brest station.

Comptel relayed a message from Helen Thorp. For what it was worth, she wanted him to know that Rene Rice had come up with a five-million-dollar contribution to the consortium's ransom fund. She added a zinger. "Maybe you should have gone into barley futures too. They sure beat condominiums."

The CIA turned out to be more helpful and less sarcastic. For openers they told Chamberlain that Hammond had made five secret trips to Brazil last year and had at least twice conferred at length with South African security forces. While the Brest station head was conveying this information, a call came in from one of their field men. Kaga Nagumo had driven from Paris and rendezvoused this morning with Hans Streicher in a fishing village up the coast from Brest.

Dead-ended in the French city, Chamberlain figured he had nothing to lose in tailing the arms dealer and the Japanese man. They couldn't be worse off than he was, and the fact that they had joined forces indicated that they thought they were on to something.

Kreegan rented a Citroën. Chamberlain observed the way he drove out of the city, concluded he could do a lot better, and took the wheel when they reached the countryside. Seeming relieved, Kreegan unfolded some maps and navigated as Chamberlain headed up the coast, driving faster and faster as he mastered the technique of making the front-wheel drive pull the massive car around the numerous twists and bends.

"Oughta see her any minute," said Kreegan, jabbing the map. They topped a rise and the land sloped down to the English Channel. At the end of the road was the village they were looking for. It had a little round harbor in its midst. The harbor looked empty, but as they barreled down the road, Chamberlain noticed that the steel harbor gates were swinging open.

"You think they're on a boat?" asked Kreegan.

"And leaving, damnit."

Chamberlain floored it and the Citroën tore down the hill. The village buildings now blocked the view of the harbor. He weaved through twisting streets, blaring his horn through a cluster of old cars and muddy farm trucks, swung around a long stone warehouse, and screeched to a halt beside a silver

Mercedes a hundred feet from a long wooden boat about to sail.

Men fore and aft were tossing lines ashore. A man stood atop a big canvas-wrapped box that took up most of the center area of the boat.

"That's Streicher," said Chamberlain.

"There's a Jap next to him," said Kreegan.

"Nagumo," said Chamberlain, jumping out of the car. "I'm going with them."

"Right behind you," said Kreegan.

"No. Call Comptel. Tell 'em what's happening. Try to get some air support. Watch which way we go. Track us until you get a helicopter on us."

"What if they don't want you along?" asked Kreegan.

The harbor gate was wide open, letting a low swell into the basin. Streicher looked back, then reached for the gear levers. Chamberlain started running for the boat. The guy who'd tossed the bowline was quite large, as was the man beside him. Chamberlain ran faster, heading for the deck just ahead of the canvas-wrapped box. Two smaller men in blue suits stood there. It looked like a better place to board.

He was fifty feet from the boat when Hans Streicher threw both gear levers into reverse. The motor torpedo boat erupted in a sheet of flame, rolled over on its side, and sank like a stone.

14

"I should kill you for that," snapped Lady Janet. Her hand was deep in her raincoat pocket.

Henri Trefle gave her an owlish leer. "No you shouldn't. You need me."

"I needed you in there, you bastard, and where the blazes were you?" She jerked her thumb at the grimy hotel across the street from the bar where Trefle was drinking. A sea chill crept into the low-ceilinged room. It was late morning in Brest.

Trefle shrugged. "I heard you tell the hotel manager that you would screw him if he told you where Grandzau's men went."

"I assumed you would have the sense to get me out of it once we had the information."

"I've given up trying to guess your tastes," Trefle replied with an innocent smile. "What was he like?"

A red dot of anger glowed high on each of her tanned cheeks. "I had to break the pig's arm." Her blouse was wet where he had slobbered on her breast. He'd torn some buttons and left marks on her skin. Her gun filled her hand in her pocket and a red rage was pushing her to shoot Trefle, but he was right. Now she needed him badly. She was shooting morphine for the pain and amphetamine to stay awake, and they were making her crazy.

"What did he tell you?"

"A taxi took them down the coast last night and left them in a country inn."

Trefle put down his glass. "Let's go."

She followed him out the door to their car. She drove. Trefle dozed until they were out of Brest, heading west. When he awakened, she said, "The pig in the hotel told me that two Americans were there before us, also looking for Grandzau's men."

"CIA," grunted Trefle.

"It sounded like the man from Belgium who I hit in Marseilles."

"Did he offer to screw the hotel manager?"

"Don't push me, Henri."

The glass knife seemed to leap from his arm. Fast as she was, there was nothing she could do. The car was moving at a hundred kilometers and the road twisted right and left. His knife lay across her throat.

"I'll do what I please to you."

She sat as rigidly as she could, neither slowing nor accelerating the car, moving only to shift the steering wheel. She'd been a fool to let her anger take the best of her. There was no defense. What did a crazy man care for the speed they were traveling?

"What shall I do to you?" he asked softly, pressing the knife until a sudden burning told her he had broken the skin at her larynx.

"Wait until you have Hammond," she breathed.

"I don't need you any longer. We're close."

"What if we're not? What will you do for money?"

"We're close. I can feel it."

She said nothing. Denying what he believed might sound like a threat. He was crazy. She'd been crazy enough at times in her own life to know how close she was to death. He would do exactly what he wanted. And he would do it suddenly.

"Henri. There's an intersection ahead. I'm slowing the car. I have to stop for the traffic signal. It's turned red."

"Don't slow down."

She felt a thin stream of blood trickle down her throat. It tickled. She held her foot steady on the accelerator as they closed swiftly on the intersection. It was empty. Then she saw a tank lorry approaching from the right, followed by a stream of cars the slower vehicle had backed up on the narrow road. Henri didn't seem to notice. But when she nudged the accelerator to try to cross ahead of the tanker, he smiled and shook his head.

"No. Don't go faster."

They were seconds from the intersection.

"Henri. Please."

He stamped on her foot, driving pain through the bones and the accelerator to the floor. The car leaped through the crossroads, missed the blaring tanker by inches, and shot down the coast.

Trefle took his foot from hers and his knife from her throat. He settled back on his side of the car, smiling to himself. Slowly, her breathing returned to normal. She dabbed the blood from her throat with her handkerchief, then pressed the cloth to the cut until the bleeding stopped.

After a while he stirred. He slipped the glass knife back into his arm sheath. When he spoke, he sounded sad.

"I want Hammond as much as you want Grandzau. I want to kill Hammond much more than I want to kill you. But I wanted to see you afraid."

Lady Janet stared at the road and said nothing.

"Did you beg when they whipped you?"

"No."

"I didn't think so. But this time you begged. I wanted that very much."

Lady Janet said nothing until they passed a sign pointing down a side road which seemed to lead to the sea. "Three miles, Henri."

"Drive for two and a half. I can't run like I used to."

They put the car behind a hedgerow and walked until they saw the inn at a quarter mile distance. It was just past noon. If the men were there they might be at lunch. It was a good time to attack.

Trefle studied the fields, the road, and the stream that approached the faded old building. They couldn't see the water, but it apparently was on the sea. It looked like a building built in the thirties and the blankness of the side they were observing indicated that the main windows faced the opposite direction.

Trefle gave her the plan and started walking toward the stream. Lady Janet went back to the car, assembled the Smith & Wesson submachine gun, loaded it, and lay it on the floor in front of the passenger seat. Then she drove to the inn. She scanned the fields along the way, but Trefle was nowhere in sight.

She parked in front of the door. Close up, the building looked shabbier than at a distance. She went in, her arrival announced by a cowbell fastened to the door. A middle-aged Frenchwoman in maid's dress hurried into the reception area, drawing a curtain behind her, but failing to block Lady Janet's glimpse of a dining room with large, dirty windows and a big table occupied by six men tensely watching the door. She thought she saw them relax as they caught sight of her.

"Oui, madame?"

"Un menu, s'il vous plaît." From the windows she had glimpsed a small harbor down the hill.

"Oh non, madame. Nous sommes fermés." Closed.

Lady Janet shrugged and left. She climbed back into the car, started it, turned it around until it was facing back up the road she had come on, lowered her window, and sprayed the front of the hotel with submachine-gun fire.

She put the car in reverse, backed up until she could see the dining room, and fired another short burst through the big windows. Then she drove away, taking care to leave as quietly as possible. She parked behind the hedgerow where they'd hidden the car earlier and waited for Trefle, her eye on the road in the unlikely event that the police had been called.

Fifteen minutes passed and Trefle climbed out of the stream bed, wet to the waist, carrying a man over his back like a sack of laundry.

15

The sandstone quay had deflected the explosion, shielding the village from noise and concussion, but doubling the impact borne by Streicher's wooden boat. The result was an eerie impression that no boat had existed. No part of it broke the water's surface. The crane stood nearby unscathed. Even the windows in the warehouse were unbroken.

The men struggling in the water looked as if they had fallen in drunk. Chamberlain threw the mooring lines that were lying on the quay. Several men grabbed for them, but when he saw Nagumo thrashing weakly, he tore off his coat and jacket, ripped off his shoes, and jumped in after him. Trailing a line, he swam through the icy water, put a chest carry on the Japanese man, and hauled himself back to the quay. A crowd had gathered, numbed by the fierce suddenness of the explosion. Half a dozen hands reached down, took Nagumo, then pulled Chamberlain out. It was very quiet.

The water stank; diesel fuel spilling from the boat's ruptured tanks had floated to the surface. Kreegan ran up and threw Chamberlain's coat around his wet shoulders. "Let's go, boss. In the car where it's warm."

"I gotta ask Nagumo where they were going."

"Nagumo's dead."

Chamberlain felt his reactions going fuzzy. "No he's not. I just pulled him out."

"He's dead. I just looked at him, boss. He's dead."

"Where's Streicher?"

"He didn't come up."

Chamberlain took a deep, steadying breath. Kreegan was fussing at his shoulders, straightening his coat, and trying to walk him to the car. Chamberlain shook him off.

"Find somebody who came up and can talk. I got to know where they were going." He pushed Kreegan away and looked around, his teeth chattering. The cold was clearing his mind. The French were staring into the dark, oil-smeared water, pointing at things and talking quietly. Small wooden bits of the boat were bobbing to the surface. An old, white-haired gendarme—the village constable—parked his bicycle and came bustling onto the quay.

Chamberlain spotted three tough-looking young Germans lying under blankets, wet and cold, but uninjured. They must have been near the bow, thrown clear of the explosion. He saw a Japanese man, shivering in a wet blue suit, kneeling over Nagumo's body, his face blank.

"Where were you going?" Chamberlain asked, squatting beside him. The man stared at Nagumo's still form and said nothing.

"Mr. Nagumo was working with me," Chamberlain coaxed. The man looked at him and his eyes lighted with recognition.

"You pulled him out of the water?" he asked in perfect, accentless English.

"Yes."

"Mr. Nagumo did not say where they were going. Only he and the German knew."

"What was under the canvas?"

The man told him. Chamberlain rocked on his heels and tried to figure what to do next. Kreegan returned.

"None of 'em know, boss."

This time Chamberlain let Kreegan take him to the warm car. Kreegan put the heater up full blast.

"Who'd you talk to?" asked Chamberlain.

"Krauts. Commando types. They'd worked for Streicher before, riding shotgun on gun shipments, that sort of stuff.

They did what they were told and they didn't ask questions. Streicher had a rocket-armed amphibious APC sitting on that boat."

"I heard."

"Something like six people didn't come up," Kreegan remarked. "What do you suppose it was? Bilge fumes?"

"No. She was diesel. Maybe one of the rockets."

Kreegan glanced in the rear-view mirror. "Cops."

Chamberlain had already heard the klaxons. "Let's get out of here. I need a phone and some dry clothes."

Kreegan waited until the police vans drove past them onto the quay, then turned the car and left quickly.

"First hotel you see," said Chamberlain. "There. Perfect. Drop me and get some diving gear. Tanks and wet suit."

Helen Thorp was with Alfred Cowan when his teleprinter chattered out Grandzau's next brief message. Cowan ripped it out before she could read it, stared at the paper, and said, "So much for your consortium."

"What?"

He tossed the paper onto his desk. "Sounds to me like Hans Streicher made a private deal."

Helen read the message:

"HERR STREICHER HAS WITHDRAWN HIS BID FROM THE PENDRAGON AUCTION—LANCELOT."

Helen looked out the window. "Why would he bother telling us?"

"Maybe he's telling you the consortium idea won't work."

The telephone rang. Alfred Cowan picked it up and spoke with his secretary. Then he turned to Helen.

"Chamberlain calling from Brest. Collect."

She took the phone. "Put him on, Mildred. . . . Pete, we got a—what? . . . Oh. That's what it means. Hold on." She covered the telephone. "Pete says that Streicher was killed a couple of hours ago, along with Kaga Nagumo of Mishuma."

"What? Nagumo. Son of a bitch. He was a nice little guy." He shook his head sadly. "Gimme that phone. Chamberlain, what the hell is going on over there? What?"

Helen Thorp looked out the window again, seeing nothing, thinking how fortunate it was that Streicher was killed before he reached Hammond. That he had come close was likely, and just as likely was the chance that Hammond would have been killed in a foolish attack. Now only the KGB presented a threat of excessive force, and the Russians, according to the Comptel office in Brest, were as lost and confused as Chamberlain.

Cowan handed her the telephone.

Chamberlain said, "I'm going to dive down to the wreck and try to figure out where they were heading."

"What else are you doing?"

After a silent pause, Chamberlain said, "I don't know. I'm trying to get through to the CIA. Maybe they have something. And I'm canvassing the Comptel branches to see if they've come up with something new."

"They haven't," Helen said coldly.

"Sorry, Ms. Thorp. I'll go swimming and I'll hope the CIA has something."

"You're long on hope and short on fact, Pete."

"Got any suggestions?"

She did not have any suggestions. She hung up and steeled herself to meet Alfred's troubled gaze.

"Is Hammond worth all this?" he asked.

Helen played it honestly. "Mr. Nagumo's wife wouldn't think so."

"Neither do I."

"But nobody told Mr. Nagumo to play commando. I mean, really, Alfred. Could you imagine doing something like that?"

Cowan shrugged irritably. "Maybe somebody did tell him to do it. You said he was at his embassy in Rome. You know how the Japs work with their government. Maybe they said, go get Hammond. Don't come home without him. Banzai! Damnit, I liked that man . . . what do you think?"

Helen was thinking about the time Hammond had followed her to Tokyo. Alfred had cornered the market on a new silicon chip, and Nagumo wanted them badly. Mishuma had put her up in a beautiful cottage in a garden in the middle of Tokyo while they negotiated. Hammond had heard about it and flown to Tokyo to ask her to dinner again. She had refused, again. That afternoon she caught him, climbing over the wall with a sack of orchids. She'd let him stay for tea, that time.

"English, English, sweetheart," Kreegan shouted into the telephone. *"Anglais!* Gimme an operator who talks English."

"Forget it," said Chamberlain. "It's no use."

"Goddamn Frenchie telephones—oh, hello. Yeah. Listen, we been calling a number and getting a disconnect recording. At least it sounds like a disconnect, but they're talking French so we're not sure."

Kreegan was red in the face. It was the first time Chamberlain had seen him stymied.

"Now listen, we been calling that number just this morning and getting through. This disconnect thing just started, so it's a mistake, see? Capish? Yeah, check it out, I'll hold." He nodded briskly to Chamberlain. "Don't worry, sir, I finally got somebody with a brain in his head. Talks English. I'll get you right through."

Chamberlain wasn't so sure, but he said nothing. He was lying on the bed in the village inn, several streets from the harbor where Streicher and Nagumo's boat had exploded. He'd had a hot bath and had his clothes dried while Kreegan had driven to Brest and back. The diving gear he'd bought there was stacked neatly in the corner.

His friend at Langley had given him the Brest CIA station number when he'd called him from Marseilles. He'd checked in with them before they'd left Brest. He'd called them again when he called Comptel, and a different voice had asked for a code word and hung up when he'd used the word he had been given earlier. A transatlantic call to Langley had elicited a new code word from his friend, but when he'd called Brest again, first he'd gotten no answer, and then the recording. Kreegan had come back at that point and taken charge of the telephoning, while he checked out the diving gear.

Kreegan stopped drumming his fingers. "I'm here . . . what? That's crazy. I told you we talked to them this morning. Twice. A couple of hours ago . . . oh. Right. Thanks."

Making an obvious effort to control himself, he gently cradled the telephone. "It's disconnected. Just like that. They got a new number, but it's unlisted.

"Give me the phone."

Chamberlain called Langley. When he told his friend's secretary who was calling, she said that his friend was in conference.

"When should I call?"

Her voice was as flat as a blackjack dealer's. "He'll be in conference late into the evening and then he's going directly to dinner."

"Tell him I understand."

He hung up and stared at the ceiling. Kreegan had the good sense not to ask. After a while Chamberlain swung his legs off the bed, stripped, and worked his way into the wet-suit pants. Kreegan helped him on with the jacket. Chamberlain zipped up and snapped shut the crotch piece. Then he put his pants and overcoat and shoes over the wet suit, while Kreegan put the tanks and regulator and the rest of his clothes in the suitcase he had brought the gear in.

Chamberlain looked around the rented room, checking that he'd left nothing behind. He found himself thinking very cautiously. They checked out, got into the car, and drove out of the village, heading for the opposite side of the harbor. Chamberlain was trying to think of how he felt, if he was lonely.

"You know what happened?" he asked Kreegan.

Kreegan seemed embarrassed by the intimacy. "I guess I can guess."

"I've been cut off."

Kreegan said, "Do you mind me asking, sir? Do you still work for them?"

"No. I really did retire. I work for Comptel. My old friends there do me a favor, I do them a favor. Listen, it's a good deal for them too, having a friend in a big multinational. It works both ways. They get a lot of information from ex-guys like me."

"So why'd they cut you off?"

"I don't know," said Chamberlain. "Find a road down to the beach."

He did know, but the sense of caution was flowing steadily now. He was still playing their game, but with no protector. Comptel could get him out of a lot of jams, but not the jams the CIA could. He was alone. For the first time since he'd joined the SEALs.

"It doesn't make sense," Kreegan objected. "Why'd they change their minds on you?"

"I don't know," Chamberlain said. He spoke shortly, to shut Kreegan up. He knew exactly why they'd cut him off. And it had nothing to do with changing their minds on him or losing trust. They had stopped helping him with the Comptel operation for the simple reason that they had started their own.

He'd been their stalking horse. The only reason to desert a stalking horse was to draw a bead. Using him and trailing the KGB, they'd found Grandzau. He felt a little stupid. He'd probably given them the clue and he hadn't known it.

All he could do now was to try to catch up. If they got there first and got in a jam, Charles Hammond was dead. They could be trusted to put together a crackerjack operation. They weren't the dummies they led the newspapers to believe. But what if the KGB was drawing the same bead? There'd be a regular little war, with Charles Hammond in the crossfire.

And that was exactly what Ms. Thorp had hired him to prevent.

The Citroën bumped to a stop at the edge of a narrow sand beach. There were groins, long rock fingers on either side of the narrow harbor mouth. Two groins on this side. He could walk down the deserted beach in his clothes, in case someone in a house on the hills happened to be looking. At the groin, he could disrobe and enter the water with a good chance of not being seen. There was a cold bite in the air and the sun was dulling rapidly behind thickening clouds.

"Okay. Turn the car around and wait for me here. After I'm gone a few minutes, stroll on down and get my clothes. I'll come out of the water right behind the car when I get back."

Kreegan looked at the cold gray water. A good sized swell was smacking the beach. "What are you going down for, sir?"

Chamberlain grinned. "For Comptel. For the company."

"Bull, if you don't mind me saying so, sir."

"Not at all. Fact is, I'm hoping to see something that'll tell me where they were going. I want to see what they had aboard and I'm hoping for a look at a chart."

He got out of the car, carrying the suitcase, and walked to the groin. He worried about a fishing boat anchored near the end of the groin, but he saw no one on it so he took off his clothes and donned his tanks.

It was damn close to dark in the roiled water. They'd closed the harbor gate again and he had to feel his way under it after a long swim around the groins. He came to the surface for a quick look. Here, inside, the surge had stopped. He broke surface just inside the steel gates, exposing just enough of his head to observe the quay on the other side. There were still police there, but no diving support equipment that he could see. The last thing he wanted was to meet a police diver underwater.

He estimated the distance at a little under three hundred feet, took a compass bearing, went down again, and swam for the wreck. The water was less roiled out of the surge and swell and he could see about ten feet. The harbor deepened as he neared the quay, which was built on the original, natural basin, so that when he found the shattered motor torpedo boat, its hull lay, on its port side, in a surprising forty feet of water.

The starboard side, which had been facing the quay, had borne the brunt of the explosion and much of the plywood hull was simply obliterated. He swam between two splintered ribs, careful to avoid fouling, and found himself in the engine room. The low compartment seemed relatively unscathed, and the unexpectedly small diesel engines were still bolted to their beds.

Then he found a tangled mess of pipe and wiring and a big hole torn out of the bottom and both sides amidships. This was obviously the place the explosion had started. He swam out of it and over the hull and examined the armored six-by-six that had been under the canvas. It had tipped off the boat and stood on the harbor bottom, up to its wheels in mud. All six rocket launchers looked in perfect shape.

It was the explosion amidships that had sunk the motor torpedo boat. Chamberlain swam back into the explosion area for another look. It looked like somebody had smuggled a big charge aboard Streicher's boat. How had he exploded it? Timer, probably, but it was a funny coincidence to blow just as the boat sailed.

Chamberlain swam back to the engine room and studied the diesels closely in the murky gleam of his diving light, pondering how he would have blown the boat. He found what might have been an extra electrical wire attached to the generator, which had been powered by belt drive from the diesel engines. He traced the wire, hand over hand. It had been stapled to the underside of a longitudinal brace and ran back to a thicket of vertical and horizontal brass rods. The rods ran up to the deck and along the bilges to the reduction gears. Chamberlain was amazed. The guy who'd set the charges had gone to a lot of trouble to wire them to the gear linkages and guarantee that they would blow only when the boat was leaving the dock. Instead of using a battery, he'd drawn his electrical power from the generator, forestalling the possibility that they'd blow early if somebody was just fiddling around with the bridge controls. Why go to so much trouble, he wondered. It was a good way to ensure killing everyone involved including Streicher, but the same could have been achieved with a timer set for later in the day.

Chamberlain's wet suit insulated him from the icy winter water and held his body heat to keep him warm. He shivered nonetheless as a deep chill rippled across his back. The explosion wasn't an accident. Charles Hammond's kidnapper was practicing an aggressive defense. Grandzau had come out of hiding to attack his hunters. Which meant he was stalking the stalkers—watching.

He'd hit Streicher with a vengeance the moment the arms merchant had gotten too close. Had he hit the KGB too? The Russians had dropped from sight since Marseilles. And what about the CIA? Were they charging into a trap?

Chamberlain floated motionlessly inside the exploded hull, weighing the possibilities. No, he concluded with a taste of bitterness. That was one of the reasons the CIA had cut him off; they'd realized instantly that Grandzau was on the attack and they'd decided, rightly it turned out, that Chamberlain would take a long time to figure it all out by himself.

Was he next? Was Grandzau watching him too?

Absurdly, he poked his head out of the hull and looked around the murky water. You did things like that underwater. Fear was compressed in on itself until it reached a critical point a diver couldn't handle. He pushed it away.

He thought of Kreegan alone in the car. What if they got Kreegan and waited calmly on the beach to shoot the first head that surfaced? He decided to take a look from the groin before he approached the beach. But first he swam to the bridge, where he hoped to find Streicher's charts.

He glanced at his watch. Twenty minutes of air left. He glided out of the hull, through a hole in the deck, and swam through a cabin toward a narrow passage which would be the companionway to the bridge. He thought suddenly of the woman he'd seen in Brussels. The woman who laid him out in Marseilles. Son of a bitch. Grandzau's agent? Hadn't the German secrets-seller had a woman partner? Was she his eyes among the hunters?

And then it began to make sense. Grandzau's agent. She had ordered the boat to explode at dockside so everyone would know it had been done. They wanted the news to spread to the others. It was a threat. A threat from weakness instead of strength. Grandzau couldn't attack them all, so he attacked one. The one with the least resources. He probably hadn't expected Nagumo to be along with Streicher, but it didn't matter. Streicher only represented himself. Nagumo represented Japan. They'd have a new man on the scene in hours. So Grandzau had lost little and gained much.

Chamberlain swam through the companionway and into the space of the open bridge, where he saw the first body. The explosion had burned the man's clothes off. He lay sadly naked, his hair burned away, tangled in the twisted remains of a chair bolted to the deck behind the helm. Another dead man was pinned aft by a fallen timber.

Chamberlain searched for cubbyholes where charts might be rolled, hoping they hadn't burned. He turned on his light and thrust the beam around the dashboard. If he was right in his conclusions, Kreegan was safe. And by the time he found any charts, the CIA would probably be debriefing Hammond in a Washington hotel room.

He bumped into the dead man in the helm chair and had the creepy experience of accidentally looking into his dead eyes. Streicher. Of course. He'd been at the helm. Something fluttered beneath him. Gently, careful not to tear the water-soaked paper, Chamberlain eased Streicher's body away from the seat of the chair and retrieved the chart that the German had been sitting on while he had manned the helm. The arms merchant's body had protected the paper from the flames.

Chamberlain swept his light over the paper as it drifted in the water. It was a British Admiralty English Channel Chart—an overview that showed the west end of the Channel and a portion of the Atlantic. It looked as if courses had been penciled in, but he couldn't tell for sure in the dull light. He folded it, took a final look around, and checked his compass for the swim across the harbor.

A third body appeared suddenly in his line of vision. By the time he realized it was alive, he could see its mask and air tanks. He cursed his stupidity for staying on the boat too long. The police divers had finally arrived.

Chamberlain snapped off his light and lunged off the boat, seeking darkness. Then the diver made a quick motion and Chamberlain realized he had been wrong; a police diver wouldn't be coming at him at full speed with a twelve-inch knife in his hand.

Chamberlain twisted around and grabbed the diver's wrist, and discovered he had made his third miscalculation in as many seconds. He had chosen to stay and fight a man twice as strong as he. The attacker wrenched his arm free as effortlessly as if Chamberlain were a child, and feinted with the knife. Chamberlain dodged the blow. The diver was waiting for him. He wrapped his other gigantic arm around Chamberlain's torso. Chamberlain was crushed against the man's chest and now the knife was descending toward his back.

He tried a knee, missed, but the giant's defensive reaction gave him an instant's respite. He twisted sideways a couple of inches. The knife clanked off his air tank, glanced through his rubber wet suit, and burned across his ribs. He felt it scrape bone. The pain made him arch his back convulsively. Both his hands were trapped between his and the diver's body, crushed near his neck. He thrust up with all his strength and ripped off the man's face mask, pulling it down over his air regulator and mouthpiece. The diver panicked in the rush of cold water and let go.

Chamberlain lunged away, lost in the dark, afraid of crashing into the quay, desperately trying to read his compass. A hand fastened around his calf like a stillson wrench and yanked him backward. The diver was trying to retrieve his knife, which was dangling from his other arm by a wrist thong. He had replaced his face mask, but it was still full of water.

Chamberlain went with the yank, pulled his mask off again, jammed his fingers into one of his eyes, and ripped his air regulator from his mouth. The guy stopped pawing for his knife and scrambled for his regulator, tightening his grip on Chamberlain's leg at the same time. Incredulous, and more than a little frightened by the diver's inhuman determination,

Chamberlain clawed his pry knife from the sheath on his other leg.

The diver found his mouthpiece, blew out the water, and grabbed his knife. Chamberlain plunged the tip of his blade into the man's hand and tore loose. He kicked the diver's mouthpiece out again with a lucky thrust of one of his flippers and swam madly for the dark, fleeing in near terror, heedless of obstructions.

He gained control of himself, looked back, saw nothing, and swam further. Then he stopped, and when he was sure he was alone, he checked his compass. The harbor gates were in the opposite direction. Detouring widely around the motor torpedo boat, he swam across the harbor as fast as he could, taxing his dwindling oxygen supply, not caring for anything but getting away.

It had happened so fast he hadn't had time to react, but when he'd pulled the diver's mask off, he'd recognized one of the KGB heavies from Marseilles, one who'd ridden in the Peugeot, but whose face he had glimpsed when the car had stopped to give orders to the goons on the street. He increased his speed. The diver must have come off the fishing boat beyond the groin. Had they sent another killer after Kreegan?

He surfaced for a split second, raising his head as far as his eyes, and found the harbor mouth fifty yards to his left. The steel gates must have foxed the compass. He went under and headed for them. Ten feet away, he stopped dead in the water, braking with his hands.

The Russian was waiting under the gate. He had fixed his mask and regulator and was holding his knife again in his good hand. He was staring straight ahead and Chamberlain, coming in from the side, was out of his line of vision. If he had enough air, Chamberlain would have waited him out. The guy had to be wondering if Chamberlain had beat him under the gate. But he didn't have the air and the quay was swarming with French cops who'd spot him if he tried to go over land. On the other hand, the cops would cover Kreegan and Dassault would probably come to his rescue as they had in Marseilles. It made a lot more sense than tangling with the Russian, who had him outweighed and, if not outclassed, out-determined. He started to back away. The Russian swiveled his head, spotted Chamberlain, and came after him like a torpedo.

Chamberlain dodged and swam for it, slithering under the gate, banging his tank on the steel. At that moment, his air started turning awfully thin, awfully fast. He reached back, flipped the five-minute reserve, and swam with all his strength.

The Russian was simply too fast. His enormous legs, long and thick as telephone poles, drove through the water at an unbelievable rate. He caught up in seconds, and Chamberlain was reminded by a sudden weariness that he was no longer a twenty-three-year-old underwater demo man, but closer to thirty-five and tiring rapidly.

He turned to fight, pulling his knife from his sheath, and the Russian, caught by surprise, hurtled past. He recovered quickly, but his overshot had given Chamberlain a second to set up. Slowly, Chamberlain backed away. Overhead, the swells were crashing into the harbor gate. Twenty feet down, they created a surge that raised and lowered the divers and roiled the mud on the harbor floor. At a distance of eight feet, the Russian was an insubstantial shadow.

Chamberlain backed away very slowly, watching as the Russian stalked him, readying his lunge. He thought his air was going thin again. He backed further away. His flipper brushed the steel harbor gate. He stopped.

The Russian's shadowy form hung in the water, eight feet away, rising and falling as he did. Chamberlain pointed his flashlight at him and turned it on. He flicked the beam from side to side, up and down, as if searching. All the while he watched the shape of the Russian's form. Suddenly it elongated and Chamberlain knew the man was making his run. The knife came first, then the big head, sharklike in its rubber hood, and then the thick neck and giant shoulders.

Chamberlain felt the surge start to push him down. He brought his cupped hands sharply up from his sides and dropped under the Russian's charge. Then he kicked up with all his might, rising rapidly to ram his knife into the diver's stomach.

There was no need. The Russian hit the steel wall head first. By the time Chamberlain got to him he was floating limply, his mouthpiece dangling, his neck bent at an awful, twisted angle.

Chamberlain felt a moment of regret he hadn't taken the guy alive for questioning, and then his air ran out. He grabbed the Russian before the surge could take him away and took air from his mouthpiece. Then he detached him from his tanks and let him sink, while he swam slowly around the groins and toward the beach, dragging the Russian's tanks by one hand. He landed a hundred yards beyond the car and lay in the surf, unmoving, scanning the beach, the water, and the car.

The beach and the groins were still deserted. The day had turned grayer and undoubtedly cooler, though he couldn't tell in the water, and it was unlikely that anyone would be out walking. He saw no sign of Grandzau's woman or anyone else watching the car. Kreegan seemed all right. He was sitting at the wheel, unmoving, but at a natural angle. The fishing boat was still anchored off the groin and still looked empty. Still, they'd be looking for their diver and they'd seen him cross the beach. He crawled out of the surf into deeper water and swam underwater, down the beach, until he was immediately behind the car. Then, lying in the surf again, he slid out of his tanks and flippers, gathered his gear in his arms and, leaving the Russian's in the water, shambled up the beach.

Kreegan flipped the passenger door open just as he reached the car. Chamberlain shoved the empty air tank onto the floor and fell into the passenger seat.

Kreegan smiled tightly. "I caught a Russian, sir."

16

Chamberlain turned around slowly. The Russian was slouched low in the back seat, a wiry man in a dark pullover and knitted sailor's hat.

Kreegan's smile was rigid. "Only thing is, he wanted to keep his gun."

The gun was pointed at the back of Kreegan's head. It shifted quickly toward Chamberlain's face. Thc Russian held it like he knew how. His expression was impassive, his eyes alert.

Kreegan spoke again, in the same light, brittle tone. "I tried him out. I don't think he talks English. I thought if I waited for you, we might be able to take him alive. He's just been sitting here like he's been waiting for somebody to tell him what to do. I been talking and talking to him and myself, so he's used to the sound of my voice. There's a gun under my seat and a gun under your seat and what do you suggest we do?"

Chamberlain watched the Russian's eyes.

"Where did he come from?"

"A guy brought him in from that fishing boat in a rubber dinghy."

Chamberlain's hands started shaking. He was exhausted. The fight had taken its toll of shock and fright. His back throbbed painfully, and he felt his entire body surrendering, craving rest, oblivion. He heard Kreegan's voice as if he were calling from the beach.

"Are you all right, sir?"

Chamberlain shook his head violently, trying to clear his mind. "How'd he get the drop on you?"

Kreegan sounded insulted. "I *let* him, sir. I pretended I was sleeping." He hadn't once taken his eyes from the rear-view mirror since Chamberlain had sat down in the car.

"Why?" muttered Chamberlain, his head reeling.

"So we'd take him alive and he'd tell us what his crowd is up to."

"But he doesn't speak English."

"I didn't know that. But don't worry, sir. We'll get a translator. The company must have a couple in Europe. Right?"

"Right. Where'd the guy in the dinghy go?"

"Back to their boat."

"Great big huge guy?"

"No. Little feller."

"That means there's at least two of them."

"Three," said Kreegan. "I think I saw a diver go over the side. I've been watching the water in case he comes up on the beach."

"He's dead," said Chamberlain. The Russian took no notice. He sat placidly, as remote as a stranger sharing a cafeteria table.

Kreegan glanced at Chamberlain. Chamberlain tried to gesture to keep quiet, but the steward's open face dropped in amazement.

"Jesus! You're bleeding like a stuck pig."

Out of the cold, salt water, Chamberlain's knife slash had opened up. Blood was forming puddles on the car seat. "Don't let him know."

But the Russian had picked up on Kreegan's alarm. He sat up straight, his nostrils flaring, his eyes growing narrow, and waved them to lean forward against the dashboard. Then he leaned over the back of the front seat and saw the blood.

He went white for a long moment, then red. Gesticulating angrily, he pointed at the car keys until Kreegan removed them from the ignition and passed them back. Training his weapon on them, never lowering it for a beat, he backed carefully out of the car, moved around to the front, and sighted them through the windshield.

Kreegan wet his lips. "What's he going to do?"

"He knows I killed his partner, you damned fool. What do *you* think he's going to do?"

The day was turning grayer and colder along the French side of the Channel coast and by afternoon snow squalls were skipping across the water, brief, intense storms that drove the fishing boats to harbor. Freighter and tanker traffic moved through the English Channel as usual, east and west from the Atlantic to the North Sea, and north and south between France and England.

A small, lean freighter edged out of the eastbound traffic separation lane and ran diagonally southeast, toward the invisible coast, many miles away in the fading light. She was old and rusted, but possessed simple, smooth lines that said she had known strength and speed. She was riding high, empty, and making fourteen knots.

Between her and France were England's Channel Islands—Sark, Jersey, Guernsey. And near those islands, but not visible in this weather, were smaller islands—rocky, deserted, their stony shores and narrow beaches wrinkled and pocked by crumbling quays, fortified buildings, and gun emplacements built forty years ago by Nazi German occupiers during World War Two. They had been the outermost reaches of the Atlantic Wall, the edge of Hitler's Fortress Europe.

The freighter headed for those islands.

The men on her bridge scanned them with binoculars and changed course for the island farthest west. It was flat and windswept, except for one end, where an ancient castle commanded the approaches to a low cliff and bunkers surrounded the quay at its foot, a quay long enough to accommodate the ship.

An old French smuggler acted as pilot, augmenting the captain's charts and aerial photographs with an intimate knowledge of channels and depths. The freighter was shallow draft, but her young captain was taking no chances. An extremely sophisticated fathometer graced the old-fashioned wheelhouse. His eye rarely left it as it probed water depths far ahead of his bow.

Charles Hammond saw her coming first, from his perch atop the lookout tower where Grandzau let him pace under the eyes of his Maltese guard. He watched the ship surreptitiously, hope and doubt vying in his mind. Rescue, or more of Grandzau's men? Rescue, or a ship off course? Rescue by whom?

Then the guard saw it and the startled way he grabbed the field phone told Hammond the ship definitely wasn't expected. The man shouted into the phone, then placed himself so he could watch Hammond and the ship at the same time.

She was making a lot of smoke, more than her single stack warranted, and then Charles Hammond realized that the smoke seemed to be coming from her decks. She was too distant, and the visibility in the snow-shrouded, fading afternoon light too poor, to see for sure. Within moments the smoke thickened and then there was no doubt that it was indeed smoke rising furiously from her decks. A black and greasy column billowed high until the north wind mixed it into the dark squall clouds over the ship.

She drew closer, surprisingly fast, but on a course that would take her past Charles Hammond, a couple of miles east of the rock island. He wondered at her speed, then realized that her captain was running with the wind as if to make it easier to fight her fire. He was probably heading for Sark and pleading on the radio for a fire boat to meet him.

When she was three miles north of the island, flame spouted from the midst of the black smoke, leaped from her decks, and began creeping up the side of her bridge house. Hammond glanced at his guard. The fire had the man's full attention now, not that it mattered. Hammond had nowhere to run.

The burning ship still steamed at speed. But her profile was changing, shortening and stacking up as she turned slowly toward the island. Excitement surged through Hammond. She was turning directly toward him. Had her captain given up trying to reach Sark, or was it a trick? Was she a ship in danger, or a clever rescuer?

Grandzau must have been thinking the same thing. Hammond looked down, forty feet, to the foot of the tower. Some of Grandzau's men were running down the rocky slope to the narrow beach, toting their automatic rifles and shrugging into flak vests. Others took up positions in the old bunkers, where Hammond had seen them installing heavy machine guns, a mortar, and electric wires leading to several points at the edge of the water. He hadn't seen what the wires connected to, but it had been part of the frantic activity the day they had arrived on the rock island.

The ship was closer. She didn't seem to have slowed, though now the smoke and flames looked devastating. Within minutes she was near enough for him to spot the sailors on her decks, desperately fighting the flames. Hammond began to doubt a rescue. If it was a ruse, it was a good one, absolutely convincing. She was covered with fire.

He looked in the direction of Sark, expecting to see a fire boat or rescue tug, but the squalls stood like a wall across the eastern horizon. Unless the freighter had made radio contact, she was alone. Her sailors humped hoses into the teeth of the fire and launched great white arcs of water into the flames. But wherever they hosed, the fire merely spread. Suddenly, with a hollow thump audible on the tower, fire exploded from the ports just beneath the bridge, spewing like arterial blood.

Hammond's shoulders sagged. It was not a ruse. The freighter lost way quickly, weaving back and forth, pointing toward the quay and then the beach as if out of control. Or perhaps her captain couldn't settle on the best way to save his crew.

Grandzau's men put down their rifles and stood to watch the burning ship. She was heading again for the quay, and now that she was quite close, near enough for them to smell and feel the heat, the sight of her was much more compelling.

Four hundred yards out, she veered toward the beach. Her captain had decided to beach her in the shallows. The crew began to fall back from the flames, retreating toward the stern, where their mates were preparing to lower a boat. When she was a hundred yards off the beach, her stern grounded and the bow swung until she was broadside to the tower. The sailors worked frantically, carrying injured men into the boat, then lowering it jerkily to the waves.

It seemed a small crew; Hammond could see eight men. They pushed off and broke out oars and tried to row for the shore. Halfway in, fifty yards off, the boat sank in a trough, spun beam to the waves, and overturned, spilling the sailors into the water. Grandzau's men stood transfixed by the sight of the bobbing heads in the short, steep waves. Several started into the surf, but found that the shelf dropped quickly. They stood in the water up to their chests, calling encouragement and shouting to the men behind them to get ropes.

Suddenly, the entire crew disappeared in the water. A high-speed engine roared gutturally, and a low, broad flat-bottom boat raced around from behind the freighter, spitting machine-gun fire. Six men crewed the attack boat. One drove, five laid down a withering fire that swept through Grandzau's men, cutting down those on the beach and those running for rescue lines. An instant later, the sailors in the water resurfaced close to the beach, lobbing hand grenades at those of Grandzau's men who'd waded into the surf.

Rendered shadowy and insubstantial by the smoke of the burning freighter, the swimmers and the attack boat reached shore simultaneously, seconds after the grenades exploded. They landed amidst carnage; hardly a man of Grandzau's was still moving.

Hammond saw his guard break out of his trance and come after him. Hammond leaped up, leaned over the wall, and yelled to the attackers.

"Look out for the bunkers!"

One of them fired a burst of automatic fire in his direction. Then his guard hit him with his shoulder, knocked him down, and dragged him into the shelter of his wall. The trigger-happy attacker's bullets sounded like rivets. Hammond was shaken, but he yelled another warning, which the guard choked off by clamping a sour-tasting hand over his mouth. Hammond tried to bite him, and then it was too late.

The bunkers opened up with roaring bursts of heavy machine-gun fire. Hammond struggled in the guard's bearhug. It didn't seem like anyone could have survived the strafing that must have covered the beach, but in seconds the heavy roar was being answered by the sharp clatter of return fire.

The guard rolled him further under the cover of the wall and suddenly Hammond could see the beach through an open stone water drain. He ceased struggling, transfixed by the battle.

The attackers had regrouped and were firing from behind

rocks with amazing precision. Whatever surprise Grandzau had achieved was a short-lived advantage. Of the fourteen men Hammond had seen come ashore, one was lying dead in the surf near the bodies of Grandzau's fallen defenders, and thirteen were pouring automatic-rifle fire into the two bunks which had them in a crossfire.

Commands were shouted. Americans. Hammond grinned. The CIA had come through with a special assault team. Behind them, the fires on the freighter were burning out and the ship looked amazingly unscathed. The shooting abated. Conserving ammunition, Hammond guessed. Some of the men were looking to the sky. Hammond eyed the darkening horizon. The squalls were closing in again. If they were waiting for air support, it had better come in soon.

Suddenly the guard yanked him away from the drain hole and dragged him toward the stairs. Inside the stone stairwell, the guard straightened up and ran down the circular stairway, dragging Hammond after him. They ran full tilt till they hit the vaultlike room at the bottom of the tower. There was a man on duty there. He opened the oak door and the guard dragged Hammond after him.

Grandzau was watching the battle from an armored glass slit. He turned toward the commotion and when he saw Hammond, the worried look passed from his face.

"I was afraid your rescuers might have slaughtered you." He motioned to the guard. "Bring him here. Have a look, Mr. Hammond."

Hammond looked.

Insulated from the noise by the thick glass and stone, the room seemed like a private screening room. They were detached from the battle raging outside and the only definite indication that what was going on outside wasn't a film came when Grandzau spoke by field telephone to his men in the bunkers.

"Work them east," he ordered. "Try to force them to shelter by the big stone."

Hammond looked. At the east end of the beach, just before the cliff closed on the water, a single massive, square rock, so straight it might have been quarried, stood ten feet from the surf.

"Number-One Bunker, fire two mortars. Number-Two Bunker, cease firing."

The mortars *wumped* into the sand. More followed, and Hammond watched the CIA men break east, dodging from rock to rock. Some went back into the water and tried to swim. More mortars were fired from the first bunker, and by the time the CIA men had reached the square stone, they'd lost three more men.

Firing started again from the second bunker, but there was nothing to be seen behind the stone. Grandzau reached toward an electric switch, then smiling at Hammond, said, "I wouldn't watch this if you've a weak stomach."

Before he touched the switch, three of the attackers broke swiftly from the square rock. Dodging and weaving, they charged the Number-Two Bunker like a reverse wedge, two men with machine guns protecting one behind them, who was carrying a bulky object in his arms. At the same time, the men behind the square rock concentrated a heavy covering fire at the first bunker.

Grandzau arrested his movement toward the electrical switch, as if stunned by the speed of the attack, or pausing to see its outcome. They reached the mouth of Number-Two Bunker. One man fell, but the other two affixed the bulky package to the bunker wall and ran to either side.

The bunker exploded with a roar that shook the tower. Ceiling stones fell to the floor, narrowly missing Hammond, and the armored glass in the viewing slit cracked like old china.

The CIA assault team increased its fire on the first bunker and Charles Hammond began to believe that they would get him out of this mess. Then Grandzau smiled. His bony hand caressed the electric switch the way a collector might fondle a perfect porcelain.

Hammond gaped in disbelief through the cracked glass. He saw the beach around the square stone erupt in hundreds of little holes, as if rain were falling heavily on loose sand. The gunfire stopped instantly and a loud, sharp *bang* echoed between the stone bunkers. A moment later, two men staggered out, dying, from behind the rock.

Grandzau nodded, a private confirmation.

"What did you do?" breathed Charles Hammond.

Grandzau was reaching for a telephone. He answered matter-of-factly. "We ringed that area with Claymore antipersonnel mines."

"That was slaughter," protested Hammond.

Grandzau spoke into the field phone. "Kill those two."

The surviving CIA men dashed for cover. Grandzau's men cautiously left their bunker and followed, darting from rock to rock, trading shots, slowly stalking the retreating pair until they too passed beyond the sight lines of the observation slit.

Grandzau stood up, pressing his bony hands into the small of his back. "That should keep them occupied." He smiled. "And now, Herr Hammond, in the event your rescuers had a reserve team, it is time our small band left this island."

The Maltese took Hammond's arm. Grandzau called and the man outside opened the door. Grandzau, Hammond, and the two guards entered a passageway at the back of the tower. The Maltese locked a steel door behind them.

"You're leaving the rest of your men?" asked Hammond.

"They are mercenaries," said Grandzau. "They understand treachery."

The sight of Grandzau's helicopter, a big two-engine job hidden under gray camouflage netting, shredded Hammond's spirit. Shaken as he was already by the failed rescue attempt, he saw in the waiting aircraft the final proof that Grandzau and only Grandzau commanded his fate.

Softly, respectfully, he said, "Please wait."

"What is it?" said Grandzau, scanning the darkening sky as the guards and the pilot furled the netting.

"Name your price."

"I beg your pardon."

"You win. I'll pay anything you ask."

"We've been through this, Herr Hammond. You have nothing to pay. Nor am I collecting an ordinary ransom. I'm selling you to the highest bidder."

"I can pay more than they will. I'll guarantee I'll pay your price in six months."

"Six months is a long time."

"You know I'll have the money then. I'll have it in *two* months. I'll own the resources of an entire country."

"But what if your grand retirement plan fails? What if your deal to end all deals doesn't work? Where would that leave me?"

"You know it won't fail," Hammond pleaded angrily. "You're the only thing that's gone wrong."

Grandzau smiled. "A temporary setback. Your friends will

save you. Really, Mr. Hammond, you underestimate your value by a great, great deal. How could they abandon a man who's going to own the resources of an entire country?''

''I can't count on that. What if something goes wrong with your goddamn auction and I'm not freed in time? I'll pay you more than they will. I—'' He had a sudden awful thought. ''What if *you* fail?''

Gunfire sounded in the distance. Hammond thought that Grandzau was wavering. ''I'll pay you in one week,'' he cried. ''One week.'' He took Grandzau's arm. The Maltese let go of the camouflage net and moved to stop him, but Grandzau waved the man away. Hammond pulled Grandzau to him and leveled the full force of his eyes on the German's face. ''You must know I *can* pay you. You know I *will* pay you. You know you can *trust* me. I beg you. *Wait one week.*''

Hammond could see the doubts churning in Grandzau's mind. The German was a lightweight, but once a plan was set, lightweights clung to it no matter how the situation changed. He had to shake him loose. ''You know you can trust me.'' His gloom vanished. He rose euphorically. He'd beat this son of a bitch. He'd sell him a sure thing.

''One week!''

But Grandzau shook his head. ''I'm afraid that your friends may not be as honorable as you are. To tell you the truth,'' he added, smiling, as he steered Hammond up the ramp to the helicopter, ''I have always found them to be as treacherous as I am.''

''I'll protect you from them. I'll give you asylum. One place in the world where you'll always be safe.''

''Citizenship?'' Grandzau asked mockingly.

''One week, please.''

''Why bother?'' asked Grandzau, buckling Hammond's seat harness as the helicopter pilot and the Maltese climbed aboard. ''Five days from now you'll be quaffing rum drinks on your island paradise, and this will all seem like a bad dream. Think of it. Native girls catering to your every need, and you'll never, ever have to make another deal again—just like you planned.''

The Russian aimed through the windshield at a point midway between Chamberlain's eyes.

"You want I should go for my gun?" asked Kreegan. "It's right under my seat."

"No, for God's sake. The man's five feet away."

"He can't see my hand."

Chamberlain felt his lips go numb with fear. Kreegan was tensing beside him—an amateur second-guessing a pro.

"No!"

"He's gonna shoot us anyhow, sir."

"He could have done it in the car. He got out for a reason. Now sit tight, for God's sake, before you spook him."

"Why's he just standing there?"

"I don't know," Chamberlain said evenly. Kreegan was still balled up, ready to jump. "Don't get us killed, Kreegan."

Kreegan edged forward on the seat. "Did you notice his weapon?" he asked. "SIG P-two-twenty. Very interesting pistol. Double and single action. Cheap weapon—aluminum and pressed metal. But it's got a real cute automatic safety catch on the firing pin instead of—"

"Shut up. He sees you talking and he thinks you're planning something."

The Russian rocked the car slightly as he braced his knees against the front bumper. His pistol stayed aimed at Chamberlain's head.

Kreegan swallowed. "I'm sorry, sir. I'm really, really scared."

Chamberlain broke eye contact with the gun barrel and glanced at Kreegan. "Just be quiet," he said gently. "Please."

The Russian raised his other hand over his head and waved from side to side. Chamberlain sagged against the back of the seat. "He's signaling his partner. It buys us time."

Kreegan sighed.

"Don't go for your gun. The steering wheel's in your way and you'll never make it. We'll wait for a better chance."

"I'm sorry about all that talk, sir."

"Just relax," said Chamberlain. He felt light-headed and didn't know if it was from blood loss or a nervous reaction. He wanted to look back, out at the water to see who was coming from the fishing boat, but he was afraid to turn his head, afraid to spook the Russian.

"What do you see in the mirror?" he asked Kreegan.

"Nothing—hold it! The guy's in the rubber dinghy."

"How many?"

"Looks like he's alone. Yeah, he's pushing off. He's alone."

"Rowing?"

"No. He's got a little outboard. Hear it?"

"Yeah. Same guy as before?"

"Looks that way."

"Maybe it's just the two of them," said Chamberlain, trying to figure when to make a move. "What does he look like? A gorilla?"

"Naw. A tall, skinny guy. It's getting dark. Kinda hard to see him now. But he was wearing all black. Very thin. Head like a skull. Like a skeleton. I think he had a Beretta, but he didn't take it out."

"Kreegan."

"Yes, sir?"

"This is important. Did he seem like a gunman, like this yo-yo, or a boss? What are we dealing with? You saw him already. What is he?"

"He's like a boss. Must have something wrong with his leg. He carries a cane."

Chamberlain wished he could see for himself, but there was no way to turn around safely, and if he tried to adjust the rear-view mirror so he could see, the Russian might shoot him.

"All right, what kind of gun is under my seat?"

"Your little shot revolver."

"Can I shoot through the windshield with it?"

"Uh, better make it two shots, sir. One for the windshield and one for the guy. And close your eyes. There's gonna be glass flying all over the place."

"Where exactly is the gun?"

"Yours is butt out, facing the door. Reach under the middle of the seat, between your ankles, and it'll fit right into your right hand. You *are* right-handed?"

"Yes."

"Thought so."

"Is the safety off?"

"Yeah. Just pull the trigger."

Chamberlain moved his feet further apart and rehearsed in his mind the arc his right hand would swing from his lap down between his legs.

"How close is the dinghy?"

"Close. Ten yards. He's having trouble with the surf."

"Maybe he'll drown," said Chamberlain.

Kreegan gave a short, nervous chuckle—a small, choked sound of acknowledgment.

"Listen up," said Chamberlain. "I'm going to take a chance that this guy with the gun is tougher than the guy in the boat. So I'm going to take him out first."

"What should I do?" asked Kreegan.

"Have you ever killed anybody?"

"Yeah."

"Can you kill that man in the dinghy?"

"Yes, sir."

"Now listen real close and get this straight. Getting out of this alive is the most important thing. Number one. Got that?"

"Yes, sir."

"Now, where's the boat?"

"Still in the surf."

"Don't take your eyes off it." Chamberlain continued to stare at the pistol five feet in front of the windshield. "Now listen close again. It would be *nice* to get that guy in the boat alive. He's probably the boss and he knows what's happening. *Nice,* but not as important as getting us out of this alive."

"I understand."

"Kill him if it's him or you. Kill him if it's him or me. Kill him if you even think it *might* be him or you, or him or me."

"He's on the beach."

"Watch him," said Chamberlain, raising his eyes from the pistol to the face of the Russian who held it.

"The guy's walking toward us," muttered Kreegan, barely moving his lips.

"Same guy as before?"

"Positive. Tall, skinny, all black clothes."

"Gun?"

"All he's carrying is that cane."

17

Chamberlain watched the Russian, waiting for him to glance toward the man in black, waiting for the instant the Russian dropped his guard. There had to be a moment when he felt safer because his boss had arrived. Chamberlain would kill him at that moment.

"Halfway here," muttered Kreegan. "Twenty feet. Funny, he's not using the cane. Just carrying it."

Chamberlain stared through the glass into the unblinking, unwavering gaze of the man aiming the gun at his forehead.

"Ten feet," said Kreegan.

Chamberlain was on the verge of motion. *He'll look now,* he thought. *Now.* He sensed that the man in black was coming up on Kreegan's side of the car.

"Oh shit," breathed Kreegan. "He drew his gun."

Chamberlain sank wearily against the back of the seat, feeling the blood squish in his wet suit. He felt cold. "Forget it," he muttered to Kreegan. "No way."

"Yes, sir."

Chamberlain noticed that the Russian was still staring at him. He'd never shifted his eyes.

"He wants in, sir." Kreegan nodded toward the man in

black, who had rapped his cane on the side window. All Chamberlain could see was the man's wire-thin torso, and the cane and gun held in black leather gloves.

"Roll down your window," said Chamberlain. "See what he wants."

Kreegan rolled it down and Chamberlain, despite the angry seething in him over the way Kreegan had gotten him into this mess, admired his gutsy, irreverent "Yeah?"

The man in black bent over until his skeletal face filled the window opening.

"Where is Grandzau?"

Lady Janet hadn't seen Henri Trefle so pleased with himself in years. He dumped his captive face down on the back seat of the car, removed one of the man's bootlaces, and used it to tie his thumbs behind his back.

"Is he alive?" asked Lady Janet.

"Sure." Trefle grinned. "I just gave him a little tap on his neck."

She remembered to smile back to encourage his good mood. "Nicely done, Henri."

They scanned the fields and trees, making sure no one saw them, then drove the car out of the hedgerow and sped inland, putting distance between themselves and the mercenaries they had surprised in the hotel by the sea.

Trefle chuckled, congratulating himself. "It was perfect. They fled in every direction—one even went over the cliff—and this one, of course, came into the streambed, as I knew he would. He dove into my arms, thinking I was a rock, perhaps, that would shield him from your bullets. Some shield."

"Some rock," said Lady Janet.

Trefle laughed. "Some rock."

Several miles inland, she started driving down narrow dirt roads. Twice she ended up in barnyards, backed and filled and drove quickly away. The third time she found what they needed, a deserted barn beside a tumbledown stone cottage.

She stopped the car and turned off the lights. Trefle went to reconnoiter the area. Lady Janet stayed behind the wheel. The prisoner stirred on the back seat, tugged at his bound hands, and tried to sit up. Lady Janet touched the cold muzzle of her Smith & Wesson to his head.

"Don't."

From the corner of her eye she saw Trefle's shadowy form enter the barn. A moment later he came back to the car.

"Drive in."

She eased the car in by the glow of the parking lights. She waited until Trefle had swung the sagging doors shut before she turned on the headlights. It was a small barn and smelled wet, abandoned so long ago that the hay and straw had rotted to dirt and mud.

Trefle dragged their prisoner out of the car. He looked to be in his late twenties, a hard-looking Pole or Czech—the sort who had escaped the Communists and found out all he knew how to do was fight. He blinked angrily in the headlights and made a lightning fast move to escape. Trefle hit him in the solar plexus and while he was doubled over, Lady Janet helped Trefle hang him upside down from a rafter.

He was suspended a couple of feet off the barn floor, his eyes level with the blazing headlights. His face turned red as his blood rushed down into it. Lady Janet knelt beside him and held her gun to his forehead.

"We won't hurt you if you tell us where you were meeting Grandzau."

He said nothing.

She repeated the question in French. He understood and spat in her face.

"Henri."

She stepped aside and wiped her face as Trefle knelt beside the man. Trefle drew his knife. The glass glittered like a diamond. He smiled into the man's eyes and turned his face so the man could get a better look at him. He smiled grotesquely over the razor edge of his blade, offering it.

"Do you know who I am?" he asked in French.

The question startled the soldier and riveted his attention. He focused on Trefle's splotched and bloated face, then the knife. Abruptly, his eyes widened.

"My name?" asked Trefle.

"Henri Trefle," the soldier muttered.

"I can't hear you."

The man cleared his throat. His face was very red now. He answered loud and clear. "Henri Trefle."

Trefle smiled again, leaned closer into the man's face, and

held the blade to his throat. "I ask you once. *Where were you meeting Grandzau*?"

"On a ship."

"What ship?"

"I don't know."

A chilling growl rumbled inside Trefle. He clamped a huge hand around the back of the hanging man's neck and started to saw the blade across his throat. The mercenary screamed.

"*Wait, wait*. A launch. He is picking us up at the harbor with a launch."

"When?"

"Tonight. Midnight. I swear it."

"What harbor?"

"Below the hotel. We're to assemble on the quay at midnight."

"How do you know that you're going to a ship?" asked Lady Janet. "Why not across the Channel or down the coast or to an island? I think he's lying, Henri."

"No, no. No I tell the truth. They told us we would be on a ship."

"Why would they bother?" Lady Janet asked Trefle. "He's lying."

"No," shouted the prisoner. "He made us prove we had been on ships so we wouldn't be seasick."

"Where is the ship going?"

"Please."

"Where?" snapped Trefle.

"Please. I don't know."

"Henri," said Lady Janet. "Come here."

They retreated to the furthest corner of the barn. The prisoner's ragged, frightened breathing echoed in the dank space. Trefle seemed anxious to get back to him. Lady Janet watched him swinging slightly. Outside, she thought she heard a snow-filled wind striking the thin walls.

"What do you think the others will do?"

Trefle shrugged. "By now they've figured how we did it to them and that we're probably only two or three in number. If the money's good, they'll go to the quay earlier, set up a strong perimeter, and try to board the launch."

"They'll be taking a terrible chance."

"They're fighters. If the money's good, they'll take the chance. I would."

"What will they tell Grandzau?"

"They might tell him that this man deserted. Especially if Grandzau isn't there personally at the launch."

"And he wouldn't be, would he?" she mused.

"No," said Trefle, eyeing the hanging mercenary with anticipation.

Lady Janet tried to form her next question and realized suddenly how tired, cold, and hungry she was. They had driven most of the night and had begun canvassing the Brest hotels at dawn. Her whole body ached from holding it stiffly against the pain of the beating. And it looked like a long night ahead.

"What duties were you hired for?" she called across the barn.

Distance made the mercenary brave. "We were not told," he said sullenly.

Henri Trefle bounded across the barn and pressed his knife to the man's throat. He broke the skin, as he had Lady Janet's earlier in the day, and watched with satisfaction as a thin trickle of blood traveled down the man's throat and dripped from his chin.

"My friend, you had better guess."

The sudden attack destroyed the mercenary's last resistance. His words poured out in a torrent of fear. "Grandzau told us we would work for only a few days. A week at most. A thousand francs a day per man. He promised there would be no heavy weapons, no artillery, no tanks, no other soldiers. He promised a simple job. We asked how simple? He said only guard duty. We would keep order, he said. Keep order. The money was good, you know that, Colonel Trefle."

Trefle smiled faintly at his one-time rank.

The mercenary clung to the smile. "We didn't mean to offend, *mon colonel*. We, I, didn't know this was your fight. I would not have taken such a job. I would not serve against Colonel Trefle. But I didn't know. The money was good, the jobs are few, surely *mon colonel* understands. . . ."

Lady Janet listened from the corner, but the man had ceased to make sense. He was babbling, terrified what would happen when he stopped. She looked at her watch. Five o'clock. They had to get some food and rest and plan what to do at the quay.

She sensed that Grandzau was about to slip away. The fact that this mercenary team had been hired for guard duty was very significant. It meant that Grandzau was abandoning his present force—the men who had executed the kidnapping—which probably meant he was leaving his present hiding place. That this new team was hired to keep order indicated that Grandzau was positive that no force could attack him. This team would protect him against the unlikely event that someone invited to the auction tried to pull something during the proceedings. The fact that Grandzau didn't expect an outside attack meant that he had an intricate, complex, and foolproof plan to protect his Pendragon auction.

"Henri. Cut him down, tie him up, and let's go."

"He'll talk."

"No I won't. No I won't, *mon colonel*. I swear it."

"Tie him well. It will take him a day to free himself. We'll be gone by then." She got into the car and reached for the key.

Trefle sighed, stood up, and backed away. He gripped the rope from which the mercenary was hanging and raised his knife. As Lady Janet turned the ignition key, the starter murmured hesitantly. "Damnit," she muttered, flicking off the headlights to get more power from the overburdened battery. That's all they needed, to be stuck in a cowbarn in the middle of nowhere with a dead battery. She hit the key again, and relieved of the headlight strain, the starter kicked the engine to life. She raced it a moment and when she was sure it wouldn't stall, she turned the headlights back on.

What she saw made her stomach twist. The mercenary hung limply. His head was below her sight line, but the blood on Trefle's knife told what he had done. He smiled into the headlights, his eyes a mad glitter, and wiped his blade on the dead man's pants.

Chamberlain wished he had taken the risk of going for his gun. Even though the setup had been suicidal, there was a mad, frightening note in the Russian's voice. He weighed the new odds. This wasn't going to get better unless he did something, but the odds were lousier than before. The man in black held his gun inches from Kreegan and the first Russian was still drawing a bead on his head. Worse, they were unquestionably both pros, while he and Kreegan added up to one out of shape pro and one amateur who happened to like guns.

Before Chamberlain could say anything, Kreegan tried to tough it out. He replied with another question.

"Buddy, you think we'd be sitting here talking to you if we knew where Grandzau was?"

The man in black waited two or three seconds. Then, in a move so fast that even Chamberlain didn't see it coming, he broke Kreegan's nose with his cane. The steward yelled in pain, clutched his face, and bent forward. Chamberlain thought he was going for the gun under his seat, but Kreegan just moaned, the fight smashed out of him.

"Where is Grandzau?"

"We don't know," Chamberlain said quietly.

The man in black reached through the open window and switched on the car's interior lights. He gazed at Chamberlain over Kreegan's bowed head.

"You dove to learn where Streicher was going. What did you find?"

"Nothing."

The man's gaze was chilling, as if he knew he was going to do something terrible and was stalling, savoring the anticipation.

"My diver is still down there. What do you suppose he found?"

Chamberlain knew there was no sense lying. The wound on his back was condemning. He kept his voice neutral, his manner inoffensive. His gut was clamoring alarms, warning that this Russian was deadly. He tried to ignore Kreegan's agonized groans.

"Your diver broke his neck. He ran into the gate."

"I never knew him to be a careless diver."

"I got lucky," said Chamberlain, trying to find a way to defuse the man. He could see there was a turmoil building in him, a molten center of emotion promising to explode.

"Then you must report what my diver would have reported. Where was Streicher going? Where is Grandzau?"

"I don't know."

Kreegan's breath rasped miserably through his mouth. He was still crumpled forward, still holding his face in his hands.

The man in black glanced at Kreegan, then said to Chamberlain, "Get out of the car."

He covered him as he opened the door and stood up. The man in front of the car shifted his gaze to Kreegan. The man in black made Chamberlain walk around the car and stand with his back to him. Chamberlain sensed him examining his knife wound in the dim glow from the car's interior lights.

A bitter wind was blowing off the water and slicing through his wet suit. It was insulated to keep body heat in when submersed, but in the air the wet suit was a sieve. Chamberlain shivered uncontrollably. The cold pebbles on the beach froze his bare feet. He thought his bleeding had stopped, but he felt faint.

The man in black stepped in front of him, his gaunt face eerily white in the light from the car. He held his cane in one hand, his Beretta in the other. His emotional seizure appeared to be rising to a peak, but he was careful to stand out of his partner's line of fire. Chamberlain braced for a blow from the cane.

"Where is Grandzau?"

Chamberlain said nothing.

The man in black nodded to his partner, who turned his full attention toward Chamberlain. Then he twisted the cane and withdrew a whip, a riding crop almost as long as its scabbard. Chamberlain wondered if anyone in the harbor village could see the dimly lighted car on the beach.

"Where is Grandzau?"

"I don't know."

The man in black checked that his partner had Chamberlain covered, then slipped his pistol back into his shoulder holster and said, "Remove your diving suit."

"Now hold on," said Chamberlain, not quite believing that this was happening. "I don't know where Grandzau is, and hitting me with that thing—"

"Shut up!"

"All I'm saying is, it isn't going to change the facts," Chamberlain insisted calmly, keeping a wary eye on the crop.

The man in black returned a dead look. "I haven't the time to argue with you. We are not fooled by your charade. We want Hammond and the CIA isn't going to stop us."

"I'm not CIA."

"Remove your diving suit," he repeated, passing the whip through his hand, "or my man will shoot you."

Chamberlain saw that he meant it and complied. He unsnapped the crotch strap and pulled down the jacket zipper. The man's hands were trembling, as if with excitement. He supposed he was a freelance operator. It wasn't like the staid and humorless KGB to employ psychotics.

"Stop!"

Chamberlain froze, to show he wasn't pulling a weapon.

"Hands behind your head!"

Chamberlain raised his hands and stood shivering, defenseless. The Russian reached into the open folds of the wet suit and gingerly removed the sodden chart Chamberlain had taken from Hans Streicher's sunken boat. He spread it on the hood of the car, pasting it down by its moisture, and lighted a penlight.

Chamberlain watched from the corner of his eye. There *was* a course penciled on the chart. Streicher had been heading northeast toward the Channel Islands. The line stopped short of Sark, about two hundred miles from Brest.

The Russian looked up from the chart and out toward where his fishing boat was anchored. He made a deep, guttural sound, which Chamberlain knew had to be a curse. The boat was useless—too slow for the distance. The Russian needed a car. A car first, and then another boat. He snapped a command and gestured toward Kreegan.

Chamberlain started to back away, his hands still behind his head. It didn't take knowledge of the Russian language to know that the KGB men intended to take the car and kill them. The man in black straightened up from the map and angrily sheathed the riding crop. His dark eyes flickered toward Chamberlain, noticed he had moved. He drew his weapon as fast as a snake tongue and raised it to fire.

His partner opened Kreegan's door and yanked him out by the lapels. The Russian cried out, seconds too late. Kreegan's shot revolver boomed like a dynamite explosion, flinging the Russian into the dark. Blinded by the flash of the weapon, Chamberlain threw himself to the sand and crawled frantically around the car. He heard the swift *crack crack* of the Beretta, Kreegan's yell, and a second *boom* from the shot revolver.

In the muzzle flash Chamberlain saw the man in black running toward the water. He yanked open the passenger door, pulled out the gun from under the seat, and fired in the direction the Russian had run. Again, muzzle flash lighted the beach like a flashbulb. He had missed. The Russian had veered to the right.

Chamberlain fired twice, bracketing the area he'd run to.

Two shots from the Beretta told him he had missed. He raised his weapon. From the other side of the car he heard Kreegan gasp.

"Get out of here, sir. You haven't got the range. He'll pick you off from a distance. Get in the car."

"Can you drive?" Chamberlain whispered, acutely aware that the interior light was still on and the switch was on the other side.

Kreegan uttered a forced laugh. "Drive?" he choked. "I can hardly hold my weapon."

"You hurt?"

"Go, sir. While you can. You don't have the range."

"Hang on," Chamberlain called. He crawled around the back and lunged through the open driver's door. He found the switch, then shut the door to keep the interior lights off. A shot snapped from the water and a bullet clanged off the door. Ricocheted, which meant he'd hit the side from a shallow angle. He was close behind the car.

Chamberlain felt his way in the dark, crawling over sand and pebbles to where Kreegan lay on his stomach, holding his shot revolver in both hands, aiming toward the water.

"Don't move me, sir."

"I gotta get you in the car."

Kreegan shook him off with a moan. "I'm dead, sir. No point making it hurt worse than it does already."

"You're not dead yet. I'm taking you to a hospital."

"Sorry I screwed up."

"Don't be an idiot, Kreegan. I'll have you there in an hour."

"Thanks for letting me come along, sir."

"What?" Chamberlain couldn't see Kreegan's wounds in the dark. He played his hand gently over his back, but he'd been hit in front and the Beretta slugs apparently hadn't exited.

"I mean I just wanted some fun, like I used to in the service."

"Where are you hit?"

"I had a good time. Thanks, sir."

"Hold on, Kreegan. We're getting out of here."

Kreegan didn't answer. Chamberlain touched him, but he lay still. He reached for his arm and tried his pulse. He felt none and when he put his ear to Kreegan's chest he heard nothing but the surf and the occasional noise the Russian made circling closer on the pebble beach.

Chamberlain found Kreegan's gun and fired several shots toward the noise. The blinding muzzle flashes lighted an empty beach. Somewhere close the man in black was hugging the ground. Chamberlain slipped into the car, started the engine, and floored the accelerator, slamming the door shut by the forward lunge.

He heard the crack of two shots over the engine roar. A bullet tugged at the side of the car, low down. The Russian was shooting at his tires.

Then he was out of range. He turned on the headlights. A high stone wall leaped in front of the car. Chamberlain slewed around the sharp bend in the road, missed the wall by inches, and raced through the harbor village, driving badly, a beat behind the powerful Citroën.

He felt himself going under. He'd opened the wound by crawling around the car and he was still bleeding. He felt his strength and will seeping out of his body.

He clenched the wheel and forced his face partially out the window into the cold slipstream. The car sped up, drifting from side to side of the narrow road. Dully, he knew he had to make Brest. He needed help badly, but Kreegan was dead.

He had to make it to the airport. With luck they'd fixed the Comptel plane in Marseilles and flown to Brest. They'd get him a doctor. And then they'd fly him to the Channel Islands. If he could make the airport.

18

He was stopped in the Citroën at a traffic light in Brest when a blue Renault rounded the corner and sped off in the direction from which he had come. The blond woman driving was the one from Brussels and Marseilles, the woman he thought was Grandzau's partner.

Chamberlain hauled his wheel around and tried to pull out of the line of cars waiting for the light to change. The knife slash in his back burned angrily. He'd torn the damned thing open again. He gritted his teeth and backed and filled madly. Knowing it wasn't deep didn't make it hurt less. Or bleed less, either.

The streets were clogged with homebound evening traffic and it seemed that no French commuter worth his salt gave an inch to a rich man's Citroën. Chamberlain finally put her facing the other way, but he couldn't risk speeding in the city streets because the gendarmes would put too many questions to a man driving in a wet suit. His clothes were on the back seat, where Kreegan had put them.

He thought he saw the Renault stopped at an intersection, but when he got closer, he saw that though it was a Renault, it was not blue, but red, and driven by a priest. He looked left, right, and ahead. There were cars everywhere and he realized he hadn't a chance to find her, so he drove around a block and headed once again toward the airport.

In the parking lot, he pulled on his clothes over the wet suit, then went to the private aviation counter, walking as steadily as he could, aware how badly he looked. The woman on duty eyed him nervously.

"Where is the Comptel plane?"

"Ah." She sounded relieved. "Oui, monsieur." She directed him in pidgin English and precise gestures.

Chamberlain went back outside and found it parked where she said it would be, its windows lighted, its boarding ramp down. The door was shut against the cold. The co-pilot let him in.

"You got the wheels fixed."

"Yes, sir. Are you all right? The company's been trying to get a hold of you."

"No. I need a doctor. And I'm afraid I have some bad news for you."

The co-pilot cut him off before he could explain about Kreegan.

"Someone's waiting to see you, sir. In the main cabin. Some kind of Fed."

"American?"

"Yup. We didn't invite him aboard, but he wasn't exactly taking no."

"Okay. Get the doctor. I need some food, right away. Hot. And I want to make a call to New York."

"I'll try, sir. Kreegan runs the galley."

"Kreegan's dead."

"What?"

"I'm sorry, I really am . . . tell the captain we're moving out tonight. Tell him to find a landing strip in the Channel Islands. Sark, if they've got one. Otherwise, Cherbourg."

He brushed past the co-pilot, through the curtained galley and the little cabin where Kreegan had made him sleep the night he had boarded in London, and into the main cabin.

"Pete! Hey, you look a little ragged, fella."

Chamberlain stared at his friend from Langley. The CIA again?

Arnie Fast waved a glass. "Let me pour you a drink," he

said, moving to the bar. "Nice little plane you got here, Pete."

"Wait a minute," said Chamberlain. "This morning the Brest station yanked their phone out of the wall and your secretary implied you'd be in conference for a year."

Fast tilted a Scotch bottle invitingly. "That was this morning."

"What are you doing here?"

"Well, to tell you the truth, I was in the neighborhood." The banter ceased abruptly. "Cherbourg, to be exact." He ignored Chamberlain's sharp look. "So I thought I'd stop by and see how you were doing down here in Brest. Only a couple hundred miles." He gave the posh cabin an appreciative once over. "'Course I fly commercial, unlike some of my retired old buddies who left the Agency when the Agency needed them most." He tipped his glass to his mouth and Chamberlain realized he was a little drunk.

"Got here pretty fast for commercial."

"As a matter of fact, the air force had something quick coming this way. Things are getting better, again."

"Must be, if the air force is taking you seriously."

"You bailed out too soon. We're really getting back on our feet," said Fast, with a smile Chamberlain had long ago given up trying to read.

"I didn't bail out. I just moved on."

"You know, Pete, semi-pro espionage is sort of like semi-pro ball. A lot more semi than pro."

"Arnie, I'm cold, I hurt, and I'm tired. What do you want?"

"Anything new about Grandzau?" He pointed the Scotch bottle at Chamberlain again.

Chamberlain nodded. "No ice." He drank deeply for heat and release. It burned like heaven.

"You know something, Arnie, I think of you in my head as my, quote, friend at Langley, but we're not really friends, old buddy. I have a thing or two to tell you, but seeing as how you cut me off this morning, I want you to answer a couple of my questions first."

Fast freshened his own drink and sat down.

"Make it quick. Let's quit fucking around."

"Fine with me. I think Grandzau has an agent on the

ground. A woman. Beautiful. Blond. Looks about thirty, and rich. Who is she?"

"Sounds like Grandzau's old girlfriend. Englishwoman. Lady Janet Isling. Some lord's daughter. Rich and loony. We tried to find her when the Pendragon cables started, but she'd disappeared from her house in the south of France. Seen her?"

"She knocked me cold in Marseilles."

"Sounds like her style. She was running dope for Grandzau when he was fighting the Chinese dealers. Used to hang out in Paris with French mercenaries. Knows how to handle herself. I figured she was dead from junk by now. That type usually is."

Chamberlain wanted to try his theory. "Or maybe she's dogging our various tracks for Grandzau."

His friend from Langley didn't seem impressed.

Chamberlain added, "*Somebody* nailed Streicher and Nagumo."

"True. What's your second question?"

"A possible KGB agent. Russian or Middle-European. Thirties or forties, hard to tell. Tall, bony. Very weird. Carries a riding crop in a cane scabbard and likes to use it."

"Sounds like fun, but I never heard of him."

"Ask your computer," said Chamberlain. He buzzed the co-pilot, who told him the doctor had arrived. "Good. Send him through to the aft cabin and set up a call to Langley, Virginia." He handed the telephone to his friend. "Back soon. I'm going to get patched up and into some dry clothes."

"I have people watching the plane."

"I told you, we're not friends."

There was a knock. Chamberlain opened the door to the doctor and led her past Arnie into the aft cabin. She was a handsome, stern French matron with large hands. She helped him out of his shirt and stripped off the wet-suit jacket. He lay face down on the bed while she examined the knife slash. She gave him a couple of deadening shots around the cut and started sewing.

"Did you bleed much?" she asked in English when she finished.

"Yes."

"Turn over carefully."

She produced a couple of plastic blood packs, beaded with condensation from recent refrigeration, and administered a transfusion through a vein in his left arm. "Your blood type was in the company records."

"Do you work for Comptel?"

"Of course."

"How bad's my back?"

"I'm sure it feels much worse than it is. A very shallow cut. You'll have to move carefully for a couple of days."

"I'm freezing. Can I take a hot shower?"

"I'll put watertight tape over it."

Twenty minutes later the doctor helped him into his gray suit jacket, freshly cleaned and pressed, and asked how he felt.

"Not bad. Thanks a lot."

She straightened his tie, and left with a smile.

When Chamberlain joined Arnie in the main cabin, two places had been set at a portable dining table, and a white-jacketed steward was waiting to serve soup. Fast lowered his sherry glass. "You look better."

"What did you find out?"

"There's no record of anybody with that description in the KGB's European ops. We'll keep looking."

"I had a feeling he'd be freelance," said Chamberlain. He drank his soup quickly and told the steward to bring the main course immediately.

"My turn," said Fast. "What do you know?"

Chamberlain had been wondering since he'd boarded the plane what to tell him about Streicher's chart. His first inclination was to go to Grandzau's island alone, but the Russian knew about it too and he wasn't in any position, tonight, to tackle his and Grandzau's people at the same time with no preparation. The Russian team had lost four men since Marseilles, so the man in black would have his own troubles. And even with the rest of KGB-Europe backing him up, it would be several hours before he'd be able to do anything like launch a night attack on a rock in the English Channel.

He looked his friend in the eye. "You know damn well I don't want you blundering into this and getting Hammond killed, but I gotta tell you that it's likely the Russians'll attack Grandzau in the morning."

"Where?"

"He's on a little island in the Channel, west of Sark."

"Shit! That's all you know?"

"That's what I think."

"Yeah, well think about this, Chamberlain. I lost an entire assault team on that fucking rock this fucking afternoon.

"How'd you find it?"

"We put the pieces together, including a few you didn't know about, and reconned the thing from the air. Weather socked in and something played hell with our air support's radar, so we couldn't back up the assault team. Grandzau had laid on quite a welcome, so they lost their asses. Fourteen. Some of your ex-SEAL buddies. . . . Naw, you wouldn't know 'em. They were young guys." He paused, then added bitterly, "Grandzau's vanished."

"Hammond?"

"Do you think I'd be here if I had Hammond?"

"So why are you here?"

The man from Langley stood up. "On the slim chance that you'd found something we didn't already know," he said. Then he brushed past the dining steward and went out the door. Chamberlain watched him from a port. He stormed down the ramp, waved angrily, and several shadows materialized into men. They trooped after him, into the terminal. Chamberlain finished his steak, reached across the table, and ate his friend's.

The intercom buzzed and the co-pilot told him he had a line to New York. Chamberlain sighed, then cheered himself with the thought that when he finished this call he could go to bed.

Helen Thorp and Alfred were finishing lunch in his office when she heard her private line ringing through her open door. Alfred punched a button and passed her his phone.

"News at last?"

"Better be."

"This is Pete Chamberlain."

She thought he sounded very tired, but it was only eight in the evening in France.

"Yes, Pete. Is it all right if Alfred Cowan listens in?"

"Sure. It's his phone. This is just a brief, bad report."

Alfred picked up. "Hello, Pete."

"Hello, Mr. Cowan. Okay, here goes. Kreegan is dead, killed by a Russian who was trying to kill both of us."

"Who's Kreegan?" asked Cowan.

"He worked on the plane," explained Helen. "Go on, Pete."

"Is he a Comptel employee?" asked Cowan.

"Yes," said Helen. "Go on, Pete."

"Streicher and Nagumo are dead."

"You told us late last night."

"The CIA attacked Grandzau's hideout."

"What?"

"They're all dead."

"Hammond?" Helen asked fearfully.

"Vanished with Grandzau."

"Where?"

"Vanished, gone, missing. Grandzau's made a shambles of all of us. Even the KGB is lost. Everybody's lost."

"Hold on," said Helen. She covered her mouthpiece and waited for Alfred to cover his. "What do you think?"

"He's giving it to us straight. No holding back."

"And what does that mean?"

"He's still got a lotta balls."

"Are you saying he can do the job?"

"I'm saying he hasn't given up."

Helen gnawed her lip. "I don't know if that's good or bad."

"He's a solid guy," said Cowan. "I'd want him on my side."

She spoke into the telephone. "What's your next move, Pete?"

"I don't know. I lost the mercenaries. Grandzau's in the clear. No one's even close."

The men from Marseilles drifted onto the quay below their hotel two hours before midnight. Gliding shadows—nervous, hunched shapes—they dispersed about the deserted fishing anchorage. The quay, garlanded by motor-dories and small wooden trawlers, was lighted by a single streetlamp that marked the end of the road that wound down the slope from the hotel. Atop the lamp pole burned a red channel light, which, when lined up with another red light on the slope, indicated safe entrance from the Channel.

Three of the mercenaries hid in separate doorways, lost in deep shadow. Another crept aboard a fishing boat and crouched behind the wheelhouse. The fifth clambered silently up a drainpipe and mounted a pitched roof with a view of the lighted quay and the mouth of the anchorage, which was a hundred yards from the quay and marked by a four-second green flasher. The fishhouse and cottages were dark, and after the men from Marseilles had settled in, nothing moved but the wind and occasional thin bursts of snow blowing in from the Channel.

"How many?" asked Trefle.

Lady Janet scanned their positions. She'd paid two thousand francs for the World War Two U-boat captain's night glasses. Their prisms were in need of adjustment and cleaning, but still showed the dark quay in amazing detail.

"Just the five."

Trefle was lying on his back on a row of boat cushions, staring lazily up at the planks overhead and seemingly impervious to the cold. He took another pull from the bottle he'd been nursing since they'd arrived.

"Fools. Everywhere but where we are."

They had hidden their sleek, low boat under a dock. There was barely room to stand and since the tide was coming in they'd twice had to adjust their lines on the dock pilings, but they were deep in shadow, invisible from the quay, yet commanded a clear view of it and the rock jetties that formed the mouth of the anchorage.

Lady Janet had almost despaired of stealing a boat. Only fishing craft were in the water this time of year and they weren't fast enough to trail the kind of launch Grandzau would send. Then Trefle had hit upon the idea of stealing a pleasure boat.

They had broken into a yacht basin in a Brest suburb, winched a fast, seaworthy runabout onto a trailer, and fitted it with a pair of giant outboard motors. Then they'd hitched the trailer to the Renault, taken on petrol at the shuttered marina's pumps, and driven back through Brest and up the coast to the harbor next to this one. Launching in the dark, they'd made a cold, wet, bone-jarring run to this anchorage.

"What time is it?" Trefle asked now.

"Ten."

"I'll spell you at eleven." He fell asleep, snoring lightly.

Lady Janet scanned the quay again, saw that none of the mercenaries had changed position, and shifted her attention to the jetties. She strained her ears for the sound of Grandzau's boat. She was soaked from spray and freezing cold and her last injection was wearing off hours too soon. She gnawed hungrily at some cheese, tore off a piece of bread, ate it, and stole a swallow of Trefle's red wine to wash it down.

She wanted another injection. She held off until ten-thirty.

Trefle awakened at eleven. "Get some sleep."

"I'm fine. I feel quite well."

She couldn't quite see his face, but she felt his gaze and thought she saw the light from streetlamp on the quay reflected in his eyes. He was looking at her.

"You're using a lot of that stuff."

"I've been off it a year. It's just for the pain."

"It always is."

She passed him the binoculars and reclined on the cushions where he had lain. Sometimes when she got this high, it was hard to remember why she was hunting Grandzau. The cold and the pain and the hate were at a distance. She imagined the pain and hate sitting on the quay, put in a box, a crate, waiting to picked up and sent to sea. Waiting with the mercenaries for Grandzau's boat.

She imagined standing up and looking at the quay and seeing the crate sitting there. She looked at it for a long, long time. Trefle shook her awake.

"Up! Something's coming."

She sat up groggily. Trefle scooped a handful of water from the side of the boat and hurled it in her face. She snapped alert. "All right."

"Listen."

She heard the faint mutter of an engine. "Something's wrong," she whispered. "It's not coming from the water."

Trefle cursed softly. "Untie the stern."

She threw the rope into the water; there wasn't time to untie it from the piling. Trefle slashed the bowline with his knife. Before the boat could drift out from under the dock, he wrapped an arm around the piling and sat down behind the steering wheel, his other hand on the starter key. Lady Janet slung the submachine gun over her shoulder and examined the quay through the night glasses.

"They're facing the street," she reported. "I don't think they know what it is either. They've drawn their weapons."

"Maybe it's just somebody out for a drive," Trefle said doubtfully. "I see lights."

A pair of headlights crested the hill and descended quickly.

Trefle cursed. Lady Janet continued to watch the mercenaries. The one on the roof had his weapon trained on the quay.

The headlights disappeared behind a building and reappeared an instant later on the quay. Then the car swerved into a tight U-turn and stopped, facing the road.

Someone shouted, "*Merlin*!"

Grandzau's old code word for all clear.

The mercenaries started running toward the car.

"Go!" screamed Lady Janet.

Trefle hit both starters at once, and the boat flew across the anchorage, Lady Janet unslung the Smith & Wesson and leveled the perforated barrel at the car. Three of the mercenaries were already in it. The man who'd hidden on the trawler was running across the cobblestones and the last was sliding down the drainpipe.

She pressed the trigger and the gun began its smooth bucking.

Trefle knocked the barrel up.

"Don't kill the driver!"

He slewed alongside the quay, lost control of the speeding boat. It slammed hard into the stone. They were thrown to the bottom, tangling in the mess of lines, cushions, seats, and hastily rigged wiring. Lady Janet tore loose first, hauling herself onto the high quay, dragging her weapon after her.

The car was rolling. One door hung open. The last mercenary chased after it, leaped in. The door slammed behind him and the car squealed toward the turn.

Lady Janet ran with all her heart, legs frantically pumping, gaining. The driver got into second gear and the car pulled away. She loosed a long, desperate burst of gunfire at the tires.

The car skidded into the turn and passed from her sight. Seconds later she saw its taillights as it climbed rapidly up the hill. Lady Janet ran a few more yards, then shambled to a halt in the middle of the street, her weapon trailing from one hand.

Lights flared on in the cottages and some doors opened tentatively. Oblivious, she stared up the hill, gasping for breath, watching the car escape. Hot tears blinded her.

"Come on!" Trefle yelled.

Lady Janet didn't move.

She was vaguely aware of the lights in the windows and somewhere heard people shouting. She didn't care. Trefle came running. He had blood on his face.

"Let's get out of here."

"We didn't think he would come by land," she whispered.

"Later."

"He pointed everyone toward the water." The weapon slid from her hand. It clattered on the cobblestones. A couple of men came out of a door. Big men. Made bold by the sight of a woman, a single man, a fallen gun.

Trefle snarled. He picked up the gun, threw Lady Janet over his shoulder, and carried her back to the boat.

At the Café Pierre, Helen Throp said that she would keep her coat.

The Texan, a handsome man in his fifties, agreed a trifle too loudly. "Coatcheck gal would hop a plane to Brazil if you let her get her hands on that," he laughed. "Gollee, but that's a fine-looking fur. Couldn't take my eyes off it all night."

A glance from Helen Thorp told the maître d' that Ms. Thorp's table would be a distance from the dance floor tonight, but not in an intimate dark spot. Her guest was executive director of Comptel's Houston and Dallas-Fort Worth sales and production. He'd been doing an excellent job, proving Alfred Cowan's contention that top flight regional management was the key to efficient conglomerate operation—a notion Helen Thorp did not endorse—and he deserved all the courtesies when he came to New York on business. She performed such duties with the careful deliberation she planned all her work. Nothing was left to chance.

Helen had taken him to the theater. They'd seen a revival of a successful musical that played to a packed house of New York executives and their out-of-town guests. Then dinner at the Crystal Room in the Tavern on the Green—a restaurant she could count on for the gay party atmosphere such a night on the town required.

He was pleasant company, but he had had a long, grueling day and had insisted on a second bottle of champagne at dinner. Thus far he seemed a pleasant drunk, but she was taking no chances at the obligatory afterdinner bar stop, so she'd chosen the Café Pierre in the Texan's hotel, and left her sable draped over her shoulders for a graceful departure.

"Penny for your thoughts, Ms. Thorp."

She smiled brightly. The fact was, she hadn't done her duty as well as she might. She'd been distracted all evening, preoccupied with what was happening to Charles Hammond. "I must apologize," she said. "I can't get this kidnapping out of my mind."

"You mean the Hammond thing?"

She nodded, guardedly. She'd almost let slip Comptel's involvement. Few employees knew the extent of the company's relationship with Hammond, and none but Alfred's immediate circle knew about the Pendragon auction.

She dissembled easily. "It's a frightening thought, being held by God knows whom that way."

"Sure," the Texan said expansively. "When one of their kind gits one of *your* kind it comes real close to home."

"I guess that's it." She permitted herself a doubtful smile. "Ted, I'm afraid I'm going to have to call it a night. I'm terribly tired and we've got more of the same tomorrow morning."

The Texan smiled at her. "Never was much at throwing passes, but you are one gorgeous lady."

She smiled back. He wasn't that drunk and he was very handsome, with pale ginger hair that reminded her of Hammond's.

"Thanks," she said. "That's nice to hear. Awfully nice."

"Didn't mean it to be nice. Meant it to tell you what I thought. Friend of mine has a place over on Park Avenue. He's outa town and he gave me the key. Nice and private."

She was tempted. He had a gentle and knowing look about him. But there was no such thing as private. She'd learned that when Hammond had pursued her so avidly. She worked in a small world and someone would always know and it might be the worst person of all to find out.

"When I first came to work," she said, "I made a rule. I wouldn't make it with the boss."

He grinned. "But *I'm* not the boss. *You're* the boss."

Helen reached for her bag. "Ted. If I won't sleep with the boss, how can you ask me to sleep with the help?"

Outside, on Fifth Avenue, the doorman whistled for a cab, but she preferred the cold winter air. She walked along Central Park South slowly, thinking about Hammond. How he had wanted her. And how he had persisted. As only Hammond could . . .

Comptel and Decca, the British electronics company, had been negotiating a partnership to build satellite ground stations in northern India. Decca had the contacts in the Indian government, but Comptel had a new, easily maintained ground station and things were going badly because Decca was not used to being number two to anybody in technology. Alfred had sent Helen over to pry things loose. Hammond heard about it.

He bought every first class seat on the Pan Am Clipper to London but hers and when she climbed the staircase to the top deck dining room, he was sitting waiting for her, alone at a single table set for two. She had agreed to dinner that night over the North Atlantic. . . .

Sixth Avenue was somewhat less peopled than Central Park South at this late hour, so when she turned down it she walked closer to the curb and kept her eyes open. She could feel the Comptel building drawing her. It towered, shoulder to shoulder, with its neighbors. Like the other skyscrapers, it housed a power center, an oddly small core that weighed on the destinies of thousands of employees and millions of citizen-customers throughout the world.

A sleepy guard let her into the lobby. Her key operated Alfred's private elevator. She headed skyward, up to the center of the power center, the core of the core, the electronic consoles where the messages, the information, and the power terminated.

She wasn't surprised to find Alfred at his desk.

The private teletype started clattering.

"Sir?"

Chamberlain was lying awake in the dark. He'd slept for eleven hours, and was listening to the morning sounds of the airport when the co-pilot stepped into his cabin.

"What's up?"

"Private line from New York, sir. Head office."

"Helen Thorp?"

"Yes, sir."

Chamberlain felt for the phone.

"I'm up late, or you're up early, or something like that."

"Come to New York."

"Why?"

"We just received a message from Lancelot. He's starting the auction."

BOOK III

19

"YOUR BID IS EXPECTED AT THE PENDRAGON AUCTION SAVOY HOTEL. LONDON. LANCELOT."

"*London*? What the hell am I doing in New York?"

"Ms. Thorp will see you now," said her secretary. She took back the cablegram she'd handed Chamberlain when he'd arrived and led him into Helen Thorp's office.

She was conferring with a young executive, Cardin-suited, who stood before her desk clasping and unclasping his hands behind his back.

She noted Chamberlain's arrival with a quick glance and resumed her instructions.

"Copy me up to two hundred and fifty thousand. Over that, tell me first."

The guy's knuckles were white. He asked, "Can I go to a million?"

"Not without telling me."

She stood up, rounded her desk, and walked him, past Chamberlain, to the door. The guy stared through him, visibly annoyed that Chamberlain had been allowed in before his meeting was over.

Chamberlain watched Helen Thorp from the corner of his eye. She was wearing a dark pleated, slit skirt and a pale blue silk blouse buttoned to the neck. Her thick dark hair swayed as she walked and when she reached for the doorknob, her breasts swelled attractively against the silk.

She smiled. "If I'm out of town and it's urgent, Mildred can reach me. Thanks for coming in, Brian. Mr. Cowan and I think you're doing a damn good job."

She closed the door and regarded Chamberlain coolly through her long lashes. "Which is more than I can say for you."

"If you told your secretary to let me in early to show me how important you are, it worked. I'm very impressed."

"It was to show you how important you are."

"If I'm that important why the hell did I have to come to New York if the auction's in London?"

"Why?" she asked with ice in her voice. "To keep you out of trouble between now and the time Hammond is auctioned."

Chamberlain glared angrily and she glared back. "Alfred Cowan was worried that you might crash the company airplane into the Savoy, but I told him not to worry, that Hammond was safe if you were aiming at the Savoy because you'd hit the Dorchester."

"If you want to fire me, fire me. But spare me the sarcasm."

"Spare *you*? Did it ever occur to you that a little sarcasm is all that's preventing me from screaming my head off at you? Can you imagine what it's been like getting your reports these few days? Five groups were looking for Charles Hammond. You tied for fourth place with the Russians."

"First, second, and third got killed."

She let go of the doorknob and waved his objection aside. "But number three, your *friends* at the CIA, almost got Hammond killed with them, which was precisely what you were hired to prevent."

Chamberlain met her angry gaze, then looked away. She wasn't the sort to waste time yelling at him if she was going to fire him. Getting Hammond back was still too good a chance to screw up by getting in a fight with Ms. Thorp. He looked at his watch. Four o'clock in the afternoon, New York time. He'd taken off from Brest the moment she had called.

"You're right, Ms. Thorp. The simple fact of the matter is that I'm not closer to Hammond than I was three days ago in this same office."

"Almost four."

"Four. Right now it's ten o'clock at night in London and I should be there."

"I'm afraid we'll have to get bidding instructions from Mr. Cowan first. He's waiting for us. He said to bring you in as soon as you got here."

"Is that why you brought me back to New York? To see Mr. Cowan?"

"Yes."

"Jees, I have a big mouth. I'm sorry."

"Let's not keep Alfred waiting." She led him through Mildred's office to Cowan's. Chamberlain followed sheepishly, feeling silly, and enjoying her perfume.

Cowan was in a conference call, sitting at his desk with his feet propped up on an open drawer, addressing a speaker phone. He nodded at Helen and Chamberlain. "Sorry, boys, I gotta get off. Try to work it out and get back to me in the morning."

He flipped the phone off and said, "Have a seat. How you doing, Pete?"

"I've done better."

"Didn't work the way we thought it would, did it?"

"No, sir."

"What's your next step?"

"I guess that's up to you and Ms. Thorp, sir."

"You think we should bid?"

"You're asking my opinion?"

"Yes, damnit. I'm a bit busy for small talk."

"Yes, you should bid. And I think you should put every effort into patching up the consortium so you can outbid the Russians. They want him very badly."

"Why do they want him?"

"I don't know, sir. But they sure as hell do."

"Helen?"

"Alfred, it just doesn't make sense. The more I think about it, the less sense it makes. But they want him."

Cowan said, "What about the CIA?"

"The Central Intelligence Agency is going to be a real

problem now. They'll probably take their defeat very personally."

"What the hell for?" snapped Cowan. "I thought they're supposed to be professionals."

"They are, but several important people there are now responsible for losing an entire assault team—a clandestine assault team that isn't even supposed to exist and now a lot of people know about it. And those people are almost certainly going to decide that to clean *their* records, at least, they're going to have to pull off a major victory and the only major victory they can pull off that will mean anything will be keeping Hammond from falling into Russian hands."

"Goddamnit!" growled Cowan.

"There's possibly a bright side to it, Alfred," said Helen.

"Yeah? Name it."

"Grandzau, or whoever Lancelot is, has done a very good job of protecting Hammond so far. Perhaps he has a way to hold the auction safely, in which case we can buy him back. With the help of our partners."

"What do you think, Pete?"

"She's right. He's probably got a damn good plan."

"How the hell can he hold a ransom auction at the Savoy Hotel?"

Helen looked at Chamberlain. He knew that she was expecting him to answer, but he wasn't sure what to say.

"I mean that's the craziest thing I ever heard of," Cowan added.

"Hard to tell," Chamberlain said slowly. "He might tell us all where to go next from there. Or, and I suppose this is possible, he might hold an auction in a private conference room. They've got all kinds of meeting facilities, I'm sure."

"All I know is last time I stayed there and changed rooms when my wife joined me, it took them eight hours to transfer my bags. Now are you telling me that they'd bring Hammond to the Savoy?"

"Very unlikely. They'd probably keep him someplace else and rig a telephone hookup to prove he's alive."

"I hope," Alfred Cowan said ominously, "that for Hammond's sake that doesn't happen. Because you"—he pointed to Helen—"are not taking any Comptel money to any auction where Hammond isn't. You're not taking a penny anywhere you don't have a guarantee you can buy him alive."

"Of course not, Alfred."

"Don't 'of course not' me. I'm not making any exceptions on this. If Grandzau wants Comptel money at that auction he's going to produce Hammond on the spot."

He looked at Chamberlain and Chamberlain nodded because there didn't seem to be any point not to.

Cowan pointed to Helen again. "This thing has the potential to be a hell of a con job."

"Except that Hammond has been kidnapped," said Helen. "Surely you're not suggesting that a man of his talents and success would engineer his own kidnapping for a few million dollars?"

"Not likely," said Cowan. "But I want proof that he's alive before I pay a penny for him."

Helen smiled. "You're repeating yourself, Alfred."

"For emphasis, dear. Emphasis."

"How high can we bid?"

"I've been thinking maybe we should raise Comptel's contribution to ten million dollars."

Helen Thorp stared at him. "Thank you, Alfred. Thank you very much."

"Just remember the conditions. And one more. I want you over there." He turned to Chamberlain, who hoped his annoyance didn't show. All he needed was her dogging his tracks in London. "Pete, I think you'd better play it defensively for a while. Watch the CIA and watch the Russians, but don't go for Grandzau. I think we'd better rely on his good sense. He's done pretty well so far, wouldn't you say?"

Chamberlain heard himself saying, "Yes, sir. He's done very well."

"Okay. Thanks for coming over so fast. Now, I think you'd better hop right back on that plane and head for London."

"Yes, sir," replied Chamberlain. He grinned. "You're spending more on my aviation fuel than my salary."

Cowan looked at him blankly. "Fuel's expensive."

Chamberlain wished he'd kept his mouth shut. "Yes, sir."

"One other thing, Pete."

"Yes, sir?"

"Keep an eye on Ms. Thorp. I don't want her in any danger at all. I'm not kidding. As far as I'm concerned, she's more important than Hammond."

"The stockholders might not agree with you," said Helen.

Cowan ignored her. He held Chamberlain's gaze for a long time with hard, flat eyes. Finally he lumbered around his desk, awkwardly patted Helen's shoulder, and mumbled, "Take care of yourself."

Hammond ran hard, pushing his limits, punishing his body, driving himself. The Maltese loped easily beside him, effortlessly pacing the older man. Grandzau appeared suddenly and held his palm up like a traffic cop.

Hammond tried to run past him, but the Maltese grabbed his arm and jerked him to a halt.

"You mustn't overdo your exercise," said Grandzau. He was carrying a towel.

"Tell this clown to let go of me."

Grandzau shook his head. "A heart attack would be most untimely."

Hammond jerked free and started to walk to the door.

"No, no, no," said Grandzau. "I was reading that a jogger must treat his body as carefully as a champion racehorse. You must walk around and cool down slowly."

"Fuck off."

"Herr Hammond, the bidders are gathering at the Savoy. They are coming from all over the world. You are too valuable to abuse." He flipped the towel over Hammond's head. "We must take care of you."

"Leave me alone!" Hammond shouted. "Go away."

"You're awfully edgy for a man who's supposed to be the calm one in the middle of the storm," Grandzau said mockingly. "Charles Hammond the negotiator, the great dealmaker, the cool go-between."

"I'm sick of dealing and you, goddamnit, know it."

Grandzau smiled sympathetically. "Don't worry, Herr Hammond. It is not in my interest to disappoint your new friends."

Chamberlain spotted a KGB man buying the *International Herald Tribune* at the newsstand. Thirty feet across the lobby, a CIA operative was reading the Reuters News Service teletype printouts that the Savoy Hotel displayed for its guests. Chamberlain sat down on a couch between them, and when Helen Thorp found him there, he had already concluded that both superspook agencies had changed tactics.

The CIA operative had the gray hair, the recent suntan, the horn-rim glasses, and the casual houndstooth jacket associated with a retired midwestern businessman trailing his wife on yet another world tour. He wore a kindly, grandfatherly expression and though he might have stood with a touch more solid grace than the average grandfather, he could easily pass for a man who played squash twice a week with his doctor.

The KGB man looked equally benign, exactly like a Middle-European university professor, with a light, wispy cloud of white hair swirling above a balding pate, wire-rim glasses, and a badly cut wool suit. He looked a bit too shabby to belong in the Savoy, but he could have been attending a convention.

"They've pulled out the heavies," he told Helen. "They're both just laying back and watching. These clowns aren't even carrying coats. They couldn't follow us into the street."

"Maybe the heavies are outside."

"I already checked. They're not. No, they just decided to stop hitting."

"Like us."

"Right. Grandzau's intimidated all of us."

"Good. Let's go."

They walked the few blocks to the City, where All Seas had its offices. Rene Rice, the receptionist informed them, was out for the day.

"But I had an appointment," said Helen Thorp.

"Monsieur Rice asked me to apologize. He had to leave on a pressing matter."

"I'm at the Savoy. I must talk with him. Let's go, Pete."

Chamberlain followed her out the door. When they got to the street, she said, "He's been ducking me. He can't handle this."

She looked up and down the narrow street and checked her watch. "Damnit. Okay, back to the hotel. We'll work on the others. Get a cab."

Chamberlain hailed a taxi. On the ride back, she sat in the corner, staring out the window, chewing her lip. She'd been nervous and irritable on the flight over and a night's sleep hadn't helped much. Chamberlain sympathized. Grandzau had the lot of them locked up in the Savoy waiting.

"Shall we try the hospitality suite?" she asked when they got back to the Savoy.

Chamberlain knew it wasn't a question. He followed her up the stairs, thinking again that Grandzau was close to brilliant when it came to manipulating the people who were waiting for his auction. He had rented a suite on the second floor, in the name Pendragon Ltd., and stocked it with a bar and a waiter who presided over a sumptuous hors d'oeuvres table.

Bored and restless, the invitees to the Pendragon auction gathered in the hospitality suite as they would at a convention and drank and schemed and speculated on what would happen next. When Chamberlain and Helen arrived, the new representative from Mishuma was telling the man who claimed to have inherited Hans Streicher's business that a bellboy had told him that Pendragon Ltd. had rented an entire floor of the hotel starting in two days.

"The seventh, that would make it. He's holding the auction right here."

The man from Dassault shook his head scornfully. "Ridiculous. He won't hold the auction in the hotel. Five limousines are reserved early the morning of the seventh. It will be done in some country house out in Surrey."

"We say *down* in Surrey," remarked the Englishman who represented British Hovercraft. "Not *out.*"

The Frenchman stared, sneered, "*Anglais,*" then spied Helen and lighted in smiles.

"Ms. Thorp. What have you heard? Where will the auction be held?"

"Not a thing, but I'm glad I found you all here. Now's a good time as any to reform the bidding consortium and finalize our commitments."

She looked around at the dozen men in the room. Several, seeing her expression, put their glasses back on the bar. She said to the bartender and the waiter, "Would you excuse us, please. That will be all for now."

They trooped out.

"And you, please," she added when they had gone, nodding at the Russian, who shrugged unhappily and levered his bulk out of the chair in the corner and lumbered out under the stares of the others.

"Is there anyone else who intends to bid for Hammond alone and not join in the consortium?"

The men looked from one to another and said nothing.

"Is there anyone else who should be here that anyone knows of?"

"There's a Qataran sheikh who's bidding," said the German.

"Has anyone seen him?"

No one had.

"It's probably a rumor."

"What about Rice?" asked the Frenchman.

"I'll get to him," said Helen.

"None of us have seen him," said the Frenchman. "Perhaps Rice is also a rumor."

Several men laughed.

"I'm sure," Helen replied icily, "that Charles Hammond's own company will contribute handsomely to the auction fund that Comptel has started."

The man from Dassault picked up his glass and clinked his ice thoughtfully. "Who's to say," he asked no one in particular, "that Comptel, Incorporated is to direct the consortium to buy back Charles Hammond?"

"Any company contributing more than Comptel is welcome to the doubtful pleasure of managing the consortium."

"Well, how much is Comptel contributing?" asked the Frenchman.

Helen stood where she had when she entered the room, several feet in from the door, her hands in her coat pockets, Chamberlain behind and to her right. "If Grandzau didn't bug this room, then the KGB, or the CIA, or Scotland yard probably did. Possibly all four did. Therefore, I suggest you write your contributions on a piece of paper and pass them to me and I will award the chairmanship of the consortium to the highest contributer."

"Can we trust you to do that?"

"I will then pass the papers around and everyone can see. Then I'll take them back and burn them."

Chamberlain found himself admiring her infinite patience. Nothing the Frenchman could say would ruffle her. She took off her coat, handed it to Chamberlain, and sat down. She had a gold pen and she wrote briefly on a cocktail napkin. There was no other paper around, so the others followed suit. And while they were writing, Helen casually blotted her lips with her napkin. They brought them to her. She collected them in her lap and when she had the last, she shuffled through them, reading without expression. Finally she stacked them in a neat pile and stood up.

"Well?" said the Frenchman.

Chamberlain saw small red spots appear on her cheeks. She crossed the room and handed the napkins to the Japanese man. The man from Mishuma bowed, glanced through the napkins, and passed them to another man. He rose and cleared his throat.

"Encouraged by Comptel, Incorporated, we as a group have raised a very large fund to ransom Mr. Hammond. We at Mishuma are pleased to lead such a generous consortium."

Someone started clapping and several others followed suit.

Chamberlain watched Helen. She clapped politely, as if at any ceremonial meeting. The red spots had gone from her cheeks and he couldn't read what she was thinking, though he had the feeling that she had begun to relax.

Chamberlain watched the napkins go from man to man. Most read them eagerly. One or two looked chagrined, as if their companies hadn't contributed enough. Several looked in awe at the man from Japan. Something had been bothering Chamberlain, and now he got it. Most of the American companies had replaced the men they'd sent earlier in the week; with Kaga Nagumo gone, and Hans Streicher, this was a younger and more aggressive group. The first crowd had been a bunch of lawyers. This time, the companies were sending a different type, as if they had decided that their top young executives were better equipped to deal with the auction.

Like the CIA and the KGB, the companies who wanted Charles Hammond were treating Grandzau more seriously. The whole event had taken on a more cautious tone. He watched them return to the bar and freshen their drinks.

Something about them still bothered him. There wasn't the panic here there had been before. He shook his head. What made him think the fix was in?

"What'd they go for?"

They were walking quickly down a carpeted hallway. She seemed very excited.

"About sixty million dollars, not counting the Japanese."

"And counting the Japanese?"

She turned to him, awed. "The Japanese are contributing

thirty million dollars. They must have government backing. Can you imagine what Hammond is doing for them to make him that valuable?''

''Ninety million bucks for one guy? He can't be worth that much.''

''Let's hope the Russians feel the way you do.''

''Grandzau's a genius,'' said Chamberlain. ''Hammond can't be worth that much to any one group. But together—''

They had reached the lobby and she interrupted him. ''There's somebody coming your way.''

Chamberlain looked up. ''Hello. Inspector Farquhar, this is Ms. Helen Thorp, my boss at Comptel. Inspector Farquhar's with Scotland Yard. He was *very* helpful right after the kidnapping.''

Farquhar took her hand, then shook hands with Chamberlain. ''Mr. Chamberlain exaggerates. Actually, we helped each other.''

''How's Wheeler?'' asked Chamberlain.

''Recovering nicely. Asking to be let out, but it will be a while. Hammond's bodyguard,'' he explained to Helen.

''Yes, I visited Mr. Wheeler earlier today.'' Chamberlain looked at her, surprised. She hadn't said anything to him.

Farquhar turned to Chamberlain. ''I wonder if you might have a moment?''

''Sure.''

''I'll be upstairs,'' said Helen. ''Call me when you're done.''

Farquhar watched her walk to the elevators. ''Good God, man. Where do I sign up?''

''There's an opening in the London office.''

''I'd prefer her office. Something to drink?''

''Sure.''

''My car's waiting. There's a nice little pub over on St. Martin's Lane. Shall we?''

Chamberlain glanced around as they walked out the door. Now the CIA and KGB men were watching him with interest. Farquhar's car was a regular Metropolitan Police car, a white Rover with a blue light on top and black panda markings on the side.

''I'd prefer leaving here in something less conspicuous,'' Chamberlain remarked.

Farquhar laughed. ''Terribly sorry. This was all they had.''

But Chamberlain noticed that Farquhar took pains to have them exit from the car before they reached his pub. Once inside, with beer in hand, Farquhar said, "I'll get to the point. Two points actually. The first is important, the second interesting."

"What's up?"

Farquhar cleared his throat. He seemed embarrassed but determined, and as he spoke his determination hardened.

"I've traced your meanderings across the Continent with some concern."

"How do you mean, traced?"

"Interpol followed you easily, shall we say. Hardly surprising, all things considered."

"What are you talking about?"

"My concern was understandable. We had worked together and I daresay found the partnership enjoyable. At least I did."

"Same here."

"Interpol had little trouble tracing the general death and mayhem that accompanied your visits to various towns and cities. My concern, however, turned to alarm when I learned you were headed back to London. Quite simply, old son, we can't permit that sort of thing here in England."

"Fair enough. What's the interesting thing?"

"We won't permit it. I have my orders. We are not to interfere in the Pendragon Auction, but neither are we to allow wholescale slaughter in the streets. We will deport anyone, regardless of alliance, who participates in any violent act."

"Do you think Grandzau will hold the auction here, at the Savoy?"

Farquhar smiled, obviously relieved to be done with his message. He scooped up Chamberlain's glass and got two more lagers from the sweeping double bar. When he returned to their round corner table, Chamberlain was watching the street through the curtains. He released the cloth and took the glass mug Farquhar offered.

"Cheers," said Farquhar.

"Cheers. Do you think that Grandzau will hold his auction in the Savoy Hotel?"

"That's my interesting news."

"He will?"

"No. You probably are aware that some of our Concordes were never put into commercial service. The poor things have been ferried about to wherever someone might buy one, and occasionally, rarely, they've been chartered for private work."

"Why bother?"

"I imagine the accountants are happy to enter anything on the credit side. At any rate, we've just learned that someone who sounds awfully like Grandzau has chartered a Concorde."

Chamberlain put his mug down. "For when?"

"The seventh."

"To where?"

"That we don't know. But he's requested pilots who know the Gulf States. Draw your own conclusions."

"The Persian Gulf? Why the hell all the way down there?"

"Why not?" asked Farquhar. "The Gulf area might encourage some of Hammond's Arab clients to participate. They'd feel safer on their own ground. He was heavily involved in some of the smaller states' arms purchases. He was virtually Hans Streicher's only agent in the Gulf."

Chamberlain nodded. "Sure. With the Shah gone, every sheikh with a spare two billion dollars is building his own army."

"Why do you think my government is so interested? Hammond has such marvelous contacts in the smaller states. We had concentrated too long on Iran and Saudi Arabia. Our arms people found Hammond could do a lot better for them than they could in places like Qatar, the Emirates, even Kuwait. They say he has a fine touch with the more primitive peoples."

"But why would Grandzau hide in Hammond's territory?"

"He seems to have planned everything very carefully. Certainly there he doesn't have to worry about CIA and KGB attacks."

"He's got to worry about the Arabs," said Chamberlain.

"One would imagine he's made an arrangement."

Chamberlain sipped his lager. It didn't make a lot of sense. "Why the Concorde?" he asked. "Can you imagine what that thing cost?'

"The figure I heard for the deposit alone would have kept an earl comfortable for a decade."

"Do you realize what this whole kidnapping has cost Grandzau?" Chamberlain marveled. "The snatch, the plane, getting to that island—you heard about the island?"

"Oh yes. The CIA debacle was cause for a certain amount of delight in European circles."

"And now the Concorde? Money, money, money. Who the hell is paying for it?"

"Grandzau could have retired rather well off."

"He'd have had to," said Chamberlain. "He must have a backer. A very rich one."

"Possibly," conceded Farquhar. "But that doesn't help us."

"Specially if he's sitting down in some Arab state right now waiting for the fun to begin."

"He's done well."

"I wonder why he bothered chartering a Concorde?" Chamberlain mused.

"Speed. It's a long flight to the Gulf."

"Sure, but he would be better off putting us on a conventional plane so we get there exhausted and in no condition to give him any trouble at the auction. That's what I would do."

Farquhar drained his glass. "I would too, but then again neither of us came up with the clever idea of kidnapping Hammond in the first place. . . . I'm afraid I must be going. Can I drop you?"

Chamberlain lifted the curtain again and checked the street. "Is that guy following me?"

Farquhar looked. "Fellow with the cloth cap? Yes. Ever since you landed last night at the airport. I have men observing everyone at the auction. We're quite serious about minimizing the carnage in our city."

"I thought I saw him down by Rene Rice's office a couple of hours ago."

"He's a new man," Farquhar said dryly. "Not yet as skilled as his partner."

Chamberlain pulled a disgusted face and Farquhar laughed. "Sorry, old son."

"Where *is* Rene Rice"

"Up until two hours ago he was holding continuous telephone conversations with Madagascar. We've of course got taps on his telephones, in the event the kidnappers make direct contact."

"What's he talking about?"

It was Farquhar's turn to make a face. "Frankly, I haven't the foggiest. We can't locate a single soul in the entire British Isles who can understand his brand of Malagasy. It's polysyllabic with a vengeance. They link scads of phrases which form single unpronounceable words of unbelievable length."

"Like German?"

"Much worse. The French sent us a translator. It was their colony, you see. He was worthless. Rendered literal translations which bore no relationship to the intelligible. Rice must know we're listening and he's circumspect."

"Could you tell how Rice sounded?"

"Agitated. Hammond's name popped up regularly."

"Until two hours ago?

"Yes. At that time the phones to Madagascar went dead."

"Just like that?"

"It was expected. One of their political parties called a general strike to protest electioneering irregularities. Candidates arrested, that sort of thing. At any rate, poor Mr. Rice went home to listen to the government radio broadcasts on his wireless. The election is in two days. Same day as your auction, in actual fact."

"Did you tap his house also?"

Farquhar nodded. "Complete surveillance. We arrested some KGB thugs hanging about the All Seas offices. We're taking no chances that they grab Rice."

"I'd like to talk to him," said Chamberlain, "if you have no objection."

"None."

"Where does he live?"

"I'll drop you. It's on my way."

While Farquhar hailed a cab with his furled umbrella, Chamberlain approached the man who'd been following him. He looked frozen. The thin sleet had dusted his cap and shoulders dirty white. Chamberlain caught his eye and circled to hold it as he turned aside.

"They closed Covent Garden market about ten years ago, so you're the only guy in the theater district wearing a cloth cap. Bad show."

The young man reddened, but he had the sense to look blank before he hurried away.

Chamberlain climbed into Farquhar's cab. "Not bad."

"I trust, therefore, that you gave the lad some encouragement."

"Sure."

They rode silently for a few minutes while Chamberlain mulled the meaning of the chartered Concorde. An extravagance, unless speed was vital. But if it was, why hadn't Grandzau sent the bidders where he wanted them now, instead of putting them on ice at the Savoy?

A big, hard-faced man going to fat opened Rice's door. Chamberlain recalled that Rice's secretary was former FBI. Before either could speak, Rice peeked around his secretary's shoulder and nodded. "Monsieur Chamberlain. It's all right, Patterson. I'll take care of this."

Patterson, expressionless, lumbered back into the room. Over Rice's head, Chamberlain saw that the apartment was sparely furnished with a few elegant, black lacquer Chinese pieces. A single splendid carpet, bordered by pickled wood floors, colored the middle of the room. A gas fire burned hotly in a small marble fireplace, beside which sat an armchair. On a table next to the armchair was a large shortwave radio. Rice's mournful eyes were half shut with exhaustion.

"May I come in?"

"What does Ms. Thorp want?" His hands were trembling.

"I believe she wanted confirmation of the All Seas contribution."

"I'll call her tomorrow."

"Sir?"

"What is it?" He was already closing the door.

"Who did Mr. Hammond visit the morning he was kidnapped?"

20

Rice answered without having to think about it. "The morning he was kidnapped, Mr. Hammond had breakfast with the Japanese ambassador to Great Britain."

"I mean who was he meeting where he was kidnapped?"

Rice hesitated.

"Did you tell the police who he met?"

"Oh yes. You could ask them."

"Or you could tell me."

Rice shrugged. "At this point nothing really matters, does it?"

Chamberlain said nothing. A man in Rice's position would have deeply ingrained habits of discretion.

The Malagasy shrugged again. "He was visiting an old friend. A Major Ramsey, who lives at the Overseas Club."

"An intelligence officer?" asked Chamberlain, wondering if he should have gone into this earlier.

"Retired."

"Oh. Did Major Ramsey and Mr. Hammond ever do business?"

Again Rice hesitated. Did he regret opening the topic? "Perhaps before my time. I've only served Mr. Hammond eight years.'' His face began to crumble. ''It was just an ordinary morning. He was late, as usual, and I phoned ahead with explanations. Then Patterson and I went to the airport to ready the plane. We had UN meetings in New York on the second.'' His voice mirrored the breakdown of his face. ''One moment all was normal, the next, chaos.''

''Was Ms. Thorp expecting you?''

''I don't involve myself in Mr. Hammond's private life.''

When Chamberlain got back to his room, he knocked on the door that led to Helen's suite, gestured her to come to the bathroom, sat on the edge of the tub, and turned the cold water on full blast.

''Privacy,'' he explained over the roar of the tap.

''Aren't you overdoing it a bit?''

''Streicher's boat didn't blow up by itself. Grandzau has had somebody on the ground all along. Stashing the bidders in the same hotel just makes it easier to keep track of us.'' He stopped talking and stared. She was wearing a silk robe, a silver gray clinging garment that set off her beautiful eyes and jet hair. He blurted, ''Jesus Christ, you are gorgeous.''

Her brow furrowed in surprise and annoyance. ''Get off it, Pete. I don't have time for that.''

''Sorry. It just sort of slipped out.'' He was wondering if she slept with Hammond. But she seemed to worry mostly about what his kidnapping would do to her job.

''Well, put it back. What did Farquhar tell you?''

''He thinks that Grandzau's rented a Concorde to fly the bidders to the Persian Gulf tomorrow.''

''The latest rumor around the hotel is that Grandzau is sending us to Scotland on the train. I like yours better.''

''I've got another one that's even better.''

''What?''

''This is just my idea. I haven't told anybody.''

''What?''

''How about Hammond setting up his own kidnapping?''

She nodded calmly, and it occurred to Chamberlain that she might have had the same thought. Obviously she knew Hammond very well. How well he could only guess from Rice's oblique comment on Hammond's private life.

''How,'' she asked, ''of all the possibilities, could you have come to that conclusion?''

"I added up what the kidnapping must have cost. Somebody's put a fortune into it."

"And because Charles Hammond is heavily mortgaged you assume that he spent his money on faking his own kidnapping. Is that your *only* reason?"

Chamberlain began to feel uncomfortable. "No. Holding the auction in a Gulf State is another. He'd feel safe there among his Arab friends."

"Anything else?" she asked coolly.

"I found Rice."

"And?"

"First of all, it still bothers me that he's such a lightweight. It's like Hammond doesn't trust somebody smart around him."

"Ridiculous," said Helen.

"Anyway, Rice told me that Hammond visited a retired spy a few minutes before he was snatched. Supposedly it was a social call."

"So?"

"Funny coincidence. Funny sort of friend for a busy guy like Hammond to have. A social call in the middle of the day. How many do you make?"

"Purely social? None. But that's me. I don't really have friends. But it was the holidays, and perhaps he stopped to make a courtesy call. People do that around the holidays. Hammond would do that, stop in and see an old man alone in his club for Christmas."

"What got this started in my mind was what Mr. Cowan said about the kidnapping and the auction having great potential for a con."

"Anything else?"

"Yeah. I doubt Rice is in on it. He seems too broken up."

"Anything else?"

"No . . . you don't sound convinced."

"I don't agree or disagree. I'm just being devil's advocate. I want to think about it, and I think I'd better talk to Alfred."

Chamberlain started excitedly for the door.

"Where are you going?"

"You talk to Mr. Cowan. I'll check out Ramsey at the club."

"No. Don't do that." She stood, the robe shimmering from her breasts.

"Why not?"

"Because I want you here with me when Grandzau makes his move."

"That's not till the day after tomorrow."

"We don't know for sure. Farquhar's guessing about that Concorde. Grandzau's completely unpredictable."

"But he's not going to start the auction without everybody."

"Pete," she said flatly, brushing past him and out into the suite. "I want you with me."

Chamberlain followed her, exasperated. "Ms. Thorp, this could mean something."

"Like what? We've already decided to stop hunting Grandzau and do what he wants."

"What if it's a con?"

"It's not," she said angrily.

"May I suggest something?"

"What?"

"To protect the company. To protect ourselves. It won't hurt to have a couple of your analysts try to sort out Hammond's finances. And it won't hurt for you and me to go see this Major Ramsey. Those are two decent leads. We'd be crazy to pass them up."

Her eyes had turned cold and very hard. He'd seen that same look in Alfred Cowan's eyes when the company chairman was issuing a direct order. It was a detached look a professional fighter got after he'd made his decision to kill.

"You're right," she said. "I'll call New York. Then we're going over to see that man." She grinned. "It'll beat hanging around this dumb hotel.

"I'll get some dry shoes," said Chamberlain. He stopped halfway through the door that connected his room to her suite. She was already reaching for the telephone.

"Hey, thanks," said Chamberlain. "Thanks a lot."

"For what?" she said, her eyebrows raised in surprise.

"For listening to me."

Helen Thorp looked at him, held him with her steady gaze. Then she grinned again. "I'll meet you in the lobby. Ten minutes. Next to the KGB spy."

She took his arm as they rounded Harrods and walked into the quiet neighborhood behind the giant department store.

"Do you mind?"

"Not at all." The snow was glazing the sidewalk and her leather-soled boots were sliding on the ice. He could feel her fingers through his coat.

"I'm so glad we came," she said. "I can't stand sitting around."

Chamberlain glanced at her as they crossed a street. She looked as happy as she sounded. Despite the storm, which was driving afternoon shoppers off the streets, she'd insisted on leaving the cab on Knightsbridge and walking the last few blocks. The cold air had colored her cheeks and snowflakes lay like stars in her black hair.

"Do you walk a lot?" Chamberlain asked.

"Oh yes. I hate having to exercise, and I'll be damned if I'll jog around town in a sweatsuit. I'd much rather put on some decent clothes and take a good long look at a piece of New York. Where is this place?"

"Right around the corner, I think. There it is, Herbert Crescent."

They followed the curving street until they came to the Overseas Club, identified only by its number, midway in the row of Dutch-facade town houses. The street continued a couple of hundred feet to a small garden park surrounded by a black iron fence. Through the fence and the trees could be seen another street lined with town houses.

They climbed the steps of the Overseas Club. Helen rang the bell. Chamberlain had a look up and down the street.

"Eerie, isn't it?" said Helen. "They took Hammond right there." A couple of little English cars were parked where the limousine must have sat.

When the butler opened the door, he led them politely into the foyer before he asked their business. Chamberlain noticed a bulge in his morning coat which might have been a gun. Helen asked if they could see Major Ramsey.

"Have you an appointment?"

"I'm afraid we don't. But if you would be so kind as to tell Major Ramsey that I am Helen Thorp, a friend of Charles Hammond, I think the major might see us." The butler went in to ask.

"You're acting awfully English all of a sudden," Chamberlain remarked.

"When in England. . . . It worked for Hadrian and it's

working for me.'' She gazed about the foyer, inspecting the paintings on the walls and smiling quietly, enjoying herself, until the butler returned. The major would probably see them in the front sitting room. Chamberlain thought that the foyer, which was much smaller than those of most clubs he'd been in, looked very easy to defend, an asset in a home for retired spooks.

The butler returned, leading them to the sitting room. It was dimly lighted and tomb silent—a large room filled with leather chairs on a drab carpet, heavy draperies, and oil portraits of men from the nineteen forties on the walls. Major Ramsey sat by a coal fire. He rose when he saw Helen, shook her hand, and then Chamberlain's, and invited them to sit by the fire.

Chamberlain thought Ramsey had to be seventy-five if he was a day. A neat and trim man with a little bristly mustache and a pink scalp. He had tiny, bright eyes and a clear voice.

''How do you know Charles Hammond?''

''He has managed business deals for the company I work for, Comptel, Inc.,'' said Helen. ''Mr. Chamberlain works in our security division and is assisting me in our efforts to get Hammond from the kidnappers.''

''Any new word on the auction?'' asked Ramsey.

''How do you know about the auction?'' Helen asked, glancing in alarm at Chamberlain.

''Come, come. I can ask old friends a favor now and then. They know how worried I am about Charles Hammond.''

''No new word since we've been summoned to the Savoy.''

''Why did you want to see me?''

''We wondered if you could tell us what Charles—Mr. Hammond came to see you about just before they kidnapped him.''

Ramsey glanced into the fire and answered softly. ''He came to say Happy New Year.''

''Is that all?'' asked Chamberlain.

''It meant a lot to me.'' He waved Chamberlain's objection aside. ''No, no. I understood your meaning. I'm sorry. It was purely a social call, with no connection to the kidnapping, except for one thing.''

''What's that?''

''It was on his schedule to see me that morning. So the

bogus chauffeur was able to tip off his henchmen. I want to help get Charles back, but I can't. I have nothing to add."

"What did you talk about?"

Ramsey looked at Chamberlain. "CIA?"

"Was."

"Quite. . . . We talked, like friends talk." Suddenly he brightened. "Do you know what?"

"What?" asked Helen. She'd been regarding him with a smile while Chamberlain asked the questions. Now she leaned forward, warm and attentive. "What did Charles say?"

"He invited me to come and live in Madagascar—Malagasy. You see, I worked East Africa for many years. Long before your time, Mr. Chamberlain. Before your CIA knew precisely where East Africa was located, as a matter of fact. He knows how the cold troubles me in England."

"That's wonderful. Are you going to go?"

"I told him I would. But now—yes I'll go, if Charles survives this. He said I could live on one of his plantations. Or in Tana. Or both. He's retiring there too, you know. Very—"

"He's always talked about that," Helen said. "Well, thank you for seeing us and—"

"He said he was through dealing. No more deals, he said. He's retiring."

"Charles Hammond retiring." Helen laughed. "I find that hard to believe."

"So did I."

"Just talk, I think. Goodbye, Major."

As they started down the front steps of the Overseas Club, Chamberlain stopped suddenly. Helen slipped and had to grab his arm. "What's wrong?"

"There. Across the park."

Through its bare trees and bushes, which were accumulating snow on their branches, he saw a man almost obscured by the glistening sleet.

"What? What's wrong?" Helen asked.

"See the guy walking on the other side of the park? See, he just turned into it, heading this way."

"In the black coat. Yes."

"He's the KGB man who killed Kreegan."

21

"What's he doing here?"

Chamberlain cursed himself for not bringing a gun. He'd taken the shot revolver from the plane, but he'd hidden it in the hotel room. London was no place to be caught carrying without all kinds of licenses, and Inspector Farquhar had made it too clear how little support he would be if Chamberlain got in trouble.

The man passed from sight, then reappeared. He was heading toward Herbert Crescent and now it was unmistakable that he was dressed entirely in black and carrying a short cane. Chamberlain looked at Helen. She couldn't run in those boots, but he had to get her out of the way. He looked up the street, from where they had come. Too far.

"Quick. Get back inside the club." He walked her, protesting, back up the stairs to the Overseas Club. "Go sit with Ramsey again. I'll get back to you as soon as I take care of this clown."

"What are you going to do?"

"What you pay me to do. Please get inside."

"Wait a minute," she said, irritated.

"You're putting me in a dangerous position. Will you please get inside?"

"It can't be the same man. What's he doing here?"

"That's the first thing I'm going to ask him, if you will just get out of my way."

She rang the doorbell. Chamberlain started back down the stairs as the door opened. He heard the butler invite her out of the snow.

Too late.

It had taken too long to get rid of her. The man in black had already emerged from the park and was well onto Herbert Crescent, flicking his cane against his pant leg and nervously eyeing the street. The instant he saw Chamberlain coming down the stairs of the Overseas Club, he turned and ran.

He had a thirty-yard lead. Chamberlain tore after him, astonished and elated. The guy was running because he didn't know that Chamberlain wasn't carrying and he didn't know that Chamberlain was alone. Which meant *he* was alone. And maybe wasn't carrying either.

The man in black ran like a scarecrow, the tails of his coat flapping, his heels kicking comically high. But he flew over the slippery ground, gaining with every gangling step, and when he had reached the end of Herbert Crescent he had increased his lead to forty yards.

Chamberlain pumped after him, slipping and sliding, encumbered by his overcoat, panicked by the guy's uncanny speed. The Russian turned unhesitatingly left when he hit the little park. Chamberlain rounded the turn seconds later, ignoring a clamoring voice in his brain that screamed that his quarry could be standing ten feet past the turn aiming a gun at his head.

He wasn't. He was still running, his lead greater. The distance between them had grown so that the sleet and snow partly obscured Chamberlain's view of him. When he turned the corner the wind hit his feet, driving the stinging sleet into his eyes, burning his cheeks. He thanked the good luck that he'd bought slip-on rubbers while waiting for Helen in the lobby. They gave him some traction. Still, he rounded the corner wide and had to slow for a second to regain his balance.

He sprinted ahead again, forcing his knees high against his coat. The Russian turned left again. By the time Chamberlain rounded that corner, he was almost out of sight, up a long, narrow street that ended at the road that ran behind Harrods.

Chamberlain tore at his buttons, flung off his coat. The Russian jinked right when he reached the end of the narrow street. Chamberlain ran blindly until he reached the corner. Slithering right, again ignoring the chance that he'd be gawking down the Russian's gun barrel, he raced around the corner and searched desperately for a sign of him.

Harrods department store took up the entire left side of the street, a high brick wall with dark windows. No one was out in the thickening snow. Street lights glowed dully in the dusk. He ran. A car horn sounded behind him. He flung a glance over his shoulder. A taxi cab. Chamberlain kept running.

Ahead was Sloane Street, cars and buses lined up and moving slowly on the busy thoroughfare. If the Russian made it there, he would never find him. A flutter of black suddenly darted through the snow, crossed the street, and vanished inside Harrods.

Chamberlain reached the door seconds later. Bursting through the foyer into the main store, he found himself suddenly in a crowd. He worked through it, breathing heavily. It was warm in the store. The snow melted instantly on his shoulders.

He rose on tiptoe and tried to see over the heads and hats of the shoppers. The man in black was crossing an aisle almost a hundred yards away. Chamberlain started after him, sprinting in empty spaces, then elbowing through clusters of customers.

He veered away from cash register areas as he plunged deeper into the store. Twice he lost sight of the man in black, only to spot him again, trapped as he was among the jostling crowd. The shoppers were concentrated around elevators and stairways and Chamberlain realized that it was almost five o'clock, near closing time. He lost the man in black again. He climbed onto a display counter a salesgirl was covering with a muslin cloth and, despite her perplexed inquiries, scanned the giant store.

The man in black was running down a staircase. Chamberlain leaped from the counter and charged after him. He descended two steps at a time and found himself in a white-tiled fish and meat room. The butchers were storing their wares and boys were scooping ice from the empty fish trays. Two customers were left, paying at a cash register, but the man in black had vanished.

Chamberlain saw two exits. He darted from one to the other. The Russian could have gone either way. He chose the door that led to the busiest part of the store and began searching faces among the departing shoppers. He had seen nothing by the time he was back outside. He looked up and down the street. The sidewalks were mobbed with people heading for the Underground.

He took a chance and went into the station and down the long escalator to the trains. There were several turns the Russian could have taken. Chamberlain walked the crowded platforms, scrutinizing faces and clothing, but when two trains had come and gone, he realized it was hopeless. Wearily, shivering now as his perspiration dried in the cold air, he made his way up to the surface and walked up Sloane and around Harrods, back toward the Overseas Club.

He found his coat where a thoughtful citizen had draped it over an iron fence and got into it gratefully. His hair was soaked from the snow and he buttoned the coat to his neck as he walked quickly toward Herbert Crescent. The snow was filling in the long, skidding footsteps he and the man in black had made on the street.

The butler remembered him.

"Mr. Chamberlain, yes. I'll tell the lady you're back."

Helen came out in five minutes. She greeted Chamberlain with a small smile. "Where's your dangerous captive?"

"I lost him."

"You certainly were dramatic about it."

Chamberlain said nothing. He rose while the butler helped Helen into her sable. The butler offered to telephone for a mini-cab, but suggested they would have better luck on Sloane Street because it was rush hour.

Helen said they would walk awhile, but when they got down the steps and into the full force of the now-blowing snow, she decided otherwise. "I guess we'd better get a cab." She took his arm again as they started slogging back the way they had come.

"Ramsey tell you anything more?"

"No."

"Anything more about Hammond retiring?"

"Not really. I think Charles might have said that to encourage Ramsey to accept his hospitality. You know, he might have said he would be lonely down in Malagasy and Ramsey would be doing him a favor. Sorry, Pete. I was hoping for a little better too. But it was just a holiday visit."

"Are you sure he's telling the truth?" Chamberlain asked doggedly. An experienced agent would find it easy to play the role of a half-dotty old man. But Helen was sure.

"He's just a nice old guy who was happy to have a visitor." She squeezed his arm, and Chamberlain turned to her. "Do you know what he did?" she asked with a grin.

"What?"

"Took me up to his room on the pretext of showing me his collection of African masks, and patted my bottom."

"You must have made his week."

"I stood still long enough to make his month. Hey, are we getting a cab or not?"

"As soon as we see one."

"What's wrong with you?"

"Nothing that catching that Russian son of a bitch wouldn't have cured."

She stopped and appraised him with her arresting dark eyes. "You look cold and you're wet and I know a better cure. Come on, I'll buy you a drink." They were on Sloane Street, caught between hordes of shoppers streaming toward the Underground and other hordes fighting for taxis.

"Fine by me," said Chamberlain, looking around for a pub.

"Not here. Come on, cross the street, we'll go down there and over to Motcomb." They walked for five minutes on streets that grew quieter and quieter until she turned into a pub nestled among houses and small shops. Inside, the air was thick with cigarette smoke and the subdued roar of a drinking crowd that lined the bar and filled every table.

It was a neighborhood place for men and women of all ages stopping off on their way from work. It was warm and friendly and it told Chamberlain that Helen Thorp knew this part of London very well. He wondered again whose apartment she stayed in when she came to London.

She plowed through the people around the bar, exchanging smiles and remarks with those she jostled, and returned to Chamberlain with two glasses.

The man in black had followed Chamberlain out of the Underground and back to the Overseas Club. When Chamberlain had come out with Helen Thorp, he had followed them to the pub on Motcomb Street. When he could see through the foggy windows that they were here to stay, he hurried back to Herbert Crescent to have a chat with the major. What did Ramsey know about Hammond's plan? And what had he told Helen Thorp and Chamberlain?

"Double whiskeys. Hope you like 'em."
"Perfect. Thanks."
"Cheers."
"Cheers." He met her eye for an instant, marveling at this side of her he hadn't seen—her ease and pleasure at the busy bar and her warm delight at being alive. He reflected that he had met her under the worst conditions, right after Hammond was kidnapped. And he wondered again, for the fortieth time, what their relationship was.
"Have you lived in London?" he asked.
"Bits and pieces. Several months at a time. Have you?"
"No. New York's my only city."
"What about Washington?"
"That's no city."
She laughed. "True. Actually, I think every real New Yorker needs a country house in London."
Chamberlain smiled at her smile. She had a beautiful full mouth.
"Where'd you grow up?" she asked.
He told her a little about Connecticut and his first curious visits to New York City and how he had settled in Greenwich Village for college.
"NYU? You must have been bright. Their business school was my second choice after Wharton. It was tough to get in."
"I think they had a quota to balance the student body, so they let small-town types like me in if we could read and write. The crunch came when they asked me to think."
"What did you do?"
"Joined the navy."
"Would you like another drink?"
"Sure. Let me get it."
The crowd began to thin out at six-thirty and by seven o'clock the pub was almost empty. Helen said, "There's a nice place in Covent Garden for dinner, just around the corner from the hotel. Care to join me?"

"Sure. Thanks."

"It'll be fun. Let's go back and change."

It was still snowing and the streets were empty. They walked to Belgrave Square and found a cab which took them slowly and cautiously across London.

As was his custom, when the Savoy doorman opened the cab door, he said, "Good evening, madame. Good evening, sir." Then he added in a barely audible mutter, "The police are waiting in the lobby, Mr. Chamberlain. For the lady."

Chamberlain nodded his thanks, caught up with Helen at the revolving door, and whispered into her hair. "We've got cops. I don't know why."

She turned her face to his as if to kiss him, and whispered back, "Inspector Farquhar is sitting on the couch. Do you want to run for it?"

"What?"

"I'm kidding, you idiot." She kissed him on the mouth. "*That* ought to give him something to think about. Let's go see what he wants."

She pushed through the revolving door and Chamberlain followed, thinking that the taste and softness of her lips were giving him as much to think about as the sight of her kissing him was giving Farquhar.

Farquhar got quickly to his feet. Chamberlain spotted two of his plainclothes backup men moving casually closer. The KGB and CIA observers watched almost openly. Farquhar's polite smile was nowhere in evidence. He looked one hundred percent cop. One hundred percent angry cop. He said hello, with a chilly glint in his eye, and got right to the point.

"Ms. Thorp. I'm afraid I'm going to have to ask you a few difficult questions. Shall we go to your suite or would you—"

"My suite would be fine, provided you tell me what this is about first."

"This is about the murder of Major Donald Ramsey in his rooms at the Overseas Club this evening."

Chamberlain looked at Helen, but she showed nothing. She was as cool as she was behind her desk in New York, and she said just what he was thinking. "Murdered?"

"He was found after you left."

"Are you suggesting I should have a lawyer while you ask your questions?" She glanced once at Chamberlain and he wondered, how hard is she? As hard as this act of hers? Or is it an act?

"That's your decision," Farquhar replied.

"I'll take Mr. Chamberlain to witness."

They rode silently up in the elevator. Chamberlain thought that the entire exchange in the lobby must have looked like a simple business meeting to anyone who could not hear the words. He thought that Farquhar was being a bit theatrical, but supposed it was his way of softening a witness—were it anyone without the balls of Helen Thorp. How Farquhar could suspect her was beyond belief, or certainly would be if Farquhar had heard her talking about the old man the way she had.

A third plainclothes officer was standing outside the Comptel suite, hands clasped behind his back, at parade rest. Farquhar nodded to him and he stood aside as they entered the suite and closed the door. Helen sat in an easy chair, her back to a corner.

"All right, Inspector, what is this all about?"

Her no-nonsense tone infuriated Farquhar. The British inspector reddened visibly. He made no effort now to hide his feelings. Mimicking her tone with devastating accuracy, he said, "This is about a fine old gentleman, a patriot, a war hero, a devoted public servant, being murdered in cold blood in the club he chose to make his final home. And it is about the fact that you were his last visitor."

"Was he seen alive after I left?"

"No."

"Then why are you subjecting me to this nonsense instead of arresting me?"

"I'm very tempted . . . If I had one more shred of evidence—"

"But you have none," Helen shot back.

"Wait," Chamberlain said. "Wait a minute both of you. Farquhar, did you know Major Ramsey personally?"

"I had that honor." Farquhar drew himself up ramrod straight.

"I'm sorry. And I'm sure Ms. Thorp is sorry too. But she certainly didn't murder him. You know that, Farquhar."

"I *am* sorry," Helen said quietly. "It's extremely upsetting."

"Yes, it is," said Farquhar. "Extremely. Perhaps I should apologize too for letting it color my actions."

"What can we do to help?" asked Chamberlain.

"Tell me why you visited him," said Farquhar.

Helen Thorp stared at the floor. At first Chamberlain thought she was thinking, then he realized that she hadn't heard. "Helen?" he asked gently. They'd shifted easily to first names at the pub. "Ms. Thorp?"

She shuddered and when she raised her eyes they were filled with tears. "Excuse me." She stood up and walked to the bedroom.

Farquhar and Chamberlain exchanged glances. So she wasn't so hard. It just seemed that her first reaction was to stay tough. Later she let go, when she thought she was safe.

"She'll be back," Chamberlain said quietly. "I can answer the question if you want."

"Please."

"Hammond was kidnapped right after meeting with Ramsey. We wanted to know what they talked about."

Chamberlain waited for a response, but Farquhar said nothing. He paced a few steps back and forth, then went to the couch. The two men sat silently for several minutes, until Helen Thorp came back from her bedroom.

She had dried her eyes and evidently fixed her makeup, but she was deathly pale and seemed to be struggling to maintain control. Chamberlain noticed the depth of her upset, and recalled again how animatedly she had described Ramsey taking her upstairs to see his African masks. The old major had struck a very deep chord in Helen Thorp.

"Excuse me, Inspector. I'll answer your questions now."

"Would you care to sit down?" asked Farquhar.

"I'll stand."

"Mr. Chamberlain has told me why you went to see the major."

"Yes. Pete felt we might learn something about Hammond's recent activities which might be helpful. It seemed worth a try."

"Well, could you tell me briefly what you and the major discussed."

Chamberlain got up and walked to the window. He moved the thick curtain aside and looked at the snow. The Russian must have doubled back and entered the club through a back way or window and surprised the old man in his room, about the time he and Helen were at the pub.

When Helen finished telling Farquhar the things she had told him, the inspector asked a few brief questions, then said, "Thank you for your cooperation." He rose from the couch and faced Helen, who had remained standing throughout. "Ordinarily," he said, "I would ask you to remain in London until my investigation was complete, but I realize that in this instance you may have to leave hurriedly to attend your auction. I will accept your word that you will return immediately, if and when I need you."

"You have my word," Helen said.

"Thank you. Ah, Peter, I wonder if you would accompany me for an hour or so?"

Chamberlain looked at Helen, although Farquhar's question was more a demand than an invitation. "Are you all right?"

"Yes. Go ahead. I'd just as soon be alone."

"You're sure?"

"I'll see you in the morning."

"Can I bring you anything?"

"I'll get something to eat from room service. Good night, Pete. Good evening, Inspector Farquhar."

Out in the hall, after Farquhar had dismissed the plainclothesman and they were walking to the elevator, he said, "I gather this falls in the midst of an otherwise very pleasant evening."

"I've seen better timing," Chamberlain admitted. "What can I do for you?"

"I warned you not to mess about in London." He stabbed viciously at the elevator button and Chamberlain saw that despite his gentle treatment of Helen, the inspector was still seething.

"We were curious," said Chamberlain. "We just went to talk to the guy, that was all."

The elevator came and they got in. Chamberlain looked for the plainclothesman, but he had apparently taken the stairs. The doors closed and Farquhar exploded angrily.

"And then you went chasing a man through the streets and dashing around inside Harrods like a pack of cheeky schoolboys. The store telephoned a complaint. Why didn't you open fire on him? There couldn't have been that many shoppers about at that hour."

"I don't carry a gun."

"You bloody well better not, or I'll have you in Dartmoor till the second coming." He patted both sides of Chamberlain's jacket with quick, expert strokes and seemed disappointed when he found no weapon. Chamberlain wondered how he would get the gun in his room back aboard Comptel's plane. The elevator doors opened on the lobby and he followed Farquhar outside into the snow.

When they had walked beyond earshot of the doorman, Farquhar asked, "Where the devil do you think you are? Some banana republic where you entertain the natives with spy adventures? Who were you chasing?"

"A Russian. Probably KGB. He shot a guy who was working with me in Brest. Yesterday."

"An employee of your firm?"

"Yes."

Farquhar stopped on the corner where the Savoy drive met the Strand. "And you were intending to wreak revenge in the streets of London?" he asked disgustedly.

Chamberlain shivered. The wet snow was melting on his bare head, starting to soak his hair again. He said, "I'm looking for Charles Hammond. I wanted to know what the hell this guy was doing outside the Overseas Club."

"And what do you think?"

"It seemed like a hell of a coincidence, but I guess he had the same idea at the same time that Ms. Thorp and I did."

"What idea?"

"To check out what Hammond was up to. I guess he's grasping at straws just like us."

"Do you think that he went back and killed Ramsey?"

"Was Ramsey beaten?"

"There was a single mark on his face," said Farquhar, looking at Chamberlain sharply. "We weren't sure what caused it."

"Did it *kill* him?"

"He was shot."

"A Beretta?"

"Yes. Apparently Ramsey was going for his own revolver, but he was too slow."

"This guy moves like greased lightning."

"The major used to," said Farquhar, staring at the snow.

"Did he get off a shot?" asked Chamberlain.

"No," said Farquhar. "Not this time." He raised his hand and further down the Strand a dark Jaguar with a long radio antenna, parked in front of Simpsons, turned on its lights and skidded away from the slush-filled curb.

"How'd you happen to know Ramsey?" asked Chamberlain.

Farquhar hesitated. "Well, as a matter of fact, we met in Kenya. I was doing a stint with the colonial constabulary and he was a captain then, somehow attached to MI-Five. He was doing counterinsurgency work against the Mau Mau. Rather successfully, too, as it turned out. I came back to the Yard, but he stayed for years, even after independence. Tremendously knowledgeable fellow. There wasn't a thing about East Africa he didn't know."

He took Chamberlain's arm as the Jaguar slid to a halt in front of them. "Tell me more about this Russian."

The man in black saw the Scotland Yard inspector and the American CIA agent get into an unmarked police car and drive away up the Strand. Hardly believing his eyes, he watched the dark car until it vanished at Trafalger Square. Luck, at last.

Still he hesitated. The fool inside—the KGB observer—could wreck everything. He couldn't go in the back because he needed the keys to the Comptel suite and he couldn't wait for the agent to come out because there wasn't time. There was no time left.

To get past the doormen, he carried his cane like a swagger stick and snapped it to his temple in a smart salute. They scurried to help him through. And of course the KGB fool inside gaped like the fool he was. Fortunately, the CIA observer was an even bigger fool. He'd become engrossed in the newspaper he was supposed to be reading for cover.

The man in black quickly crossed the lobby, commanding the fool to follow him, with his eyes. He ducked into an open elevator and held the door for him while he stayed out of sight of the CIA observer, who had at last lowered his newspaper and was watching his KGB counterpart enter the elevator. The CIA observer was beginning to get up from the couch, his face wreathed in puzzlement, when the elevator door closed. The man in black pressed several floor buttons.

"What are you doing here?" blurted the KGB observer.

He flicked his cane under the fool's chin and tapped him hard. "I will flay you alive the next time you give me away."

The professorial Czech barely flinched and the man in black reflected that pawns had an often unerring instinct for sensing their master's difficulties.

"You surprised me," he said. "You weren't supposed to enter the hotel. They told me you weren't."

"Give me the woman's keys." The Kremlin's replacement for him was probably already in London, waiting. Or gone ahead to Arabia.

The Czech pulled a handful of Savoy room keys from his pocket and picked through them until he found the right one. The elevator stopped and the man in black stepped into the hall.

"Ride up and down several times, stopping at each floor, then return to the lobby. Call me on the house phone the instant Chamberlain returns."

He traced the room numbers down the long hall. His observers had located the rooms of every participant in the Pendragon auction. He found the right door, pressed his ear to it, and listened. He was not supposed to enter the hotel. But the penalties for disobeying would be mild compared to the penalty for not getting Charles Hammond back in time.

Helen Thorp had felt herself falling apart when Chamberlain and Farquhar had gone. Tears flooded her eyes again. She looked at herself in the mirror. Her mouth was trembling. Bringing an iron will to bear, she forced herself to meet her own eyes. When at last she could think of more than the old man dying, she left the mirror, drew a deep, hot bath, and soaked the chill from her body. She lay in the water a long time, letting her thoughts drift. When they threatened to grow too hard to bear, or too complex, she turned to cleaner, simpler ideas. And then, to memories. Hammond. . . .

When the Clipper had landed in London, after their dinner over the Atlantic, Hammond had asked her down to Dorset for the weekend. She had refused. And back in New York, she refused his next invitation to dinner. What he had done on the Clipper was charming, but it didn't change anything. She was terrified of him.

She knew that he had the power to devour her. She knew it as surely as she knew that she did not want to be devoured by anyone. He sent her a mirror. It was crystal and gold and had its own rosewood box for when she traveled. "Look how lucky I am," said his note. "See what I see."

To her surprise, Helen Thorp started to cry again.

The tears passed. They meant nothing. She was tired. It was time to get out of the tub and go to sleep.

She dried with a warm towel from the steam-heated rack, removed her shower cap, and shook out her long, dark hair. Then she wrapped herself in a thick terry robe and stepped into her bedroom.

A man waited in the armchair beside her bed. He held a black cane in one hand and a gun in the other and the first thought that penetrated her shock was that she had never realized how far you could see down the barrel.

"What did Major Ramsey tell you?"

"What?" That was the last thing she had expected to hear, and she gasped out her surprise before she realized that this was the man Peter Chamberlain had chased at Herbert Crescent—the cane and the black clothes—which meant he was the Russian who had killed Kreegan and Major Ramsey. Now she was afraid.

"What did Major Ramsey tell you?" he repeated loudly.

"Nothing. I don't know what you're talking about."

She could see a pulse beating in his temple. He was skeletal. The bones showed in his face. His skull seemed to strain against his skin. Though he sat with one leg draped over the other, his whole frame was rigid with tension.

"I have no more time," he snapped. "I won't be misled by the CIA."

"I'm not the CIA," Helen blurted with relief. It was a mistake. When he realized it was mistake, he would leave.

He ignored her. "I will kill you if you don't tell me what Major Ramsey told you."

"He didn't tell me anything."

He raised the gun.

"You can't shoot a gun in here," she heard herself saying in rational tones. "Everyone will hear you."

"The walls are thick. No one will hear. And if they do, what happens to me won't alter the fact that you are dead."

Helen felt the blood drain from her face. "He didn't tell me anything. He just talked about his past."

"You're lying."

She bolted through the sitting room door, half in terror, half realizing that he wouldn't shoot her before she told him what he wanted. Ten feet from the front door he caught her. He thrust his cane between her legs, tripped her, and fell on top of her as she sprawled.

Clamping a powerful hand over her mouth, he silenced her scream and forced her to the floor, pressing his other arm against her throat, squeezing her windpipe until she was pinned flat on her back, fighting to breathe. His face was inches from hers, his clothing rough against her skin where the robe had ridden up her legs.

"I have no time," he muttered. "No time."

She kicked futilely. His eyes passed down her body and fixed on her bare legs. "No time, no time," he mumbled again, but even as he uttered the urgent words, the anxious light was vanishing from his eyes, obliterated by a fierce new glow—mad, sexual, and utterly terrifying.

He was far stronger than he looked. He lifted her off the floor, one bony hand still clamped over her mouth, and carried her effortlessly back to the bedroom. Kicking the door shut, he threw her on the bed so hard that she was stunned, her arms and legs pinwheeling wildly.

Before she could recover he forced her onto her belly, ramming her face into the bedspread, sat on her buttocks, and tied her hands behind her with the belt from her terry robe. She arched her back and tried to scream. He pulled a perfumed handkerchief between her lips and tied it tightly.

Bound, gagged, powerless to move her hands or speak, Helen Thorp felt a terror that doubled her own strength. She rolled onto her back and levered a knee into his groin. He grunted and fell off her. She kept rolling, heading for the telephone.

He got there first, rolled her back across the bed and forced her again onto her stomach. She felt her strength failing. She made herself stop struggling in order to husband it, but even as she got a grip on her panic, he snatched her pantyhose from the dresser top and tied her ankles.

Then he got off the bed. She drew deep, shuddering breaths, fighting to contain the panic that was starting to overwhelm her, fighting to remember that she had to stay sane to get out of this.

"What did Ramsey tell you?" the man in black asked silkily. His whole voice and manner had changed. He was enjoying himself, gloating. He picked up his cane.

She lay quietly, watching him, surreptitiously testing the belt around her wrists. She had to somehow get the gag out of her mouth and scream. He twisted his cane's ivory handle. Her eyes widened in disbelief.

Smiling, he separated the handle from the cane, unsheathing a long, thin black riding crop.

"What did Major Ramsey tell you?"

She shook her head to indicate she couldn't speak through the gag. He drew the whip through his fingers. "Perhaps you will nod your head when you are ready to talk." She tried to say that she had nothing to tell him, but she couldn't talk through the gag. He rolled her onto her stomach again.

She watched over her shoulder, unable to believe this was happening to her. He raised the whip, swished it sharply through the air, then took the hem of her robe in his other hand. He lifted it slowly, prolonging the moment. She shivered spasmodically as she felt the terrycloth sliding up her legs.

"I hope, for your sake, he told you something."

She shook her head violently. No. Nothing.

He smiled, his teeth as white as his awful, bony cheeks. "A shame. I ask you once more. What did Ramsey say?"

He raised the whip higher and slowly, inch by inch, bared her buttocks.

22

"He'll be terribly disappointed if you tell him," a woman called mockingly from the door.

The man in black froze with Helen's robe in one hand and his whip poised high in the other. Only his eyes moved. The pleasure flashed out of them and they turned hard and flat, flickering from side to side, assessing the threat.

"Turn around very slowly," said the woman. Helen couldn't see her, but she recognized the drawl of an English aristocrat. She felt her robe settle protectively over her legs as the man in black let it go and slowly faced the door. She released her fear-stiffened muscles and sagged into the mattress.

"Completely around. And raise your hands higher. *Both* hands."

Helen twisted her neck so she could see. The man in black was turning like a robot, turning to face a beautiful woman holding a gun. She was a startling sight, a great beauty with lovely, golden hair and exquisite clothes. Vast blue eyes burned in an exhausted face. They never left the man with the whip.

Beside her hulked a huge man in an incongruously new

overcoat and a broad-brimmed hat pulled low over his blotched face. He looked as if he had dressed for the specific purpose of walking into the Savoy Hotel.

The man in black exploded into motion. One moment he was standing beside the bed with his hands high in the air, one holding the whip, the next instant he was flying over the bed, over Helen. His free hand flashed into his jacket and pulled out a gun while he was still in the air.

The blond woman fired three times—three muffled bangs hardly louder than a door slamming—and when the man in black hit the floor on the other side of the bed, his gun fell from a lifeless hand.

The giant crossed the room in two strides and knelt by the body, his hands poised.

"*Mort,*" he said to the woman. She pocketed her gun, went to the body, and stared down at it, her face working. The big man waited, saying nothing. Finally, she bent over Helen and removed her gag.

She babbled her relief. "Thank you. Thank God, thank you."

The blond woman surveyed her coolly. "You are a lucky woman."

"Oh I know. Thank you. Could you . . . undo my hands, please?"

"Where is the auction?"

"What?"

"Where is Grandzau's auction?" She swept an impatient hand through her hair. Helen, sick with relief but now stunned by the woman's question, heard a ridiculous thought run through her mind. How did she keep her hair so perfect? She was clearly hours from collapse. She looked like she hadn't slept in days and her eyes glistened as if she were running on pills. She repeated her question.

Helen gaped stupidly up at her, unable to believe that this savior wouldn't untie her.

"Henri!"

The man was examining the fallen riding crop. He murmured, smiling, "How sad we haven't the time for a lengthy interrogation." He dropped the whip, rolled Helen onto her back, and pulled a long, transparent knife from the folds of his coat. He moved it subtly so Helen could see the light glittering on its razor edge.

"Where is the auction?"

"Wait," cried Helen, trying to shrink from the knife. "Wait a minute. I don't know. They haven't told us yet. They just told us to come to the Savoy." The woman watched her expressionlessly. Helen looked from her to the knife to the man. "We think it's still on the seventh. The day after tomorrow."

"Where?"

"I told you, we don't know. They haven't said."

"Henri."

"Wait, please. Wait! The police. Scotland Yard, they think that the man holding the auction—"

"Grandzau."

"They think he's chartered a Concorde to fly us to the Persian Gulf."

"What?" the woman asked incredulously. She looked at her partner. He shook his head.

"It's true," Helen cried desperately. "I swear it."

"When?"

"Probably tomorrow night or the next day."

"What airport?"

"I don't know what airport. This is crazy. Ask them. What airport do Concordes fly from?"

The woman and the man looked at each other again.

"That's all I know," Helen said wearily. "Please untie me."

"Let's go," said the woman.

"What about her?"

"Somebody will come along. Let's go."

"But she saw you kill him," said the man, nodding toward the body on the floor.

Helen paled. "No. No I didn't, I won't say a thing."

"She'll never see me again," said the woman. "Besides, neither I nor you, nor probably he, entered Britain through Immigration. I'll take the chance."

"We must kill her."

"No, Henri. It will just bring pressure. Leave her."

"You go ahead," said the giant, tapping the flat of his blade in his hand. "I'll take care of this."

Chamberlain said as he climbed out of Farquhar's car in front of the Savoy, "Oh, one thing. Helen Thorp mentioned that Major Ramsey was kicked out of Kenya by the new government when England left. But you said he stayed on."

"It was rather sticky," answered Farquhar. "First they gave him the boot. Shortly thereafter they grew open-minded enough to realize they needed his sort of expertise, so they invited him back. Are you sure you won't have a drink? There's a nice little American place in the next street. Theatrical, but I daresay they wouldn't deny a compatriot."

Chamberlain wanted to see if Helen had waited up for him. "I better pass. Tomorrow might be a long day."

"Cheerio."

"Good night."

He entered his room from the hall, hoping to find that she had opened the connecting door to her suite. She hadn't. His room was dark, hot, and stuffy. She'd gone straight to bed. He debated looking for the bar Farquhar had mentioned. Then he noticed the light under the connecting door. He started to knock, then thought better of it. She might have gone to sleep and left the living room lights burning.

He thought of the phone. But if she'd forgotten to alert the switchboard, he'd wake her, which wouldn't be a good idea considering how upset she'd been earlier. Best to leave her alone.

Then he heard voices. A man's low tones rumbled through the door. "Son of a bitch," Chamberlain muttered, wondering if it was the guy she usually stayed with in London. So much for her upset.

A woman spoke, insistent, persuasive. It didn't sound like Helen. Then he heard her voice. He pressed his ear to the door. He couldn't hear the words, but she sounded frightened. The voices were distant, as if they were coming from Helen's bedroom.

Chamberlain pressed an electronically amplified sound pickup against the door and listened closely. He slipped it back in his pocket and gently turned the key, concentrating on turning the latch without making it click. Softly, he opened the door and peered into the living room. It was empty and the voices were coming clearly from her bedroom. The man and the woman were arguing. She sounded English, he, French. Upper-class English.

He thought of Grandzau's agent, Lady Janet Isling, and crept silently back to his closet, where he had hidden Kreegan's gun. Then he slipped into the living room and glided cautiously toward the voices. He was halfway across when Helen Thorp gave a fearful cry. Chamberlain abandoned caution and walked straight into her room.

Helen was huddled on the bed, partly clad in a bathrobe, her hands and feet bound. The man who had knifed the KGB agents in Marseilles had his blade to her throat. Dead, at his feet, was the Russian in black. Three bullet holes occupied a six-inch circle in the center of his chest. That left Lady Janet Isling with the gun.

He felt her rush from the left, stepped under her swing, grabbed her arm and twisted it sharply behind her, bending it high to force her to drop her gun. It thudded to the rug. He pinned her tightly in his arms and put his shot revolver to her head. He spoke to the man with the knife.

''Back off.''

Helen gaped at him in astonishment, then cringed as the man touched the edge of his blade to her throat. He looked at Chamberlain with a bloated smile.

''Perhaps I care less for my lady than you do for yours.''

Chamberlain squeezed her tighter and thrust his hip into her buttocks so she couldn't kick him in the groin. ''Back off,'' he repeated, walking her to the side, edging toward a clearer shot at the guy.

The Frenchman pivoted with him, holding his knife to Helen and keeping her between him and Chamberlain. ''No, monsieur. *You* back off. She means nothing to me.''

''Maybe not, mister, but after you cut my lady and I shoot yours, I'll still have my gun but you'll only have a knife.''

The Frenchman eyed him fearlessly. ''I have taken revolvers from men your size before.''

''This one fires buckshot,'' replied Chamberlain.

That shut him up for a moment, and Chamberlain was relieved to see that if he didn't give a damn about the woman's life, he at least cared for his own enough to think about it.

''Henri,'' the woman hissed. ''Hammond. Remember. Remember Hammond.'' What the hell was she talking about, wondered Chamberlain.

"*Alors*? For that scum I should merely *back off*."

"*Yes*!" she commanded, shuddering with effort. "Do as he says, Henri. *Remember*." She shook in Chamberlain's arms like a taut steel cable. The Frenchman wasn't buying it.

Chamberlain watched him helplessly. He couldn't fire the shot revolver so close to Helen.

"Henri Trefle does not *back off*. It is a question of honor."

Chamberlain cursed himself for getting the guy's back up. He shouldn't have threatened his pride. "It's a Mexican standoff," he said soothingly. "The best way out of a Mexican standoff is we *both* back off. You look like a pro, mister. Why don't we both get out of this thing professionally?"

The guy peered at him owlishly and Chamberlain realized he was half-drunk. The woman took up his point, relaxing in his arms to communicate her agreement.

"Yes, Henri. The man is right. You are both professionals."

Henri said nothing and didn't move. He loomed over Helen like a puzzled bull. His expression was unreadable when Lady Janet tried again to persuade him.

"We just want to get away, Henri. It doesn't matter what happens here."

Chamberlain shot a glance at Helen. She was starting to shake. Another minute and she'd be unable to remember that her life depended on not moving a hair. He looked back at Henri. Nothing. The expression on his blotched face was unfathomable.

Then Chamberlain felt his own concentration waver. The source of distraction was Lady Janet. Since she had stopped struggling, to indicate that she supported him in the matter of Henri, her body had transformed itself from tensed, hostile bone and muscle to soft breasts and gently swelling hips.

It was crazy. He'd get killed that way. But her odor was electrifying, and despite the fact that her gun lay close by on the rug and she might be throwing him off guard, Chamberlain remembered that the smartest woman he'd ever slept with had told him that harmonious smells fueled the richest sex.

Crazy. He kicked her gun farther away. Then she trembled. It lasted a single, unguarded instant and he felt her steel herself against a repeat. She'd felt it too. Then the moment was gone.

Helen started trembling violently. He couldn't wait any longer.

"I'll make the first move," said Chamberlain. "I'll step away from your lady."

"You have a gun," Trefle complained sullenly. "What does stepping away mean when you have a gun?"

Chamberlain released Lady Janet and backed up two paces, training his weapon on her.

"Pick up your gun."

She found his eyes before she reached for it. Her pupils were black pencil points. A drunk and a junkie, thought Chamberlain. What a combination. "I won't shoot," he promised. "Pick it up."

She picked it up and pointed it at him. "All right, Henri. You can let her go now."

Henri Trefle said nothing. She glanced at him, wetting her lips. "Henri!"

Helen tried to jerk back from the knife. Trefle clamped a huge hand around the back of her neck and pushed her forward to his blade. Lady Janet fumbled in her coat pocket and lifted some red pills to her lips.

Chamberlain shook his head. "Not now, lady. Please not now."

Helen whimpered. He could hear in her voice that she was flaking out beyond caring.

Lady Janet stared at her pills.

"We need you whole," said Chamberlain. "Please don't."

Lady Janet looked at him, slowly tipped her hand and let them fall to the floor.

"Thank you."

"Henri! Let's go!" Her order carried a new intensity that cut through his resistance. He backed away from the bed and sheathed his knife in a swift, liquid motion. Then he swaggered toward the door, pointedly ignoring Chamberlain, but stealing a glance at the revolver that fired buckshot.

Chamberlain and Lady Janet looked at each other. He would have given years of his life to know what she was thinking.

"I'll stay here," he said. "You just go."

They backed out silently, through the sitting room and into the hall. Helen broke into muffled sobs. When he heard the door click shut, Chamberlain sat down beside her, covered her beautiful legs, and untied her hands and feet.

"Oh my God," Helen moaned. "Oh my God."

"It's over." He drew her gently into his arms and held her, pulling the bedspread over her to keep her warm, stroking her back to comfort her. Gradually her sobs eased and when she no longer trembled with them, he poured her a neat Scotch from the bar in the living room and held it to her lips until she was able to take the glass and sat up and drink by herself.

"How do you feel?"

"Awful. Please hold me some more."

Chamberlain embraced her until she stopped shaking. "Do you want to talk about it now? Or after I call the police?"

"What for?"

"We've got a body in our suite."

"Call them now. I want it out of here."

He telephoned Scotland Yard and asked them to call Farquhar at home. Farquhar arrived at midnight, by which time Helen had recovered enough to change into her clinging silk robe, brush her hair until it shone, and apply some makeup. She sat in the armchair, quietly sipping her second Scotch while Chamberlain outlined what had happened and an angry Inspector Farquhar studied the body.

"I gave you a clear warning," he said to Chamberlain.

"I didn't kill him," Chamberlain protested. "The woman did."

"Yes, and who was this woman?"

"I don't know," Chamberlain lied. He felt a debt to her for helping them out of the standoff with her partner. "She was blond and had a thick German accent."

Helen Thorp looked into her glass.

"Would you like to explain the sequence of events again?"

Chamberlain repeated what Helen had told him. Then Farquhar turned to Helen and asked her to explain what had happened. She related the same story.

Farquhar listened, tight-lipped, then made a couple of telephone calls and, a short time later, admitted to the suite several detectives and the Savoy's night manager, whom he engaged in a whispered conversation. The detectives photographed the room and everything in it, then took the dead man's fingerprints and fed them into a portable facsimile machine they attached to the telephone.

The night manager left, looking worried, and Farquhar glared impatiently at the facsimile machine.

"You won't find his fingerprints filed in the Yard," said Chamberlain.

"I'm not asking the Yard," replied Farquhar.

"MI-Five?"

"Why don't you mind your own business, old son?"

"You won't find him there either."

"What makes you so sure of that?"

"I already told you. The Central Intelligence Agency doesn't have a file on him and they share that kind of info back and forth with your intelligence people. You know that."

"Perhaps we file our 'info' differently," Farquhar replied dryly. "Now tell me more about this Frenchman."

"Big man. Two-fifty at least. Stones? How many stones is two hundred and fifty pounds? I don't know. You figure it out. Very big. I saw him in Marseilles for a second, swinging his glass knife. Tempered glass. He looks like a drunk, but in Marseilles he moved awfully fast for a drunk."

"Go on."

"The woman called him Henri. He referred to himself as Henri Trefle, as if his name meant something special. Big rep, I guess. I figure him for a merc."

"Certainly sounds likely. And the woman with the French accent?"

"German."

"Ah yes." Farquhar placed another telephone call and spoke at length. Chamberlain sat down beside Helen. She reached for his hand and held it tightly while the police stenographer typed her statement.

When Farquhar hung up, Chamberlain asked, "Shouldn't she have a lawyer?"

"It's all right, Pete," said Helen. "I'm fine."

"You're welcome to one," said Farquhar, "but you can be sure this isn't going to be any sort of trial. MI-Five has sent the word down through the Foreign Office. They've identified the dead man and they'll slap a D notice on the whole affair."

"Who is he?" asked Chamberlain.

Farquhar flashed a snapshot of Lady Janet. "Could this have been the woman?"

"I don't think so," said Chamberlain.

"It's rather a clear photograph."

"It's not her."

"Ms. Thorp?"

Helen glanced at it. "I'm sorry, Inspector. I hardly remember a thing about her. I was too frightened."

"Have another look, Peter."

Chamberlain dutifully inspected the picture. It was of professional quality. She looked younger, dressed in horse clothes, smiling. She'd become more beautiful since then.

"It's not the woman I saw."

"Strange. She's supposed to have spent some time with Trefle. You're right, incidentally. He's a mercenary soldier. I'll have more on him shortly. The thing is, this woman also was involved with Herr Grandzau."

"You're kidding," said Chamberlain, beginning to wish he hadn't gotten involved in the lie. But he was in now and there was no point in screwing things up with Farquhar by admitting it. "Who is she?" he asked, continuing the charade along logical lines.

"Lady Janet Isling. A very confused young lady. Her father was a baronet and one of the very few of the landed gentry who actually increased his holdings under the Labor governments. The old boy had an uncanny knack for parrying Socialists."

Chamberlain knew most of it already from Langley. The important thing he'd learned tonight was he'd been wrong about Lady Janet being Grandzau's agent. "But why were she and Trefle looking for the auction?" he asked.

"Haven't the foggiest, old man. Don't you want to know who the fellow on the floor is?"

"She knew him," Helen interrupted. "And he knew her. He was terrified when he heard her voice."

"I rather doubt he was ever terrified in his life," said Farquhar. "He was as hard as they come."

"What's his name?"

"Ivor Peitscheski."

"Never heard of him. KGB?"

"Not exactly. He'd been given carte blanche with their European support facilities—men, cars, weapons, money—but he was just visiting. This wasn't his territory."

"What was?"

Farquhar had seemed to enjoy his role as dispenser of information. But now he looked genuinely puzzled. "East Africa."

"Like Ramsey?"

"Like Major Ramsey."

"I don't understand," Helen said.

Farquhar shrugged his shoulders. "Neither do I. According to my sources, Peitscheski's enemies shipped him out to Africa years ago because he was too dangerous to keep around the Kremlin. But instead of getting his throat slit in a tribal dispute as they had hoped, he thrived. He's engineered coups and committed assassinations in every state on the Indian Ocean."

"But why would the KGB choose *him* to nail Hammond?"

The telephone rang and a detective passed it to Farquhar. While he was talking, his men wheeled in a laundry cart, dumped Peitscheski's body into it, covered him with sheets, and trundled him out. Helen stared disbelievingly when Farquhar, listening intently on the telephone, gave Chamberlain a grave wink.

"Just like that?" Helen asked quietly.

"Guess Farquhar takes the Foreign Office at their word."

"Get rid of him," she whispered. "I want to get into bed."

"Right away."

When Farquhar hung up the phone, Chamberlain intercepted him and steered him out of Helen's bedroom into the living room.

"Can we kind of wrap this up? My boss is beat."

"Of course, old son. Almost done. I do think, however, that I'll post a man at her door. At both of your doors. Best for all concerned, what?"

"Thanks," said Chamberlain.

"Incidentally, I've learned some more about Trefle." He shuffled through the notes he'd made on the telephone. "*Colonel* Henri Trefle. French mercenary. Foreign legion veteran of Indochina and Algeria. Congo veteran. Angola veteran. Rhodesia. South Africa. Somalia." He paused and looked quizzically at Chamberlain. "There's a widely believed rumor, but thoroughly unsubstantiated, that his force was annihilated during a failed coup in Somalia four years ago. Seems he was betrayed by a certain Mr. Charles Hammond."

"Hammond?"

"Organized it—or at least that's what they all say. Who knows, but the East Africa coast is a regular cauldron of coups and countercoups because the superpowers are always taking sides. Sea lanes, you know. Down the East African coast, through the Mozambique Channel. Oil tankers to Europe have to pass along the East African coast. Europe's pipeline, as it were . . . or lifeline, if it's squeezed."

23

Chamberlain glanced past the bedroom door at Helen. A dozen questions rocketed through his mind, but he couldn't ask them of Farquhar—some because they'd undermine his lie about Lady Janet, others because Farquhar's behavior tonight had confirmed what Chamberlain had suspected since morning. Farquhar had too much access to too much information for a simple Scotland Yard detective. And far too much clout. Special Branch was more like it, or one of the myriad supersecret M agencies.

He said, "Don't bother putting your guys on the door. I can take care of things here."

"No trouble, old son," Farquhar smiled.

"Thanks." Chamberlain smiled back, wondering how the hell he'd sneak out of the place without being tailed. "I can use the peaceful sleep."

"Good night, old son."

Farquhar ordered his squad out. A cluster of chambermaids surged in from the hall and hastily straightened the room under the stern eye of the night manager. While they worked, Chamberlain dialed the telephone.

"Who are you calling?" Helen asked.

"Friend at the Agency," he replied, noting it was nearly one in the morning and wondering where Arnie would be in Washington at seven o'clock in the evening. As it turned out, he was at his desk, and sounded friendlier than he had in Brest. "What can I do for you?"

"I'll do for you," said Chamberlain. "Figure I owe you a couple. Remember the Russian?"

"The cute one with the whip?"

"A certain lady we've discussed shot him in my boss's hotel room."

"Dead?"

"Very. His name was Peitscheski."

"Oh damnit, of course. Ivor the terrible. He's been shoving a chunk under the corner in Africa for as long as I can remember. About time somebody nailed him. But what was he doing in London? Wait a minute! He's the guy the Russians sent after Hammond. That makes no sense at all."

"Did Hammond ever work for you guys?"

"Fat chance," snorted Fast. "We should be so lucky."

Fast couldn't be expected to admit it on an open line, Chamberlain reflected as he hung up, but his denial had been so spontaneous that it sounded like the truth.

"Why'd you tell him that?" asked Helen.

"I might need another favor."

Through the bedroom door he saw a charwoman scrubbing the blood stains from the rug. A hall porter covered the soapy residue with a towel and covered the towel with a beautiful Chinese rug. The night manager inspected the suite, repeated his apologies to Helen, and shooed his staff out.

A sudden quiet descended upon the rooms and it seemed as if the night's terrors had never happened.

"Like another drink?" asked Chamberlain.

"Please."

When he brought them back to her room, she was sitting up in bed, her legs under the blankets.

"How do you feel?"

"Much better. Why did you ask if Hammond had worked for the CIA?"

If Farquhar hadn't bugged the suite before, he most certainly had by now. Chamberlain leaned closer and whispered, "Come into the bathroom. I'll tell you something."

She shook her head. "I can't move," she whispered back. "Come here." She touched her ear.

Chamberlain sat down beside her on the bed. She pulled him close.

"Something crazy is going on," Chamberlain whispered. "Remember that Peitscheski operated in East Africa?"

"Yes."

"And Ramsey worked in East Africa."

"Okay." She nodded, stifling a yawn.

"Now get this." He told her what Farquhar had said about Trefle and Hammond. She considered it for a moment. "First of all, it's just a rumor. Second of all, it wouldn't surprise me that much if it were true. Charles is into everything. Who knows the connection? What was Trefle really doing? What was Hammond doing? The real question is, what does that rumor have to do with Hammond being kidnapped by Grandzau?"

"Everything's pointing to East Africa," said Chamberlain. "Are you sure that Major Ramsey didn't say anything else about Hammond's business there when you went back?"

"Positive," she said sleepily.

"Farquhar told me that after the Kenyans kicked him out, they invited him back."

"That's not what he told us."

"Which is it?"

"I don't know. And I don't see how it matters. Peter, I feel so strange. I'm surprised to be alive. Peter . . ."

Chamberlain pounded a light rhythm on his knee. "East Africa, East Africa, East Africa—I'm going back to that damn Overseas Club. Maybe some of the old guy's friends knew what he was doing with Hammond." He stood up and glanced around the suite. "Farquhar left a couple of watch-dogs in the hall," he whispered. "I gotta get around them—hey, are you all right?"

Helen nodded, but her eyes were welling.

"What's the matter?" he asked, sitting down next to her again.

"I'm so scared."

"It's over. Peitscheski's dead and the other two won't be back. Besides, Farquhar's got people all over the hotel. I'm going to have to lose them in the street."

"Could you please hold me again?" she asked, raising her

face beseechingly to his. Her tears dispersed in the fine lines under her eyes. Her mouth trembled. "Please?"

Over her black hair he watched the mirror picture of Helen crumpled against him, him holding her awkwardly, unsure what was expected, what was needed.

He held her for ten minutes. Gradually, her breathing steadied. When he thought she was asleep, he turned out the bedside light, extricated his arms, laid her gently on the pillow, and started to draw the blankets up to her chin.

"I'm cold," she whispered.

"I'll get you another blanket."

"No."

"What?" he whispered.

"Come in with me."

Chamberlain laughed his surprise. Very tempting, but not tonight. "I'm too wet for that," he replied lightly. "Farquhar's almost as bad as you are about tromping around in the snow."

She opened her eyes. "I mean it."

"Helen, you don't want that. You're reacting to your fright. Give me a raincheck for when you're feeling better. I'll sit right here until you fall asleep."

She looked up at him through a veil of jet hair. And when she spoke he saw her smiling in the near darkness. "Do I have to telephone Alfred Cowan to order you into my bed?"

"I wouldn't want him to think I'm insubordinate." Chamberlain smiled. "But are you sure? I mean you've been through a lot."

"Jesus Christ! Yes I have been through a lot. But I happen to find you attractive and I enjoyed the afternoon talking and damnit I want to sleep with somebody and I'd just as soon it be you."

"Now there's an invitation I could hardly resist."

"I want to be held. But not by somebody in wet clothes."

Chamberlain took them off and slipped in beside her. She turned to him and nestled into the crook of his arm, kissed him warmly, closed her eyes, and pressed closer. He let her lead. Sometimes after a frightening action he felt dead inside. Other times relief to be alive ignited enormous sexual desire. He would go slow until he was damned sure which way it was for Helen Thorp.

Her body was surprisingly lush, possessed of fuller breasts

and thighs than her tailored skirts and blouses had led him to imagine. She moved softly against him, but she was terribly awkward, stopping and starting fitfully, fluttering to excitement only to drift away, floating alone, a sporadic passion stalled by the terror she'd had. She closed her eyes tight and strained against him as if trying to crush the fear.

He tried to nurture her excitement and when she cooled, he filled the dead places with tenderness, smoothing the low spots, building the high. Slowly, she responded. He became very detached, observing her needs, and several times Lady Janet drifted across the skyline of his consciousness.

He brought her, at last, to a small orgasm, an internal sigh, and continued to hold and kiss her with gentle care. Feeling slightly superior, and duly proud of his talents, he waited for her to plunge deeply into a satisfied sleep. When it seemed that she had, he tried to climb out of bed carefully, so as not to disturb her.

"Where are you going?"

"Overseas Club," he whispered. "Go to sleep."

"You've earned a night off," she whispered back, and without another word, she slid down his body and took him determinedly in her mouth, jolting him out of detachment, arching his back with pleasure, ripping a cry from his lips. . . . He came with staggering force. She stayed with him, drawing him out, demanding more, until he was quivering weakly, and then she licked and stroked him hard again and made him come a second, long, convulsive time.

Still she kept him. Shaking from head to toe, his breath ragged, his mouth dry, he reached for her face, begging her to stop, so intense was the electric pulsing of her mouth.

Helen removed his hands and pressed them to his sides. "You can't move them," she whispered, but this time when she had caressed him to hardness, she freed him from her mouth and slowly mounted him, drawing him into her with successive gasps. She retrieved his hands and pressed them around her bottom and shook convulsively. Chamberlain bucked under her, reveling in the fullness of her flesh and she pulled him deeper inside and came with him in long, rippling waves, that shook the bed and blotted the light from his mind. Seconds, minutes, years later, he awakened, hardening in her hands, turning with her, sliding on top of her, melting into her, crying with her.

He knew next that she was sitting up, cross-legged, wrapped in blankets, caressing his feet, watching his face, and sipping brandy. She took his eyes and held them a long time. "Tell me," she said.

He told her all he remembered and she listened with a half smile. Then she extended her brandy. "We'll sleep late tomorrow."

He drank. Nothing had ever tasted better. She took the snifter back, downed what remained, and set the glass aside. Chamberlain watched her every move, awed. He was utterly drained. Her travel alarm said it was morning.

"Go to sleep," she said.

He reached to touch her breast and failed, his arm dropping limply at his side. "Yeah. Gotta get up early. Check out the club in the morning."

She whispered softly while he dozed and he heard her gently mocking him. "So many theories. So many theories. Now they're all from East Africa. Before the blond woman was Grandzau's agent. But she can't find the auction. Then Hammond staged his own kidnapping because he was broke."

"Not because he was broke," Chamberlain mumbled drowsily. "He went broke setting it up."

"Go to sleep."

Her fingers moved ceaselessly. He was astonished to feel himself grow hard again, and then he was awake, and the sun was streaming through a crack in the drapes, and Helen Thorp was dressed, sitting in the armchair, sipping a cup of aromatic coffee, and reading a yellow cablegram.

24

The night surfed into his mind and slid away.

"Good morning."

"From Grandzau," she replied briskly, waving the cablegram. "The hall porter brought it with the coffee. We leave London tonight."

Chamberlain found it hard to imagine anything urgent. "Good morning," he said again. "Or afternoon."

She thrust it at him. "Read it. You better get dressed. We'll have to talk to the others and go to the City."

"Good morning."

She dropped the cablegram on his chest and flashed him a quick smile. "It was great. It was the kind of great people get married for. Now get dressed, we have tons to do."

It was the longest, most detailed Pendragon message by far.

"PENDRAGON AUCTION BIDDERS WILL ARRANGE TO TRANSFER FUNDS TO BANQUE ET SOCIÉTÉ DE SUISSE ZURICH. ASSEMBLE HEATHROW PRIVATE AVIATION LOUNGE 6:00 PM TONIGHT. BIDDING WILL BEGIN 8:00 AM GMT. RECESS 9:00 AM GMT TO INFORM PRINCIPALS. AUCTION RESUMES 10:00

AM GMT. CONCLUDES 10:30 AM GMT. PENDRAGON AVAILABLE 12:00 NOON GMT. TRANSPORT PROVIDED. LANCELOT."

"Why's he making such a big deal about the time?" asked Chamberlain.

"Specifics are reassuring."

Chamberlain climbed out of bed and padded into the living room, where the breakfast was laid out. He poured himself coffee, grabbed a hot croissant, and came back. Helen Thorp watched him shyly for a moment and the change in her manner made it easier to believe the night had happened and he hadn't dreamed it.

"I meant to ask you last night, but we didn't talk. What happened to your back?" she said.

"Just a gouge. I ran into a KGB shark in Scuba gear."

"It didn't seem to slow you down."

Chamberlain put down his coffee and tried to kiss her.

She moved away, the intimacy concluded. "Get dressed. We've got just a few hours to move a lot of money into Zurich."

Chamberlain found a robe in his own room. He sat down to drink the coffee, eat the croissant, and reread Grandzau's cablegram. He read it several times until he realized what was bothering him.

"You know something. This is a *private* message."

"Of course it is. They all were. Alfred is still going crazy trying to figure out how they slipped them into the Comptel private links."

"Yeah, that's a cute trick, but that's not what I'm talking about. This message is really private. It's really intended for only one of the bidders."

Helen stopped dabbing perfume behind her ear and looked at him curiously. "What do you mean?"

"It's reassuring, like you said. But only in terms of time. Grandzau doesn't promise that Hammond is alive, which you'd expect a kidnapper to do. You know, send a lock of hair or a finger."

"Stop it." She shuddered.

"Sorry. And he doesn't promise that the bidders will be safe, which is a natural worry. And he doesn't make any threats—you know: come alone, don't bring guns and knives."

"He's taking for granted that he's dealing with a sensible crowd. We're business people. I'm not going in with a gun and neither is Mr. Nagumo."

"Mr. Nagumo is dead."

"You know what I mean. His replacement. Mr. Soma."

"But this message makes one promise very clearly. He'll spring Hammond at noon, Greenwich Mean Time."

"More theories, Pete?"

"And deliver him by Concorde. To me that can mean only one thing. Grandzau knows that somebody needs Hammond immediately. At a specific time and place. And they'll pay anything to get him there. You and I don't give a damn what time we get him tomorrow, just so the auction goes smoothly and nobody gets hurt. But somebody needs him at noon for some very special, specific service. Something only Hammond can do only at noon, or a Concorde flight from noon. It's not like you and Mr. Cowan needing him because he agents ten percent of your business. It's much—"

"How did you know that Hammond negotiates ten percent of Comptel's business?" she asked sharply, suspicion and anger tightening her face.

Idiot. He'd gotten so excited over his idea that he'd let slip what he'd learned eavesdropping. "I listened in from your office when you and Mr. Cowan were talking."

"You couldn't have," she shot back. "The entire top floor is electronically secure."

"I held a glass to the wall."

To his surprise, a broad smile lighted her face. "Did you really? I had no idea you were so . . ." She faltered.

"Clever, for a hitter?"

"No," she said, coloring slightly. "Cunning."

"I'm not cunning. But I've been taught to take initiative. Sometimes it works."

"Well, you're not supposed to know that about Hammond and Comptel, so keep it to yourself. As for your latest theory, I don't see what it's all about and I haven't the time."

"Okay. Let me just keep talking while I dress. What got me thinking about this originally was talking to Farquhar about the Concorde that Grandzau's chartered. There was no need to pay for that dinosaur unless Grandzau was making a point of promising speed. Why speed? Why noon? What time is that in the Persian Gulf?''

Helen shrugged irritably.

''The hotel knows.'' He telephoned the desk and the clerk answered as if that particular question was raised daily at the Savoy. ''Okay. It's four P.M. there when it's noon here.''

''I have to go, Pete. Get dressed.''

''The point is, don't you see, if anybody needs Hammond that badly at that time, they might need him for a long time. They might never give him back.''

''Pete, you're driving me crazy.''

Chamberlain stared, hurt, then snapped angrily, ''If you don't want ideas from me, just tell me. You don't have to let me rattle on making a fool of myself. I thought you were listening.''

''Pete, it's my job to listen. Every day people pitch their ideas at me. I listen to them. Then I decide. It's what I do. I listened. I think your ideas are interesting. And I also think they don't have any bearing on the reality of the auction. I'm sorry.''

''Okay.''

''I've known you a week. I've never seen you so angry.''

''You won't see it again. I'll be dressed in a minute.''

''The spooks are gone,'' Chamberlain said as they crossed the lobby.

Helen looked at the newsstand, then back at the Reuters sheets. No professor. No retiree. ''I wonder where they went.''

''I have no idea,'' Chamberlain said.

She chewed at her lower lip, reached a decision.

''Find out.'' She scribbled a note. ''Meet me at this address. It's in the Temple Gardens. I'll be there in about an hour. Tell the receptionists I'm expecting you to join me in the meeting.''

''Whatever you say.''

''Call me there if you're held up.''

''Right.''

''Hey?''

''Yes?''

''Thanks for a nice time.'' She kissed him slowly and passionately on the mouth, then strode out the door. Her sable coat hid all but the tilt of her head and the wind twirling her thick hair.

Chamberlain watched until her cab pulled away. Then he let loose his breath. He found a telephone booth with a comfortable armchair and asked the hotel operator for the Langley number, wondering if his friend would talk to him. Fast's secretary was so cordial that when she said that Fast was out of town, Chamberlain believed her.

"Did he happen to leave a message for Pete Chamberlain?"

"Yes, he did. I assume it will mean something to you." She proceeded to read the message in a flat monotone. "'Grab your robe and grab your burnoose.'"

"Right. Thank you."

He hung up and pondered a moment. The CIA had bolted for Arabia. The KGB couldn't be far behind. How many airports could they all cover? Or would they track the plane en route? That seemed the more likely, but it also seemed an odd flaw in Grandzau's plan. Neither the KGB nor the CIA would have any trouble tracking a Concorde across Europe. Even the Swiss could do it.

He dialed another number. "Good morning, Inspector. Pete Chamberlain."

"It's afternoon on this side of town," replied Farquhar, and Chamberlain wondered if he'd listened to last night's tapes from the bugs in Helen's bedroom.

"We got cablegrams from Grandzau."

"Thank you. Actually, I've already read one."

"Just thought you'd like to know."

"Kind of you," Farquhar said coolly, obviously still put out about the death of the Russian agent. "Can I do anything for you?"

"Yes. Is it still the Concorde?"

"Very much so. Don't ask me how we know, but they've laid on a secret landing at Abu Dhabi."

"Not much to go on," Chamberlain said.

"Not in Abu Dhabi," Farquhar agreed. "Herr Grandzau could auction Hammond on the runway if the Arabs permitted and there'd be damn-all we could do about it. I think you'd better resign yourself to something, old son."

"What's that?"

"You're going to an auction."

He had time to kill, so he debated breakfast in the dining room—late lunch by their clock—or a walk in the sun, and settled on the walk. It was almost warm and last night's snow was gone from the sidewalks. He left his coat open and headed slowly down the Strand.

He noticed a lot of bobbies. There were several in the area of the Savoy and it seemed that every time he turned around he saw a big, uniformed man patrolling the street in solemn, measured steps.

Farquhar, he guessed, was taking no chances. Just a few more hours and the Pendragon menagerie would be flying east and Scotland Yard and MI-5 could go back to their daily business of worrying about the Irish. Until then, however, Farquhar had evidently blanketed the streets around the Savoy.

He went into a travel agency and studied the big world map they had on the wall. Somalia, Kenya. What the hell did Hammond want in Somalia? And Kenya? It was hard to imagine two more different countries, the Kenyans having developed into a prosperous and independent version of the rich English colonial outpost it had been, while the Somalians were turned inside out by civil war and Ethiopian invasions stirred up by a modern guerilla version of imperialist Russians and Cubans. Another talk with Major Ramsey could have been very interesting. And there off the coast of Africa sat Malagasy, the other side of the Mozambique Channel. Chamberlain felt old. When he'd studied geography, his seventh grade teacher had called it the Straits of Madagascar.

It was getting late. He left the travel agency and hurried into the Temple Gardens, the quiet park like an old college quadrangle. The buildings surrounding it housed London's solicitors and barristers between Fleet Street and the Victoria embankment.

The Temple Gardens were quiet, the walks deserted. Yesterday's snow had melted in patches, revealing wet and impossibly green grass between fields of white. Many of the red buildings were in shadow, the winter sun having settled early behind the taller buildings of central London.

Chamberlain paused under a brick archway, temporarily lost, and checked the address Helen had given him. The paths split in several directions. Ahead was a small white, green-patched field. A tall London bobby rounded a corner across that field and headed toward him. He'd ask the cop.

"Pete!" He heard Helen calling from another direction and he turned to the sound, his pulses soaring more than he would have predicted. She was running toward him, her coat flying open, her hair blowing. She waved and slowed to a quick walk. Her cheeks were flushed.

"I thought I saw you."

"Just in time. I got a little lost."

"Come on, we're late." She took his arm and steered him down one of the paths, past the tall London bobby, who nodded gravely as he might to any lovers. Chamberlain was shaken by the intensity of his feelings. He thought he would never forget for the rest of his life the way she looked in the fading afternoon light in the still gardens in the middle of London.

They went through a painted wooden door and up a narrow staircase, through a foyer lined with unruly bookshelves heaped with briefs tied in red ribbon, and into a small dark office. An old clerk looked up as if expecting them and led them into a larger back room, where the other members of the consortium which had formed to buy back Charles Hammond were gathered.

They took the two seats left in the back of the room. The man from Mishuma was addressing the group.

"He called the meeting secretly so Grandzau wouldn't know everything," Helen explained quietly.

"When'd you find out?"

"While you were dressing. It's a pep rally."

"Kind of putting one over on Grandzau?"

"Exactly."

The consortium had expanded to nine members and as each, like Helen, had an aide, there were seventeen men and one woman in the room. Soma, Nagumo's replacement from Mishuma, talked about the need for solidarity, on which they had all already agreed, and then about the need to ask their companies to be prepared to bid higher if necessary on the second round, which made most of his audience squirm uncomfortably.

Soma had done his homework, running the details of half a dozen pending financial deals and the political maneuvers in the Middle East that would be affected. "Essentially, gentlemen, nothing is getting done while he's a prisoner. Nothing. The resultant chaos will be on our heads."

Chamberlain slumped in his chair and stifled a yawn. Idly he wondered if the Japanese man had stumbled onto something. Was the Russian pursuit of Hammond merely another part of an obstructionist foreign policy? Would they put Hammond on ice just to queer Middle East politics? It could take a long while to pick up the pieces of all of Hammond's deals.

He sank lower and dealt with another yawn. From this new angle he was able to frame the Japanese speaker in the right eyeglass lens of the man sitting in front of him. Oddly, there was no distortion. The lens looked like ordinary glass.

Helen stirred impatiently. He wondered how difficult it must be for her to play second fiddle to the Japanese man. Their lovemaking had left him as awed by her as before and even more mystified. He counted himself lucky to have known two or three women who were capable of complete abandonment. She was less abandoned than determined. The wild ones were sometimes crazy in the morning, as if fantasy remembered changed to nightmare, but Helen Thorp stayed determined, a promising link between day and night.

Someone across the room asked a question and when the man in front of him turned his head toward the welcome distraction, Chamberlain saw that his left lens was also plain glass, as clear as a pond on a bright winter morning. Fake eyeglasses?

Chamberlain took a closer look at the guy, tabulating what he could see from the back. Expensive haircut, properly shaped in the back. A bit of vacation tan on his sturdy neck. Good-looking suit, but a little lightweight for London this time of year. He was an aide to the Lockheed rep, the tweedy middle-aged lawyer sitting beside him, and California would explain the light suit. Good shoes, brand new, the backs of his heels still carrying a feather of rubber.

Fake glasses. He leaned forward to try to get a look at his hands. The man obliged by raising one and asking the speaker, diffidently, what he suggested they tell their company to get the ransom contribution increased. A big hand. Went with the neck. The guy had an incredible neck, when Chamberlain thought about it. The kind of neck you didn't get playing racket ball. Built like a middle-weight boxer. Good hands.

Chamberlain sat up abruptly, startling Helen, and began methodically examining the backs of the other fifteen people in the room and the front of the burly Japanese speaker. *Son of a bitch!*

"I'll be back," he whispered to Helen. He eased quietly out of the room, found the old clerk, and asked for a telephone. The clerk let him into the solicitor's private office, but made a point of leaving the door open. The solicitor, host of the secret meeting, was nowhere to be seen. Chamberlain gripped the phone, thinking furiously. Even if Fast's secretary would agree to send a message to Abu Dhabi, it would take too long.

Chamberlain shrugged and dialed Farquhar's Scotland Yard office.

"Inspector, this is Pete Chamberlain."

"Again?"

"This is about a favor, but I'm not sure if the favor is for me or you."

"Perhaps I should be the judge of that."

"I'm going to give you a message concerning the Pendragon auction and I want you to pass it on to your counterpart in the CIA."

"Whatever are you talking about, old son?" Farquhar laughed jovially. "I haven't any *counterparts* in the CIA. I'm a policeman."

"Cut the crap, Farquhar. If he happens to be Arnie Fast, tell him I'm really pissed off. But whoever he is, tell him to pull his plants out of the auction."

"Plants?" Farquhar barked. "What plants?"

"I counted five, maybe six."

"Give me your number, I'll call you back."

"734-8080."

Chamberlain waited by the phone and wondered what the old clerk was thinking. Fucking Agency never stopped trying. Nice trick, though, and they'd done a damn good job of making the hand-to-hand guys look like businessmen who pummeled tennis balls on weekends. If they pulled it off, Grandzau would never know what had hit him. But if Grandzau's mercs tumbled, and it took one to know one, then there'd be a real mess and a dead Charles Hammond.

He watched the clock on the wall. It was an old ticker, with roman numerals and a sweep hand that chopped each minute into sixty ponderous seconds. He watched it for ten minutes and began to think of calling Farquhar back, when the phone rang.

"For me," he called to the clerk, and picked it up. "Chamberlain."

"Hey, old buddy. I told them they couldn't fool you, but nobody listened. I'm not one bit surprised. Sometime you got to tell me what tipped you!"

Chamberlain thought he heard a satellite echo in the line and presumed that Fast was in Abu Dhabi, but he didn't care.

"Get 'em out or I'll blow the whistle."

"Hold on, Pete."

"I don't work for you, Arnie. I work for people who are paying me to get our man back in one piece. You're risking his life."

"Now you listen to me—"

"Don't give me any crap about loyalty to the old company. I retired, legally and fairly, and I haven't broken any agreements."

"I'm talking about loyalty to your country."

"You're calling it that, but you're talking about loyalty to the Agency. And to you, to get you out of that mess you made in the English Channel."

"No. Listen. I can't give you the whole story, but it's vital that we get him back."

"I'll get him back."

"I don't think you can handle it, old buddy."

"I'm doing better than you are so far."

"Where would you be without my help? Probably just pulling into Marseilles."

"Probably," Chamberlain admitted, "but now we're going to play by Grandzau's rules and get him back alive. So get your guys out."

"Pete. Please listen. They're just a precaution."

"Precaution? And what happens when we win the bidding and your phonies can't deliver their share of the money?"

"They can. It's legit. The outfits they represent are pledged to give the money, just as if they were their own people."

"How'd you talk them into that?" Chamberlain asked suspiciously.

"By appealing to their patriotism."

"Arnie."

"The companies were glad as hell not to risk their own people. If the auction goes well, my guys'll never make a move. They'll just pony up the money like everybody else and ride shotgun until he's home free. They're on your side, Pete. Insurance in case something goes wrong."

"I don't like it. What if they go off half-cocked?"

"Come on, Pete. They're good guys. The best we have."

"You can't throw a good team together in one day."

"You think this is their first job? Tell you what. I'll set up a meet with the team leader. You check him out yourself. You'll see what I mean."

"We're leaving in three hours."

"He's going to check with me right after that meeting you're in is over. I'll tell him to talk to you. Pick a spot."

"The Cheshire Cheese."

"How corny can you get?"

"It's close by and busy enough to be private and safe."

The meeting had broken up and Helen was swept past him on a crest of attentive colleagues. Chamberlain followed her. He caught up on the narrow path outside the solicitor's door. She was looking around.

"There you are. Listen, it's three and we have to leave the hotel at about five. Why don't we have a late lunch?"

"I promised to meet a guy."

"Is it important?"

"Let me fill you in later."

"Are you going back to the club?"

"No, no more theories."

"Do what you please, but it seems silly to me."

"I'm not going to the club. Can you get back to the hotel all right?"

"I'll share a cab with Soma," she said, smiling through the group at the man from Mishuma.

They parted on the Strand, Helen hailing a cab with the Japanese man and his aide, Chamberlain hurrying toward Fleet Street. He debated whether to tell Helen if he went along with the CIA. The fewer in on the secret the better. It annoyed him that he was tempted to go along, take the insurance, if the team leader looked good.

The team leader looked very good. So good that Chamberlain hadn't recognized the tweedy Lockheed lawyer as a plant. He surveyed the Cheshire Cheese with the happy eye of an Ivy League English Literature professor on a Christmas vacation pilgrimage to Ben Jonson's favorite pub. He gave the television above the bar an appropriately pained look and winced again when his gaze fell on the jukebox.

Beautiful, thought Chamberlain, a real pro. He looked somewhat fat and middle-aged until you took very close notice of his hands and feet, where years of training had created physical clues that weren't easily erased. He stood slightly pigeon-toed, balanced and ready to spring from the balls of his feet. And there was a tension in his hands, an inclination toward motion.

He crossed the barroom and joined Chamberlain, standing at the bar. His cover name was Doug Pickert and he said there was a real Doug Pickert in Lockheed's legal department. He knew how to talk in a clear, quiet voice that was easily understood but wouldn't carry. Chamberlain passed him a Newcastle Brown Ale.

Pickert thanked him politely. He took out a briar pipe and began stuffing it with tobacco and Chamberlain wondered how many times he'd rammed the stem through somebody's eye and strolled innocuously away before the body hit the floor.

He got it lighted without incident and spoke, probing Chamberlain with merry, soft eyes. "We support you fully in your desire to retrieve the subject without violence."

"With a gang of hand-to-hand killers?"

"Think of us as a precaution," Pickert replied mildly.

"Insurance?"

"Exactly." Pickert beamed. "That's a perfect word."

"It's Arnie Fast's word."

Pickert sighed indulgently. "Pete—you mind if I call you Pete?"

"Get off it," snapped Chamberlain.

"No, you get off it," Pickert shot back. "You've got your back up for no reason. And I know you know it. You're just being a pain in the ass for the hell of it. We're the A team, Pete. The best. We don't fuck up. You can count on it. So if Arnie *says* we're insurance, he *means* we're insurance."

"I'll tell you what I told Fast. You can't throw an A team together in two days. I don't care how good the guys are."

"I've been drilling my guys since two hours after Hammond got snatched. And don't you tell me, sonny, that I can't put together an A team in six days.''

''I've been around awhile,'' said Chamberlain. ''How come I've never seen you or any of your guys before?''

''You really want to know?''

''Yeah, I want to know. I want to know who the hell you guys are. How come I've never seen you?''

''Because the Agency doesn't make guys like us work with sluggers like you.''

The best Chamberlain could muster was a sarcastic, ''Were you in on Fast's classy little op in the Channel Islands?''

Pickert was unruffled. ''Good God, no. Fast is as bad as you are, waltzing around the world looking for battle ribbons. If you'd just stop and think about it, you'd see the safest way to get Hammond is to spring him from the auction itself, and then, only if necessary. . . . Can I tell Fast that you're with us?''

Chamberlain cast bleak eyes on the dirty floor. ''I'm not against you.''

''Trust us.''

''Sure.''

''Great, Pete. Really great. Share a cab back to the hotel?''

''No. No thanks. I think I'll walk.''

''Well, see you on the plane.''

Chamberlain watched Pickert wander out of the Cheshire Cheese, beaming and swaying like a tourist high on history and stout English ale. A few minutes later he made his own melancholy way out to Fleet Street. Considering the doubts the Agency might have about him, he wouldn't have risked the close space of a cab with a man of Pickert's skills even before the slugger insult.

Listlessly, his mind lumbered through the things he could have said, but no words he knew could have erased the bitter hurt. It was his own damn fault. He'd done it to himself. He'd hit a pro and the pro had bloodied him back. A real pro, not just a hitter.

He walked west on Fleet Street toward the Strand as darkness fell. Office workers were filling the sidewalks, flooding up from the City and pouring out of the newspaper buildings. Chamberlain wallowed blindly among them, his eyes on the pavement, the hurt burning the more he tried to ignore it.

Kreegan surfaced suddenly on his thoughts—Kreegan and

Wheeler, Hammond's brass-balled bodyguard. Endowed with guts, a measure of common sense, and the patience to stand guard in other people's cars and foyers, they occupied the lower levels on the scale of hard men upon which Pickert had found him wanting.

Chamberlain walked slowly, thinking of the qualities that separated him and Pickert. At the bottom of Pickert's scale of hard men were the property guards, three-dollar-an-hour security men, lobby guards, elevator starters, floorwalkers, bank guards, Brinks drivers, Pinkertons, airport security, most cops, Feds, Treasury agents, Scotland Yard, Interpol. People guards were a notch higher, private bodyguards to the Secret Service, rated by the value of whom they protected, the penny-ante ones like Kreegan doubling as bag carriers, the special ones like Wheeler weaving elaborate precautions.

Idea guards held the high ground on the scale of hard men, the defenders of the faith, the spooks and spies and saboteurs dominated by Pickert, maybe not because they knew more ways to kill with their bare hands, but perhaps because they owned enough brains to avoid the stupid mistakes that could be expected of lesser hard men, sluggers like Chamberlain.

A double-decker bus splattered Chamberlain with icy slush from a flooded gutter at the corner of Chancery Lane. He jumped back from the curb too late and spotted a tall bobby watching him over the heads of the rushing crowd. Chamberlain looked away, then quickly back, wondering if Farquhar had put a uniformed tail on him as a loud warning to be good, but the bobby was sauntering assuredly into the street, gesturing a double-parked taxi into motion.

The cab shot ahead and it occurred to Chamberlain that the policeman's determination to move the traffic was so obvious that the cab driver hadn't offered even token resistance. Pickert was like the bobby, not too smart to make stupid mistakes, but determined not to.

Sick of himself, and certain that the crowds who brushed past were aware of his limitations, Chamberlain crossed Fleet Street and cut into the nearest Temple Gardens alley. A detour through the deserted gardens would give him space to think. And he'd return to the Savoy via the quieter Embankment in better shape than he was now to deal with the night ahead. But by the time he had found a way into the Temple Gardens he still couldn't break loose from Pickert's insult.

He'd racked up a real bonehead list of stupid mistakes in the last six days. Some were ordinary miscalculations, but others were colossal idiocies that a guy like Pickert would never have pulled.

Pickert would not have let an amateur like Kreegan pal around like an old war buddy while he tried to find Charles Hammond. Pickert wouldn't have lied to Farquhar because he liked the feel of Lady Janet Isling. Nor would Pickert have taken Helen Thorp—or anyone else connected with the Pendragon auction—to bed before the job was over, unless it was to find out some specific information. All he'd found out in Helen Thorp's bed was that he wouldn't mind staying there a long time.

The Temple Gardens were dark, the walk illuminated intermittently by pale yellow pools of lamp light. Pausing in one of the pools, Chamberlain thought it might not be too late to undo some of the damage. He looked at his watch, his pulse quickening with the relief of going back into action. The hell with Pickert.

He'd just have time to check out the Overseas Club if he went directly on to Heathrow from there. Phone Helen and tell her to bring his clothes to the plane. A little role reversal. Leave the shot revolver in the room. Comptel could afford the loss, and he'd had no intentions of smuggling it past Grandzau's mercs anyway. Knowing he would never make it to Knightsbridge in a cab during rush hour, Chamberlain turned in a half circle, wondering which Underground line was closer.

A tall London bobby strode heavily through the light pool behind him, his whistle lanyard swinging rhythmically with his measured step. So Farquhar was having him followed after all. No wonder he'd been seeing bobbies all over town today. Fired up because he was moving again, Chamberlain flung aside the last vestiges of Pickert's depressing condescension and broke into a broad grin. Screw all of them. Why not ask Farquhar's tail which Underground line was closer?

He hurried toward the approaching bobby and intercepted him in the near dark between the two lamps.

"Excuse me, Officer. Which way is the closest Underground station?"

The guy was good, he had to admit. Didn't blink. Went to the offensive.

"Are you not aware, sir, that the Temple Gardens are closed to the public after dark?"

"Sorry, I didn't know that. I'm just taking a shortcut. I'm looking for the subway." Subway, to emphasize that he was a lost tourist. Charades within charades. Incredulously, he watched the bobby take a summons book from his pocket and begin to write.

"You're kidding," said Chamberlain.

"Have you any identification, sir?"

Chamberlain gave him his passport. Despite the fact that it was so dark that his face was a white blur beneath his helmet, the bobby copied Chamberlain's name on the summons.

"You may answer this in any station house, sir, within forty-eight hours."

"Sure."

"Here you are, sir." He extended the summons and the passport together, one for each hand, and Chamberlain took them, one in each hand.

25

The last pterodactyl, thought Lady Janet, must have looked as formidable as the first. And so it was with the Concorde, the needle-nosed supersonic jet liner perched in splendid isolation on a remote apron at Heathrow Airport near the start of the runway the tower had assigned to yesterday's tomorrow.

Lady Janet smiled grimly. She was starting to have thoughts again. She'd had a decent sleep in a quiet hotel, and she hadn't taken an injection or a pill for more than twenty-four hours. The pain was still there, but it was more a distant ache, a quiet reminder of what Grandzau had done to her and what she would do to him.

She watched the Concorde while Henri negotiated with the driver of a catering truck. Trefle had already offered a thousand pounds to take them from the caterers' staging area across the apron to the jet liner. The driver was Indian. He wanted the money. He stared at the notes in Trefle's huge hand as if they were raw gold and diamonds. But he seemed to know that if he agreed to secrete her and Trefle aboard they would hurt somebody, and that scruple was definitely stopping him.

Henri switched tactics. He left the money in one hand and

drew his glass blade with the other. Then, to the driver's enormous surprise, he spoke in Hindi, a rough pidgin version he'd learned in East Africa. He said he would kill the driver this minute. Then he would take his wallet, find his address, and order his men to kill his family.

It was a crude threat, but it worked because it was more intimate in the poor immigrant's own language. A killer who could speak Hindi could easily penetrate a London Indian slum and find his family. The driver reached for the money and called Trefle sahib.

Lady Janet peeled off another thousand pounds and pressed it in his hand.

"Enough," Trefle objected.

"We've done a terrible thing to him," she whispered in French. Trefle told her she was going crazy. She countered that her gesture would make the driver loyal.

They crouched in the back of the truck, in the container which the driver lifted hydraulically up to the chartered aircraft. It contained twenty-six champagne, caviar, and steak dinners. Eighteen for the bidders and four for the crew. That left four for guards, who, the Indian informed them, had inspected the Concorde earlier and didn't intend to return until the passengers boarded.

It struck Lady Janet as a little lax on the guards' part, but Trefle deemed it *un coup de chance* and had demanded that they steal aboard early because the Concorde was a very small plane and it was going to be hard to find a place to hide. The laxness worried her. It wasn't like Grandzau to leave the plane unguarded.

"Where is Mr. Chamberlain?" asked Soma. He was holding a limousine door open for Helen Thorp, who, ignoring the agitated flutterings of the doormen trying to load the eighteen bidders for the Pendragon auction into a long line of Daimlers, Humbers, and Rolls-Royces, was standing on tiptoe looking up the Savoy drive.

"I don't know," she said.

"Perhaps he went on ahead to the airport."

"I hope so."

"We should leave."

"Yes. He'll catch up with us."

Charles Hammond raised a haggard, pleading face to his

captor. He was clutching a copy of Grandzau's last cablegram.

"Do you really mean this? Will you let me go by noon tomorrow?" He clutched at hope. It might work. His deal might go through and he'd be done negotiating other people's deals forever.

"Of course. I would reap no profit by betrayal."

"By noon?" He was sick of being middleman in other people's petty squabbles. Sick of kowtowing to both sides. Grandzau was right. He'd look back on this as a nightmare, but it would be over. And by tomorrow night, he would close his ultimate deal. His last.

"Provided, of course, someone bids for you."

Hammond was frantic. "They're not coming?" he shouted.

"Of course they're coming," Grandzau said soothingly. "They're leaving right now. I was joking. Of course they're coming. And of course they will bid for you. They will bid a king's ransom. . . . As well they should for a man who would be king."

Arnie Fast accidentally ran into his KGB counterpart in the sweltering lobby of a low-rent Arab hotel that should have been shut down years ago. Neither man wasted time wondering why the other was there. Both knew that the routes around the Arabian princes lay in the back alleys of the bazaar.

"Comrade," said Fast as they edged warily past each other, each with a hand in his pocket, "we're going to blow your ass away."

The Soviet had managed a station on East Forty-fifth Street, half a block from the United Nations Secretariat building and even closer to the American Mission to the UN. By the time the CIA had figured out what he had been doing there, he had changed his cover corporation and had moved, like any up and coming Manhattan entrepreneur, to a flashier address in the Citicorp building. He gave Fast a tight smile and a reply in perfect English.

"Don't count on it, meathead."

Outside, as he drove swiftly through the tangled alleys of the old dhow harbor, the Russian regretted that he had let the American goad him into speaking. In the hotel, Arnie Fast scratched his head and wondered for the dozenth time why they were so uptight about Hammond.

The bobby thrust the stiletto underhand and the gleaming sliver leaped up at Chamberlain's belly, searching entry to his heart. Chamberlain never knew if it was Wheeler in his thoughts or the belated realization that the policeman couldn't have seen his name in the dim light when he wrote the phony summons. All he did know was that the warning had come way too late.

He was a big man to use a stiletto, and a big man to take one away from. Filling his victim's hands was a deadly, effective trick and the underhand thrust involved no unbalancing lunge that Chamberlain might have used to pitch him forward.

Chamberlain's single advantage was that Wheeler had told him about the trick. He accepted the summons and his passport, sidestepped, dropped the flimsy summons, but wrapped his fist around his passport, curled it into a tight shaft and rammed the hard edge of the document into the killer's nose.

He gasped in pain and surprise and stopped in midthrust. Chamberlain gripped his extended forearm in one hand and his bicep in the other and used all his strength to break his elbow over his knee like a piece of firewood.

He screamed once and went down in a tangle, clutching his arm, bringing his legs up protectively. Chamberlain went for him in a frenzy, determined to find out why Grandzau's man had come after him right after a meeting with the head of the team that the Agency was planting in the Pendragon auction.

But before he reached him, the bobby did an incredible thing. He blew his whistle the way a real bobby blew his whistle to call for help. Chamberlain froze, astonished. Did the whistle mean he had partners nearby? Or was he a real bobby doing some freelance killing on the side? Or was he just a smart operator, all alone, but hoping like hell that the whistle would frighten Chamberlain away? Almost immediately another police whistle answered in the distance. And then another echoed shrilly. And another. Chamberlain did the only thing he could do. He ran.

"Gentlemen, and lady," said Inspector Farquhar. "There

are public conveniences at either end of this lounge, and I strongly recommend that you divest yourself beforehand of any objects that Heathrow Airport security might deem inappropriate aboard an airliner."

He paused but neither Helen Thorp nor any of the eighteen men left the armchairs in which they'd been waiting for an hour.

"They are empowered to make arrests for weapons violations, and any such arrest would obviously prevent the detainee from boarding Herr Grandzau's aircraft."

Still no one moved. Farquhar looked from face to face and issued a final warning. "Make no mistake. Great Britain's primary interest is to see each and every one of you safely out of the country."

Helen Thorp glanced at the boyish-looking Englishman who represented the hovercraft and tank manufacturers who depended upon Hammond to sell their wares in the Gulf States. Neither he nor his rugged older partner nor the two overweight City types who were contributing a hefty sum from a British bank and insurance consortium blinked an eye at Farquhar's ridiculous claim. All four men represented Britain's real primary interest. A safe departure was merely a detail.

Soma nudged her. She moved aside. He was becoming too familiar.

"Grandzau was wise to have us depart from London," he whispered. "They're doing a very good job for him."

Helen said nothing, but he was right. The British were being perfect nursemaids.

"What could have happened to Mr. Chamberlain?" asked Soma.

"I don't know."

A security woman came into the VIP departure lounge and whispered to Farquhar. He cleared his throat for attention.

"I should like at this time to announce the departure procedure. In several minutes you will be led from this lounge to a bus which will take you across the airport to your aircraft. Before boarding the bus, you will be searched, electronically and by hand, for weapons by Heathrow Airport's own security forces. Now, once aboard the bus, I have been led to believe, you are in Herr Grandzau's hands. His guards may search you as well.'' He looked at several of the bidders, then his gaze fell on Helen Thorp.

''What I am trying to say,'' he continued, ''is that once you board that bus you are, for all intents and purposes, on your own. We have no reason to suspect that you will be in danger, and yet there would be little we could do to help. I suggest you follow directions to the letter. Do only what you are told to do. You must keep in mind that Charles Hammond's kidnapper has come too far to take any chances at this late date.'' Again he scanned their faces. This time, Helen noticed, he chose several others to bear his gaze upon. ''If you get in his way, may God have mercy on your soul.''

''That's a bit dramatic,'' muttered Soma.

Helen still said nothing, determined to turn him off once and for all. Farquhar, with one last admonishing glare, stopped talking and stepped aside. He frowned at the empty chair beside Helen and joined her. He gave the Japanese man a curt nod, then spoke to Helen. ''Where is Peter?''

''I don't know.''

''When did you see him last?''

''At the Temple.''

''When?''

''About three.''

''Are you sure it was three?''

''About three.''

''Was it still light?''

''Of course. What's the matter, Inspector?''

''Nothing. Ah, maybe that's him now.''

There was a commotion at the door. Several of the airport people were converging there. One hung back, his hand stealing into his jacket. Farquhar rose, reaching into his own jacket and motioning one of his men forward.

Then the throng parted and a white-robed Arab and an Englishman pushed into the lounge, waving a copy of the last Pendragon cablegram. Farquhar spoke to them for several minutes, then offered them chairs. They declined, and stood huffily near the door, clearly annoyed. Farquhar returned to Helen Thorp and took the chair that should have been Chamberlain's.

''Another bidder,'' he told her. ''He was staying at the

Dorchester. Seems to have made up his mind to come at the last minute."

"Who's the Englishman?" asked Helen.

"His solicitor. I know him. He does a lot of Arab work."

"I will invite him to join the consortium," said Soma. He got up and engaged the two in conversation. Farquhar caught a signal from one of his aides.

"All right, gentlemen, we are ready to depart."

Chamberlain watched them shuffling down the narrow corridor into the security bottleneck. Stealing a trick from the phony bobby who tried to kill him, he'd followed an airport guard into a mens' room on the far side of the terminal, tied him up, and taken his identification badge. Now he stood inside the checkpoint, guarding the door that led to the bus outside.

His luck so far surprised him. He attributed it to the fact that the Heathrow search team was not a team but had been thrown together out of extras on their duty roster. At worst, he had hoped, they would have held him until Farquhar arrived. He wasn't sure about Farquhar, but Pickert's boys seemed a more likely group to have ordered his execution. How the Agency tied into the phony bobby he hadn't a clue, particularly if it had been the same man who'd gotten Wheeler the day they kidnapped Hammond.

Both Fast and Farquhar, and only Fast and Farquhar, knew he had stumbled upon the Agency plants. Had one of them told Pickert to get him? Had Pickert hired the bobby when Chamberlain wouldn't go with him in the cab? No sense. He was gambling that Farquhar wouldn't risk arresting him in front of the others. Once on the bus, he would watch Pickert and his men like a coiled snake, though once on the bus, on the way to the auction, what would be the point of harming him?

One thought made sense. The simplest thought. If the bobby had worked for Grandzau and Grandzau had sensed he was getting too close for some reason or other, he might have ordered the bobby to kill him and the man had made his move coincidental to his meeting with Pickert.

But that idea presupposed three conditions, none of which were likely. That Grandzau had a man on the ground who was watching him, who perhaps had overheard things he told

Helen at the hotel. That Chamberlain had indeed gotten closer to Hammond than he had realized. And that the bobby just happened to go for him right after he'd discovered the plants and met Pickert.

None of it would matter much once he was on the plane. Then they would just go to the auction, bid, outbid the Russians, and take Chamberlain home. He turned away from the security table and watched from the corner of his eye as he pretended to look out the door at the bus.

Most were subdued. The Japanese man who'd taken over the consortium was first. His aide, one of the CIA plants, followed close behind. Then came four English businessmen, two young, two middle-aged, all of whom were, as nearly as Chamberlain could ascertain, legitimate bidders. Then there was a fifth Englishman Chamberlain hadn't seen before, but he was no killer, and an Arab in robes. So Grandzau had flushed out some Arab money after all.

Three young American attorneys shoved their carry-on bags onto the X ray conveyor belt and stood still for the electronic wand. All three of the plants, thought Chamberlain, did an admirable job of concealing their excess musculature. The Germans passed through and a couple more Americans, Boston bankers representing the CIA. Then the young Lockheed man whose overdeveloped neck had given the whole thing away, and then Pickert, offering his pipe for inspection with a jovial smile. The French, two men with long, pinched faces, sidled through the electronic passage. An alarm shrilled.

Farquhar's men frisked both of them. Shaking his head in disbelief, Farquhar watched them extract a miniature derringer from one of the Frenchman's sleeves. His companion purpled, but was allowed to pass. Farquhar personally arrested the other and ordered him taken away. A uniformed sergeant took his arm.

"My embassy shall hear of this," hissed the Frenchman.

"Come along, sir."

Helen was last. She carried only a handbag, which evoked no response from the electronics. She held her coat open and let a policewoman frisk her blouse and skirt.

Chamberlain tensed. Farquhar was coming his way, apparently to signal the guards on the bus. Chamberlain faced him as he drew near and spread his hands open at his sides.

"'Fraid your boy's got a broken arm."

"Peter! My God, what are you doing here?"

Chamberlain said nothing.

"Are you all right, old son? Was it you did that bloke in the Temple Gardens?"

"Yours?" Chamberlain asked coldly.

"Good God, no. He's probably the same blighter who almost killed Hammond's bodyguard. I had a feeling it was you. Why'd you run away?"

"Would you have stayed?"

"Of course not. Well, his trick backfired. Our patrols found him before he could get away. You didn't see his knife, did you?"

"No."

"Too bad. He must have hidden it. Anyway, good to see you. Are you going aboard?"

"If you let me."

"Come on, then," said Farquhar, taking his arm. "We'll run you through the machines—see here, Ms. Thorp, Peter is back."

"So I see," said Helen, who'd been watching from the edge of the milling group as it waited to go to the bus. "Are you all right?"

"Fine."

"Good. I was worried."

Farquhar walked Chamberlain through the search, holding his arm throughout. He let him go at the door, whispering, "I see you've agreed to go along."

"I don't know if they believe me."

Farquhar smiled. "Stay out of their way and I think you'll be all right."

"Who do you suppose sent the pig sticker after me?"

Farquhar gave him a look that Chamberlain could only define as genuinely sympathetic. "I have no idea, old son. No idea at all."

He squeezed Chamberlain's arm, opened the door, and stepped out into the night and returned with a young man in battle dress. The business-suited bidders gaped at the violent costume. He wore jump boots, jungle fatigues, twin ammunition bandoleers, and a string of grenades around his waist. He had a dark beret on his head, a bright red silk scarf at his throat, and a vicious-looking machine pistol in his hand.

Chamberlain heard the bus backing closer to the door.

"Incidentally," said Farquhar, ignoring the soldier, his eyes flickering over his own men, cautioning them to stay calm, "where did you get that security badge? Who does it say you are, Constable McGeedy?"

"He's in the john on the other side of the building."

"Unharmed, I trust."

"Just tied up. He's fine."

"What would you have done had I arrested you?"

"I would have assumed you were going to kill me."

"And reacted accordingly?"

"Right."

"I rather thought as much."

The bus stopped next to the door with a squeak of scarred brake linings. There was a quick knock and the soldier opened the door. Two more soldiers, similarly attired and armed, stepped in.

"*Allez!*"

He motioned to Chamberlain first, frisked him professionally, and passed him through the door to a fourth soldier, who led him onto the bus. It looked like an ordinary airport bus with an open luggage hold underneath, except it had an electronic checkpoint built into the door in case airport security had missed anything. Chamberlain, assuming as much, had deposited his various pocket gizmos at the left-luggage counter.

He walked to the back of the bus, as the soldier instructed, and sat down and looked out the window. The Concorde was nowhere to be seen in the blue-, green-, red-, and white-lighted distance of the giant airport. No surprise. Airports always shoved trouble to their outer edges. Grandzau's Concorde would occupy a lonely place on the rim of the lights.

He waved when Helen stepped aboard. She said something to the Japanese man, who was following close behind her, and walked back and sat beside him.

"Saved you a seat."

She wrapped her coat tightly closed. "I'm freezing."

"It's just terror."

She looked around. "What's the TV for?"

Chamberlain had already noticed the screen above the driver's seat. "No idea."

"Pete, where were you?"

"I took a long walk to clear my head."

"Did you go to the Overseas Club?"

"Yep." He decided now was not the time to alarm her with a recounting of the attempt on his life. They all needed to be calm for what lay ahead.

"And?"

"Most of those guys are retired. They're pretty shook up about Ramsey. So they're all packing their old service revolvers. The place looked like a genteel Dodge City, a gang of steely-eyed old codgers just hoping I'd make a false move. Unfortunately, Ramsey hadn't confided in any of 'em."

"Too bad."

"Doesn't matter now. Here we go."

The guards trooped onto the bus. The last aboard closed the door and slipped into the driver's seat. Gears clashing, the bus pulled away from the terminal into the sea of lights. An airport vehicle guided it out of the terminal area, through a maze of taxi ways, stopping and starting to let airliners pass.

Attaining a road that seemed to circle around the runways, the guide truck dropped aside and the bus continued on its own. Chamberlain glanced back, but in seconds the truck lights were lost among the thousands of runway lights, glide pattern markers, flashing wing and tail lamps, whirling support-truck dome lights, and the now distant but still bright terminal.

In the control tower, the ground controller followed the bus's progress by means of the ground radar which crowned the tower beneath a white radome. The bus appeared as a small blip among scores of small vehicle blips and three dozen brighter targets which represented airliners moving on the ground. He paid little attention to the bus because he had already been told it would be taking the long circle route out to the apron where they'd parked the Concorde, which showed as a medium-size stationary blip. Of more immmediate interest were the swiftly moving lines of light that represented braces of 747s hurtling along the ground at two hundred miles per hour.

The small part of the ground controller's attention not on the screen was tuned to the voices of his fellow operators, the air controllers. Without losing sight of a single moving target on his vast round screen, the ground controller picked up the beginnings of consternation in the air.

"*Fermez*!" hissed Trefle. "Close it!"

But Lady Janet kept the overhead luggage door open and hung over the side to watch out the tiny port that gave her a small view of the road by which the airport bus would bring the passengers.

The engines rumbled loudly here in the stern, where they had decided to risk that the passengers, with plenty of seats available forward, wouldn't take the noisy aft seats. If one did, they could hold the luggage doors shut until he tried another. The young man and woman who were flight attendants were forward, shuttling between the cockpit, already occupied by the pilots and engineer, and the curtained-off galley, where they were preparing dinner. The Indian driver had been wrong. The crew numbered five.

"Get in here," growled Trefle. "They'll see you."

He was stuffed in forward of her, his giant bulk barely fitting the cramped rack, his knife in his hand because he'd never have room to reach for it if he needed it.

Lady Janet glanced up the narrow aisle. The attendants might walk into the main cabin at any moment, but she was less worried about them than about the guards. There weren't any. They had never come back to the plane and a voice was whispering in her that this was wrong.

"Intruder!" cried an air controller.

The supervisor was a broad-shouldered Yorkshireman who could move surprisingly fast when he wanted to. He crossed the control tower at a dead run.

"Came up from the east," said the air controller, pointing out the slow-moving blip. "I can't raise him."

Unlike the other lights on the screen, this bore no transponder-generated flight number and no altitude data. The ground controller, seated nearby, was already hunting a slot in case the intruder was a crippled ship limping into Heathrow for an emergency landing.

The blip kept moving deeper and deeper into Heathrow airspace. Then it fell off the screen, only to reappear in a moment.

"Very low," said the air controller.

"Affirmative." The supervisor grabbed binoculars and scanned the eastern sky. "Bloody—" He'd started to say *Sunday fliers*, but realized it could just as easily be some RAF twit. A man of quick decision, he settled on, "—hell," and when he couldn't make visual contact despite the air controller's continued radar observation, "bloody, bloody hell."

Chamberlain got a clear view ahead when the guards, who had spread down the center aisle to cover the passengers, seemed to realize the pointlessness of that exercise and regrouped in the seats by the front door. The bus reverberated from the almost ceaseless roar of jets taking off and landing.

He checked his watch. They'd been riding for ten minutes. Then the bus turned and suddenly the Concorde was there in front of the headlights, waiting, its drooping needle nose pointed whimsically down the blue-light-lined runway.

All the lights went out at once and dark descended like a thrown blanket.

The distant explosion accompanying the blackout, and automatically attributed to the IRA, was the least of the air controllers' worries. Emergency lamps relighted the control room in seconds. Six controllers, their faces as tight as papier-mâché masks, gaped incredulously at six blank radar screens. Others, clenching useless binoculars, stared aghast.

A black night crouched outside their observation windows, pocked fitfully by the wing, tail, and belly lights of jet planes that were blundering blindly above the dark airport and milling around the runways like lost cattle.

The Yorkshireman yanked them back from the brink of panic.

"Right, lads. You've got your radios. Send them away."

"Where?" a voice cried plaintively.

"Budapest, for all I bloody care! Get *rid* of them!"

Lady Janet saw a flourish of dark reflections settle upon the bus and knew instantly what Grandzau intended. She flung her body out of the rack, crashed to the cabin floor, and tore down the aisle, waving her weapon at the Concorde crew in the doorway and screaming back to Trefle, "Henri! It's a trick! The bus, Henri! The bus!"

Chamberlain sat tight, betting when the driver doused his headlights that the airport power failure wasn't an accident. He wished he knew as surely what Pickert's boys were doing in the dark. At least he had his back in a corner.

The ominous whine of jets lumbering overhead in the dark was suddenly louder. Grandzau's mercs had opened the door. Then a new noise, the muffled beat-thump of a helicopter. It was close and getting closer. Sounded like a big job. He could distinguish the separate beats of twin rotors. A big Chinook, or one of the Sikorski sky cranes. It was over them in an instant, thunderous, turbines screaming, giant rotors swishing, beating the night, shaking the bus like a tent in a windstorm.

When it seemed that the brain-scrambling racket couldn't get louder, a dragging, ripping noise vibrated the bus like a big anchor chain roaring through a hawser pipe. Seconds later the noise diminished slightly. The mercs were back in the bus. They'd shut the door. Again he heard chains, jingling this time.

Someone cried out, an involuntary, frightened yelp of surprise. Chamberlain felt his stomach drop. Christ! They'd picked up the whole goddamn bus.

It hung still for a moment near the ground, then lurched forward, tilting slightly to starboard, and began a lunging, swaying, thunderous, stair-stepping climb into the night sky.

26

Flashing patches of light began blinking on and off out on the runways. The bastards had also mucked up the emergency generators and all Heathrow was flickering like a madman's Christmas tree, but the control tower supervisor had worse problems.

He had emergency power for his radar and the big dishes and airy parabolic reflectors were spinning again, but his screens blazed white, thousands of blips, a hundred times the targets that should be there. He strode from screen to useless screen.

The Yorkshireman could think of only one reason for such a malfunction. He was being jammed by ECM. Somebody had attacked his radar with electronic countermeasure equipment. Lights or no lights, Heathrow was still blind.

Chamberlain looked out the back window when the runway lights started blinking. He caught a glimpse of the Concorde, still waiting. The lights flashed off, blackening the airport again. The laboring helicopter gained speed and altitude, and soon all he could see was a scantly lighted, snow-covered countryside.

The snow, less than a thousand feet down, sent up a pale backglow that illuminated the ghostly pale, stunned faces of the bidders twisting in their seats. The soldiers watched passively. Two manned the door in the event, Chamberlain figured, that somebody panicked and made a crazy run for it.

He noticed several of the CIA plants shoot meaningful glances at Pickert as if asking, What now, sir? Pickert looked unperturbed. He stuffed his pipe absentmindedly, then slipped it into a pocket.

Chamberlain listened to the wind racing past the bus. It had certainly never gone this fast in its life before. He guessed, from the sound, at one hundred knots. The rotor beat had eased considerably as soon as the ship leveled off. You could talk if you yelled. Chamberlain leaned close to Helen and yelled.

"Nicely done."

"What?"

"Grandzau. You could almost like him if you didn't think about the jets trying to land."

"Where do you think he's taking us?"

"Ship's probably got a five-hundred-mile range."

"That's a lot of help."

"Well, you know we're not going back to London."

"Which direction are we flying?" she yelled back.

"South, I think. I don't know."

An eerie blue light shone suddenly from the television screen, and brightened to a picture of a gaunt, lined face. A voice roared from loudspeakers, louder than the wind, the turbines, and the thrashing rotors. Everyone watched the television.

"I am Lancelot. Charles Hammond is safe at the auction site, where we shall arrive in several hours."

His silky, German accent put Chamberlain in mind of the Red Baron radio commercials—the mild voice of the tame Hun. It didn't quite go with Grandzau's hooded eyes, and hard, greedy mouth.

"I am in the helicopter which is lifting your bus. Rest assured that you and I both are in far less danger than if the CIA and the KGB knew where we were going. The helicopter is capable of its task. The Americans named it the Jolly Green Giant in Southeast Asia, and they should know." Deadpan, he added, almost as if reading from a script, "In fact, I shouldn't be surprised if some of the corporations you represent submitted the low bids for its moving parts.''

Grandzau chuckled mechanically as the TV screen went dark.

The plants started eyeing Doug Pickert, chafing for orders. Chamberlain sympathized. It would be very satisfying to climb out a window, up the side of the helicopter, and strangle the son of a bitch. Unfortunately, it was no way to find Charles Hammond.

The racing slipstream blew Lady Janet off the helicopter like a high-pressure firehose. She pitched backward into the night, landed on the roof of the bus, and slid over the side. Stunned by the impact and stiffened by the bitter cold, she clawed desperately at the rivet-studded metal, then hit one of the sling chains. She grabbed the heavy links with both hands and began climbing back up to the helicopter.

''Crazy woman,'' yelled Trefle, crouching in the lee of the open luggage hold. ''Wait till they land.''

Lady Janet braced her rubber-soled boots on the links and went up the sling as if it were a ladder. This time when she reached the roof of the bus, she crawled aft and hid from the wind behind one of the helicopter's wheel struts. She was not waiting for them to land because she knew that Grandzau would never have the confidence to leave an operation like this to subordinates.

Grandzau would be in the helicopter cockpit and she was going up there to kill him while his mercenaries were trapped in the bus. She'd seen them get into the bus seconds before the helicopter took off. The bus was already airborne when she and Henri flung themselves into the luggage hold.

She smelled salt. The ground was no longer white, so she guessed they were over the sea. The rotor downdraft and the slipstream tore at her like living things. She started up the strut. She'd been ready this time for whatever Grandzau pulled. She had good gloves, boots, and several layers of tight-fitting warm clothes. She had a pistol under her breast and the Smith & Wesson 76 strapped to her back, set to full automatic.

Reaching the belly of the helicopter, she left the protection of the wheel strut and hauled herself inch by inch up the handgrips that studded the side of the aircraft. The thunder of engines and rotors was as punishing as the beat of the wind. She headed for the point where the cable that held the steel girder sling-support entered the belly. It was extended several feet down, so she was able stand on the steel supports while holding the cable.

The bus swayed back and forth so the cable moved inches forward and inches back, making the well through which she intended to enter the craft a dangerous place should the cable swing against her as she climbed up. She waited a few minutes, got used to the swing of the arc, and made her move.

She was up and through quickly, but the Smith & Wesson got caught and she struggled to free it, as the cable scythed at her legs. She twisted violently to one side and was up into the hold of the giant helicopter.

She lay still, trying to see in the dark. They'd never hear her over the racket, but she'd never hear one of them either. It was a luxury to be out of the slipstream. Slowly, trusting her black clothes to hide her, she worked her way forward, guided by a faint red light, until she could see the cockpit, and the silhouettes of the pilot and Grandzau, black against the glow of the instruments.

Though she'd known the truth for a week, it was still shocking to see him alive. She remembered the burial she'd arranged in the mountains for the blackened, mutilated body the Italian police had pulled from his car. She remembered how she had loved him. Then she eased the Smith & Wesson from her back, braced the sling around her arm, rose to one knee, and flicked off the safety.

He turned to speak to the pilot and she saw his face.

She waited, deep in shadow, to feel something. Repulsion, love, hate. There was hate, a beautiful, contained force that would never leave her, but what flew through her mind, as odd as a summer bird in winter, was something her father had said shortly before she left home.

They'd stopped to breathe the horses on a crest above the old village where once lived the grooms and gamekeepers—those shepherds of her childhood—long dead, or moved to Council housing. Her father had lighted a cigarette, a Senior Service, jammed it into his ivory holder, slipped the holder between his teeth, and remarked of the London middle classes who were renovating the stone cottages for weekend homes, "How the petty have risen."

What, she wondered bleakly, had she ever hoped Grandzau would change in her life?

He'd aged markedly in three years and looked as if he might have been ill, but mostly he looked the same—the same pretentious, striving, treacherous, and rather ordinary criminal he had always been.

She could forgive him the deception, she thought, lowering her weapon. She actually owed him for that, the years alone had cleared her perceptions, purged the demon that sought places she didn't want to be. The very clarity with which she now saw Grandzau was proof of the debt she owed him. For whatever reasons, he had freed her. But the cruelty she'd suffered, the knowing, deliberate cruelty, she would never forgive. She wouldn't kill him, however. Now that she saw what he was, what he wanted, she knew a sweeter revenge.

The bus swayed on the chains, buffeted by gusty headwinds that slowed the big helicopter to eighty knots. It swung side to side in widening arcs that staggered the aircraft and sickened the passengers, who were already miserable from the ceaseless racket and the bitter cold.

Helen Thorp sank deep into her warm sable. She had Hammond to thank for the magnificent, hooded coat. . . . After he'd given her the crystal mirror, she'd let him take her to lunch on a business day in New York. Not for the gift, but for his beautiful note. He took her to Barbetta and everything she had feared had happened.

He was as exciting and charming as any man she had ever met and he seemed as delighted by her as she was captivated by him. He seemed to know her deepest thoughts, and every yearning in her body. She tried to explain how she knew he would consume her, but it came out confused and she heard herself sounding like any woman trying to convince any man that she had a career as important to her as his was to him. And as brilliant.

"It needs all of me," she said lamely, miles from her meaning.

"Brillianter," smiled Hammond. "When I was your age I was a lot less impressive. You can do both."

"Not with you, I couldn't."

They drank champagne and the only thing that saved her

that afternoon was a meeting with an assistant secretary of state that she couldn't cancel.

Hammond had smiled his understanding. He knew what she had done. When she got home that night there was a package from Revillon. A Norwegian silver fox coat. She sent it back, took two years bonus money out of a rising market, and bought the sable by herself.

She'd won a victory more symbolic than real.

Because for Hammond, there was never defeat, merely delay. . . .

The cold, thick and damp and smelling of salt, was a frightening reminder of the black sea somewhere below. Occasionally they saw the lights of a ship and each time it seemed they were flying too low, much closer to the invisible water than would seem safe.

"Are you cold?" she shouted to Chamberlain.

"Freezing," yelled Chamberlain, beating his hands together. His gloves were useless and his feet felt like he'd been wading in a brook.

"Put your hands in here." She leaned against him and closed her coat around his hands. "Better?"

"I'll tell you after the circulation starts. Thanks."

She leaned closer and put her lips to his ear. "Listen. There's something strange about Soma's assistant. Can you hear me? Just nod."

Chamberlain nodded.

"I know Soma slightly. I've met him at conferences, but his assistant is somebody new. He's a little strange. I can't quite put my finger on it, but he's almost not Japanese. He seems to have to remind himself how to behave with Soma. Am I making any sense?"

Chamberlain nodded.

"There's not enough respect. Do you know what I mean?"

Chamberlain nodded again. He was familiar with the elaborate rituals of deference that characterized Japanese corporate life.

"You wouldn't have noticed it," she said. "But Soma's been coming on to me, so they've been around a lot. . . . What do you think?"

She turned her head and pressed her ear to his mouth.

"I think you're even smarter than you look. The guy is a

CIA plant. There's six of them. Him, Pickert from Lockheed and his assistant, and the eager-beaver attorneys from the other American companies.'' He felt her stiffen. ''Let me finish. Pickert's the boss. They're hand-to-hand guys. Elite squad.''

She tore away from him and screamed into his ear, ''Why didn't you stop them?''

''I just found out. I braced them, but then I let them talk me into going along with them.''

''Are you crazy?''

''I thought they were right. And I believed them when they said they wouldn't make a move unless things went wrong. They said they were insurance and I bought it.''

''That's a pretty big decision to make alone, Pete. Too big.''

''I was alone. You weren't there.''

''Next time pick up the goddamn telephone. Jesus Christ, Pete. I hired you to protect Hammond, to save him from violence, and you let those . . . those *crazies* come along. I don't believe you. How dumb can you get?''

''Dumber than you think,'' Chamberlain shouted into her ear. ''Somebody tried to kill me right after I met with Pickert. Did Hammond ever work with the CIA?''

''I don't know,'' she said angrily. ''Why?''

''Because the guy who tried to kill me was a lot like one of the kidnappers. The fake bobby.''

''Doesn't that sound like Grandzau tried to kill you?''

''That makes no sense.''

''Neither do you. Goddamnit, Pete. Now what are we going to do?''

''We gotta go along. You'll start a war if you blow these guys. It's too late.''

''It's not too late. I can tell the guards right now.''

''Forget it,'' said Chamberlain. ''Pickert's guys would fight.''

''But Hammond is safe.''

''And what if Grandzau gets shot or the goddamn helicopter crashes?''

''Why didn't you tell me?'' she raged.

''It's easier not to give it away if you don't know.''

''Well now I know, damn you.'' She shoved his hands out of her coat and stared into the thundering darkness.

Chamberlain shoved his hands into his coat pockets and craned his neck to look out the back window, down toward the invisible sea, wondering.

White light flowered in the darkness. The helicopter dropped toward it and Chamberlain made out a ship wallowing in heavy seas.

"Are we going to land on that?" yelled Helen.

"I hope not." He could see the deck rising and falling fifteen feet on every wave.

The ship turned and ran with the wind. The helicopter skimmed the aft bridge house, dangled the bus in front of the white structure, then lowered it toward the heaving deck. The deck swooped up to meet them and the bus hit with a bone-jarring impact that flattened its springs, bounced it off the deck and then down hard again.

An explosion like a high-powered rifle sounded overhead and the passengers ducked reflexively. "They're shooting!" cried Helen.

"Explosive bolt on the sling assembly. He winched us down and cut loose. Safer than trying to land with us."

As Chamberlain spoke, the big aircraft floated to the deck ahead of the bus with surprising agility. Men ran to it from both sides, dragging lines to tie it down. The rotors stopped turning, the lights went out, and the bidders sat again in darkness, until the guards turned on the bus lights and motioned them out.

Chamberlain and Helen reached the rolling, pitching deck last. The guards pointed them after the others, through a door in the bridge house, down a central winding stairway, through a corridor, and into the crew's dining room. The bidders sat at two long eating tables. On the thickly painted beige walls were advertisements for bags, caps, and jackets which sailors could purchase with duty-free Marlboro cigarette cartons. It wasn't much warmer inside than it had been out.

Chamberlain smelled food and was suddenly hungry. It was almost midnight. The guards remained standing, one in each corner, and a couple of young men in dungarees and white serving jackets began placing large bowls of stew and pitchers of hot coffee on the tables. They returned with bread and butter, served that, and retired. Everyone ate but the Arab, who sniffed disdainfully and asked the nearest guard if the stew contained pork. The guard shrugged. The Arab, his black eyes fathomless, pushed the stew aside, buttered some bread, and sipped black coffee.

Grandzau appeared after the stewards cleared the table. He was wearing a heavy bridge coat and he stood just inside the door saying nothing, watching, until everyone noticed he was there. A hard-looking merc stood beside him and Chamberlain saw the shadows of others in the corridor.

"I trust you've enjoyed the sailors' fare. Your cabins are ready. There will be a certain amount of sharing of the accommodations, with the exception, of course, of the lovely lady from Comptel, Incorporated." He nodded toward Helen. "I was disappointed to learn that Mr. Alfred Cowan would not join you. I have long admired his skills."

A look that Chamberlain thought would split concrete flickered through her long lashes, but she said nothing.

"Where is Herr Hammond?" shouted the German who'd replaced Hans Streicher.

"Herr Hammond is asleep in his cabin."

"We want to see him," said the Frenchman from Dassault.

"You will see him in the morning."

"No," shouted the German. "Now."

Grandzau shook his head. "You will see him tomorrow morning. You may examine him thoroughly before the auction to be sure that the goods are undamaged. Now you will sleep. My men will take you to your cabins."

Chamberlain lay awake on the top bunk of a two-man junior-officer cabin. The ship was rolling ten degrees, slow and easy for a navy man, probably hell on the people who were used to crossing oceans on airplanes.

"You sure the pipe doesn't bother you?" Pickert called up from the bunk below.

"It's fine."

"'Cause these days a lot of people don't like smoke anymore."

"I kind of like it," said Chamberlain. "It reminds me of a professor I had in college. He smoked the same stuff."

"Middleton's Cherry Blend?"

"I guess so."

Pickert chuckled contentedly.

"What's funny?"

"I was just thinking of a fellow I know who's trying to do business in Arabia."

"Funny coincidence we'd end up in the same cabin. You think the Hun's bugged the joint?"

"I'd count on it."

"I almost got mugged on my way home this afternoon."

"That a fact? London's not the town it used to be."

"I suppose so. I mentioned our conversation to a couple of people."

"I don't think much of a fellow who blabs barroom confidences," Pickert said slowly. "Especially when they're true."

"These people wouldn't say a thing unless I woke up with a terminal hangover."

"My old sea legs tell me it's going to be a real calm night."

"Glad to hear it."

"Are you balling that boss of yours?"

"You're way out of line, Pickert."

"Bimbo."

"Pickert, if you rate her a bimbo I pity Lockheed next time you negotiate a deal with Comptel."

"I wasn't talking about her."

The guards brought breakfast to the cabins, coffee and a plate heaped with sweet rolls. At seven-thirty, they ordered everyone down to the crew's dining room. In the confusion, Chamberlain slipped through an open cabin door for a look out its ports, which faced forward. They were heading east, into the sun.

She looked like a ten-thousand-ton freighter. They'd covered the helicopter and the bus with canvas tarpauline. From the sky she'd look exactly like any other freighter carrying deck cargo. A guard noticed him in the cabin and, brandishing his machine pistol, ordered him out.

They'd removed the long tables from the crew's dining room and set up folding chairs facing the galley door at the aft end. There were many more guards. Four stood in the corners watching the bidders, cradling their weapons. They'd changed from the bulky battle dress to black wool pullovers and blue jeans. Each wore a wool watch cap and carried a machine pistol. Two more guards waited by the galley door and another two stayed outside the other door.

Helen had saved him a seat. He thought that the dark circles under her eyes made her look beautifully dissipated. He asked how she had slept.

"Rotten. And I'm sick."

"It's calming down. You'll be better."

"Where the hell is Grandzau?"

When the electric clock on the bulkhead hit eight o'clock, Grandzau marched into the room, flanked by two more guards. That made ten Chamberlain had seen.

Grandzau faced the dour bidders. Most looked exhausted, battered by the helicopter flight and a largely sleepless night on the rolling ship. They eyed him with a mixture of disgust, impatience, and hopeful anticipation.

Grandzau smiled back. He'd dressed with great care; a white carnation gracing the lapel of his three-piece, blue banker's suit proclaimed this was an occasion, a momentous day, despite the shabby room.

"Good morning," he said formally. "The Pendragon auction will now begin. May I present to the bidders Herr Charles Hammond."

27

Charles Hammond pushed through the swinging galley door, followed closely by an unarmed Maltese guard and a sea-kitchen odor of steam, animal fat, and strong soap. He was dressed like a sailor, in borrowed clothes, baggy blue jeans and a ribbed black sweater that stretched over his barrel chest. Grandzau reached for his elbow. Hammond shook him off impatiently and stared, chest heaving, at the people who had come to bid for his life.

They stared back.

Hammond's face was drawn. There were dark circles under his eyes and his mouth sagged at the corners. His ginger hair and the harsh fluorescent lights conspired to give his pale skin an unhealthy pallor. He looked down at his trembling hands and quickly clasped them behind his back, as if to confine them. His restless eyes skipped about the shabby dining room and fell on Helen Thorp.

"Hello, Helen."

The folding chairs were crammed tightly together and her shoulder had been touching Chamberlain's. He felt an electric tension ripple through her body. She leaned forward intently and Chamberlain knew, with a curiously sinking heart, what their relationship had been.

"Are you all right, Charles?"

The bidders exchanged worried glances.

Then a jerky smile lighted Hammond's weary features. "Still worth bidding for."

Ignoring Grandzau, he stepped closer to the seated bidders. "I'm okay. They treated me all right—if you can treat anybody all right when you lock him up for a week."

Hammond looked at his watch. Abruptly he began pacing back and forth in front of the group, still ignoring Grandzau, nodding hello to bidders he knew, standing taller, pacing faster. Chamberlain sensed the fires that drove him, his love of action. Confinement must have been killing. Now he was moving again, and growing more animated with every word.

"We gotta get going. How 'bout those of you who know me personally tell those who don't that I look like my normal, healthy self. Then let the Hun here"—he jerked his thumb at Grandzau—"get on with this so I can leave gratefully with whomever buys me." He flashed a big smile that tried to encircle the entire group in its nervous spirit. "I truly don't want to be here any longer."

It hadn't quite worked. They were still staring like a crowd at a bloody accident. Hammond snapped his fingers twice—a sharp, impatient, let's-go beat.

"Helen! Get this moving, sweetheart. Tell 'em you know me and I'm fine."

Wait, thought Chamberlain. That's former boyfriend talk. Too brusque for Helen to take from a lover. But Helen Thorp jumped to Hammond's command. Casting him a wry, intimate grin that an amazed Chamberlain read as you-haven't-changed-and-I-guess-you-never-will, she stood up and addressed the bidders.

"I've known Charles a long time and there's no question in my mind that other than looking tired and fed up with being at the mercy of Mr. Grandzau, Charles Hammond is his usual, very fine self. I've never seen him better or in more of a rush."

She turned to Grandzau. "I think that if Mr. Grandzau would please start the auction, we really should get going."

Grandzau looked relieved to be given back charge of his own auction. He'd assembled a high-powered group and a bad night's sleep on a rolling freighter hadn't taken enough out of them to give the German the edge. Their expressions reminded Chamberlain of the look on the face of a limo driver getting a parking ticket.

"I will state the rules of the Pendragon auction," the German began methodically. "The item for purchase is Charles Hammond. He may be removed from this ship immediately upon verification of the winning bid being deposited in my accounts and moved successfully to another bank in another country. Two rounds of bidding will be divided by a recess during which you may communicate with your principals. I guarantee that Charles Hammond will be in the winner's possession before twelve o'clock noon. The winning bidder may leave the ship by helicopter. The Concorde at Heathrow will be at his disposal as part of the purchase price. The other participants will be returned to England aboard this ship, whose captain and crew are my prisoners."

Grandzau took a deep breath.

"The Pendragon auction has begun. What am I bid for Charles Hammond?"

A quiet settled over the dining room, a human quiet that allowed the drone of the ship's engine to fill the space left by voices. Heavy china clinked behind the galley door as the freighter rolled from side to side. The expressionless guards fingered their machine pistols, and Charles Hammond stared at the deck as if too modest to watch the bidders vie for him.

Grandzau licked his lips, watching them expectantly.

No one said a word.

Several members of the consortium looked at Soma, wondering if he would begin. But Soma sat stone-faced, waiting perhaps for the Russians. The Russians stared at the galley door. The Arab examined his elegant rings, while his English solicitor studied his own unadorned pink hands with equal interest.

Charles Hammond looked up with a grin. "Somebody?"

"Ten million dollars," said the Arab.

"Fifteen million," said Soma.

"Twenty," said the Russian.

Stepping up in increments of five million dollars, the bidding for Charles Hammond rose to fifty million dollars, with the Russians maintaining the lead. There it stopped.

Chamberlain expected the Arab to drop first. The sheikh had neither government backing, as did the Russians, nor the awesome combined resources of the international conglomerates.

"Sheikh Mādir?" asked Grandzau.

The sheikh's as yet silent English solicitor rose to his feet, bristling dangerously. "May I remind you, sir, that Sheikh Mādir is under no obligation to bid in any particular sequence whatsoever. Until you have given fair warning that you will accept a bid as final, Sheikh Mādir remains a contender, with all the rights and privileges of the other contenders. May I suggest," he added acidly, "that you ask Mr. Soma his intentions."

Grandzau flushed and bowed stiffly.

"I stand corrected by the Briton." He turned to Soma, then took the Japanese man's glance as a warning not to make the same mistake with him. "I have a bid of fifty million dollars from Herr Petrov. I remind you that no final bid will be accepted until after the recess. Do I hear fifty-five million?"

"Fifty-five," said Soma.

"Sixty," said the Arab.

The Russian said seventy million, the Arab came back with eighty, and Soma shot the consortium's bolt at ninety million dollars.

Grandzau beamed. "Would a bidder care to close the first round at an even one hundred million dollars?"

Chamberlain's gaze moved from one bidder to the next. Hammond and the Russians kept watching the clock. Suddenly he was sure that the Russians would keep the lead in this first round. They were here to win and the price meant nothing.

"Don't be shy," teased Grandzau. "Who will make it one hundred million dollars?"

"One hundred million," said Sheikh Mādir.

The Russians stared in disbelief.

The room buzzed with conversation.

Chamberlain looked at Helen. She was chewing her lip and gazing at nothing. The enormity of the numbers sank slowly into Chamberlain's head. What in the world would the sheikh want him for? What were the others' limits? Why hadn't the Russians tried to top, as he'd expected?

Hammond gazed at the sheikh; a puzzled expression clouded his anxious face. He saw Chamberlain watching him and looked away.

"Done!" said Grandzau.

Soma did a creditable job of feigning indifference, though from the looks on the Russian bidders' broad faces, one could see that their limit was higher than one hundred million. Chamberlain couldn't understand why they hadn't topped the Arab.

"This concludes the first round of the Pendragon auction," said Grandzau. "Sheikh Mādir leads at one hundred million dollars. The participants have five minutes to compose messages to their principals. I shall transmit them, and the bidding will resume at ten o'clock."

Hammond looked at the clock on the wall.

Grandzau snapped his fingers. Hammond's guard took his arm and marched him forcefully back through the galley door. Grandzau followed with two more guards and once again the dining room filled with the smells of the kitchen.

Helen Thorp was already on her feet. "Will you excuse us?" she asked the Russians.

"Nyet!" The Russian followed his answer with a long, slow, insolent look, until Helen turned to the nearest guard. "Move eighteen of us to another room, or move them. Or I start yelling for Grandzau."

The guard waved his machine pistol at the Russians. "*'Raus!*"

Moving with deliberate languor, they climbed out of their chairs and sauntered down the corridor.

"They're not sending any messages," muttered Chamberlain.

"Bluffing," she muttered back. "All right, Mr. Soma."

"Thank you, Ms. Thorp." Soma faced the consortium members, huddling hopefully around him. "As Ms. Thorp suggested yesterday, we've each arranged codes to communicate with our companies, even though most of us promised not to ask for additional contributions. The need is apparent. Would you each give me two pieces of paper? Your code message on one, and the additional sum you are requesting on the other."

The consortium members retired to separate places, conferred with their aides, and scribbled their messages. Chamberlain watched Helen draw $10,000,000 in a clear, bold hand. She glanced at him. "Alfred always says big numbers are the only way to get attention." She handed it and the code message to Chamberlain, who took them to Soma's aide, who, when he had received everyone's, shuffled the messages and numbers into two neat piles and gave them to Soma.

Soma read the numbers and his expression brightened. He handed the messages to a guard, who hurried from the dining room. Several minutes later, they heard a helicopter take off from the foredeck.

Chamberlain noticed Doug Pickert's small, appreciative nod. Grandzau had patched together an uncrackable communications net. Flying a safe distance from the ship, the helicopter would fire a brief, almost untraceable electronic message burst. A land receiver, waiting in England or France, would pass them on to the principals and by the time their answers were radioed back, both ship and helicopter would be a hundred miles from where the messages were sent.

Grandzau's mercenaries passed around mugs of strong, sweet tea. Helen didn't want any. Chamberlain sat beside her drinking his, while she moodily chewed her lip and ignored his efforts to make conversation. He gave up and walked down the corridor to the central companionway. The other bidders stood around the various levels of the open stairwell under the scrutiny of the guards, who had stationed themselves from the bridge level down to the main deck.

Chamberlain jogged up to the bridge and back down, to get the blood flowing. Pickert gave him a friendly wave, but didn't interrupt his conversation. The ship's gentle roll and its suburban playroom Formica and Naugahyde decor were the only things that made the recess of the Pendragon auction look any different than any midmorning break at any convention conference anywhere in the business world.

The helicopter returned in an hour, swooping over the bridge house onto the main deck, its big engines reverberating against the steel bulkheads. The bidders hurried down the stairs and gathered at the door to the main deck, awaiting the pilot with their replies. Grandzau bustled up, took them from the pilot as he opened the door, and passed the envelopes to their owners. The guards pointed down the corridor and the bidders hurried aft to the dining room to resume the Pendragon auction.

Soma collected the answers from the consortium members, read them, and settled expressionlessly into his seat.

"How'd you do with Mr. Cowan?" Chamberlain asked Helen.

"He came through."

The guards crowded back into the dining room, taking up their positions in the corners and at the door. Grandzau reappeared from the galley, followed by Hammond and the Maltese guard.

Hammond anxiously eyed the clock on the bulkhead. Ten o'clock. Two hours until the promised noon release. Time enough to transfer the money.

"We resume," said Grandzau. "The last bid was submitted by Sheikh—"

"One hundred and twenty million dollars," said the Russian.

"I have a bid for—"

"One hundred and thirty million," said Soma.

"One hundred and fifty million," said the Russian.

"One sixty," said Soma.

"One-seventy," said the Russian.

After a long wait, Grandzau said, his voice barely in control, "I have a bid from Herr Petrov for one hundred and seventy million dollars. Do I hear one eighty?"

He looked at Soma. Soma did not raise his eyes.

"Fair warning. I have—"

"One hundred and eighty million dollars," said the Arab.

Grandzau looked at him sharply, and Chamberlain had a crazy thought gallop through his mind. *The Arab was a shill.* Grandzau had put a plant into the auction to force up the bidding.

Grandzau swallowed hard and paled visibly. "I have a bid," he began haltingly, "for one hundred—"

"One hundred and ninety million dollars," said the Russian.

The Arab shrugged.

Grandzau sagged with relief.

"Fair warning. Herr Petrov bids one hundred and ninety million dollars. Fair warning." He glanced from bidder to bidder. "Fair warning at one-ninety. Fair warning . . . Charles Hammond is sold to Herr Petrov for one hundred and ninety million dollars."

In the absence of a gavel to end the Pendragon auction, Grandzau smacked his fist gleefully into his open palm. His guards took the joyful gesture as a signal to surround the bidders, and cocked their weapons with a simultaneous steel clatter.

Pickert and his men, who had started to their feet, sank quietly back into their chairs and stared into the guns. Grandzau gestured to the Russians to join him. They, the Maltese, an armed guard, Grandzau, and a strangely relaxed Charles Hammond exited through the galley door and reappeared a moment later, walking up the corridor outside the dining room.

"Where are you taking them?" asked Pickert.

"Radio room," said a guard.

"What about us?"

"You wait."

Pickert looked around at the nine armed mercenaries pointing machine pistols at the seated losing bidders. "Anything you say, fella."

It seemed to Chamberlain that the guards were aiming mostly at Pickert's men. One, however, held his weapon trained squarely at Chamberlain. It was almost as if they knew about the plants. Chamberlain toyed with the thought that he should feel flattered that the guards figured he rated his own guard, but he wasn't. He was worried. Grandzau and the Russians had the whole thing firmly under their control.

Chamberlain turned to Helen. She was huddled deep in her coat, her face expressionless.

"Hammond looked kind of happy."

"Relieved it's over," she replied without looking at him.

"He doesn't seem worried about the Russians."

She shrugged, defeated.

Chamberlain eyed the armed guards. He wondered if the extra ammo clips they had stuffed into their belts under their sweaters were a bad sign. He'd guessed right after all at the end of the first round. The Russians hadn't topped the Arab's bid then because they had known that they would win when it counted, at the end of the Pendragon auction.

Helen had been wrong. The Russians hadn't been bluffing when they sent no message to their principals because they themselves were the principals. They had been arrogant, knowing they had no limits on what they could spend to buy Charles Hammond.

But Chamberlain had guessed they would win before the recess. How, he wondered. Was it that Hammond couldn't keep his eyes off the clock and his watch? What had tipped him? Time. Hammond had been frantic about the time. Hammond had no value to the Russians after a certain time.

Chamberlain wondered. Grandzau had promised release at noon.

Had Grandzau kidnapped half a partnership?

28

Had Hammond made a deal with the Russians before he was kidnapped? A deal he had to close today?

A machine gun clattered loudly, firing short, clean, expert bursts. Somewhere, high in the bridge house, a man screamed death.

Chamberlain threw his chair at the guard nearest the door and hurled Helen after it.

"*Run!*"

The guard was wrenching his arm free of the thrown chair and was starting to fire his gun, the bullets marching swiftly across the ceiling and walking down the wall. Chamberlain kicked at his groin, missed, but connected with his stomach. Soma, the Arab, the English solicitor, and the Frenchman fled through the door and followed Helen up the corridor, away from the melee in the dining room.

Pickert's men had rushed the guards the moment the machine gun sounded. The advantage of surprise had allowed them inside the mercenaries' fire screen. The room was echoing with weapon fire, the thud of hands and fists and the cries of startling pain.

Chamberlain clubbed the man he had kicked with his bare hands until he collapsed to the floor. Reaching for his weapon, he saw a mad kaleidoscope of wildly swinging arms, legs, and guns. The guard had fallen on his weapon. Chamberlain couldn't get it out from under him and even as he tried, Pickert yelled, "The galley!"

His team seemed to separate from the mercenaries and hit the swinging door en masse. Several had captured machine pistols. Pickert went through last, pausing to help a man shot in the leg and catching a bullet in the shoulder as the mercenaries regrouped and started to direct a blaze of gunfire at the swinging door. Pickert was flung backward into the galley, shouting as he fell, "Run, Chamberlain!"

Chamberlain was the last man who wasn't a guard in the dining room. The rest of the legitimate bidders had escaped up the corridor and all of Pickert's plants were in the galley, already returning the mercenaries' fire. Chamberlain flung himself out the door and raced up the long corridor, weaving, smashing from bulkhead to bulkhead.

He heard the sharp, metallic snap of a weapon being cocked behind him, heard the first bullet leaving the clip, cracking into the chamber, and flung himself face forward, hit the deck, and rolled. Three slugs filled the space he'd been in.

He kept rolling into the stairwell, grabbed a post, and frantically tried to pull himself out of the line of fire. Two more shots whined off the hard linoleum, splattering hot chips in his face. Then the gunman shouted sudden pain, and the firing stopped.

Chamberlain scrambled onto the stairs and shot a glance back down the corridor. The gunman lay on the floor. One of his comrades was pouring fire further down the corridor at the outside door to the galley. Pickert's men inside and Grandzau's mercenaries in the dining room had bottled each other up. Chamberlain could hear them trading shots through the galley door. At the same time each group covered the corridor from its outer door, so neither could move from its position.

"You okay, Chamberlain?" Pickert called from the galley, the wound in his shoulder tugging his voice like a beggar at his sleeve.

"Made it."

"Get Hammond!"

Chamberlain ran up the open stairwell, up past passenger and officer cabins, past the lounge where the other bidders hid fearfully, past the officers' dining room, the boat deck, and the captain's deck. The shooting below crashed and echoed on the steel bulkheads and the noise smothered the thud of his shoes on the rough treads.

He stopped short halfway between the captain's deck and the bridge deck, and quietly reversed. The unarmed Maltese guard and the other guard were sprawled dead at the top of the stairs. One of the Russian bidders lay moaning feebly outside the radio room. Charles Hammond was standing in the radio room, visible through the open door, his hands high over his head, his face taut with fear.

Chamberlain went down two levels to the boat deck, went out into the cold, and climbed the steel stairs up the side of the bridge house to the bridge deck. Helen Thorp was already there, pressed against the white bulkhead, peering through a port into the radio room. She whirled about, wide-eyed, awkwardly leveling a machine pistol at Chamberlain's belly.

"It's me. Where'd you get the cannon?"

"Thank God. What a mess. You won't believe this. Look."

Chamberlain ducked under the port and peered in from the other side. "*What*? Where the hell did she come from?"

Charles Hammond, the other Russian, and Grandzau all had their hands in the air. Grandzau and the Russian were standing beside the ship's radios, big consoles which formed an *L* on the forward and inboard walls. Hammond was just inside the doorway, facing Henri Trefle, who was holding his knife. Lady Janet Isling sat cross-legged on the radio operator's bunk, her back in the corner and a machine gun in her hands.

Chamberlain stepped back from the port. "Where did they come from?" he repeated.

Helen Thorp handed him the machine pistol. "Stop them."

Chamberlain looked at her. How hard was Helen Thorp? That hard. *Stop them* meant *kill them.*

She insisted on coming with him. All right, she might

cover his back when Grandzau's guards made it past Pickert's outnumbered men. They raced down to the boat deck, entered the stairwell cautiously, found it still empty, and tore up the stairs. The fight below raged, staccato bursts of gunfire, shouts, and yells, which were followed by long seconds of ominous silence.

Chamberlain didn't have much time. He'd been on enough ships to know that Grandzau's mercenaries could find another way out of the dining room if they looked hard enough.

Stay, he motioned to Helen at the landing between the captain's and bridge decks. He climbed over the stair railing and swung across the pit of the stairwell until he could grab a railing on the far side. The ship rolled and he started to fall back, almost dropping the gun. Who, he wondered, was at the wheel? Or had a frightened helmsman put her on autopilot and gone to hide?

He hauled himself over the railing and crawled past the dead guards and the unconscious Russian bidder to the edge of the open door, which, he could see from here, was hooked open to a ring in the deck. The radios blocked his view of Grandzau and the Russian to the right. Lady Janet, Hammond, and Trefle, all to the left of the doorway, were also invisible unless he stuck his head around the corner, which would offer Lady Janet a perfect opportunity to blow it off.

He was inches from Trefle and Hammond, however, and could hear every word that transpired between them whenever the shooting below abated. Hammond sounded scared witless, Trefle, implacable. Hammond was pleading that what had happened in Somalia wasn't his fault.

"They took everything I had," he said. "You must believe me, Colonel."

"You betrayed my men," Trefle said simply.

"*I* was betrayed. I lost a fortune."

"My men lost more."

Grandzau shouted, "Janet. You can't do this. Stop him!"

"Shut up, Karl," came the cool, even reply.

"You don't know what you're doing," cried Grandzau.

"But I do, Karl. I most certainly—"

The crash of gunfire riddled the rest of Lady Janet's reply. When the shooting subsided, Chamberlain heard Hammond again. The dealmaker's tone had changed. He was still afraid, but he sounded hopeful, as if he'd worked out a plan.

"Colonel. Listen to me. I can offer something much better than revenge."

"Nothing can buy your life."

"I'm offering to buy yours, Colonel," Hammond replied boldly.

Chamberlain heard the heavy slap of Trefle's hand on flesh and saw Hammond sprawl to the deck. He shook his head and rose to a cautious crouch, his eyes gauging Trefle, never seeing Chamberlain kneeling beside the door.

"Colonel. I have an army. But I have no general."

"An army like mine that you shot to pieces?" Trefle asked dangerously.

"Ten thousand men."

Lady Janet laughed. "He's having you on, Henri," she drawled.

"What army?"

"Colonel. Will you be my general?" Hammond rose to his knees as in prayer, supplicating, and offering. Proud of the sacrifice. He raised one finger as if to stop a second blow. Chamberlain saw Trefle's shadow darken over him. "Listen, Colonel—"

"Don't!" shouted the Russian. "Don't tell him."

Chamberlain looked at his watch 10:40. Still time to radio to transfer money by the deadline. He glanced down the stairs. Helen was angrily waving him on. *Do something*. She couldn't hear Hammond. Chamberlain raised a hand to still her, then pointed down. She was neglecting to watch their backs and the firing belowdecks had stopped. Then he realized that the wounded Russian was staring at him.

"Explain," demanded Trefle.

Chamberlain stared back at the Russian, transfixed, waiting for him to do something that would give him away. Instead, he closed his eyes and lay still.

"Be careful, Henri," Lady Janet drawled again. Chamberlain thought she sounded like she was enjoying herself.

"Shut up, woman. Explain."

Hammond was still the only person Chamberlain could see in the radio room. The dealmaker stayed on his knees. He spoke soothingly, slowly, as if his eyes weren't flashing up at the bulkhead clock and down to his wristwatch.

"She stands like the Colossus of Rhodes, Colonel. You know her. She dominates—"

Gunfire rattled through the ship, multiple short bursts that sent deafening echoes up the open stairway. Chamberlain couldn't hear what Hammond was saying, but before the shooting stopped he was damn sure that "she" was Malagasy. And it wasn't toc hard too fill in the space after "dominates" either. The Mozambique oil-tanker channel. Europe's pipeline. Lifeline, when squeezed.

"Insurgency? You want me to put down insurgency? You're crazy. The Americans will blow you off the face of the map."

Not necessarily, thought Chamberlain. That depended upon who Hammond's partner was. In the old days, when Malagasy was still Madagascar, Russia didn't have a navy. But they did now, and they'd offer a lot for a base on Malagasy. Maybe even one hundred and ninety million dollars for a man who could offer them one.

"It's taken four years," Hammond said. "Everything's falling into place. I've made the ultimate deal and I'll never have to make another deal again, for anybody. Now they'll come to me."

"You're crazy," said Trefle.

"Don't tell me I'm crazy," snapped Hammond scornfully, rising, daring the mercenary to hit him. "I don't want to rule the world, just a piece of it. It's all planned. The police, army units, radio station, and an ally."

"What ally?" Trefle asked suspiciously.

Russia, you dummy, thought Chamberlain. Hammond made a deal with the Russians.

"Henri. Look out for him," Lady Janet warned again. "He's tricking you."

"What ally?"

Shooting broke out again, but Chamberlain knew Hammond's answer. Russia would support a Hammond coup in Malagasy. A lot of pieces fell neatly into place. A lot of other pieces, on the other hand, fell right off the table. But one thing was sure. Henri Trefle was wrong—Hammond was not crazy. He was, however, almost unbelievably unlucky that he had been kidnapped.

"It was all set, then *this* happened. Help me, General."

"How?" asked Trefle.

Incredibly unlucky. And so were the Russians unlucky.

Hammond's voice shook with suppressed emotion. "Let this stupid, meddling, idiot German finish his goddamn auction. Let my ally pay the ransom they've bid. Come with me. They have planes waiting everywhere, don't you, my friend?"

"You talk too much," the Russian said coldly.

"And you worry too much," said Hammond. "It's in the bag, isn't it, General?"

Perhaps Hammond was *too* unlucky, thought Chamberlain, recalling something Daitch had said about Grandzau before he'd blown up his house in Brussels. *Not for the money. For the secret.* He was getting the money anyway, but what was Grandzau's secret? Hammond and the Russian were both obsessed with time. But so was Grandzau. Chamberlain had spotted his private message in the last cablegram. Guaranteed noon delivery. Grandzau knew about Hammond's deal. Had known all along. Had known how the Russians would fight to get Hammond back. Had defended himself at enormous expense.

"*Henri!*" Icy determination rammed the laughter from Lady Janet's drawl.

Chamberlain saw the mercenary's thick, dark shadow lengthen suddenly like a springing cat. Wild reflections flashed across the radio room. Someone gasped in shock and Lady Janet gave a startled cry as Trefle's huge blade swished through the air like a long silver whip.

Hammond's eyes, locked to the blade's swift flight, suddenly widened. Lady Janet fired five times, then fired again, a noise echoed by shooting elsewhere in the ship. Henri Trefle backed slowly out of the radio room and toppled over the wounded Russian. Blood bubbled from his riddled chest. He was still alive as he fell. His dying eyes lighted with dim recognition when he saw Chamberlain crouched beside the door.

"Slow," he murmured, imparting his reason for his death. "Too slow." One of Lady Janet's bullets had shattered his tempered glass blade. He held its crumbled stump in his hand.

In the radio room, Charles Hammond moaned relief. "Thank you. That psychotic—"

"I'll kill you for what you did to him."

"No, Janet," pleaded Grandzau. "Please."

She sucked in a deep breath. Chamberlain held his own. She sounded badly shaken. Would she lash out and kill Hammond? He tensed as if to charge into the radio room, but there was nothing he could do.

She took another deep breath. "I should kill him, Karl, but I won't. I much prefer to watch your grotty little hands itching to use that radio. When is your deadline, Mr. Hammond? Noon? One? It's a long way to Madagascar."

Chamberlain pressed tight against the bulkhead because Hammond had started glancing at the door as if planning a break. *Don't,* Chamberlain prayed. *Don't tempt the lady.*

Then Hammond spoke and he sounded easygoing and good-natured, only slightly baffled by the turn of events. "Listen, dear. I'll level with you. I don't know who you are and I don't know what your problem is with Grandzau, but I have got to be in Tananarive when the polls close. We've got an election today and there's going to be some fraud and some dispute and a little violence, and I've absolutely got to be there to step in and smooth things over. The whole deal is planned, has been for months.

"You're obviously a woman of the world and you can understand that. It has nothing to do with you and Grandzau. Please, let him make his radio call. Let him collect the money my friend here has pledged. Then let me go and you can do whatever you want to Grandzau to make him tell you his account numbers. Have your fun with the little bastard *and* keep the goddamn ransom. One hundred and ninety million bucks ought to be worth putting off making one dirty little Kraut unhappy."

Lady Janet laughed brittlely. Shots echoed in the ship. "Put your hands back in the air, please. All of you. That's better."

"What do you say?"

"Terribly sorry, but I'm enjoying this arrangement immensely."

Hammond's tone changed from conciliatory to threatening. "Listen, sweetheart. You screw me up and you'll have the entire Russian KGB hunting your tail around the world. They're not going to take too kindly to losing a naval base on the Mozambique Channel."

"You've tried bribery, Mr. Hammond, and it didn't work. Now you threaten me and I can assure you that won't work either. What is left?"

"You dumb cunt," Hammond yelled. Chamberlain glanced down the stairwell. Helen had heard that. She started over the railing. Chamberlain waved her back, but she kept coming.

Lady Janet laughed again.

"Insult? From a stranger? Impossible."

Hammond sobbed in frustration. "All right. All right. You name your price. What do you want?"

"You made me kill Henri. You betrayed him twice."

Helen edged around the open stairway, jumped for the railing out of Hammond's sight, and slipped. Chamberlain darted to her and pulled her up. They crawled back to the radio room door. Gunfire coming up the stairwell was followed by screams, then silence.

"Janet, for the love of God," pleaded Grandzau. "This is madness. Why are you doing this to me?"

"Why did you leave me?" she asked. "Why did you fake your death and leave me alone? And leave me out of your scheme? I could have helped you with this. I always helped you. Why did you trick me?"

"Because you went back to Trefle," Grandzau answered tonelessly.

"What? I went once. I had to be sure. It wasn't to hurt you. You weren't to know."

"Did you think you could keep that secret from me?" Grandzau asked with scorn. "Keep a secret from Karl Grandzau? I sold secrets, I bought secrets. You were a fool."

"So you punished me with your secret?"

Grandzau's voice took on a intimate note. "Janet, your revenge is crueler than the crime. I was hurt that you would go to Trefle behind my back. I couldn't stay with you anymore."

"So you punished me."

"Punish is not exactly—"

"Karl, what that man did to me compressed a lifetime of pain and indignity into a single, agonizing, eternal hour." The laughter and the drawl were gone from her voice. "It will never leave me."

"*I* didn't whip you," Grandzau shrieked.

"Did you think that the KGB would discuss the whereabouts of my resurrected lover in the presence of my solicitor? You planned it so *they* would avenge my infidelity to you. You didn't have the courage to do it yourself."

"But *I* didn't have anything to do with it," protested Hammond. "I didn't have anything to do with any of you people until this bastard kidnapped me. Why are you taking your revenge on me?"

"You were my device, Mr. Charles Hammond. As Henri Trefle was yours. You recall you did have something to do with him even before your unfortunate kidnapping. You betrayed him in Somalia and again this moment, trying to turn him against me. You forced me to kill him. Perhaps this is my last gift to Henri. . . . He was a kinder lover than you might suppose."

"Kill her," whispered Helen Thorp.

"She's doing us a favor," murmured Chamberlain. "The Russians have a deadline. The whole thing'll be over in an hour."

"Kill her. Before she kills Hammond."

"She won't."

Helen shook her head violently. "She's crazy. Listen to me, Pete. Hammond's got to get away from her. Do what I say."

"It's not necessary," Chamberlain argued. "It's not worth the risk."

Helen placed her hand on his arm. "Look at me, Pete." She drew him into her dark eyes. "Save Hammond and you can name your price at Comptel. You can have a great job in the company, or you can take the money and run. Alfred and I have already discussed a two-hundred-thousand-dollar bonus if you save Hammond. But it's really up to me and I can go a lot higher to show the company's gratitude. Save Hammond, Pete. Kill her."

Chamberlain took the gun and climbed silently over the railing, down the stairs, and out the door onto the boat deck. Two hundred thousand dollars—back to real world numbers he could understand. Helen followed a few paces behind. It had been a while since the last shots were fired belowdecks and the silence threatened. The ship was trailing a curving wake in the gray waves. The sea, the small circle visible toward a hazy horizon, was empty, the ship alone.

She followed him up to the outside bridge deck. He glanced into one of the radio room ports, ducked under it, and looked in another. Helen ducked under both ports and surfaced behind Chamberlain. "Can you see her?"

"Cover your face," he muttered. "I have to shoot the glass out first."

Lady Janet felt very well, considering how close Trefle had come to killing her. She had her back wedged safely into a steel corner, her weapon comfortably in her hands, and Grandzau writhing in a dual agony of greed and dashed hopes.

She was sad about Trefle. She'd known the deadly risk when she'd first approached him for help, but with a drinker and a crazy man there was always a small hope, a wish, that he'd miraculously change. His knife had slashed a long, deep hole in the radio operator's mattress inches from her groin.

She didn't know who was fighting aboard the ship. She'd seen the mercenaries. Perhaps the crew had struck back. But she had stumbled onto the perfect revenge. Charles Hammond, Grandzau, and the Russian had a single goal—to use the radio. It and the clock held all their attention. There was a perfect symmetry to it all. Hammond for Henri. The Russian who might well have commanded the man in black, and Karl for her. She heard the port glass shatter before she heard the shots that broke it. She was still trying to raise her weapon when a second machine pistol burst poured through the port. The bullet stream seemed to flow forever, tremendously loud and longer, much longer, than such a weapon should be fired.

"You hit the radio!" screamed Helen.

"You're goddamn right I hit the radio. I blew it to pieces and now I'm going to get the one in the helicopter. Here. Take the gun. Safety's off. Cover me if they come up the stairs."

"Don't, Pete."

"Don't tell me how to do my job, goddamnit. Hammond's safe as long as Grandzau can't call the Russians. Cover me." He started swiftly down the outside staircase, plunging like a sailor with both hands on the rails.

"Stop!"

Chamberlain turned and looked up into the deep black bore of the gun he had given her.

In the radio room, Grandzau, Hammond, and the Russian gaped at the ruined radios. Chamberlain's bullets had riddled their aluminum cases, smashed the power dials, shattered the frequency counters, and ravaged their inner circuitry.

"There's another radio on the helicopter," Grandzau shouted.

Lady Janet laughed. The sound of her laughter frightened her. The sudden, unexpected, unknowable attack had thrown her to the edge of hysteria. The ports and the open door yawned dangerously, threatening new assaults.

She pressed her back deeper into the steel corner and fought for control. It lay in the power she held over Grandzau. "I should imagine that whoever smashed this one is already on his way there, wouldn't you think?"

"Janet. I'll give you anything."

"You already did, Karl, but you took it back. Close that door."

"Are you pointing that at me?" asked Chamberlain.

"Yes."

"Helen, what are you doing?" He started back up the stairs.

"Don't move."

He stopped halfway up. "Helen. If I don't get to that helicopter radio someone else on the other side will. It's the only way they can sell Hammond in time. Let me go. I know what I'm doing. It's the best for Hammond."

"Fuck Hammond, you idiot."

"Huh?"

"The Russians are buying Hammond from me."

"I don't get it."

"They're paying one hundred and ninety million dollars into *two* accounts. Half to Grandzau. Half to me. I'm the silent partner. I'm the money man. Who the hell did you think paid for all this? I'm the inside man. Who do you think planned the auction? Grandzau?"

Chamberlain stared at her. "What are you going to do?"

"I'm going to shoot you and then I'm going to kill her."

"She'll blow your head off, Helen. She's a pro."

"For ninety-five million dollars I will take the chance."

The sea wind blew her jet hair like silk. Her cheeks flushed, her nostrils flaring, she was, Chamberlain thought sadly, the most beautiful thing he had ever seen in his life. He looked past the gun barrel into her eyes, and only felt sadder.

"You're taking too many chances, Helen. I'm a pro too. Never point a gun at a hitter." He started down the stairs. Her pupils narrowed decisively as she pulled the trigger.

29

The weapon filled her hands, heavy, mute.

Wearily Chamberlain watched her work the unfamiliar safety and try again.

"I emptied the whole magazine into the radio."

"You tricked me?" The wind was still blowing her hair and neither fear nor anger made her less beautiful.

"I'm sorry."

"Why?"

"I guess I wanted to see how dumb I really was."

"You're not dumb."

"Apparently not."

The gun slid from her hands and clattered to the deck. Chamberlain stayed where he was, halfway down the steps, looking up at her. A single tear floated, balancing, on the rim of each of her dark eyes.

"Why is there a deadline?" he asked.

"I don't know."

Chamberlain started down the stairs again.

"Pete? Let's make a deal?"

He stopped and looked up at her again. "A deal?"

"Help me. We'll share."

Chamberlain shrugged. "I guess I could learn to handle the fact that you just tried to blow my brains out. There's a lot of shooting going on anyhow. And I could joyfully forgive your having taken me into your bed on the chance that Ramsey's cronies might have spilled something."

"It was a *very* slim chance." She smiled.

"Tipping off the KGB that we were going to the Overseas Club was something else, and I find it even harder to accept your sending Grandzau's killer-bobby after me. Much harder."

She didn't deny it. "I was frightened. I thought you were on to me. You kept asking all those questions . . . but I stopped him the first time. In the Temple Gardens."

"For the first time I am grateful. But since you didn't stop him the second time, I feel that my best future lies with Alfred Cowan. He hasn't tried to kill me even once."

She shook her head scornfully. "Do you want to be somebody's employee the rest of your life? Or do you want to share ninety-five million dollars with me? Make up your mind, Pete. We don't have any time."

Chamberlain sighed. "Helen, you're making it hard to say no. I can't think of anything I'd like better than the opportunity to screw your brains out on a regular and loving basis."

"I'll expect a touch more elegance of expression from you in the future," she said with a smile. "I'm very demanding."

"Why are you lying about Hammond's Madagascar plan? You know damned well why there's a deadline."

She went white. "I . . . why are you trapping me?"

"Why are you lying to me, Helen?"

"I don't trust you."

"*You* don't trust *me*?" He started down the stairs again. She followed.

"Where are you going?"

"*You* don't trust *me*? I haven't tried to kill you. I haven't lied to you."

"Pete, please wait."

He started down and she followed. When they reached the main deck, her heel slipped on the wet steel and she fell hard.

Single shots sounded sporadically from inside the ship. Pickert's men would run out of ammo first. Had Grandzau put a guard on the helicopter? It stood beyond the airport bus, far across a wide stretch of open, shelterless deck, but the dangerous approach wasn't what was holding him back. He wished now that he'd figured it all out, that he could be as sure as he was when he shot out the ship's radio. Helen was confused and scared and she'd hurt herself when she fell. He couldn't bear to see her vulnerable. He wanted reasons he could buy. He knelt down and took her into his arms.

"How'd you get mixed up with Grandzau?"

"I had an affair with Charles Hammond."

"I wondered."

She was trembling in his arms. "Everyone wondered. We thought we'd kept it secret. Charles said that if people knew they would think I was acting for him instead of Comptel. He was the most exciting man. You have no idea the aura he projected. When he left a room it was empty. I thought we had invented love."

She threw back her head and laughed bitterly.

"Grandzau approached me in New York. Like a little dirty man who bothers secretaries on the bus. He told me that Charles was using me to push phony deals at Comptel . . . since you figured out his plan, you can figure out the rest."

"Why'd Grandzau tell you?"

"He said that Charles was plotting a coup against the Republic of Malagasy and supporting it with my deals. I was still young enough to feel more hurt than the fool I was. He told me because he wanted my help. The help of a brilliant woman scorned, as the little bastard put it. He's just smart enough to know his limitations.

"Grandzau had a great idea. Since the key to Hammond's coup was Russian recognition in return for a naval base on the Straits of Mozambique, Grandzau figured that if he kidnapped Hammond the week before the coup, the Russians would pay anything to get him back. And *do* anything. He couldn't figure a foolproof way to protect himself until he got the ransom. How could he fight the entire Soviet Union?"

"And you told him how?"

"I was devastated. But hurt changes pretty quickly to anger. But I thought, okay, maybe Charles intends to take me in with him. He was the kind of man who would give me the island of Madagascar as a love gift. I believed he might do that. So I went along with Grandzau. I knew I could stop Charles at any time. Right up until last week. But he never took me with him. Last summer we slowly stopped seeing each other and I finally had to admit that he did not love me. And probably never had. That he'd used me all along. Had courted me not for love, but as part of his plan, his ultimate deal."

"So you had an auction."

She tossed her head. "It wasn't really an auction, as you guessed. Just a smokescreen to confuse the Russians. Everyone ran in circles and it dissipated the Russian heat, just the way I planned it. It would have worked perfectly if it weren't for that bitch in the radio room." She shook her head. "I can't believe that Grandzau's past had to come back now."

"He brought it with him," said Chamberlain. "Why didn't you trust me? Because I wouldn't kill her?"

"No. I was worried about your reaction to the Russian connection. I'm international. I don't care what individual governments do as long as they keep the civil peace intact and corporate taxes negotiable.

"But I'm ex-navy and ex-CIA. You didn't know how I'd feel about planting a Russian navy base on the free world's oil lanes? You could have asked."

"'Free world's oil lanes' doesn't sound as if you'd like it."

"I don't," said Chamberlain. "But not for the reason you think. The last thing the world needs is a bunch of amateurs starting World War Three. Because once the amateurs like you start fooling around, you bring in the hitters like me and Henri Trefle and pretty soon somebody's massacring a bunch of dumb natives, and the few of them that survive become insurgents, and it just gets worse and worse."

"I was right. You're going to wreck the radio in the helicopter and destroy everything I've done."

"I don't believe you people. Grandzau's just a weasel, but you and Hammond, you're businessmen. What are you starting wars for? You've got all the money in the world already and most of the power. Airplanes, hotels, good restaurants. What the hell else is there?"

"I knew you'd be this way. No one is starting a war, Pete. Hammond is just realigning things a little. Everything goes in cycles. Nothing matters for very long. You know that. All this is now is a magnificent opportunity for you and me to be rich and happy for the rest of our lives . . . quickly, *we must get the Russian to the radio.*"

"Maybe you're right," said Chamberlain. "Maybe the U.S. and the Russians would sort the thing out as usual. But you didn't hear Hammond plea-bargaining with Trefle. He knows there'll be resistance on the island to his coup so he offered to make Trefle—France's candidate for world psychotic of the year—general of the armies of Madgascar."

"I'm sure that was because Trefle was threatening him."

"Events threaten the nicest plans. Then the plans don't stay nice . . . Did you really think this wouldn't get dirty?"

Helen nodded.

"But this wasn't a nice little Comptel takeover umpired by the Security and Exchange Commission. You and Grandzau made a plan that required *shooting* people."

"Only to defend ourselves. To protect the auction."

"Yeah? What about Hammond's bodyguards? Two dead and one with a shiv in his throat."

"Grandzau promise there'd be no killing. He promised."

"And you believed him?"

"Yes. I'm not a monster. I'm a businesswoman. I'm not a killer."

"What about Major Ramsey? Was his murder worth all of this?"

Helen stiffened. Finally his words had found a vulnerable place in her. He remembered her tears in the Savoy when Farquhar had announced the old man's death.

She turned, refusing to meet his gaze. Looking out to sea, she answered, "Pete, it boils down to taking chances . . . to having the balls to do something that counts."

Anger gorged Chamberlain's throat. He didn't want to be reminded that refusing Helen's offer might not be the smartest move, particularly if he was afraid to take the chance.

"I'll show you something that counts."

Crossing the deck with long, hard strides, he headed for the giant helicopter. It was parked in the middle of the main deck, its long rotor blades drooping like the wings of a sunning dragonfly. Helen ran beside him. "What are you doing?"

Chamberlain kept walking.

"Don't ruin the radio."

"Not just yet." He stroke up the single open ramp, through the cavernous hold, and up to the cockpit.

"Stop right there, fella," said the pilot.

He was American. He was pointing a .45 U.S. Army automatic at Chamberlain and he looked scared. Chamberlain gave a quick look over the pilot's right shoulder, fracturing his attention long enough to hit him in the nose and take the gun away.

"Any more weapons aboard?"

The pilot held his nose in both hands and looked into the barrel of the .45. He was sullen, but cooperative.

"In there."

Chamberlain opened the locker, scanned the contents of the mercenaries' arsenal, and selected a heavy-caliber sharpshooter's rifle. It was bolt action and fully loaded. Ignoring Helen, who was eyeing the radios, he said, "Take off."

"Where?"

"Up."

The pilot wound up his turbines, got them going, and said, "Come on, buddy. Where do you want to go?"

"Just pull alongside the bridge house. Nice and low. Starboard side."

"Shit, I hope you know what you're doing, mister."

"I got the gun," said Chamberlain, glancing at Helen. "It doesn't matter if I know what I'm doing. Up!"

The helicopter rose hesitantly, put its head to the wind, and gained altitude.

"Alongside and lower," said Chamberlain.

"This ain't exactly the most maneuverable son of a bitch."

"Just get down there. That's right. Stay off about a hundred yards."

"Pete, what are you doing?" asked Helen.

"Pickert's pinned down in there. See that port? That's the galley. See those two ports? They're the dining room where we had the auction. Grandzau's mercenaries are in there."

"What are you doing?"

Chamberlain raised the rifle and shoved the barrel through a small window behind the pilot's head.

"Mister, I can't hold her like this. You got air currents coming off the side of the ship'll blow us ass up into the drink."

Chamberlain was holding the rifle with one hand. He stuck

the .45 into the back of the pilot's neck, glancing again at Helen. "Do your damnedest to make sure that doesn't happen."

"You're crazy, mister."

"Just making a point for the lady. Get in closer."

He dropped the gun in his lap and opened up suddenly with the rifle. The booming concussions were deafening over the scream of the turbines. Glass flew from the ports in the side of ship, glistening mushrooms that fell to the sea and scattered into the dining room.

The scope's crosshairs jogged and slid around the shattered port, the exaggerated consequence of the helicopter's vibrations and the rolling of the ship. Most of the time Chamberlain saw only the welded plates. He had fired fast and indiscriminately until he'd scored a lucky hit on the glass. Now he tried to line up a harder shot.

The rotors flung salt spray through the window, wetting his face, ruining the pilot's vision.

"I can't hold her, mister."

"Give the lady a life jacket."

The scope passed over the port and he could see the mercenaries ducking for cover from this new assault. Two covering the hall door held their ground. Chamberlain zeroed in on them and fired six times as fast as he could work the bolt. Two of the high-powered slugs made it in the port and blasted through the barricade of tables they'd heaped around the door.

The mercenaries scattered. Chamberlain swung the barrel and bounced three shots off the hull nearer the galley. A signal. Then he sighted the port again and waited. Movement flickered in the corridor. Pickert's men were slipping past the now unguarded dining room door. Chamberlain waited until one of them charged onto the main deck and leaned over the gunnel, covering the dining room ports.

"Okay. Take her back on deck." He turned to Helen and met her level gaze. "That counts."

They landed. The pilot sagged in his seat, his hands trembling. Chamberlain returned the rifle to its rack. Then he fired the .45 into the radio until the gun was empty and the radio was filled with holes.

"And that counts."

Helen shook her head in disgust.

"Take off," he told the pilot.

"Now where?"

"Anywhere. Just get out of here. If you're lucky they won't catch you." He headed for the hatch. "Going with him?" he asked Helen.

"Should I?"

"No. You're safer in your own world."

She followed him off the helicopter and watched it thunder up and grow small in the sky.

"I assume you covered your ass at Comptel?"

"Like a virgin."

"I won't tell Hammond. I doubt anybody'll believe Grandzau. Did you do it for money, or revenge?"

"Money . . . but I would have stopped the second Hammond asked me to join him in his plan."

"Queen of Madagascar?" Chamberlain asked bleakly.

"Hammond's queen. . . . "

They walked back toward the bridge house. Pickert came out grinning, his shoulder wrapped in blood-soaked kitchen rags. Helen started toward him. Chamberlain laid a restraining hand on her arm.

"Helen. Don't make any deals with Pickert."

She looked at him. "I don't know what you're talking about."

"Sure."

Pickert waved his pipe. "Thanks for the hand, Chamberlain. Tough sons of bitches. 'Course, when they ran out of ammo we'd a had 'em at a distinct disadvantage."

"I had a feeling they might have had more ammo than you."

"We wondered about that. Where's Hammond?"

"Radio room." He led Pickert up the stairway. Helen followed, her face a mask. A couple of angry rounds of gunfire echoed through the ship.

"Still holding out," said Pickert. "Tough sons of bitches."

Halfway up the final stairway Chamberlain called through the closed radio room door.

"Miss Isling?"

"Who's there?" Hammond cried hopefully.

"Wrong side. Pete Chamberlain. I want to talk to Miss Isling."

"*Lady* Isling," muttered Pickert. "Can't take you anywhere, Chamberlain."

"Lady Isling," Chamberlain called. "I'm the guy who shot out the radio. I did the one on the helicopter and sent it away. You can let Mr. Hammond go now. The Pendragon auction is over."

Pickert persuaded an ashen Grandzau to order his men to surrender. They found the ship's crew locked in one of the deck containers and sent a shivering captain and helmsman to the bridge. Plied with hot coffee from the bullet-riddled galley, they determined the freighter's position at less than a hundred miles from Southampton. Five hours later they made VHF radio contact with the Isle of Wight and got patched into the phone lines to London. An evil-looking Royal Navy missile carrier came out to escort them into Portsmouth, where they docked in a thin rain, the only merchant vessel in the fleet of gray fighters.

Inspector Farquhar, lean as their silhouettes, waited at dockside. At his back was a contingent of Scotland Yard detectives, uniformed police, Royal Navy Marines, and some quietly dressed young men, whom Chamberlain assumed were from British Intelligence.

The freighter's captain and crew were led away to make statements. Pickert's men surrendered their weapons to the Royal Marines, who took charge of both them and Grandzau's mercenaries. Farquhar's detectives, many of whom affected his pencil-thin mustache and fitted, single-breasted raincoat, took Chamberlain, the bidders, Karl Grandzau, Lady Janet Isling, Helen Thorp, Charles Hammond, Doug Pickert, and the surviving Russian into a nearby Quonset hut, where Farquhar took statements.

Petrov demanded diplomatic immunity. Farquhar offered a police escort to his embassy in London or Heathrow Airport. The Russian hesitated, as if weighing the sort of homecoming in store for him, and with a fatalistic shrug chose the airport.

Farquhar arrested Karl Grandzau for kidnapping, murder, nineteen charges relating to the events at Heathrow Airport, and hijacking the freighter. The German countered with an accusation. He said that Helen Thorp, executive vice-president of Comptel, Inc., was his partner.

Charles Hammond, his weary face lined like crazed glass, his ginger hair pasted by the rain to his bare head, had shambled through the proceedings in a stupor. Now he came alert as Helen professed astonishment at the charge.

Farquhar, openly dubious, sent inquiries to his men who were interrogating Grandzau's mercenaries. None knew a thing about the American business executive. Chamberlain wasn't surprised. Grandzau, obsessed with his secrets to the last, had told no one, not even his prisoner, about his secret partner. Now no one would believe him, no matter whom he accused.

Farquhar seemed relieved. He told Helen and Hammond that they were excused. A limousine was waiting to take them to London. Chamberlain watched bleakly as she took the dealmaker's arm firmly in both hands and led him away without a look or a word for anyone in the room. He supposed he ought to blow the whistle on her himself, but he wasn't up to playing God. Not with Helen. She'd lost the Pendragon auction. Like Hammond, she was back down at the bottom.

Farquhar then excused the other bidders and told them they'd be able to leave England in a day or two. They shuffled out to a waiting bus and when it growled away, Farquhar and two of the quiet intelligence men huddled by the door. Chamberlain, Lady Janet, and Doug Pickert waited. They were in a classroom, with rudimentary torpedo diagrams still chalked on the blackboard. They sat side by side in plastic school desks, Chamberlain in the middle.

Chamberlain had a pretty good idea what was coming. He nudged Pickert. He had a clean bandage on his shoulder, and his eyes were glazed over from pain-killers.

"You owe me one," Chamberlain said.

"I suppose so."

"I'll take it now."

Pickert glanced over at Lady Janet, who sat composedly, her hands folded on the desk. "Bimbo."

Chamberlain did not bother explaining that from what he had overheard in the radio room she had had more right to be on the ship than all of them. He said, "Go with me?" and Pickert nodded.

Inspector Farquhar returned, flanked by the intelligence officers, and announced that the national elections in Malagasy had ended without a coup. There was, however, one final matter. Had Lady Janet Isling ever seen Peter Chamberlain before this day?

She answered in a quiet, steady voice. "I believe I saw him for the first time in Brussels, last week."

"And then?" asked Farquhar.

"Marseilles."

"Under what circumstances, Lady Janet?"

"I hit him with a pistol."

Chamberlain thought he saw the merest hint of a smile tug the corner of her mouth, but he wasn't sure because she was looking at Farquhar. Farquhar did not smile.

"And then?"

"Aboard the freighter. Today."

"Did you not see him at the Savoy the night you shot a Russian KGB agent in Ms. Thorp's suite?"

"I haven't been in the Savoy in years."

"Lady Janet, we have witnesses who saw you in the Savoy the night the Russian was shot. Surely you—"

"The Savoy was Karl Grandzau's favorite hotel," she interrupted coolly. "We stayed there often, whenever we had to go to England. It was the only place he ever stayed." Chamberlain nodded to himself. That's how she'd caught up with the auction. "But when he died . . . I mean when I *thought* he died . . . I ceased to enter its doors." She was silent for a moment, then raised her head and spoke very softly. "I had good memories there. I didn't want to go there alone."

"As a matter of fact," Farquhar said dryly, "you weren't alone. You were seen with Henri Trèfle."

"As a matter of *fact,* Inspector, I haven't been in England in more than three years, as a simple inspection of my passport will prove. And you will note that my only visits to England since I left home at nineteen were with Grandzau to the Savoy."

"Immigration is not the only way for an exile to enter England," snapped Farquhar. "Just the other day a French speed boat was found abandoned on the Channel coast. We traced it to Brest, where it had been stolen."

Lady Janet said nothing.

Farquhar turned to Chamberlain. "Let's stop messing

about, Peter. Is this not the woman you saw in the Savoy? The woman who shot the Russian agent?''

''No.''

''Peter.''

''She's not the same woman, Inspector. What do you want me to say?''

''The truth. Look at her. Stand up, Lady Janet, if you would be so kind. Look at her, Peter. Look! Are you sure?''

Chamberlain looked up at her as she stood up and faced him, turning gracefully, conveying somehow in the way she moved that she did it by her choice, not Farquhar's. She looked down and met Chamberlain's eyes with a steady gaze he could only call complex. He saw pain, depth, and peace.

''I'm not about to forget a woman who bent a gun barrel over my head,'' he said. ''She wasn't in the Savoy.

Laughter flickered in her eyes for an instant before she sat down.

Farquhar changed tactics. He asked how she happened to be aboard Grandzau's hijacked freighter. Lady Janet sat serenely and said nothing.

Farquhar bored in and the men flanking him moved closer.

''Lady Janet, you've backed yourself into a nasty corner. Either you boarded the freighter as Karl Grandzau's partner, in which case I will charge you with being an accomplice in the kidnapping of Charles Hammond, or you boarded by helicopter with the other bidders, which means you were in London when the KGB agent was shot.''

Lady Janet said nothing.

''Which is it?''

She sat mute. Chamberlain watched a fine vein pulse to the surface of her white temple. She touched her hair, covering the telltale vein with a wisp of gold.

''*Which*?'' shouted Farquhar, suddenly smacking her desk.

''She boarded the ship by herself,'' said Chamberlain.

''What?''

''She went aboard alone to rescue Charles Hammond.''

''Shut up, Peter. Which was it, Lady Janet?''

''She's working for the U.S. government.''

Farquhar opened his mouth and looked at him incredulously. ''*What*?''

''I said Lady Janet was working for the U.S. government.''

''What the devil are you talking about?''

"I don't know the whole story, but one of the agencies hired her because of her connection with Grandzau."

"What are you saying?"

"I'm saying she did a damn good job and she's being kind of loyal not admitting it."

Farquhar angrily cut him off. "Do you expect me to believe that nonsense? I'm warning you, Peter, I have enough on you to put you inside for a long time. Starting with the gun you left in your hotel room."

"I'm just telling you what I heard."

Doug Pickert raised his pipe. "Inspector?"

"What do you want?"

"I'm afraid big mouth here is telling the truth. Now I am not empowered to go into this officially and I do not intend to, but since this is a very private meeting and Pete has already blown the lady's cover, I can tell you that there's something to what he's saying. This could have been cleared through channels in a few weeks."

Farquhar stared. At last he turned back to Lady Janet.

"What do you have to say about all this?"

She smiled serenely.

"She can't come right out and admit it," argued Chamberlain. "You woudn't want her to if she'd worked for you, would you, Inspector?"

Farquhar threw up his hands.

"All right. Mr. Pickert, we've an ambulance waiting to take you to hospital. Go with this fellow here. As for you, Peter, see me in London tomorrow. We'll have lunch, clear up a few details. Go. I'd like to conclude my chat with Lady Janet without your coaching."

Chamberlain got up slowly. "She doesn't need any help unless you try to railroad her."

"I won't. You have my word. I'll see you tomorrow."

Chamberlain followed Pickert out and said goodbye at the ambulance. A constable offered to drive him to London. He declined and walked out into the rain. He eyed the British navy base with a memory of dozens of such clean, precise places, and walked slowly down a long driveway to the main gate.

The guard saluted. Chamberlain saluted back for the hell of it, then stood alone in the lee of the security hut, protected from the rain by its overhanging roof. A line of wet, black taxis glistened in the street lights, waiting for passengers.

Chamberlain stood a long time, wondering what Helen and Hammond would say to each other in the car to London, and thinking that it might be smart to call Alfred Cowan before she did. Touch base. Not that Helen would do anything to him. She had no reason to, and he had kept her story out of Farquhar's investigation. Besides, Helen was not the sort to waste time getting even. She'd rather get ahead. But he ought to find out what kind of bonus Cowan had in mind.

Smart, but he wasn't feeling smart. He wasn't feeling much of anything. That wasn't true. He was feeling mangled. He was thinking how she'd looked running in the Temple Gardens, her black hair flying like it had splayed the night before across her pillow, and like it had blown in the sea wind when she'd pulled the trigger.

Lady Janet came striding through the rain, her hands in her pockets, her head high, a small smile on her face. She saw him outside the gate and stopped.

"That was awfully decent of you."

"No problem. I figured we owed you a couple. Not counting Marseilles, of course."

"Would you rather I'd shot you?"

She said it with a smile. He smiled back.

"Thanks for taking the chance."

"I did the first thing that came into my head . . . you know."

Chamberlain nodded. "Sure. When you think it's too late . . . you're fast."

Shop talk expended, they eyed each other awkwardly over a gulf of mutual loss.

"Did Farquhar give you a hard time?" he asked.

"Nothing that can't be worked out," said Lady Janet. She glanced at the taxis as if to motion one over, then changed her mind. "Was what Karl said true?"

"About what?"

"That your woman was his partner?"

"She wasn't my woman. She was my boss. Yes, she and Grandzau were partners."

"From the beginning?"

"Since before he faked—disappeared."

"Were they lovers?"

"No. She was Hammond's. Grandzau found out that Hammond was using her and her company to support his coup plot." Chamberlain looked up from the wet ground and found her eyes. He wanted to be alone. But first he wanted to tell somebody he could trust. "We made love one night at the Savoy. After you and Trefle left. I don't think I ever woke up happier the first minute in the morning. But it was a setup."

Lady Janet shook her head emphatically. "It's a rare setup that's *completely* a setup."

Chamberlain shrugged. "What do you feel? Used? Stupid?"

"Sorry."

"Good word."

"And you?"

"Numb. A little mangled."

The rain fell harder.

Lady Janet nodded at the nearest taxi. It pulled alongside. She got in, lowered the window, and looked at Chamberlain, standing under the overhang.

"Where are you going?" she asked.

"I don't know."

"Would you like a lift to the train station?"

Chamberlain thought about it. "I think I'm just going to stand here until it stops raining. Thanks."

Lady Janet regarded him through long, pale eyelashes, studying him carefully.

"When it does, my home is in Gloucestershire. It's called Isling House. Anyone can tell you the way."